Alan Scholefield w[...] 1931. His first nov[...] was an immediate [...] up journalism and become a full-time writer.

He now lives in Hampshire with his wife and three daughters.

Alan Scholefield's many books include: *The Eagles of Malice*, *The Stone Flower**, *Great Elephant** and *Venom*, which has been made into a film.

* also available in Sphere Books

The Sea Cave

ALAN SCHOLEFIELD

SPHERE BOOKS LIMITED
30–32 Gray's Inn Road, London WC1X 8JL

First published in Great Britain by
Hamish Hamilton Ltd 1983
Copyright © 1983 by Alan Scholefield
Published by Sphere Books Ltd 1984

For Pauline and Colin Traill

Publisher's Note

TRADE
MARK

Printed and bound in Great Britain by
Cox & Wyman Ltd, Reading

CONTENTS

PART ONE: THE FIRST INQUEST   7
PART TWO: THE SECOND INQUEST   123
PART THREE: THE TRIAL   235

PART ONE

The First Inquest

The body was found on a lonely stretch of coastline on the Saxenburg estate. In the 1920's it was a wild place where you could walk for mile upon mile and see nothing but the bleak plains on the one hand and the restless, wind-chopped sea on the other. Over the centuries these turbulent waters at the southernmost tip of Africa had been the graveyard of nearly two hundred ships; more than a thousand dead bodies had been washed ashore.

But not this one.

It was found in a small bay about three miles from the town of Helmsdale, overlooked by Saxenburg House itself. The bay was in the shape of a horseshoe. The house stood on one headland, the other had been worn away over the millennia into a jagged point, part of which occasionally collapsed. Here there was a sea cave, a grotto, a dark place.

When the tide was high, the cave was filled with rushing water which scoured it of dead seaweed and dead sea creatures. The water made a low, hissing noise as it came over the shingle, a kind of counterpoint to the waves breaking on the India Reef.

The body lay unmolested in the sea cave for several hours. Then, as the tide turned, water began to creep up to it. Slowly, the sea lapped over its feet, moving upwards until it covered the chest and head and finally lifted the body from the sand and dragged it down the shelving floor into the deep water beyond the entrance.

It started on its last journey.

The India Reef lay about a mile from the cave and the body drifted towards it. Had it reached the dark rocks no

9

one would have seen it again, for they were the home of sharks, barracuda, crabs and crayfish – all good scavengers.

But the reef was surrounded by rip tides, whirlpools and contrary currents, and one of these currents began to pull the body in a sideways motion parallel to the shore.

Soon it reached an area where the swells ran into the bay, unimpeded by rock or reef. It was picked up by a wave and moved a few yards towards land. The next wave brought it a few yards closer, the next closer still.

Saxenburg Cove, as the small bay was called, had a sandy beach that looked inviting but was, in fact, dangerously rocky. However, there were three rock pools which changed the nature of the place. Each was about six feet deep and half the size of a tennis court. They were linked by short connecting channels. Rocks formed their walls and at low tide the sea could not reach them. Then, the water in the pools was crystal clear and you could swim from one to the next. At high tide the swells flowed over the rocks, renewing the water. Sometimes a fish or an octopus or a piece of flotsam would be deposited in the farthest pool.

High tide brought the body to the rocks which formed the barrier of the outer pool. Water pushed and pulled it, scraping its face and shoulder on the barnacles, until at last it slithered into the pool. The tide retreated, the body remained.

Dawn came, hot and windless.

The body lay face down, its arms outstretched, its legs dangling. Seemingly with a will of its own, it gradually floated through the connecting channels until it reached the pool nearest the beach. There it stopped, for there was nowhere farther to go, and there it was found by an early bather.

[2]

The inquest was held four days after the body was discovered. The day was hot, with only a slight breeze.

Kate Buchanan was standing on the verandah of Saxenburg House when she heard the motor come to the front door. Smuts called through the chauffeur's window, 'Is she down yet?'

'No.'

He lit a cigarette and waited, then he said, 'It starts at eleven. We have to be there fifteen minutes early.'

'I know. She won't be long.'

The fact that Mrs. Preller was coming downstairs in the morning was an event in itself. She had decided to attend the inquest since the body had been found on her estate.

Kate rubbed her hands on her dress. They were damp with perspiration, not only from the heat, but from the knowledge of the ordeal to come. And there were other fears, private fears, that she had made a terrible mistake and that it would eventually catch up with her.

She looked down at Saxenburg Cove, below her. The rock pools were invisible, but she knew where they were. She knew exactly where the body had been, for she had found it. A picture flashed across her inner eye of Miriam's face, and she felt her stomach turn. It had been like raw meat after its scraping on the barnacles. She fought the images. How long, she wondered, would it take for the picture to be erased from her mind?

'Miss Kate.' It was Lena's voice.

Kate turned and saw the Cape coloured house-keeper at the door. 'Madam is coming down now, Miss Kate.'

She crossed the verandah and reached the door as Mrs. Preller emerged into the sunlight. She was dressed as usual for an outing in a suit with a hobbled skirt, a long, light coat, buttoned boots, a dark hat and a veil that half hid her face: a post-Edwardian fashion plate nearly twenty years out of date.

Kate could make out the dead white face behind the veil and the red slash of the lips. She looked out of place in the sunlight, like some etiolated night creature.

'Is everything ready?' she said.

'Everything is ready.'

'We must go, then.' Her Viennese accent was marked.

She pronounced 'we' as 've' and rolled her r's and often her syntax was idiosyncratic.

Smuts held the door open for them and gave Kate a wink as if to say, 'Cheer up, my friend, you're not dead yet,' which was an aphorism often on his lips.

The large black motor proceeded out of the drive and across the headland towards the road that ran along the cliffs.

'I do not like doing such things in the morning,' Mrs. Preller said. 'But it is my duty. Her body was found on Saxenburg. Why here? She could have swum anywhere.'

'She liked the rock pools. We went there together once. She was a good swimmer.'

'Not so good, I think. And look what her carelessness does to her poor father. I hope you will be careful on this coast. Is that not right, Smuts?'

'Right, Miss Augusta. It's the most dangerous coast in the world.'

'I order you to be careful.'

'I will be.'

The motor turned onto the cliff road, making for Helmsdale, which lay in its own bay about two miles away. As they changed direction, Kate looked back at the house. It was the angle from which she had first seen it two months before, when she had arrived at Saxenburg. Smuts had picked her up at the station and brought her here in the dusk of a spring day. 'There it is,' he had said, and she had looked through a gap in the undulating country and seen the house standing on its headland.

She had seen it a hundred times since then, but that was the picture she would always retain: the great house, etched against the darkening sky.

'See that white line beyond the bay?' Smuts had said. 'They call it the India Reef. Three Indiamen went down on her. *Somerset,* 1756; *St. Giles*, 1767; *Heron*, 1807. There have been others, but it's the Indiamen people remember.'

The foaming white line started about a mile from shore and travelled at right angles to the cliffs for about the same distance. Rip tides surged one way, then another, and rollers from the Southern Ocean boomed as they struck.

'When it's calm you can hardly see the reef,' he had said. 'That's what makes it dangerous.'

The wind had been blowing that evening, a tearing gale from the south-east which battered at the motor and blew the road surface away in clouds of dust. Kate had stared at the house. It had been built to withstand wind. It crouched on its headland, seemingly part of the organic structure of the dark rock itself: square, massive, a kind of Krak des Chevaliers out of time and place, designed to endure against the battering of the gales.

'They didn't call this place Cabo Tormentoso for nothing,' Smuts had said.

'Who didn't?'

'The Portuguese when they first came. Cape of Storms. Cabo Tormentoso. More accurate than Cape of Good Hope, my friend.'

The dying day, the house, the wind, the reef which had claimed so many lives, the strange little man at the wheel, had combined to increase Kate's feeling of unease, but she had pushed it aside. She had made her decision; any decision was better than none. She had learnt that the hard way.

It was then she had noticed the faded elegance of the car's interior; the seats of grey plush, the windows' blue glass and the small silver vases in brackets on either side of the back seat, filled with purple everlastings.

They had bumped along at less than twenty miles an hour, winding in and out of rocky outcrops and the occasional great dune of white sand partly overgrown by mesembryanthemums. Sometimes the road would leave the cliffs and cross the edge of a great flat plain covered in what she now knew was called 'fynbos' in the local Afrikaans language. Finebush. A mixture of grasses and heaths and gnarled, twisting shrubs, none of which grew to a height of more than five or six feet, crouching, like the house, close to the ground, offering as little resistance as possible to the gales. Nowhere on that desolate plain had she seen a single tree.

'Be careful where you walk in that stuff,' Smuts had said. 'We get snakes around here: cobras, puffadders.'

13

He was a small man, almost bald, and his sunburnt neck was criss-crossed by lines. He was about sixty and so short he could hardly see over the big, wooden steering wheel. The first thing she had noticed about him was that he looked and walked like a jockey. He even dressed like one, in riding breeches and brown leather boots.

As she studied him in the half-light, something had reared up beside the car, only inches from her face. She had given a gasp of fright. It was tall and sinuous and she thought then that it was one of the snakes he had mentioned.

'Don't worry, he won't hurt you,' he had said.

The creature, pale, white and about as thick as her wrist, had kept pace with the car. Then suddenly it had bent in the middle and a head had appeared at the window, with thick, spatulate lips, staring eyes and bristles that seemed to cover it all over.

'It's only old White Neck,' Smuts had said.

'What is it?'

'Ostrich. Have you never seen an ostrich before?'

'No.'

'Look there.'

She had followed his pointing finger and seen a flock of fifty or sixty huge birds standing beside the road, some grey, some black with white tail feathers. All their heads, on the long white columns of their necks, were turned to look at the car.

'You should have seen this place in the old days,' he had said. 'There were thousands.'

'Ostrichs?'

'Didn't you know this was the biggest ostrich farm in the world?'

'Nobody told me. You mean, for eggs?'

'That's rich! Feathers, my friend! Feathers. Before the war, everyone wanted our feathers. France, Germany, America, England. We couldn't get enough. People say the fashion will come back. Who knows? Boss Charles built this place on *feathers*, my friend.'

'You mean the ostriches were killed for their feathers?'

14

A picture of an inferno of gore and feathers had risen in her mind.

'You don't kill an ostrich.' There had been contempt in his voice. 'A good bird used to cost hundreds of pounds. What would you want to kill it for? No, you pluck them every season.'

She had remembered then a hat belonging to her mother. There had been two ostrich feathers on it, one white, one black. When she was a child she had seen rich women in Edinburgh going into the luxury hotels, the Caledonian and the North British, wearing ostrich feather boas and shawls. It had never occurred to her to wonder where the feathers came from. All she had known was that they were beautiful, and too expensive for the likes of her.

'Boss Charles always said you couldn't depend on fashion. That's why he put his money into other things.'

'Is that his nickname? Boss? I haven't heard anyone call him that.'

'No, no! Boss Charles is dead. Boss Charles was Miss Augusta's husband –'

'Miss –?'

'Mrs. Preller. Your employer,' he had explained. 'I've always called her Miss Augusta. You know *Master* Charles, the son. He's not Boss Charles!'

Now, on the morning of the inquest, Mrs. Preller had clearly been brooding on Miriam's death. She always sat as far back in the corner of the seat as possible, as though to hide her face. She turned to Kate and said, 'I did not want her on the place. She used to bicycle over, sometimes even walk. I told Charles it was unwise. The coloured people get drunk, you know, and anything can happen. Is that not so, Smuts?'

'That is so, Miss Augusta.'

'Boss Charles told her father. That was soon after her mother died. He told him about the dangers. But Sachs could never control her. She used to swim naked.'

'She swam naked with me,' Kate said.

'You see? I mean, you cannot do such a thing. There are always coloureds somewhere.' Kate thought of Jonas with his fishing-pole. He was like one of the rocks: a permanent fixture in Saxenburg Cove. 'It is not very nice to say so, but she was . . . what is the English word, Smuts?'

'For what, Miss Augusta?'

'For Miriam Sachs.'

He thought for a moment, and said, 'You mean she was Jewish, Miss Augusta?'

'Of course she was Jewish, but that is not the – head-strong, that is the word. Head-strong. Her father could not control her. There were stories when she went to school. They found her with boys.' She sat back and was silent for a moment, then said, 'I never liked their friendship.'

'Whose?'

'She and Charles. When they were little she always wanted to be alone with him. I found them in a cupboard once and she had . . . well, I will not say. But she was . . . what is the word in English, Smuts? Oh, ja, forward; forward for her age.'

Kate thought of the big, full breasts, the rounded thighs, the jet black hair and the jet black eyes. Yes, Miriam had been forward, if by forward Mrs. Preller meant what Kate thought she meant.

'. . . dark places,' Mrs. Preller was saying. 'She used to take him to the grotto. I forbade it. Boss Charles found them there. No clothes on and the tide coming in. Well, I said: No more! And now look what has happened.'

Kate had met Miriam for the first time on the train coming to Helmsdale. They had shared a compartment but had hardly spoken until the train was crossing the wide plain that ended at the coast. Then Miriam had asked Kate why she was travelling to Helmsdale.

'To work,' she had said. 'I'm a secretary.'

'In the bank?'

Miriam had made it sound as though this was the only place in Helmsdale for such work.

'No, for Mrs. Preller.'

'You mean out at Saxenburg?'

'Is there another Mrs. Preller?'

Miriam had given a short, bitter laugh. 'No, only one, thank God.'

[3]

The inquest was to be held in the Magistrate's Court on
the edge of town. Beyond it was the small gaol, the local
school's playing fields, then nothing but the plain stretching to the distant mountains. Little knots of people stood
in the shade of blue-gum trees, waiting to see who would
enter. As Smuts parked the car, Dr. du Toit came towards
them.

'Good morning, Augusta.'

'Hello, Hennie.'

He smiled at Kate. It was the smile she thought of as
his 'intimate' smile, the one she liked least. He was a big
man, as tall as Tom, but as wide as a barn door, and was
running now to fat. His skin was olive and his mane of
hair silver. He was vain about his hair and used pomade
to keep it in place. He parted it in the middle, then drew
the long frontal strands back in two wings. She estimated
his age as in the early fifties, but it was not easy to judge
because his face was plump and unlined and he had two
dimples in his cheeks. He had done his internship at Guy's
Hospital in London and had captained the rugby team
there. He was a widower of fairly recent vintage and his
children had left home some years before. He was Mrs.
Preller's physician and came to tea at Saxenburg every
Friday.

Once, soon after she had arrived, Kate had gone to his
surgery to collect a package for Mrs. Preller. It was about
six o'clock in the evening and he had been on the point of
closing. The surgery formed part of his single-storeyed villa
and he had asked her to have a drink with him.

He had given her a glass of sherry and had taken a large brandy and water for himself.

'The sun is over the yardarm, as they say,' he had said, and taken a long swallow.

He had talked about London. Kate had been there only to catch the boat-train for Southampton so she had listened in silence and soon she had realised that this was all he required, to relieve his loneliness.

His house had a cold, unloved look, though she assumed he had a house-keeper, someone like Lena, to clean and cook. The furnishings were brown and the curtains let in very little light. It was a gloomy place, she thought, that needed a woman's hand.

He had talked about rugby and indicated the pictures around the walls and the silver trophies and tasselled caps in a glass-fronted cabinet. She felt that he must have brought them into the room since his wife's death, for they were not the kind of ornaments and pictures one usually saw in a family house. It was as though he had turned the living-room into a memorial to his past.

He had brought over the sherry decanter to refill her glass, but she had shaken her head.

'The doctor knows best,' he had said, dimples showing as he smiled.

He had filled her glass and given himself a second brandy, larger than the first. He had asked her about Edinburgh and she had answered briefly. Then he had asked about her family, but before she could talk about it he had begun to tell her about his own children. They were in Cape Town, two sons who were both doing well.

Soon she had begun to feel a need to get out of the claustrophobic room. Outside, the sun was shining and the sea was shimmering, but inside the house it was stuffy and hot.

'Have you met anyone your own age here?' he said.

'Not yet.'

'You should meet Miriam Sachs.'

'She was on the train when I came to Helmsdale.'

'She's a very, how can I put it? – out-going girl. I've known her for years. I taught her to swim. Her father is away a lot, you know. She gets lonely when she's here alone.'

Kate had put her sherry glass down on a table next to her chair and, for the first time, noticed a magazine, lying open. There were illustrations, but she could not make out what they were.

'You should get to know Miriam. Have some fun.' He paused. 'I've watched her grow from a little girl into a woman.'

Kate's eyes had strayed to the magazine again. There was something familiar about one of the diagrams. She realised she was looking at an illustration of a vagina.

Du Toit saw her reaction and picked up the magazine. He held it out to her. 'If you're interested, borrow it.'

Words she had never seen written before sprang from the page: penis, testicles, vagina, clitoris. It was a medical journal, but the words were a shock.

She rose. 'I must go. Mrs. Preller will be waiting.'

'You haven't finished your . . .'

She slipped past him and went out through the surgery door and into the sunshine.

Since then she had turned down several invitations from him for drinks or supper and had seen to it that any packages were picked up by Smuts.

Now he was dressed formally in a black coat, sponge-bag trousers and a wing collar. He towered over the diminutive Mrs. Preller.

'What news of Sachs?' she said.

'He's not too good. When the police told him, he collapsed. Heart. It hasn't been strong for some time. I got him to hospital.'

'You see?' Mrs. Preller turned to Kate. 'It is as I said.'

'He can't come today, of course. Maybe it's for the best. I heard the ice-factory wants to get rid of her as quickly as possible.'

'Who can blame them?' Mrs. Preller said. 'You don't want to make ice near a dead body.'

They moved out of the hot sun, but it was not much cooler inside the courtroom. Dr. du Toit led them to a row of reserved seats. The only windows were high on one wall and were covered in blinds to keep out the sun, so that the light was dim. An electric fan stood on the clerk's table, but it only seemed to move hot air from one part of the court-room to another. Kate glanced about her. The room was all mahogany and green leather. The Bench was in front of her, rising like the prow of a ship, and behind it was the Coat of Arms. Her mind went back to another Bench, a different Coat of Arms, another courtroom. Then it had been a trial, not an inquest, and it was her brother Douglas who had stood in the dock.

It was there, in the Sheriff's Court in Edinburgh, that she had felt her deepest despair. All her life until then she had fought to get away from her family. As a child her need had been subconscious, as an adult consciously planned. When she heard her brother found guilty she had tasted real bitterness; she had known she could never escape them, for without her, they were lost.

They had always lived in the same tenement near the Canongate, with the smell of urine and vomit on the common stair. Even as a child, she'd had to help her father up those stairs when he'd had too much to drink on a Friday night. Often he would have spent all his money in the Rose Street pubs and they'd only had the few shillings her mother made with the ironing to buy their mutton pies and pease pudding. As far back as that she had decided that some day, somehow, she was going to escape from the wynds of Edinburgh.

She'd had one stroke of luck – and that was all she had needed. The headmistress of her first school had felt sorry for the child with the pinched face and thin, bony body, and had given her more attention than most. Kate had responded. She had done good work. She had been praised. The praise had brought a stronger response. It became, instead of the vicious circle of failure into which some children fall, a circle that bred success. The more she achieved the more she was praised and the more she wanted to achieve.

But still she'd had to live in the stifling atmosphere of the tenement where Duggie was growing into the image of his father. As a counter-balance, she had given more and more time to her school work. She had taken extra classes so she would not have to go home, even learning to play the piano.

And then one day she had been told about scholarships, and had seen a way to break out of her rut. Each year, one or two girls of her class were awarded scholarships to the Academy, a boarding establishment out past Morningside near the Braid Hills. If she had to board, she could not live at home. She worked as she had never worked before and six months later was living in a kind of paradise. She had slept in a dormitory in a bed with clean, crisp sheets and eaten three good meals a day. She did not go home even on those weekends set aside for visiting.

She had spent four years at the Academy, the happiest years of her life. She hardly knew that a war was on or that her brother was fighting. She had not wanted to know. She had not wanted anything to intrude.

But it could not last for ever. The four years had come to an end and she had returned home. She had taken a job in a shop in George Street and begun bringing money home. It had been the signal for her father to become even more erratic. He was a carpenter and was paid by the hour; now he worked fewer hours and spent more time in the pubs. Kate had realised that she was in another circle, only this time the vicious one. She had begun putting a little of her money away, secretly, and used it to pay for shorthand and typing lessons at Nelson's College in Charlotte Square. Soon she had moved from a shop to an office, where the pay was better.

All that now seemed to be part of her distant youth. Her adult life, if she could date it, must have started the day she had gone to meet the hospital train at the Waverley Station and seen Duggie brought along on his stretcher. She had almost forgotten what he looked like and had thought how handsome he was. She had felt the tears rise and he had said, 'Now don't, Kate, it's only a wee bit of a scratch.'

But it wasn't a scratch and it had been weeks before he could walk on his wounded leg. His discharge came and, with it, a small disability grant. He had found it difficult to settle down and had started drinking heavily. She remembered how he would limp out of the tenement, sometimes with his father, sometimes alone, and they wouldn't see him for the rest of the day.

One day after he had come to her with his handsome face alight with the charm he could switch on and off – as his father could – and borrowed a pound for the evening's entertainment, she had spoken about him to her mother. She could not recall precisely what she had said, but she remembered the reaction clearly. She had always known that Duggie was her mother's favourite child, but she had never seen it so marked as at that moment. Her mother had been ironing and she had put down the flat-iron and looked at Kate, her gaunt face hostile.

'He's restless,' she had said. 'Who wouldn't be after what he's been through, so you just haud your tongue about him.'

As far as Jean Buchanan was concerned, it was enough to have him back. She had fretted every day he had been away. Now he was home. Her wee Duggie. And if he was restless and drinking, well, who wouldn't with a leg as sair as his? But the restlessness had led to other things. Money borrowed, first from Kate, then from friends. When her father was in work there was money to be had there and sometimes he and Duggie would meet on a Friday night to spend it. Or there were other men home from the trenches. Old pals. They were restless, too. And work was hard to get, especially for a man with a bad leg. One thing had led to another, and then there had been the cheque book incident. Duggie had found it in a pub, lying under one of the tables. Or at least, that's what he had told the police. He'd cashed a cheque in another pub. And another. Altogether, he had cashed a hundred and eighty pounds.

Kate had watched her father in court. He hardly seemed aware of the enormity of what had happened. This was the first time any member of the family had seen the inside of a courtroom. Duggie had been pale and drawn, her mother tearful. Their lawyer had pleaded for Duggie on the basis of his war service, the wound in his leg. It was the type of plea that was often heard in those days and he had been bound over to be of good behaviour for 12 months.

Kate had seen her future in that courtroom. She had wanted to walk away, but that was the moment when she had realised the impossibility of leaving them, and had begun to plan. If she couldn't leave them, then they must all leave this city where she would never rise above her circumstances.

Again luck, if one could describe pain as luck, came to her aid. Duggie's leg was not healing. An osteopathic surgeon at the Royal Infirmary had advised that he needed sunshine, milk, fresh vegetables and fruit. It was impossible: there was no money for expensive fruit, and where was the sunshine to come from?

From a sunny country, Kate said. If the sun wouldn't come to them, they must go to the sun. And in sunny countries there was plenty of fruit and fresh vegetables Her campaign was directed at her mother. The specialist had mentioned the possibility of amputation if Duggie's leg did not heal. Kate used the threat. Soon, scarcely realising what had happened, Mrs. Buchanan found herself convinced that if they stayed where they were, at the best Duggie would lose his leg, at the worst, die. She had made the final decision to leave Edinburgh.

They had sold the lease of the tenement and most of their possessions and had taken steerage passages to the Cape of Good Hope. Kate could remember the *Dulnain Castle* swinging out into Southampton Water, the tugs pulling and pushing, the band playing, the streamers breaking, and her father, stiff and frightened, saying: 'God knows when we'll see the Old Country again.' Even Duggie had looked sombre, as though he had understood at last what he and his father had achieved.

But in the months that followed, their lives in Cape Town had fallen into much the same pattern as before. All they could afford was a tiny semi-detached villa in the run-down suburb of Observatory. Her father had managed to get the odd week's work here and there. At first, even Duggie had brought in money selling insurance from door to door. But not for long. The sun was *too* warm for him.

'You wouldna expect him to walk all over the town with his leg,' Mrs. Buchanan said.

Money had become everything and, for once, Kate was finding it difficult to get a job that would pay enough to keep them all. So when she had been offered work at Saxenburg, she had jumped at it; not only for the money but for the distance it would place between her and her family.

They had all been to see her off at the Main Line Station in Cape Town, her mother in a shining black straw hat with the pins sticking out of it like skewers, her father in his Sunday best, but even then looking what he was: a man not to be trusted. And Duggie, handsome, hair glistening, limping up and down the train looking for her compartment. She remembered the dusty brown coaches, the howling south-easter blowing grit up from the trackside, the acrid fumes from the locomotive, the yells of the Cape coloured porters. And even then, the talk had been of money.

'Have you got everything?' her mother had said. They had been through this like a litany.

'Yes, mother.'

'I put in a wee bit of chicken and a hard-boiled egg and a tomato.'

'I know, mother.'

'You don't want to spend anything in the dining-car.'

'I won't go near the dining-car.'

'Do you remember where to send the money?'

'I have it written down in six places. The Cape Province Savings Bank. St. George's Street.'

'What number?'

'A hundred and eighty-two.'

Mrs. Buchanan had nodded. 'Do you think there'll be a bank where you're going?'

'There's bound to be. There are banks all over the country.'

'It's just that. . .'

'I'm not going into the jungle. It's not more than a hundred and something miles. The train only takes four hours.'

'Yes, I know. I know that.'

'And there are roads and telegraphs and telephones. You can even telephone me there.'

'You wouldn't expect me to spend money on a thing like that! No, it's just that . . .'

'And if there's not, there'll be a post office and I can send the money that way.'

Mrs. Buchanan had looked vaguely around the station. She had not settled down in Cape Town. She was only really at peace when she was inside the house with Duggie. Just getting to Cape Town had been like getting to the end of the earth. The huge hinterland of Africa might have been the Gobi Desert or Antarctica or Outer Mongolia as far as she was concerned.

'She must be a grand lady,' she had said.

'Who?'

'That Mrs. Preller.'

'Remember, mother, I haven't got the position yet. This is a trial.'

'Och, if the lawyer says you're good enough, I'm sure you can take his word. Just do what she tells you . . .'

'Mother, I'm twenty-five years old!'

'And if she asks you to do things you think . . . a little beneath you –'

'They'll have servants.'

'I'm only saying if.'

'Like what?'

'I don't know. You mind your place, that's all. You're very self-willed at times.'

Kate was about to say, 'I need to be,' when her father had said: 'I'm sure she knows what to do.' He had patted her gloved hand. 'You'll be just fine. I've seen how you've studied and worked. It's a marvel what you've achieved. All you have to do is your best. You canna do more than that.'

'Now, dad, don't you start.'

The guard had waved a green flag, there was a hiss of steam, and the train had begun to move out of the station.

'Good-bye,' she had called.

Her mother was dabbing at dry eyes, her father had taken off his hat, Duggie was waving his cane. She had hardly noticed them. She was looking over their heads, as she had been for the past ten minutes, hoping to see Tom. She had told herself, as the train moved out of the station past the seventeenth-century Dutch castle on the one hand and the steely waters of Table Bay on the other, that it was a good thing he hadn't come. She had told herself that distance would cut her off from Tom and what remained of their feelings would die a natural death.

But now, sitting in the courtroom at Helmsdale, she knew this to be one of the great ironies of her life, and in spite of the heat she felt herself go cold with the thought of what she had to do, what might happen in the future.

The courtroom began to fill. She saw Mr. Sachs' lawyer, Arnold Leibowitz, take his place at the advocates' table. Van Blerk, the police sergeant who had interviewed her, came in and nodded respectfully towards Mrs. Preller. That had been a feature of the morning: the respectful greetings for the old lady. It was one of the first things Kate had noticed when they were together in Helmsdale. It was natural, she supposed, Mrs. Preller owned a great deal of Helmsdale. Smuts had come in and was sitting on Mrs. Preller's far side, beyond Dr. du Toit. She turned and looked towards the rear of the court, where the coloureds stood. She could make out Lena and Betty, and in the far corner, almost hidden in the shadowy room, she saw Jonas.

At that moment the coroner came in and the inquest started. She inspected him closely, for she was to be questioned by him. He had come from the town of Caledon some fifty miles away. He was an elderly man with moist eyes and walked with a shuffle. He took his seat on the Bench, nodded to Leibowitz, unscrewed a fountain pen and shifted his legal pad into the correct position.

Sergeant Van Blerk was first on the witness stand and he began to giving evidence of identification.

'You say the father is not in court?' the coroner said.

'That is correct, sir.'

'But you contacted him?'

'Yes, sir, the deceased was taken straight to the ice-factory. The day was very warm. I then went to call Mr. Sachs.'

Van Blerk was a large man, running to fat. His head was bald and dotted with perspiration. He held a notebook in one hand and a handkerchief in the other, with which he wiped his forehead from time to time.

'Go on.'

'I accompanied him to the ice-factory where he identified the body as his daughter . . .' He consulted his note-book. 'Miriam Rose Sachs. And then he collapsed, sir.'

I see. And he is still sick?'

'Yes, sir. I understand so, sir.'

The coroner asked Van Blerk about the body as it had been found in the water. The questions were perfunctory, and concerned the depth of water and the tides. It seemed to Kate that he had already made up his mind about the cause of death.

'I understand there have been many drownings on this coast?'

'That's true, sir. Many.'

'And at this place?'

'Not exactly in the rock pools. Not that I know of. But in the bay, yes. It's rocky.'

'From the evidence, what do you think happened?'

'I believe she went swimming at night, sir, and maybe slipped and fell, probably hitting her head.'

'We'll hear what the doctor has to say about that. Thank you.'

Old Dr. Richards, the District Surgeon, was next, and his evidence was almost as brief as Van Blerk's. He was a small, gnomelike man, with a stringy, fibrous quality about him. He could have been made of dried meat. Even in the poor light, Kate could see tufts of hair growing from his ears.

'What is your opinion of the cause of death?'

'Oh, she drowned. Typical. I've seen scores of drownings along here. Fishermen mostly. They never listen. I tell them over and over again to be careful, but you see them all the time, standing on low rocks or ledges just above the water. Then a big wave comes and . . .' He threw up his hands. 'Typical!'

The coroner asked him about the abrasions on the body's arms and face and the side of the head.

'Could she have fallen?'

'That's probably how it happened. I mean, those rocks are slippery.'

The picture of Miriam's face rose in Kate's mind. It had been like something on a butcher's slab.

Mrs. Preller leant over and spoke into her ear. 'All he cares about is his fishing. He takes the government's money, but he does nothing.'

Kate was called next. She had been apprehensive about this moment, but felt calmer having seen the informality with which the inquest had so far been conducted. The coroner took details of her name, age, occupation, and then said, 'Tell me exactly how you found the body.'

She could remember it all as clearly as though it was on a bioscope film running through her mind. What made it so sharp was that it had come after the events of the previous night, so that it seemed part of a continuing sequence.

It was a Monday morning, and she had woken feeling nervous and tired and hot and had decided on an early swim to clear her head. For once there was no wind and the sea was aquamarine under an enormous blue sky with wisps of high cloud. She had put on her bathing costume, bathing shoes and dressing gown, and slipped out of the sleeping house.

The pools were like glass. She had crunched over the sand and then over the flat rocks to the first pool and was taking off her dressing-gown when she had seen the thing in the water.

The body was hunched forward, the arms were limply outstretched and the face was in the water. The shoulders were the only part of it that was above the water. The legs hung down so that it seemed almost to be standing on the bottom of the pool.

'Did you recognise the body as that of Miss Sachs?' the coroner said.

'Not at that moment.'

'What happened next?' He did not look up and she saw his pen flowing along the lines of the pad.

It was difficult to describe the next few minutes in exact words. Her mind had reacted quickly. For an instant she had thought someone was swimming and waited for movement; for an instant she had been gripped by terror; and then she had known she was looking at a dead body.

One of the hands had been almost touching the rock wall and she had bent and tugged it. The body had rolled and she had seen the red horror that had once been Miriam's face and the big, heavy breasts. She had recognised Miriam by her breasts, but how could she tell the coroner that?

'You *thought* it was Miss Sachs?'

'From her hair. The way it was cut.'

'The way it was cut?' The coroner looked up and his moist eyes fastened on her.

'Square across the forehead.'

'Is this unusual?'

'I don't think so, but I don't know anyone else here with hair cut like that. And the colour was black.'

And the eyes, she thought. The eyes had been black, too, and as the body had rolled, they had looked up at her, large and dead, the light behind them had gone out. Charles' eyes were like that sometimes. A blank. But with Charles that was usually a sign of rage.

'And then?'

'I ran back to the house and telephoned the police and Sergeant Van Blerk came out and took the body from the water.'

After Kate, Dr. du Toit was called.

'You are the Sachs' physician?' the coroner said.

'That is correct, sir.'

'You are also a friend of the family, I understand.'

'I've known them for many years. I brought Miriam into the world and attended her mother in her last illness. I am attending her father now.'

'You knew the deceased well?'

'You could say that. I watched her grow up.'

'What sort of a person was she?'

Kate heard Mrs. Preller give a slight snort.

Du Toit paused. 'She was a very nice girl.'

'Yes, but was she the kind of girl who would go swimming at night?'

'Yes, sir.'

'Alone?'

'She was known to do things like that. She was an extrovert personality. Ever since she was a little girl she did things her own way, if you understand what I mean.'

'Would she have gone swimming in the nude?'

'Yes, I believe so.'

'Thank you, doctor.'

The inquest was over soon afterwards, the coroner handing down a verdict of accidental death by drowning.

'All this nonsense, taking up the taxpayers' money,' Mrs. Preller said as they filed out of court. 'Of course she drowned. It was just like her.'

'But how did she get out to Saxenburg?' Kate said.

'On a bicycle. Or on her feet. It's not too far.'

'There was no bicycle.'

'She often walked out when she was a young girl. And there was a full moon. Miriam would do things like that. Did you not hear Dr. du Toit?'

They reached the car. 'I'm glad her father was not there,' Mrs. Preller said. 'I am not glad he is ill, but I am glad he was not there. It is bad enough to look at the dead body of your child.'

On the outskirts of town Kate saw Lena and Betty walking bare-footed along the dusty road. Smuts stopped for them and they got into the front seat beside him. As she had been before, Kate was struck by Betty's beauty. The girl was eighteen or nineteen and her skin was creamy brown. She might have been Greek or Southern Italian. Instead of the pepper-corn hair of most coloureds, hers was long and came almost to her shoulders. She was wearing a thin blouse with nothing beneath it and her breasts were high and sharply pointed. But her eyes were her most lovely feature. They were a greyish blue and Kate had sometimes wondered what stranger had crossed Lena's path all those years ago. A sailor, perhaps, from one of the wrecks?

'Well, Lena, that's over,' Mrs. Preller said.

'Yes, Madam.' She pronounced it 'Marrem'. 'Is Madam going to the funeral?'

'Yes I must. Do you want to come?'

'If Madam goes, I will go.'

Almost from the day she arrived, Kate had felt a bond between the two women. She knew Mrs. Preller's opinion of coloured people – not that it was any better or worse than most of the white population of Helmsdale – but there was something different in her attitude to Lena. It was as though they shared an understanding and a world closed to everyone else.

It was difficult to tell what Lena had looked like as a young woman, for like most coloured women she had aged prematurely and had lost the two front teeth in her upper jaw. She was much darker than Betty, but not quite as black as Jonas. Kate had been confused early on by the fact that social position among the coloured folk depended on gradations of colour: the lighter the better. The real black people, the Bantu, the Africans, the Kaffirs as they were called, she had hardly seen. They lived hundreds of miles up country. These were Cape coloureds, the product of white on black over the centuries, who now formed a separate half-caste race mostly centred on Cape Town and the southern districts of the Cape Province.

She knew that Lena had worked for Mrs. Preller for many years. 'She came to me on my wedding day,' Mrs. Preller had told her. 'She is like my right hand.'

The relationship between Lena and her daughter, on the other hand, was bad. Lena dominated Betty and there was constant friction and tension. Betty was often in tears after rows with her mother. At first Kate had tried to patch things up and had been sympathetic to Betty. But neither seemed to want her to interfere, especially Betty who, under the constant, watchful eye of Lena, was a sullen and resentful young woman. Kate put down much of the tension to the presence of Jonas.

She thought the relationship a strange one, especially as Lena seemed a good-natured person in other respects. There was no doubt in her mind that had it not been for

31

Lena she would have bitterly regretted coming to Saxenburg in those first weeks.

The house itself had had an overpowering effect on her. She had found its brooding, enclosed atmosphere claustrophobic, almost frightening. She remembered how she had entered the house for the first time at dusk and sensed its eeriness.

Lena and Betty had met her at the door and she had followed Smuts into a large hall. There had been only one small oil lamp hanging from the centre of the ceiling, throwing a feeble light, and the corners of the room and parts of the walls had disappeared into shadow and darkness. She'd had an impression of muted colours and a musty, dusty smell. A large and magnificently carved staircase rose from the centre of the hall and on either side of it were great amphorae-like porcelain jars filled with what at first looked, in the half light, like dried ferns, but on closer examination turned out to be ostrich feathers. There were more feathers in vases on the walls. They were in constant slight movement as draughts of air touched them, and appeared to be alive.

The hall's dominating feature was a towering sculpture that appeared from its general shape to be a crucifix, but as Kate drew nearer she had realised that it was the figurehead of a sailing-ship: a woman with a large, naked bust, flowing gold hair and dark red robes. On a panel of wood below it was one word: Saxenburg.

'Smuts!' She had heard the harsh, shrill call and had looked up to see the figure of a woman at the top of the staircase, her hands gripping the balustrade. The face was dead white below long, dark hair.

'I'm sorry, Miss Augusta, the train was late.' Smuts had moved towards the staircase with the rolling, bandy-legged walk that Kate had noticed on the station.

'Did you get it?'

He had tapped his pocket.

'Give it to Lena,' the woman had said. 'Lena, you bring it up, now.'

'Miss Buchanan is here,' Smuts had said.

But the figure at the top of the staircase had turned away

and disappeared, Lena following her. There had been a flash of light as a door opened and closed and then the house was silent once more.

Smuts had shrugged and said, 'She'll call you when she wants you. She will send Lena.' He had closed the front door after him and she had heard his booted feet on the gravel. She had not known whether to wait for him to come back; she'd had no idea what to do. Then Betty had taken up her cases and Kate had followed her up the big staircase. She had seen a shadowy corridor. About half way along it, a thin band of light shone at the bottom of a door and she had heard the faint sound of voices. She had followed the girl up a second staircase, this one narrower and steeper, to a square landing. Betty had opened the first door on the right, allowing Kate to go in ahead of her. It was a large, low-ceilinged room again lit by an oil lamp and, being a corner room, there were windows on two walls. The windows had no curtains and the blinds were up, giving them the look of dark, shining eyes.

'What's your name?' Kate had said.

'Betty.'

'Thank you for bringing up my suitcases.' It was then she had noticed the girl's beauty for the first time.

'We're going to be friends, I hope,' she had said.

'Yes, Madam.' She had replied without emotion and had turned and left at once.

Kate had looked about her, then pulled down the blinds. With the night shut out the room became less stark, but at the top of the house the wind roared and whined as squalls struck the headland. Such wind had been a new experience in her life then; now she was used to it.

The room must once, long ago, have been a nursery. At one end was her bed, with a wardrobe and a dressing-table; at the other there was a fire-place around which three armchairs had been grouped. They had all seen better days. One was badly stained and a second had horse-hair coming from a large hole in the arm. Near one window was a table and two hard chairs. There was a rocking-horse, missing an eye, and along one wall was a blackboard and chalks. Apart from the door through which she had entered there were two other doors, one near the head of her bed, which she found to be locked. She had assumed that a nanny or a governess might once have slept in the adjoining room. The third door opened into a small bathroom. There was a copper geyser set with paper and kindling ready to light. She had noticed that the taps on the bath and hand-basin were massive brass affairs. The bath had rust streaks and the tap in the basin dripped continuously. The water, when she had switched it on, was a pale, peaty colour. The bathroom smelled of damp and seaweed but the bedroom, when she had returned to it, had the same dusty smell as the hall downstairs.

Soon Lena had come in with a tray. There had been bread and butter on it, a glass of milk and a plate heaped with some mustard-coloured substance which Kate had not recognised.

'What have you brought me?'

'Yellowtail, Madam.'

'What's yellowtail?'

Lena had said, 'Fish, Madam. Pickled fish. If you don't want it, I can bring some cold meat.'

'I'll try it.'

'It's good.'

She had turned to the door and Kate had suddenly not wanted to be left alone and inquired her name.

'Lena, Madam.'

'Won't you call me Miss Kate instead of Madam?'

'Yes, Miss Kate.'

'The lady at the top of the stairs . . . that was Mrs. Preller?'

'Yes. She says she will see Miss Kate tomorrow.'

'Lena . . .'

'Yes, Miss Kate?'

'Nothing. Goodnight, Lena.'

Then Lena had said a strange thing: 'I hope Miss Kate is happy here. We need Miss Kate.' She had turned and left the room.

Kate had stood in the centre of the room for some moments, feeling touched, but at the same time, curious. Why did they need her? They didn't even know her.

She had tried to eat some of the food, but the pickled fish was curried and had burnt her mouth. She had sat on her bed and felt that she had never been quite so alone as she was at that moment.

But she was not the kind of person to sit brooding. She had explored the cupboard space and had begun to unpack. That finished, she had decided to have a bath, but had changed her mind when she calculated the effort of lighting the geyser. Instead, she had stripped and given herself a flannel wash. There was an old stained mirror behind the bathroom door then – she had replaced it with a better one later – and she remembeed looking at herself in the half light, seing the dim reflection of her body. 'You're a throw-back,' Duggie had said once. 'A dark Celt.' And she had remembered Tom on the ship coming out to the Cape stroking her naked breasts in the heat of the cabin and saying, 'You've got a body like a young boy,' and she had said, 'Do you like young boys?'

The mirror had reflected her eyes, deep brown and set wide apart, large and flecked with gold, with an inner light that gave an impression of immense energy and vitality.

That night, when sleep had come at last, her dreams had been filled with white, writhing snakes with gaping mouths and bulging eyes, and ships breaking up on jagged black rocks, and a woman coming out of the sea, her breasts white and bare, the remainder of her body covered in a film of blood.

When she had thought about the dream the following morning, she was able to place all the images. Now, in the car going back to Saxenburg after the inquest, she wondered if there had been precognition: surely the body had been Miriam's?

[4]

Everything was strange those first days. She remembered that when she awoke the morning after her arrival the first

35

thing she had noticed was the silence. It was almost as though she had come to her senses in a tomb. The blinds were still down and the room was dark. She had climbed out of bed and let the light in, then stood at the window, staring down at the view. It was breath-taking. Her room was on the seaward side of the house, so close to the edge of the cliffs that it appeared from her angle that cliff and house were one. The sea was directly below her.

To her left, the cliffs stretched along the coast, dropping away to the town of Helmsdale and the long white beach beyond. To her right there was the cove with the headland on the far side. In the brilliant morning sunshine the sea had been light green and almost flat calm. Tides had still sucked back and forth across the India Reef, but they were small by comparison with the day before.

It was a little after seven o'clock and she'd had no idea what the household arrangements for breakfast were. She had washed and dressed and gone down to the hall. The blue and purple ostrich feathers in the big vases at the bottom of the carved mahogany staircase had stirred and turned in the current of her movement.

All the doors which let off from the hall had been closed and she had turned to her left and opened the first one. She had found herself in a huge drawing-room. It occupied a corner of the house, with windows facing the sea. The shutters were closed, but bars of sunlight lit the room as they might the interior of a church. Again the colours were muted: purples and blues, a grey carpet, grey velvet curtains, more ostrich feathers in vases on the floor and on tables, again the smell of dust. There were piles of magazines on a low stinkwood table. The date on the top one was September, 1913, more than ten years before. She had picked up one or two more. Their dates were all before the war, some near the turn of the century. They had been published in London, Paris, Berlin or Rome and on the cover of each was an illustration of a woman wearing some form of feather decoration, either on her hat or as a boa.

'We don't use this room much,' a voice behind her said.

She spun round. Mr. Smuts had been standing in the doorway.

'I'm sorry . . . I didn't know where to go.'

'It's a lovely room, isn't it? You could sit in that window and throw a stone into the sea. And in the evening, looking out onto the reef . . . I can tell you, my friend, I've never seen anything like it. Look around you. Ever seen such a mixture of things?' He had touched a low teak chest, his fingers straying lovingly over the oiled surface. 'Medicine chest, *Clan MacGregor*, 1902.' On the far side of the room he had indicated a marble-topped table on which stood a vase of ostrich feathers. 'Wash stand. *Queen of the Thames*, 1871. See that wine cabinet? Rose wood. That was off the *Arniston* in 1815. And those decanters. H.M.S. *Greyhound*.'

'You mean all the furniture came from ships that went onto the reef?'

'Only some of the pieces. And not all the ships went down on the India Reef. No, no. Some sank off Cape Infanta, some off Cape Agulhas. Quoin Point. Danger Point. This is what we call the wreck coast. There's more than fifty gone down within a few miles of here. Started with the Dutch ship *Zoetendal* in 1673 and they're still going down.'

'But where did all this furniture come from? Was it washed ashore?'

'Some of it. Most of it was bought at auctions by Mr. Preller's family. Come and look at this.' He had led the way into a room next door. It was a dining-room with a long refectory table. 'Oak,' he had said, smoothing its surface. 'English oak. Came out of the *Nicobar*. English East Indiaman that went down just a few miles from here. They say the table floated to our beach. See those chandeliers? From the *Saxenburg*. She went down off Agulhas in 1729. That sideboard came out of her, too. So did the figurehead in the hall. Bought by Mr. Preller's family at auction. That's why they named this place Saxenburg House when they built it. Come and have some breakfast.'

They had taken their breakfast – as they still did – in a small room overlooking the cliffs.

'You should have seen this place in the old days,' he had said, pointing at her with a finger of toast. 'Parties, balls. People came all the way from Cape Town. Swimming, tennis. We had an opera company here once. Mrs. Preller used to be fond of music. Something called a string quartet, too. Never heard such a terrible noise. Now . . . well, now it's not the same.' His voice had fallen and he seemed to be looking inward, as though sensing old age coming, and the change in himself. 'Boss Charles always said the good times would come again. But I don't know . . . Come on, I'll show you round the place.'

Outside in the bright morning sunshine she had seen the house for the first time in some detail. It was three storeys and almost completely square, built of mountain stone with two curved Dutch gables facing the sea. Each window had a pair of teak shutters, most of which were closed. On the landward side of the house were sheds and out-buildings, which she had not seen the night before. Everywhere she had looked there were ostriches, some in pairs, some in flocks.

'Feather dusters,' Smuts had said. 'That's all they're good for now.'

She had seen the sheds where the wagons were kept and the room where the feathers were packed; she saw the 'plucking boxes,' and the area where a few sheep were kept. Gradually, she had realised that everything was in a state of decay.

'See those?' Smuts had pointed to what looked like a series of dusty chests of drawers against the wall of one of the sheds. 'Incubators. We used to incubate hundreds of eggs in the old days. Now what's the point?' She had recognised even then – and had heard it dozens of times afterwards – that the phrase 'the good old days' was a kind of litany.

'Morning, Master.'

'Morning, Jonas.'

This was the first time she had seen Jonas. He was a very dark-skinned Cape coloured in his late twenties, dressed in dusty khaki clothing and broken shoes. On his head he had worn an old felt hat from which rose a beautiful, pure white ostrich plume.

'Have you finished that fencing?'

'I got no more wire, Master.'

'Is there no more in the shed?'

'No, Master.'

As he spoke, Jonas had looked at Kate.

He was good-looking, powerfully built, and she could see his dark skin under the open shirt. His look was aggressively sexual and she had turned away, uncomfortable.

'All right, we're going into town in a little while.' Smuts had walked on. 'That's Jonas. We used to have twenty or thirty like him in the old days. Now he's the only one left. Do you want to see the town in daylight?'

'What about Mrs . . .?'

'Mrs. Preller doesn't want you this morning.'

'Well, I need to go to the bank.'

'We'll take the lorry.'

This was a small truck and at first Kate had wondered how they would all fit on the front seat, but then Jonas had climbed into the open back.

They had bumped over the pot-holed road. The country in daylight had given her much the same impression as it had the night before: dry, sandy, with the dusty green carpet of *fynbos* stretching as far as the distant mountains. The lorry had clattered and banged with such violence that she'd had to hold onto the side of the seat to stop herself flying into the air. Dust had risen from the wooden floorboards.

Soon they had reached the outskirts of Helmsdale. They had approached it from the cliffs winding down to sea-level. 'Look over there,' Smuts had shouted as the road dipped down. They were passing a mock-Tudor mansion with fake beams, set against what had once been white walls. Through a pair of massive gates of iron lacework she had seen the jumble of an overgrown garden. The windows of the house were covered with rusty corrugated iron, gutterings hung from the roof, down-pipes stood askew, and a windmill, its blades rusted and broken, looked like a pterodactyl standing on its long thin legs.

'That's "De Rust," ' Smuts had said. 'Used to be the Van Staden place. And see that over there?'

A little farther along, on the opposite side of the road, there was another vast house, this time in the Scottish baronial style, built of stone with a round tower. Here the gates hung brokenly from their posts, windows were smashed and again the garden was wild and overgrown. 'That's the old Richardson place.'

They had passed three more such houses with towers, wrought-iron balconies, leaded windows, doors of heavy teak, bleached and cracked by the sun and the wind.

'Ostrich houses, that's what they were called. Built in the old days when things were good. You know how much they cost? Twenty thousand, thirty thousand pounds! They had to quarry the stone up in the mountains. Brought in architects from Paris and London. Stone-masons from Cornwall. All paid for with feathers, my friend. They reckon between 1910 and 1914 nearly fifteen million pounds came into Helmsdale.'

'What happened in 1914?' Kate had said, bumping up and down and clinging onto her hat.

'The war, my friend, that's what happened. You don't wear ostrich feathers in wartime. At first these people had farms back there.' He had waved at the hazy mountains in the interior. 'Lived like poor whites. They couldn't read or write, some of them. Didn't know how to hold a cup and saucer. But they had ostriches, and when the boom started, they became rich overnight. You should have seen what they bought: marble from Italy, porcelain from France; they had sunken baths and furniture from England; ty bought their table silver in Sheffield and their linen from Ireland. They couldn't spend it all. Feathers were selling for two hundred pounds a pound. There was one chap who bought a whole library from Germany. Couldn't read German. Couldn't even read English, but he wanted a library, so he bought one. And they built their houses here, their ostrich houses, by the sea.'

'Where are they now?'

'Gone. Sold up for what they could get.'

The centre of the town was a grid of half a dozen wide streets. She had noticed one or two bullock wagons with spans of twelve or fourteen oxen being driven up the unmade main street, a few Cape carts, some riders on horse-back, horses tethered to the hitching-rails along the street and a sprinkling of cars and trucks. No building was more than two storeys; most were one.

Smuts had parked at the dusty sidewalk and Jonas had jumped down from the back.

'You go and get the wire,' Smuts had told him. 'And come back to the lorry, d'you hear?'

'Yes, Master.'

'I don't want you buggering off like last time, you understand?'

'Yes, Master.'

As Jonas turned away, Smuts had said to Kate, 'If he gets his hands on a bottle, the women have to look out.' He had pointed to a single-storey building on the far side of the street that looked like a private house. 'That's the bank. I have business to do. I'll be back in a couple of hours. If you want a cup of tea, there's the Evergreen Café. They should have the Cape Town papers by now, they come in on the early train.'

She had watched him go off up the sidewalk with his bandy-legged strut and then she crossed the road. A bullock wagon was being turned. Its rear was at one sidewalk, the front bullocks at the other. She had realised then why the streets were so wide.

There had been no customers in the bank and she had quickly made arrangements to transfer money she received in Helmsdale to her mother's account in Cape Town. On the street again, she had decided to have a look around. What there was of the centre was quickly seen. She had walked down the main street and along one or two of the side streets. It was the first small South African town she had ever been in, but it was not long before she had realised that something was desperately wrong with it.

She had been born in a city and had emigrated to another, she was used to people and bustle, here there was neither. The sidewalks had been almost empty. She had walked slowly down the main street. Each building was a replica of its neighbour. Most were white, with small pointed gables and corrugated-iron verandah roofs to enable shoppers to stroll in the shade. But there had not been any shoppers, in fact, there were few shops. Every third one had been closed, dark blue blinds covering the windows. Some had had 'For Sale' notices in them, some 'To Rent'.

The town's commercial centre became residential without any dividing line and many of the small bungalows were closed up and for sale. It was as though a plague had come to Helmsdale. She had turned down another street and seen a sign which said Preller Motors. A mechanic was working on a car, but the showroom where the new models should have stood was empty. Coming back into the main street, she had seen Preller's Hotel. And down at the little fishing harbour a sign on a corrugated iron building read, 'Preller Fertilizers'. She had paused to watch the fish market. A crowd of Cape coloured folk had gathered. The fish were being sold in bunches, tied together by strips of cane passed through the gills. They had all looked so different from the plaice and the cod and the haddock of Edinburgh. There had been red fish and silvery-yellow fish and copper-coloured fish and some with sharp, spike-like jaws and some with flattened noses. As she turned away she had seen on a slope of rising ground above the beach, what seemed to be a separate village, a kind of suburb of small, pretty white-washed cottages with dark thatch above. They looked like the bothies she had seen in the Central Highlands.

She had walked through the village, followed by a group of noisy coloured children, and soon realised that it was a coloured area. She was the only white person in it. She turned and began to retrace her steps. As she did so, something white flashed in one of the doorways. It was the ostrich plume on Jonas's hat. He was drinking from a bottle of wine. He had wiped the neck of the bottle and handed it to someone inside the house. As Kate saw him, he had glanced in her direction and with one fluid movement regained the interior of the cottage. It all happened so quickly that she had wondered whether, in fact, it *had* been Jonas. She had walked slowly down to the beach and turned up the main street.

She and Smuts had reached the lorry simultaneously.

Jonas had been lying in the back, his white-plumed hat covering his face, a roll of barbed wire at his feet.

'They sleep any bloody where, these people,' Smuts had said. 'Climb in.' She had decided that it could not have been Jonas she had seen in the fishing village.

They had driven back along the road above the cliff, passing the empty 'ostrich' houses, and Kate had been struck by the eeriness of recent decay. She had noticed other things about the gardens: the broken bottles near the gates, but also the remnants of cultivation, plumbago and agapanthus pushing their way through the weeds at the side of the overgrown carriage drives. She remembered thinking how splendid it must once have been: the music and picnics and tennis parties. It was the kind of society she had read about in Britain, but of which she had never even touched the fringe. Yet it had thrived in this remote and inhospitable place.

Betty had come from the house to fetch Smuts's parcels. Jonas had jumped down from the back and was lifting out the barbed wire. Kate remembered vividly how the girl had walked out with a swing to her hips, the wind pressing her thin dress to her body, outlining her sharp young breasts and her rounded thighs. Jonas had watched as she bent to pick up the parcels from the front seat. Then he had leaned towards her and said something which Kate could not catch but which Smuts, coming round the front of the lorry, had heard. Betty had straightened and looked at Jonas with a glance that was at once angry and inviting.

Smuts had smiled. 'Jonas, you bugger, I don't want to hear you say things like that.'

The two men had laughed.

'Betty!'

Lena had been on the front steps, her face angry. Betty had hurried up the steps and her mother had hissed at her and pushed her into the house. Then she turned and screeched at Jonas. Kate had not understood what she said, but her meaning was clear enough.

'Lena will fix you, Jonas,' Smuts had said, laughing. 'Look out for her.'

'What time is the funeral?' Mrs. Preller said as they arrived back at Saxenburg after the inquest.

'Three o'clock,' Smuts said.

'We will leave at twenty to. Lena as well.'

'Yes, Miss Augusta.'

'Have they got a rabbi?'

'I don't know.'

Kate took the old woman's arm and helped her up the steps. She was as thin as a rail. 'I have some letters,' she said.

'Now?'

'No, no, the usual time.'

After seeing her to her door, Kate went up to her room. A breeze had begun to blow from the sea and she opened her windows gratefully. It was a lovely, brilliant day and she should have been feeling part of it, instead Miriam's tragedy loomed over her. And yet she knew this was not the only reason for her depression.

Ever since she had sailed with her family from Southampton she had kept a diary. It was a simple affair with just enough information to remind her of a day or a week. Then, after she had begun the affair with Tom, she had kept her entries in shorthand. She took it from the drawer of the bedside table and sat down on her bed. She paged back until she came to a small cross above an entry just over two months earlier. It was the last time she and Tom had made love. She counted forward. She had done this several times in the past two days, hoping that somehow the numbers would come out differently. But there was no mistake: her period was two months overdue. She closed the diary and sat staring at the wall. If only Tom was free. If only he had told her on the ship that he was married. If only . . .

She felt as an animal must feel driven into a corner by dogs. She had two alternatives: the first, to have the baby, was unthinkable. Mrs. Preller would never keep her on and, anyway, who was to maintain the family and herself *and* a baby? The other alternative was to have it removed. But how could that be done? She had known a secretary in Edinburgh who'd had an abortion in Leith. She had returned to the office as pale as death and it had taken her weeks to recover fully. But Leith was six thousand miles away. After the last row with Tom and the break between them, she would not go to him for help. In any case, what could he do? He was as much a stranger in Africa as she. She had no friends; not even an acquaintance she could approach. She knew that Mrs. Preller liked her, but asking her advice was out of the question. That left only Lena. She and Lena had become friends, but there was a strong bond between Lena and Mrs. Preller. Would she not be likely to pass on confidences to her employer? Lena's religious views could also inhibit any understanding. Kate knew she had very little time in which to decide what to do; as each day passed, an abortion became more difficult and more dangerous.

She put the diary away as she heard the gong announcing lunch. She and Smuts ate together. He tended to gobble his food, without talking much and she enjoyed her meals more when Charles spent week-ends at the house. He had described Smuts as a 'coarse feeder', and she agreed with him. Normally she got on well enough with Smuts, but meal-times were a trial. A small handbell stood at his right hand and he rang it constantly, summoning Betty for the most trivial things. He smoked a brand of cigarette called Commando and a box of fifty was kept on the windowsill. At the end of each meal he would ring the bell, Betty would appear and pass them to him.

Once Kate had remonstrated with him, saying she could easily pass them. He had said, 'What do you think servants are for, my friend?'

He had a strange relationship with them: one minute he seemed friendly and on their own level, joking and teasing. But at the slightest hint that anyone had overstepped the mark and threatened his dignity he could come down harshly on the offender. Kate decided that, like the relationship between Lena and Betty, the one between Smuts and the servants was none of her business.

At two o'clock, as usual, she went up to Mrs. Preller's apartment on the first floor. She still felt its strangeness, but it was nothing like the shock she had received when she had first been summoned.

The room had been in semi-darkness and her first impression was that she had entered some sort of museum. She had smelt incense and the room was so full of furniture that she could see hardly any empty floor space. There were cabinets decorated with gold leaf, statues in black marble, gold-painted salon chairs, a small table inlaid with ivory. In one corner stood a large, dark grand piano, on the walls were heavy portraits of sober faces, and several tapestries. There were potted palms and hanging baskets of ferns and everywhere dyed ostrich plumes waving slowly from side to side. A bamboo-framed screen stood in a corner, opposite the piano. Here there was a desk and telephone and a straight-backed oak chair in which Mrs. Preller was sitting. All Kate had seen at first was a face and hair, disembodied, for the long dark dress she wore blended into the shadows. The face was dead white and the shoulder-length hair was dark. Her lips and fingernails were bright red.

'Good-day, Miss Buchanan,'' the face had said.

'How do you do, Ma'am?'

'Ah, you are Scottish. My lawyers did not tell me that.' She pronounced it Schottisch. 'I have been to Scotland. It is so melancholy, so sad. And rain, rain. Here it is wind, wind. Please let me see your hands.'

'I beg your pardon.'

'Your hands.'

Kate had held out her hands, puzzled, but glad, at the same time, that she had washed them. Mrs. Preller had taken them in her own hands and Kate had seen that her skin was a mass of scars. Instinctively, she had drawn back, but Mrs. Preller had held her, and turned her hands over so that her palms were upwards. 'You have a good heart line, not so? That is important. And a long life. At your age, you must be pleased, but there may come a time when the possibility of such a thing will make you tremble. Please sit in this chair in front of me. You are here for three months' trial. Mr. Godlonton explained such matters to you?' Mr. Godlonton was Mrs. Preller's Cape Town attorney, who had interviewed Kate for the position.

'Yes, Mrs. Preller.'

'Good. So we have three months. By then we know if we like each other. Tell me about yourself.'

Kate had told her briefly about her schooling in Edinburgh, how she had gone to secretarial college, how she had emigrated with her family. But Mrs. Preller seemed hardly to listen, so she gradually wound down and stopped.

Suddenly Mrs. Preller said, 'You do not like pickled fish?'

Kate's mind had somersaulted backwards. 'I'm sure it's very nice, Ma'am. I've never had it before.'

'Pickled fish,' the woman said, more to herself than to Kate. 'Pickled fish and mutton. Mutton and pickled fish. Now we do some shorthand.'

When Kate got to know her better she was not so put out by her sudden changes of direction, but on that first meeting she was taken unawares. 'I beg your pardon?'

'Shorthand. You *do* know what that is?'

'Of course. I'm sorry.' She had taken out her pad and Mrs. Preller had begun to read her a paragraph from one of the magazines that lay strewn about the table near her chair. Kate wrote furiously. She had taken down a story about a young woman going to her first ball and being dressed by a maid in a mansion in London. It had seemed very remote from this darkened room overlooking the sea. Mrs. Preller had paused and Kate had sat with pencil poised, hoping she was not going to be asked what she had written.

Then, in an altered voice, Mrs. Preller had said, 'My husband always said the good times would come back. He said fashion repeats itself like history.'

Kate had realised that the story had set her off on thoughts of ostrich plumes.

'I hope so,' she had continued, 'But where would I be, I wonder, if Mr. Preller had depended on that?' She had looked up sharply at Kate. 'He worshipped me, you know. *Worshipped.*' Although the room was warm, she had shivered and rubbed her arm. 'Nothing was too good for me.

47

And after Hugo died he was so kind, so kind. And then
. . .' In the midst of her memories she had yawned. 'You
may go.'

As Kate was walking along the corridor she had heard
the bell ringing furiously for Lena.

That was the first of many such meetings. Sometimes
Kate would be given six or eight letters to type before
evening. Sometimes she would have to accompany Mrs.
Preller to Helmsdale to check on her business interests
there, and later go over the books. But often the old lady
would simply want someone to listen to her talk. It was
always of the old days, the days at the topmost pinnacle
of the feather boom, when the Prellers and the owners of
the great houses that now stood derelict had been wealthy,
of the parties and the balls and the fun. But often she
talked of even earlier times, in Vienna before she had been
swept off her feet by Mr. Preller.

'That is your expression? Swept off? Such it was with
me.'

One afternoon she had come down and said she would
like to go for a walk. She had given her arm to Kate and
they slowly went along one of the gravel paths until they
came to a gate in a white-washed wall. Kate had never
been through it. She found herself in what had been a great
walled garden. The walls had been built high to stop the
gales. It was a jungle of dead grass. Thorn trees had grown
up and were flowering in what had once been a cypress
hedge. Paper-thorns had taken over the paths. 'Here we
used to play tennis,' Mrs. Preller had said. The tennis
court was a mass of weeds, the stop-netting bright with
rust, and some of it had crumbled away, leaving gaping
holes. The tattered remains of a net still hung on the posts
and in one corner Kate could see what was left of an
umpire's chair. 'And bathing parties there . . .' She had
pointed to a swimming pool, empty now and cracked
beyond recovery. Small shrubs grew up through the cracks.
'I did not like bathing in the sea, it is too dangerous, so
Mr. Preller built this for me. There . . .' She indicated a
small rotunda. '. . . we used to play bridge.' It had once
been an elegant folly with an octagonal roof edged with

iron lace-work and supported by wooden pillars. Now its marble floor was broken and a tree, growing up one side, had forced its way through the roof. In her mind's eye, Kate could picture the hot summer afternoons, the lazy slap of the cards, the soft voices, the servants bringing tea from the house.

'My father had such a summer-house in the garden of our house in Vienna. They used to play cards there. Sometimes I, also. But mostly for me it was practice, practice, until my fingers were sore and my back ached. On the very piano you saw.'

She had led the way back to the house. 'Cards! It was the end of an era. But perhaps they say that about the time before all great wars. My father would smoke his cigars and paint, my mother had her cards, my sisters went to this ball and that concert, to the Staatsoper, to the Musikverein, to Baden for the waters, to our house in the Salzkammergut. Such times! And then he came.'

'Who?'

'Mr. Preller. So handsome. Young. A great rancher. Money no object. But for *me* to come here, from Vienna! What do you think?'

'It must have been a great sacrifice.'

'That is true. But one makes sacrifices for the man one loves. You will find this out, Miss Buchanan.'

They walked on. 'One day this will be put back the way it was. Charles will do it when he has made his fortune. One day I will take Charles to Vienna and show him my home, his grandfather's home. So beautiful. So green and leafy in summer. Almost in the centre of Vienna, but like the country. Vineyards. Heurigers. One day he will be a great rancher too. It is why I have worked so hard. It is why Mr. Preller worked so hard. For our sons, Hugo and Charles. So they would have everything.'

'What happened to Hugo?' Kate said, breaking into her train of thought.

'He died. His father loved him so much. Worshipped him . . .'

'How old was he?'

'Ten years old. The first-born. Boss Charles would have

made him king of all this. It is why he bought the hotel and the garage and put up the factory. It was his kingdom and he would have done more, much more, and then Hugo would have had it. And he would have increased the property until it was like the very old days when the Prellers owned everything hereabouts. Now it is my other son, my big boy, my Charles, who must do it.' Her voice faltered. 'That is my worry. Sometimes I wonder if . . . I will not be here forever, Miss Buchanan.'

The white cemetery was two miles north of the town. An attempt had been made to site it in a spot which had some little beauty. There was a grove of stunted trees and the background was the white side of a dune. It was not very attractive, but the best that could be done. There was no church or chapel, or even a hall. It was simply a fenced-off area on the plain with several small obelisks and one ornate Victorian mausoleum of pink marble, out of time and out of place in such bleak surroundings. As she passed it, Kate saw the name PRELLER carved in large letters on its side and then a list of names: Arnoldus, Petrus, Maria, Hendrina, and many others, with dates going well back into the early nineteenth century. 'That is where I will lie,' Mrs. Preller said. She indicated a place on the mausoleum where her name would be carved. Just above it was the name CHARLES ALBERTUS PRELLER and above that HUGO FRANCOIS PRELLER.

A small knot of people stood at a newly-dug grave. Arnold Leibowitz, Sachs' attorney, came to meet them. He was tall and thin and stooped and had a shock of jet black hair that stood up like a brush.

'I am sorry to tell you, the rabbi cannot come. I am going to do what I can,' he said, and led them to the graveside where the plain oak coffin stood on two railway sleepers. Kate noticed that most of the small Jewish community of Helmsdale was present. With the four people from Saxenburg there were fifteen or sixteen mourners.

Leibowitz looked nervous and was sweating heavily in the hot sun. 'As we all know, Morris Sachs is lying in hospital and cannot be here as Miriam is laid to rest,' he said. 'And also the rabbi from Cape Town is ill. So I have been asked to say a few words. We all knew Miriam and we all loved her. I got to know Morris and Miriam Sachs when I first came to Helmsdale, soon after Mrs. Sachs died . . .'

Kate's attention wandered to the plain coffin. The sun struck it, making the wood glow, and for a moment she wondered if Miriam's body, cold from the ice-factory, was warming up. She must not think about that damaged face. She must try to remember Miriam as she had been in life.

The first time she had seen Miriam was on the train coming to Helmsdale, the second was a few weeks later. Miriam's father had come to Saxenburg to see Mrs. Preller and Miriam had sat in the car outside. When Kate invited her in she had said, 'No, thanks, I'm going for a swim in a little while.'

Kate recalled the day clearly for it had marked the beginning of something that would become important to all their lives.

Morris Sachs was a short man with a heavy body and a large heavy face that contained on its cheeks a network of small red and blue veins. She had seen him in town, but had not previously met him. As she brought him into the hall he had swept off his black Homburg and said, 'I have something from London!' His voice was filled with suppressed excitement and he had tapped a roll of magazines under his arm. He was breathing heavily and Kate had to restrain him from bounding up the staircase. She sent Lena ahead to prepare Mrs. Preller and then escorted him up.

The old lady was sitting in her chair by the screen. 'Good morning, Sachs. It must be important for you to interrupt me in the morning.'

'It could be more than important! Look!' He had opened a magazine and thrust it under her nose.

'Do not come so close! Give it to me. Miss Buchanan, take this and read it to me, please.'

As Kate passed Sachs she had caught the sour smell of his sweat.

She had found herself looking at a double-page spread

of photographs of a garden party at Buckingham Palace. There were eight pictures, showing elegant groups standing on the lawn, cups of tea and small sandwiches in their hands. The men were in morning dress with grey toppers and spats. The women all wore long garden-party dresses, most had their hair marcelled.

'What is it?' Mrs. Preller said.

'A garden party, ma'am. At Buckingham Palace in London.'

'Yes, yes, I can see that. But what has it to do with me? Why have you brought a garden party to me, Sachs?'

He stepped forward eagerly, delighted to show them what they were too stupid to see for themselves.

'Look!' He pointed with a short, fat finger. 'And look!' He stabbed again. 'And look!'

Each time, his finger indicated a woman, but still Kate could see no cause for his excitement.

She took the magazine. Sachs opened a second one and handed it to her, pointing to pictures of guests at a charity ball at the Dorchester Hotel.

Then she heard Mrs. Preller give a sharp intake of breath. 'When did you get these?' she said.

'They came by post yesterday.'

'When were they published?'

'Three weeks ago in London.'

And then Kate had understood. All the women in both sets of pictures were wearing or carrying ostrich plumes. Some wore single feathers in head bands, some carried fans, some had feathers curling around their hats.

Sachs was like a volcano about to erupt as he drew a piece of paper from his pocket. 'From London!' he said. 'From Mr. Mendel!'

Mrs. Preller looked at him sharply. 'Give it to me.' She took the cable. 'Mendel,' she said slowly. 'We have not dealt with Mendel since before the war. He has asked us for nothing, nothing.'

Sachs advanced towards her and this time she did not flinch. He turned the pages of the magazine and read a heading: 'The Luxury Look is Back. Wartime austerity replaced by High Fashion.'

Mrs. Preller sat still for a moment, then she said to Kate, 'Find Smuts and send him to me. I do not need you at the moment. You stay here, Sachs.'

Kate found Smuts in one of the sheds. He looked surprised when she summoned him. 'Now?'

'Yes, now.'

She had gone back to Miriam, who had said, 'They'll be there for hours. Let's go for a walk.'

The sun was hot and the wind was only a light breeze. The sea was that translucent green Kate had come to expect under the high blue skies.

'What's happening?' she had said. 'I realise it must be something to do with feathers, but . . .'

'Something!' Miriam said.

'Is your father a farmer, too?'

'Father? A farmer? What a priceless idea! He's a feather-buyer. He buys feathers here and ships them to England.'

'Who's Mr. Mendel?'

'He has the biggest feather business in Europe.'

They had walked down the cliff path and were on the beach. Miriam took off her shoes and stockings and went down to the water's edge. Kate had followed her example.

'What will it mean?' she said.

'The feather business is always boom or bust,' Miriam said. 'When women in London and Paris and New York want ostrich feathers we live like royalty here. When they don't, it's more like poor whites. My father says that before the war everyone here was rich. Then during the war, no-one wanted feathers. Austerity, that was the word. Now perhaps austerity is over, perhaps women want to look pretty and fashionable again. If they do, they will want feathers. Saxenburg will become like a palace again. Helmsdale will be rich. Everyone will be rich.' It was as though the word had a flavour, a taste in her mouth.

'But what if women don't want feathers again in a year or so?'

Miriam had turned on her angrily. 'Don't talk like that! Why say such a thing now?'

'I'm sorry, I didn't mean to be pessimistic.' She changed

her tone. 'What will you have? A fan? Something for your hair?'

Miriam had looked at her oddly. 'Women don't wear feathers out here,' she said.

'Why ever not?'

'Haven't you seen the coloured people wearing them?'

'You mean that if coloured people wear something the white people don't?'

'Of course.'

'Well, I will.'

'You're new. You'll learn.'

They had walked on through the sand. Kate felt it cool between her toes and it gave her a sense of freedom.

'Is Charles coming home this week-end?'

'I don't know. He didn't come back last week.'

'I know. I'll be cross with him if he doesn't. He knows I'm here.'

'Are you . . .?' Kate had paused.

Miriam had let a smile answer for her. 'We used to play together. Hide and seek. Come, I'll show you something.'

She had led the way to the headland which Kate had seen from her window.

'We weren't allowed to play here,' she said. 'It's dangerous. You can only get to the point when the tide's out.'

The rocks were wet and slippery and covered with mussels and Kate had picked her way across them with care. She could see that they were making for a ledge, visible now the tide was out. When they reached it, Miriam said, 'Can you see the hole?'

Just above the ledge, amid a jumble of boulders that had come down in a landslip, was a hole in the rock about two or three feet in diameter.

Miriam had gone down on all fours and wriggled through the hole. Kate followed and found herself in a cave four or five times the size of a large room. It faced seawards and the tide lapped at the entrance. The roof was low and when she stood there was not much space above her. The floor was white sea sand but there were larger, round stones near the mouth.

54

'When the tide comes in, it fills the cave. That's why we were never allowed here,' Miriam said.

'But you came, anyway?'

Miriam had not answered for a moment, then she said, 'Everyone comes here. Even the holiday visitors. People in town call it the "grotto" to make it sound more interesting.'

Kate walked to the low, arched entrance and looked out to sea.

'They say if you're washed out of the cave the tides take you to the reef,' Miriam had said.

She led Kate back across the slippery rocks, but instead of going onto the beach she turned seawards, walking through shallow, sandy channels. 'I'll show you the rock pools,' she said. 'You can swim here when the tide's out.'

Kate had never seen anything like the pools. There were three of them, interlinked. The rocks around them were dry in the hot sun, but she noticed that the water was not more than a foot or two below the tops and once the tide began to come in the pools would be taken over by the sea itself and, like the reef, disappear below waves and rolling swells.

'Charles and I used to swim here a lot. At low tide they're as clear as a swimming pool. But never go in when you can't see. Look.' She pointed down to something that looked like a purple pincushion. 'That's a sea-urchin. If you stand on one you'll be sorry. Hennie stood on one once.'

'Hennie?'

'Dr. du Toit. He taught me to swim. He stood on one and got blood-poisoning from the spines.'

Suddenly, she unbuttoned her dress and let it drop. She stood in a pair of peach-coloured satin cami-knickers. Kate have never seen such luxurious underwear. She wore plain white lock-knit knickers and a brassiere or a spencer in winter. The cami-knickers looked startlingly exotic in the surroundings of Saxenburg Cove, with their lacy top and lace-trimmed legs. Miriam was not unaware of the impression she was making for she posed, leaning on her arms in such a way as to arch her back and throw out her chest. Kate was not sure how to react. Scotland's climate was not conducive to outdoor nudity and even at school she and her fellow-pupils* had preserved as much modesty as possible. What experience she'd had with boys had been under rugs on a golf-course or petting in dark corners of the wynds off the Royal Mile. Tom was the only other human-being with whom she had ever been completely naked, and even that had been in the gloom of his cabin with a shutter over the port-hole. As she looked at Miriam, she wondered if she was a member of that strange new species of which she had read, but to date had no first-hand experience: a Bright Young Thing.

Miriam had broken into her thoughts: 'Well, what do you think of her?' she said.

'Who?'

'Mrs. P.'

Kate smiled. 'I can't imagine anyone calling her that.'

'Have you seen her face?'

'She sits in the dark. I've seen her hands though.'

'They were burnt.'

'What happened?'

'I don't know, exactly. People talk, but they make most of it up. It happened when Hugo died. They say her husband was like a wild man.'

'She says he worshipped her. She says he did everything for her after that.'

Miriam had laughed unpleasantly. 'Boss Charles only worshipped one person, himself. He had a flat in Cape Town. He used to go there often.'

'You mean for . . .?'

'I mean with other women.' She had opened her huge dark eyes and was looking at Kate. 'I mean, he took them there to fuck them.'

Kate knew the word, but had never heard it spoken so casually, or by a woman. It disturbed her. She felt the skin on her breasts contract and move against the material of her blouse. Her face was hot. Pictures of Tom came into her mind.

'There was a fire at Saxenburg,' Miriam said. 'Hugo died in it.'

'How did it happen?'

'No one really knows, except Smuts, perhaps. Charles went away after it, to boarding-school, and when he came home I hardly saw him. She kept him there. Just the two of them.' She paused, then said bitterly. 'She told me not to come to the house. I hate her.'

Kate had seen beads of perspiration on her upper lip as she stood up.

'I'm going to swim,' she said. 'You?'

Kate had shaken her head. 'I haven't got a bathing-costume.'

'I haven't, either.'

She had taken off her cami-knickers and stood there, letting Kate see her body, then dived into the pool and swum to the far side. Kate had dabbled her toes in the water. Miriam used her body as a shapely machine and Kate was jealous of it, jealous of the big breasts and the rounded thighs, so different from her own thin figure.

After a few minutes Miriam had come out. She lay back, allowing the sun to dry her.

'Have you got someone? A man?' she asked.

'Not really.' She was unwilling to discuss Tom.

'Charles and I are still . . .' She paused, then said, 'friends', emphasising the word so Kate could not mistake her meaning.

'That's nice,' Kate had said carefully. 'It's good to have someone like that.'

Faintly over the soft noise of the waves they had heard a call. At first Kate thought it might be a seabird, then she had seen Lena standing on the low cliff.

'My father must be finished.' Miriam began to dress.

Kate had noticed a movement on a rock about thirty yards away. Someone was standing beside it, watching. Then she had seen the ostrich plume.

'There's Jonas,' she said.

Miriam went on dressing unhurriedly.

'I wonder how long he's been watching?' Kate said.

'I don't care, he's only a servant.'

They had met Lena at the foot of the cliff. 'Has Miss Kate seen Betty?' she asked.

Kate had shaken her head. 'Are they still talking in the house?'

'They finished now.' Lena's expression was angry.

'. . . of the circumstances, otherwise there would have been a service at home.' Leibowitz's voice brought her thoughts back to the grave. 'So I will read the kaddish that would have been said in the home.' He opened his Daily Prayer Book. 'A woman of worth who can find?' he began. 'For her price is far above rubies. She stretcheth out her hand to the poor . . .'

The reading was soon over and the coffin was lowered. The mourners threw in the symbolic handfuls of earth but Mrs. Preller turned away and Kate went with her. She took a longer path to the car so that she would not pass the mausoleum and Kate sensed she was feeling the chill of her own mortality.

On the way home she sat stiff and silent for a while and then suddenly said abruptly, 'Mr. Preller built this road for me. In the early days there was no road. We went to town in the trap. But when the motors came Mr. Preller said I must have the first. So he built the road and then bought a motor. Is that not so, Smuts?'

'That's right, Miss Augusta.'

'Smuts knows about motors. He can mend them. Mr. Preller made him learn.'

[5]

Some days after Miriam had been buried Kate went out for a walk. She saw Lena and Betty at the top of the cliffs. She could not hear what they were saying for the wind was increasing, but it was obvious that they were arguing. Beyond them, she saw Jonas fishing down on the rocks, the big sea pole and the man forming a black silhouette against the red of the setting sun.

Betty began to run towards the house. Lena followed her

more slowly and as she drew level Kate, conscious of their constant warfare, said impulsively: 'Don't you think you're hard on her, Lena? After all, she's nearly grown up.'

'Does Miss Kate think so?'

'Yes, I do.'

'Has Miss Kate got a daughter? Beautiful like Betty? Eighteen years old?'

'Of course I haven't.'

'Miss Kate wouldn't say I'm hard on Betty if she had a child.'

'I suppose not. I'm sorry. It's none of my business.'

There was a sympathy in Lena which Kate had noticed was part of the coloured people's character. She had heard it said they were feckless and immoral, but she had found other qualities that were just as marked, like humour and sympathy. Now Lena said, 'Miss Kate mustn't worry about what she said. But if she knew what goes on with the young people, she would understand.'

'What goes on?'

'It's not always the fault of the girls. It's the men. They get drunk. I know young girls, twelve, thirteen, who have babies. Then they can't get married. Who's going to marry them?'

They had been walking slowly back to the house and now Kate stopped. 'But can't they have the babies taken away?' She had said it almost without thinking.

'What does Miss Kate mean?'

'I mean abortion. Wouldn't that be better than letting girls of thirteen have babies they can't deal with?'

'That's true, Miss Kate. They do that, too. But sometimes, you know, bad things happen.'

'Oh?' She felt chilled.

Lena was watching her closely. 'Girls can have babies taken away.'

'Here?'

'In the village. I know two people.'

'Who had babies taken away?'

'No, no. Who can take them away. But it is against God's law.'

'That's true. But some people are weak . . .'

'That is why I watch Betty. I think myself maybe Betty is weak.'

'But if Betty sinned . . . I only say if, you understand . . . if she was going to have a baby, what would you do, Lena?'

'Miss Kate, Jesus Christ says we must not commit sin.'

'If . . .?'

'Maybe she would have it taken away.'

'Here?'

'No, not here.'

'Where?'

'In Cape Town.'

'There are places there?'

'Yes, a lot of places.'

'Where would you go with Betty?'

'To my cousin, Sarah. My cousin can do such things.'

'Where is your cousin?'

'In District Six.'

'District Six?'

'Has Miss Kate heard of it?'

'Yes.'

'It's where the coloured people live. Sarah lives in Hanover Street.'

'I know Hanover Street,' Kate lied.

'Then Miss Kate must know the Eastern Emporium.'

'I . . .'

'It sells spices and curry and samosas and chilli bites.'

'Oh, *that* emporium.'

'My cousin used to live next door. Maybe she doesn't no more. I haven't been there for five, six years.'

'And that's where you would take Betty.'

Lena hesitated. 'Betty isn't having a baby, Miss Kate.'

'Of course not.'

'That is why I watch her.'

'I'm sorry. I didn't mean to suggest . . .'

'Miss Kate musn't be sorry. Miss Kate will have her own children one day, then she will see.'

'I'm sure you're right. How much is it, Lena?'

'How much?'

'To take the baby away?'

'It is dear, Miss Kate. Very, very dear.'

'How much?'

'Ten, twelve pounds. If the police catch them, it's trouble. That's why they ask so much.'

'That is expensive. Lena, if anything . . . I only say *if* anything were to happen, I want you to know you can come to me.'

'For what?'

'Money.'

'Money for what?'

'You know.'

She saw anger in the woman's eyes. 'Better safe than sorry,' Lena said, and walked quickly back to the house.

The train wound across the plain. Dust devils spun across the horizon, and the mountains, baking brown, shimmered in the heatwaves. Had Lena guessed, Kate wondered? In the past few days she had been distant. Or was she reading too much into Lena's expression, thinking it unusually severe? During their conversation she had felt that they had been playing a kind of game, saying one thing, each knowing that the other was thinking something else.

She opened her bag and counted her money. If Lena was right, she had just enough, the last of her Edinburgh savings, to pay Sarah, if she could find her, and to rent a room in a cheap hotel for a night. She remembered the girl she had known in Edinburgh. She'd had her abortion on a Saturday and had been back in the office the following Monday. She had looked like death, but she had been there. Today was Friday. Kate had left early and should be in Cape Town by six o'clock. If she could have the baby taken away tonight or tomorrow, she could catch the train back on Sunday afternoon. No one would be any the wiser.

She tried to doze, but images kept coming into her mind. Fumbling hands. Blood. 'Bad things can happen,' Lena had said. It was the thought of those 'things' she was trying to keep at bay. She was afraid, as she had never been afraid before in her life.

She tried to occupy her mind by looking at the scenery. They were among the wheatlands now, already cinnamon

61

in the burning summer heat. Occasionally the train would stop at a small village, nothing more than a cluster of white houses round the station; sometimes it would pause at a wayside halt. The only people she saw were Cape coloureds, driving along the dusty roads in their donkey carts. She felt that if she left the train and started to walk she might never strike anything except more emptiness, more space. At that moment, she hated the country, hated its harshness, hated what was happening to her within that harshness.

And yet, who was to blame but herself? She had started it, and it would be self-delusion not to admit it. She could not even blame Tom. She had known the gamble.

It had begun as a typical ship-board romance. Her parents, prostrate with heat in the tropics, had kept to their cabin, leaving Duggie and Kate to do what they liked. Duggie soon found drinking cronies and she began to enjoy a freedom she had never experienced before. The ship was like a cut-off world. Life had no beginning and no ending, she was encapsulated in a limbo of hot days and blue seas. She had begun to look around. There were several attractive men who were eager to partner her to the nightly dances and even more eager to take her up onto the top deck afterwards. She found herself kissing three different men on three consecutive nights and enjoyed herself immensely. Then she had met Tom.

Duggie had been teaching her deck quoits. Leaning on his cane, he had held one of the heavy rubber discs and was about to explain how to throw it when he looked at a man standing with his back to the rail. 'By God, that's Tom Austen,' he said.

'Who's Tom Austen?'

'He was a war correspondent with one of the London papers. He was with our regiment in Turkey. He has written books.'

She saw a big sandy-haired man in his thirties with a squarish face and a wide forehead. He was wearing a light cotton tropical suit and carried a book in one hand. He was watching the activity on the deck through half-closed eyes.

'Is this the way?' she said, taking the quoit from Duggie.

She bowled the rubber disc like a wheel. It had raced across the deck, gathering speed, struck a projection, leapt into the air and vanished over the starboard side, narrowly missing Tom Austen.

'My God, if you're going to chuck them about like that I'm off!' Duggie said, limping away.

Austen watched the sinking quoit. Kate went towards him and said, 'I'm sorry. That was a mistake.'

He had turned, smiling. She saw that he had blue-grey eyes under heavy brows. His smile was infectious and lit up his face. He said, 'It's an interesting new technique. I haven't seen it done that way before. Let me show you. I've travelled on so many ships I'm something of an expert.' He picked up a quoit and she noticed his hands, broad and powerful, but with surprisingly long fingers. 'You hold it like this.' He took her arm and she was aware of the strength in his fingers and of the power of his personality. 'You throw it like this.' The quoit landed flat and slid along the wooden deck. 'Now you try.'

He had spent half an hour teaching her, then as the afternoon cooled they had sat outside the Verandah Bar and drunk Tom Collinses. She had never heard of the drink before. He had told her about his travels as a special correspondent in India, Japan and Russia and about the books he had written. Now he was going to Cape Town as the staff correspondent of the London *Chronicle* with the whole of Africa as his beat.

By the time they had talked for two hours she had realised that all the other men she had known, either in Scotland or on the ship, were like young boys compared with him.

She had heard the xylophone announcing dinner and said, 'What sitting are you?'

'Neither. I eat up at the sharp end.'

'In First Class?'

'I'm in First because my newspaper pays the bill. That's the only reason. And it's pretty dull. Full of elderly generals going out to the Cape for their health. But the food's good. There's a grill room. Why don't you go and change and

63

I'll come and pick you up. We'll have dinner in the grill and . . .' He smiled. '. . . I can go on talking about myself.'

That was how it had started. The rest of the voyage, for Kate, was a kind of paradise. She had spent most of it in his airy cabin on B-deck. The difference between it and the bunk she had in a six-berth with three other women was enough to make her realise for the first time the scale on which some people could live all the time.

He was the first man she had slept with and after the first few times she knew that she had never really been fulfilled before. There was not only a physical completeness, but its influence seemed to spread to her psyche, giving her a confidence she had not known. They had made love every day and sometimes more than once. Gradually she had lost her early shyness and, given free rein, the strength of her passion was such that a door seemed to close in her mind, blotting out her normal personality. Her small, thin body seemed to be made up of fibres like electric cables, that surged with voltage when she was in his arms. Once, sweating and exhausted, they had lain side by side and he kissed her damp face and said, 'I've never known anyone like you. I never knew there could be anything like this.'

It was the greatest compliment she had ever been paid.

Like most shipboard romances, it should have ended when the *Dulnain Castle* rode slowly into Table Bay. It was five o'clock in the morning and she and Tom had been up all night.

All the circumstances had been right for love. There had been the farewell dinner and the farewell dance. The band had played Auld Lang Syne. The bars had stayed open late. Lovers – shipboard lovers – had clung to each other in every corner of the deck. Everyone knew the good time was coming to an end. The atmosphere throughout the ship was tinged with sadness. It was then Kate had known she was in love with Tom.

They had watched the sun rise from the porthole in his cabin, and seen Table Mountain and Devil's Peak come slowly closer. She had said, 'When will I see you?' He had said nothing. 'You'll be looking for somewhere to live and so will we. The Settlers' Association say they'll help. You said your office will be in the *Cape Times* building. I'll find it.' Still he did not speak. 'Or would you like me to telephone you? No, I think I'll just come and knock at your door and –'

'Kate,' he had said. 'I don't think we should see each other again.'

She wondered if she had heard him correctly.

'We've had a good time. A wonderful time. But the voyage is over.'

'That doesn't matter. We'll both be in Cape Town.'

'I don't want to hurt you.'

'How would you hurt me? Don't be silly, you could never . . .'

'My wife's coming over to join me.'

'Wife?'

'She'll be here in a month or six weeks. I have to find a house in the meantime.'

'Wife . . .?'

'I'm sorry. I meant to tell you, but we were having such a damn good time it seemed a pity to spoil it.'

'You're a bastard,' she said.

He had nodded. 'I'm not unaware of it.'

That should have been that. But it wasn't.

She did not see Tom for nearly a month. During that time she and her family moved into the small rented house found for them by the British Settlers' Association. It was a mean little single-storeyed house in a terrace which had been built about sixty years before in Observatory. Both White and coloured lived in the street and Mrs. Buchanan, who had never met a coloured person before, found that she had coloured folk as neighbours. She was immediately frightened of them.

Kate hated the house. In its way, it was as squalid as their tenement near the Canongate in Edinburgh. What made it worse was that she had, for the first time in her life, tasted luxury. The rooms were small and sparsely furnished. The kitchen, with its poor lighting, its old gas stove, the worn linoleum on the floor, the peeling paper behind which cockroaches hid and the smells of decades of cooking that had penetrated the very walls, was a dreadful place. Everything she touched felt greasy. Above all, the house was damp, for they had arrived in winter.

They had bought cheap furniture at a local auction mart and there was so little room in the house that the ice-chest had to stand in the corridor. Often she would come home in the evening to find the drip-bucket over-flowing. Soon the wall behind the ice-chest was dark with fungus. There was a small fireplace in the sitting-room and they kept in a coal fire, but the rest of the house was clammy and they used paraffin heaters in the bedrooms. The fumes, mixed with old kitchen smells, gave an overall odour which permeated the house and lingered in her clothes.

It had taken her a few days to find a job, and she took the first one that came along. It was a temporary position as secretary to a clothing manufacturer who had a small, dirty factory in the old industrial suburb of Salt River. She hated the job and the noise, but her family needed the money.

She soon found herself not only earning the bread, but baking it, too. Mrs. Buchanan, who had a weak chest, found that a wet Cape winter in a damp house kept her wheezing in her bed for much of the time. When Kate came home from work she had to clean the house and cook a meal. She had started to put money into a tin box which she kept locked. This was for rent and house-keeping, with a few pounds for herself. But Duggie and her father were constantly sidling up to her to borrow a few bob. She could not refuse them, in spite of the fact that she knew they were spending it on cheap wine.

During all this time she thought constantly of Tom. She thought of him on the tram going to and from work, she thought of him as she washed the dishes in the scummy water, she thought of him as she lay in her narrow, damp bed. She no longer cared that he had a wife; she wanted him on any terms. The only thing she would not do was get in touch with him. She had too much pride for that.

Then one evening as she came home from work, she had seen someone standing across the road from her house. He was wearing a trilby and a mackintosh and at first she did not recognise him. It was his size that gave her the first clue. She had stopped in front of him. Neither spoke for a moment, then he said, 'I traced you through the Settlers' Association.'

'Why?'

'Because I love you.'

'Where shall we go?'

'I have a car.'

He had taken her to an hotel in Sea Point, overlooking the Atlantic breakers, where they had made love in a kind of frenzy. It had been the first of many such meetings. His wife was due to arrive in three weeks and they made the most of the time they had. He had taken her to the bioscope and to the Opera House. They had walked along the Pipe Track under the grey buttresses of Table Mountain. He had taken her to the long empty beach at Muizenberg and they walked along it in the winter sunshine. And all the while, his wife's ship was rounding the bulge of Africa and steaming towards the Cape.

After an initial unwillingness to talk about her, Kate realised that if she was going to fight for Tom, she must know as much about her adversary as possible. But when she did find out, she knew with a sinking heart that there never would be a fight, there never could be. Joyce Austen was a cripple.

One day in early spring as they lay together under the pine trees on the slopes of Devil's Peak she had said, 'You can't go on blaming yourself all your life. It's not reasonable. Hundreds of people get infantile paralysis.'

'It's not as simple as that.' He had turned away from her, holding himself up on one elbow. Things had been going badly between Joyce and himself for years, he had said. They both knew it. He was reaching the stage where he wanted his freedom, but he knew that she would never agree. She must have sensed his thoughts because she had begun what appeared to be a planned campaign. Whenever he had wanted to go anywhere she would pretend to be feeling unwell. He had known it was pretence because if he cancelled his plans she would make a remarkably quick recovery.

'It got so that I could hardly go anywhere, which isn't too good for someone who makes his living by travelling. She kept nagging me to get a desk job and I kept fighting off the moment. Then the Russian trip came up. It was the most exciting single assignment I'd been offered since the war ended. I wanted to go. Joyce said she was feeling ill, but I went. While I was away, she developed infantile paralyis. End of story.'

'But it wasn't your fault,' Kate said. 'People do get ill, they do get infantile paralysis, they do become crippled in one leg – some people even die of it. You can't go through life blaming yourself!'

'If I'd stayed, I might have been able to help. The effects might not have been so severe.'

'Or they might have been worse – who's to know?'

'I realise all that, and I can live with it. But the one thing I can't do is leave her.'

Kate had to accept that. She went with him as he looked for a house and helped him to find one, a beautiful colonial villa in its own grounds in Kenilworth. She thought bitterly that she had never seen such a lovely house. She knew how she would have furnished it, what colours she would have painted the walls, she even knew what curtains she would have put up.

Joyce arrived and they had to meet more discreetly. Tom hired two servants to run the house and in that way he was able to make time for Kate. They would go to one of several hotels in the city or suburbs once or twice a week. Sometimes he might manage a drink in the late afternoon, or a meal. She lived for these moments, especially on Saturdays, which was her half day. She would take the tram into the city after work and meet him outside his office and they would go to an hotel and have lunch. He would take a room and they would spend the afternoon together.

But the strain began to tell. The erratic nature of their meetings, the spectre of the crippled Joyce and the fact that she was now spending more time at the house in Observatory with her family, had combined to make Kate irritable and jumpy. The bliss of a snatched hour with Tom was often followed by a snappish argument over something trivial. She told herself that this was natural, given the circumstances, but even so, she did not like it.

And then, in a restaurant called the Del Monico, they'd had a serious argument.

She had come into town after work and they had made love on the floor of his office; later they had gone to the Del Monico for supper. She still had the dust of his office-carpet in her nostrils.

After they had eaten he had said, 'I won't be able to make it this Saturday.'

This had happened once before since Joyce's arrival. Kate herself considered Saturdays to be sacrosanct and had fought with her own family to make sure she had the afternoon to herself.

'Is it Joyce?' she said.

'She likes to go to the races and they're on Saturday afternoon. She's always been keen on horses.'

'Every Saturday afternoon?'

'Not necessarily. But I told you, it's one of her few pleasures. We can find other times.'

'And make love on the floor?'

'You didn't seem to mind just now.'

'You go through life feeling sorry for her. Well, I don't. Sometimes I wish she were dead!'

'That's a bloody awful thing to say.'

'I can't help it. Sometimes I wish we'd never started this, that we'd never met.'

'You made sure of that.'

'What do you mean?'

'Oh, come on, Kate, you know exactly what I mean.'

'No, I don't. Do you think I would have got entangled with a married man?'

'How the hell do I know what you would have done? You started it. You chose the moment. You didn't know if I was married or not, and you didn't care. Well, you got into something you couldn't have bargained for.'

'That's a lie!' But even as she said it she knew he was right. She had chosen the moment. She had looked at the man standing beside the rail on the deck and she had bowled the quoit as close to him as she could. It might not have been consciously done, but consciously or unconsciously, she had wanted him the moment she had seen him.

A voice at her elbow said, 'Hello, Mr. Austen. Remember me? We met at the Hodgsons'. I'm Charles Preller.'

Kate had looked up and seen a man of medium height with a smooth, rather plump face, dark eyes and a sensual mouth. She had been reminded of pictures she had seen of Roman proconsuls.

Tom had risen and made the introductions and then said – Kate had heard relief in his voice – 'Won't you join us for coffee?' That was the moment at which she had decided to end their affair.

'If you'll allow me to offer you liqueurs,' Charles Preller had said.

She had not seen Tom again, but the damage had been done. She was convinced that it was that clutching, frenzied coupling on the hard, dusty floor which had planted the child in her womb and which had led her to this all-pervasive fear of what was going to happen to her.

The train was a few minutes late and she hurried through the station concourse and booked into an hotel which she and Tom had used several times. It was cheap, but clean. She left her suitcase in her room and put a nightdress and a change of underclothing in a brown paper bag and walked towards District Six.

It was dusk and the heat was rising from the pavements. She turned towards Table Mountain and realised she had been here before; Charles had brought her to a restaurant called the Crescent for curry. The pavement was crowded and she felt people were staring at her. She could not see another white face. Everywhere she looked she saw Cape coloureds or Cape Malays, the men wearing the fez, the women half-veiled. People were doing their evening shopping. She could smell joss-sticks and curry and over-ripe fruit. Street barrows were piled with watermelons, pawpaws, mangoes, grapes, melons, peaches, plums and nectarines. There were stalls selling samosas and cool drinks and other barrows selling fish. There were hallal meat

shops and basket shops and shops advertising dried snoek.
Her senses were assaulted by smells and colours and
movement. This was how she had imagined Calcutta or
Singapore. She was jostled and stared at and touched.
Then she saw the Crescent on her left and, immediately
opposite, the Eastern Emporium.

It was painted green and had the crescent moon of Islam
on the windows. She paused. The interior of the shop
was dimly lit. Outside, on the pavement, were sacks of
rice and maize flour, chillis and cardomum pods, fresh
cucumbers and lychees. She stood at the window and
stared in.

She felt something touch her arm. She jerked involunta-
rily, but felt herself gripped. She turned and gasped.
Among the sacks was a legless figure, the trunk ending in
trousers caught up with safety pins. The creature gripped
her arm with one hand and pointed to his mouth with the
other. She saw its pink interior. He had no teeth. His
mouth was like a lamprey's.

She fought off his hands and stumbled into the shop.
The Malay owner in a fez, collarless shirt and braces,
looked at her in surprise. She saw two veiled women. They
stared at her.

'Yes?' the man said.

'I'm looking for someone called Sarah. I was told she
lived next door to the Eastern Emporium.'

'What Sarah, lady? You mean Fat Sarah?'

'Is there another Sarah living here?'

'Next door, that way.' He pointed up the street.
'Upstairs.'

The house was double-storeyed, with a deep verandah
on the first floor which ran the length of the building. It
was decorated with wrought ironwork painted blue. The
street door was closed but she tapped on it and it swung
slowly inward. She found herself in a narrow hall covered
in newspapers and empty boxes. A staircase faced her and
she slowly began to climb the uncarpeted wooden stairs.
The door at the top was open and she knocked.

'Ja?' A woman's voice came from the darkened interior
of the apartment.

'I'm looking for Sarah,' Kate called.

'I'm here.'

She stepped into the apartment.

'Here. On the stoep.'

She went out onto the verandah. A huge woman ws sitting in a basket chair, fanning herself. She was wearing only a housecoat and Kate could see her great breasts resting on her belly.

'What you want, lady?'

Kate looked into the round face that lay on its pad of double chins. The eyes were small, porcine, shrewd.

'I – are you Sarah?'

'I'm Sarah.' The voice was light, almost girlish.

'I've come to ask you to . . . I understand you perform operations on women.'

The eyes hardened. 'What kind operations?'

'You know.'

'Who told you to come here?'

'A friend.'

'I don't do no operations.'

'My friend said you . . .'

'You going to get trouble, lady, you come here telling lies like this. Rosie! Rosie!'

Out of the dark apartment came a small figure. Kate did not see her clearly for a moment, then she realised that the girl was not more than eleven or twelve and that she was a hunchback.

'Rosie, go and look in the street.'

As the child turned to go Fat Sarah said, 'If Rosie see someone you going to get trouble.'

'Sees who? I don't know what you're talking about. I've come . . .'

'I know why you come.'

They were silent for some minutes and then Rosie came back.

'There's nobody,' she said.

'You look all round?'

'Nobody.'

'Plain clothes?'

'Nobody.'

Kate said, 'If you think I brought the police, you're mad.'

'I know who is mad,' Sarah said. But there was less antagonism in her tone. 'How long?'

'Nearly three months.'

'It's going to cost you twelve pounds ten.'

'My friend said ten pounds.'

'Twelve pounds ten. *Before*.'

'When can you do it?'

'Tomorrow.'

'Now.'

'You got the money?'

Kate counted out twelve pounds ten and gave it to her. She had very little left.

'Go with Rosie.'

The child led her along the corridor and opened a door. Kate went into the room. It smelled of Jeyes Fluid. There was a bed and a table. The child switched on the light, a naked bulb hanging from the ceiling, and Kate saw what was on the table. She looked away, but the images were burned in her mind: the length of red rubber tubing, the douche, the thing that looked like a garden syringe, the thing that looked like a meat-skewer, the white enamel basin, the folded towelling squares. She sat on the edge of the bed, feeling sick.

She knew that these were the worst moments she had ever experienced and always afterwards she tried to forget them. In time they did fade in the memory, but never completely. The smell of Jeyes Fluid would trigger off sudden sharp images, so would rolls of stomach fat glimpsed on a beach, or a twisted back in a crowded street.

'You must take off your clothes,' the girl said.

When she had undressed she lay back on the harsh blanket, naked from the waist down.

'I fetch Fat Sarah,' the child said.

Kate had not said her prayers for years, but now she prayed and, at the same time, tried to force her mind back and back until finally she conjured up images of happy days at the Academy in Edinburgh. She could feel Fat Sarah's fingers opening her. She saw the dormitory she had slept in; she saw the class-room. She felt something cold slide into her. There was her desk. She could see her books ... she cried out then, a half-cry, half-sob. There was a gush of warmth between her legs ... the pain was intense. Oh, God, she thought, I'm bleeding to death ... the desk was in the front of the middle row, it had a lid and she lifted it to get her books ... the flow seemed unending ... she began to feel giddy ...

'Drink.'

She drank.

It was brandy. Half a tumblerful. It burned her throat and stomach. It seemed to burn deep down ... deep down ...

She had no idea how long she lay on the bed for she fainted then and when she came to she was alone. The pain was bad. She put her hand down and felt the towelling. One square was put on as on a baby, with safety pins. The other had been used as a pad underneath it. She tried to move her legs and pain shot through her.

Rosie stood in the doorway. 'Is madam all right?'

'Yes.'

'I call Sarah.'

The fat woman stood in the door, completely blocking it. 'You going to be all right,' she said. 'There's some blood. It will stop tomorrow. You can sleep there.'

'I want to go.'

'You going to walk?'

'No. I want a taxi.'

Twenty minutes later she was at the hotel. It was not quite eleven o'clock and she ordered two double brandies to be sent to her room. She took off her dress and knickers and soaked them in the basin. Then she put a towel down on the bed and eased herself gently onto it. She drank both the brandies quickly, ignoring the burning. Then she lay back and for the first time in many years, she cried. She cried partly because of the pain and the squalor and the humiliation but also partly because she felt a sense of loss, almost a bereavement.

She was still sore the following day and spent it in the hotel, sending down at noon for a plate of sandwiches. She could have telephoned Tom, or her parents, or even Charles, if he hadn't gone to Saxenburg for the week-end. But she did none of these things. Instead, she sat in the window overlooking the Grand Parade and watched the flower-sellers and the fruit-sellers. She sat there for most of the day thinking about Tom and about Charles and about herself. Towards evening she went out and walked a little. She bought a cup of coffee and a polony sandwich at a stall on the Parade, then returned to the hotel, ordered more brandies and went to bed. The following day, Sunday, she took the afternoon train to Saxenburg. No one had seen her; no one knew.

[6]

The death of Miriam – and her life – became the sole topic of conversation in Helmsdale for some weeks after the inquest but even that faded as a new interest arose; specially so at Saxenburg. The feather boom predicted by Sachs began to accelerate and the estate, like some creature brought to life after a long sleep, began to function again.

Mrs. Preller began ordering fashion magazines and kept, as best she could from her home on the southern tip of Africa, her eye on the fashions of New York, London and Paris. From the text and pictures in the magazines it was apparent that the feminine appetite for luxury was growing; its most obvious symbol was the ostrich feather. Queen Mary was one of the leaders in the ostrich feather revival; she wore plumes in her hats and was often seen to be carrying them as fans. 'We should give her a commission,' Smuts said to Mrs. Preller. 'She's doing our business for us.'

'Talking of commissions, I hear from Dr. du Toit that Sachs is out of hospital. Have you seen him?'

'Not yet. But he'll be around, Miss Augusta. If there's money to be made he'll come, even if it's on a stretcher.'

Then Mrs. Preller received a letter from Mendel in

London. Kate read it. The demand for feathers was increasing. Mendel was certain that it was not simply a flash in the pan. 'The court is leading the revival,' he said. 'The Prince of Wales's symbol is being copied all over the country wherever fashionable people gather.' At the end he said he was planning a trip to South Africa and would visit Helmsdale.

Kate found herself pitched into the feather industry. At first the additional work was burdensome and she was quickly exhausted. She explained this to herself as an effect of the abortion. She had healed quickly, but for some time felt weak and depressed. Slowly she reclaimed her strength and as she improved physically, so the depression seemed to leave her. She viewed what had happened in the apartment in Hanover Street as part of a nightmare. Now she had woken up.

She applied herself to learning about ostrich-farming. Saxenburg had been allowed to fall into decay, the ostriches to run wild. Fences had to be replaced, gates rehung and the birds driven into 'camps' or paddocks; lucerne had to be planted as foodstuff.

She began to study the birds themselves. One of the most infuriating characteristics was their habit of making hysterical dashes, sometimes throwing themselves at a fence in order to get to the other side. Often this would result in one of the long legs snapping and then the bird would have to be destroyed.

'There's no way we can help it,' Smuts said, looking down at an injured male. He shook his head angrily at the waste. 'A bird like this cost four hundred pounds in the old days, and maybe we'll have to pay those prices again if the rise goes on. Look at it! Just wanted to get into the other camp. No bloody different from the place it's in, but it *must* get over the fence.'

The ostrich lay on its belly with one leg twisted behind it. Its feathers – Kate had learned that the males produced both black and white feathers, which were the most valuable – were covered in dust from its fall.

'Jonas!' Smuts called. 'Get the gun.'

'I'm off!' Kate said.

Smuts shrugged. 'Shooting's the kindest thing we can do. We can't set the leg.'

She was beyond the incubator shed when she heard the shots. Smuts seemed unaffected by the killing when he joined her. She was never to get wholly used to it, even when she had to order it herself.

On another occasion she discovered how dangerous the birds could be. She was crossing a camp with Smuts one morning when a big male began to 'broom.' This was a noise she had, in earlier days, associated with the waves on the rocks. Now she found that when the birds began nest-building, the males turned savage and began to roar. They would give three deep roars in succession, two staccato, the third long. They reminded her of roaring lions in Edinburgh Zoo.

'Get behind me,' Smuts shouted.

The male was flapping its broad black wings on the ground, inflating its neck, throwing its head back and striking it against its bony body with sharp, resounding blows.

'Hurry!'

Suddenly, the bird came at them. Smuts had a branch in his hand. The ostrich raced forward. He waited until it was almost on top of him, pounding at him with its clawed feet, then thrust the branch towards its head. The bird attacked three times before it broke away and returned to the nest.

'They'll rip you apart with those bloody feet,' Smuts said. 'Never cross a camp without a "tackey."' He held out the branch and showed Kate the long white thorns on the end.

But there were gentler aspects of the ostriches' life. Male ostriches remained bachelors for eighteen years, courted a female for two and, when they mated, they stayed together for the rest of their lives – and they lived to twenty and sometimes thirty years old. She learned that they had an ability to cool themselves in the hot desert winds that blew in from the west by standing with their mouths open, a ludicrous sight. When she began to deal with their eggs, she found that the birds had an uncanny knack of knowing when to move from the nest for a few minutes so that the eggs' temperatures did not rise too high.

As the days passed, she began to feel part of this world. She identified with the excitement of the feather boom, she became used to the strange house and the even stranger ways of its inhabitants. She also became more sensitive to its subtleties. It was riven by undercurrents and tensions, of half-seen looks and gestures, of facts buried somewhere in the past, upon which present actions and attitudes seemed to be predicated. Because it was so cut off in place and time from the rest of the world, Saxenburg was like a hot-house where strange plants grew unchecked. And deep inside the hot-house, like some tropical creature, sat Mrs. Preller. Little happened in the house that she did not know about. Her intelligence system seemed to Kate to embrace most things, even to her knowledge, that first night, of Kate's reluctance to eat pickled fish. She knew, within a matter of hours, that Kate had moved a chest of drawers in her room. 'Everything has its place in the nursery,' she had said. 'I have told Lena to move it back.'

Clearly Betty or Lena had reported the movement of the chest. Why? What was important about it? Or about the pickled fish, or a dozen other small incidents that had come to Mrs. Preller's notice. She supposed that Smuts also reported to her, telling her how Kate ate, perhaps informing on Lena and Betty as well. Perhaps they all reported on each other.

She had to remember that Mrs. Preller was Viennese and probably had the sophisticated European woman's penchant for gossip, no matter how trivial. Or was it something else: was this how a tribal queen ruled her little kingdom? Kate had already thought of Smuts as one of her subjects. Lena and Betty, too, were members of the tribe. She supposed that if she stayed long enough she would become a member as well.

She discovered that there were tensions within tensions, currents that ran into and over each other like the rip-tides of the India Reef. The most obvious hostility, because it was played out in the open, was between Betty and Lena. They always seemed to be on the edge of a battle. Lena watched her daughter with remorseless suspicion. At times it seemed to Kate that she could do no right. Lena would criticise her for not laying the table correctly or not dusting thoroughly, she would hiss at her for being too slow and, a few minutes later, for hurrying and being careless. Every afternoon after clearing away the lunch and washing the dishes the two of them would disappear in the direction of a group of small dwellings on the far side of the sheds. Kate had been there once, looking for Betty, and had entered their house. It was a single room with smoke-blackened walls from the open cooking fire at one end. It had no bathroom or sink, no lavatory (she was to discover that for most of the coloureds in the area the only lavatory was the wide open veld) and one small window covered in sacking. In this one room they lived and slept. And this was luxury, for Lena only had the one child. In some of the hovels Kate saw later whole families of seven or eight lived out their crowded lives.

Sometimes Betty chose not to go back to the room with her mother but would walk down to the little beach below the cliffs. Kate saw her several times on the far side of the cove near the rock pools.

Once she found her huddled in the small dining-room. She had been crying and her light brown cheeks were stained by tears.

'What's the matter?' Kate said.

'It's nothing, Madam.'

'Why are you crying if it's nothing?'

'I don't know, Madam. I just crying.'

'Can't you tell me?'

But she shook her head and left the room. As she did so, Kate noticed several weals on the upper part of her right arm. She knew what had caused them, because her own mother had sometimes used a strap on her when she was little. But Lena's behaviour seemed the more savage in view of her religious leanings. On her Sundays off she would walk into Helmsdale and attend the service at the Risen Christ Mission on the slope above the fishing-village.

'Betty used to go with her when she was smaller,' Smuts

told Kate. 'But now she won't. That's half the battle between them.'

'Why won't she go?'

'Because, my friend, she's got other fish to fry. Pardon my language, but they get on my bloody wick sometimes.'

After that, Kate saw her through new eyes. Other fish? Jonas? She ruled that out almost at once, for neither seemed to have the time to conduct a liaison. Betty worked hard, and so did he. When he wasn't working, he was fishing, and this seemed to dominate his life, to the extent that he even fished at night. Kate soon had become accustomed to seeing his big fishing pole when she looked down towards the rocks near the pools. Sometimes, when she walked on the beach, she would see him surf-casting. He would be stripped to the waist and would move in such a way as to display his body to its best advantage. Sometimes he would be fishing from the rocks, etched against the sky like a statue, at others all she would see would be the black silhouette of the rod emerging from the rocks and she would imagine Jonas sitting in some sheltered crevice. He was a good fisherman and supplied the house.

She found that her attitude to him had changed from one of slight apprehension when she first came to Saxenburg, through irritation, to dislike. She did not care for his knowing air. When he greeted her, it was with a mixture of subservience and sexual arrogance. Sometimes she thought she saw a frank invitation in his eyes. At first she had been able to avoid him, but now that she was involved in the refurbishing of the farm she was in daily contact with him.

One afternoon, Sachs arrived. He was driven out by the attorney, Arnold Leibowitz. He was pale and had lost weight. The face which had once been full of humour and excitement was now permanently sad.

'I'll go and tell Mrs. Preller you're here,' Kate said.

'We've come to see you,' Leibowitz said, uncoiling his thin, angular frame from the front seat.

'Me?'

'If you would be so kind, Miss Buchanan,' Sachs said, getting slowly out of the car. 'A few questions.'

'Of course. Mr. Sachs, I want you to know how sad I am. How sad we all are. It was a terrible tragedy.'

'Yes, yes, my dear, thank you.'

'Mr. Sachs would like to visit the place.'

'It's a bit steep.'

'I'm all right if I take it slowly. And if I don't, who cares?'

They walked down to the beach in silence and then Sachs said, 'This is where . . .?'

'Over there. In the rock pools.'

'Miriam learned to swim here. She knew those pools better than anyone. Let me ask you something: have you swum in them?'

'Yes.'

'Would you swim now?'

She looked at the swells surging into the farthest pool. 'No. The tide's high. I like to be able to see the bottom.'

'Exactly. It is what Miriam always said. You must see the bottom. There are sea-urchins. If you stand on one, it gives blood poisoning.'

He turned to Leibowitz. 'I tell you this, Arnold, Miriam would not have put her toe into that water that night. The tide was high. I tell you, it's impossible. Never, never, never. Not a toe.'

'Gently, Morris.'

'To hell with gently. They say Miriam slipped and hit her head. I say rubbish. Miriam knew these rocks like her own hands.'

'You don't *know*, Morris.'

'I know. I know my daughter. Who better?'

'Parents often don't really know their children.'

'You are saying that to me, Arnold? Me? Morris Sachs, who brought up Miriam since a little girl after her mother died. Of course I knew her, and I know she was not the sort of person who would –' He choked, and gasped for breath.

'Morris, you'll get sick again!'

'I don't care.' But he lowered his voice. 'Listen to me,

Arnold. They said bad things about my girl at the inquest. I read what they said. People are still saying it. They say Miriam Sachs was the sort of girl who would go swimming naked at night. They say she was the sort of girl . . .'

'Mr. Sachs, please don't distress yourself . . .'

Unable to speak, he waved his hand from side to side. Slowly he gathered himself and in a soft, husky voice, he said, "You are a lawyer, you think by logic. Think, then. A girl of Miriam's age and experience walks two miles along a lonely road in the middle of the night. She takes off her clothes a hundred yards from the pool and walks naked across the beach to swim when the tide is high.'

Leibowitz nodded. 'You may be right, you may be wrong.'

'I tell you, Arnold, there's no maybe wrong. And I'm going to find out. They did that inquest too quickly.'

'I told you, they had to get her body out of the ice-factory. The manager was complaining.'

But Sachs was not listening. 'And that old fool of a doctor. The District Surgeon. She slipped and fell. She hit her head. Where was he? Watching? And the things they said, maybe not in plain words, but I know what they mean. Miriam was not like that.'

But Kate was remembering. Miriam *was* like that.

She could not get the sight of Sachs crying from her mind. He had seemed so old, so pathetic. And he had been so loyal. What did he really know of his daughter? What did her parents know of Kate? What did Mrs. Preller know of her beloved Charles? The situation went round and round in her mind as she lay in bed.

Charles had arrived at her house in his red roadster the day after she had met him at the Del Monico. She had come home from work at five o'clock and found him with Duggie in the front room, a bottle of brandy on the table between them. Her father, who had a temporary job laying floor-tiles, had been out and her mother was fussing over Charles as though he were royalty. Duggie was already partly drunk and the two of them seemed to be getting along like old chums.

He had taken her out to dinner. 'How did you know where to find me?' she had asked.

'I followed you last night from the Del Monico. Do you mind?'

'No, I don't mind.'

'I thought you might, because of Tom Austen.'

'What has he to do with me minding?' she had said angrily.

That had been the first of many meetings in the next few weeks. Charles worked in a broker's office in town and seemed to have money and time to spare. She liked his car and she liked being taken out and she liked being seen with him, for he dressed well – she especially admired the long leather driving-coat and the tweed cap he wore in the car. But of Charles himself she was not so sure. He was very different from Tom. There were obvious physical differences: where Tom was large and powerful, Charles was medium-sized and sleek; where Tom gave an impression of strength and straightforwardness, Charles seemed softer, more pliable. But the main difference was that Tom had a sense of humour that matched her own and she was less in tune with Charles.

But none of this was important and in those early days she had just been pleased to be taken around the town, wined and dined, and even if she had to fight off his advances in the car, it had all helped to take her mind off Tom and her family.

One day he had said, 'I've been talking to my mother about you. She's getting on. She needs a secretary to help with the accounts and the farm correspondence. Are you interested?'

She had thought about it for a few moments. Such a job would take her away from her family and also from an environment where she could hardly avoid Tom if he tried to see her. 'Yes, I'm interested,' she said.

In the meantime, she had seen a great deal of Cape Town with him. He had been to school with the sons of many wealthy businessmen who lived in mansions in the suburbs of Kenilworth and Wynberg. She went to several parties in homes more luxurious than she could ever have imagined: large double and treble-storeyed houses set in grounds of several acres, with gardeners and majordomos and maids and cooks, all Cape coloureds, except for the majordomos who were often coal black and said to come from the North. Some of the houses had swimming-pools and most had tennis courts. At the parties there were private orchestras that played the Black Bottom and the Charleston. The guests danced and drank until dawn and then they would climb into their Pierce Arrows and their Napiers and drive to the beach for breakfast.

Kate was swept along on this tide. She could not play tennis and she did not know the latest dance steps, but no one seemed to mind. The talk was all of London. She found that the parents of the young set spoke of 'home', meaning England. On tables in their drawing-rooms she saw copies of the *Illustrated London News* and the *Tatler* that arrived every week on the mail-boat. She herself had arrived on one of the mail-boats with her family. The voyage was the single greatest adventure of her life, and would have been even if Tom had not been aboard, but Charles's friends and their parents seemed to take the liners for granted and made the journey to and from England with a regularity that amazed her. Some even kept apartments in London or houses in the Home Counties. Many had made their money on the Stock Exchange, but others owned wine farms thirty miles from Cape Town, some were lawyers, some doctors, some factory owners. All lived in a style far beyond anything she had ever envisaged.

They all knew a great deal more about London, about Ascot and Henley and Goodwood than she did. They knew who had won or lost the Test Match at Lord's; some had just come back from Wimbledon, others would be going over in time for the Grand National at Aintree. The fact that Kate could not contribute to their discussions might have counted against her had she not come from Edinburgh. They could not quite place her in their scheme of things, but they recognised that Scotland was acceptable. There was salmon-fishing and stalking and grouse-shooting in Scotland. And they could not identify her social class from her accent, for they did not know Scottish accents as they did English. The fact was that she came from 'home', and that was sufficient to give her *cachet*.

Charles's closest friends were a recently-married couple, Jerry and Freda Alexander. Jerry was short, thickset and powerful. Freda was slightly taller than her husband, an ash blonde with grey eyes. Kate thought she was one of the most beautiful young women she had ever seen. Jerry was in the construction business – his father's business, as Kate later discovered – and for a few weeks the four of them went everywhere together.

It was a strange time in Kate's life. She herself was living in a working-class suburb in a working-class house and came from a working-class background. The young social set into which she had been drawn hardly knew the words 'working-class', nor what they implied. She would be picked up by Charles in her run-down street and taken to houses whose interiors and gardens seemed even more grand than they were by comparison with her own, then, like Cinderella, she would be returned to her house when the party was over. The small semi-detached villa became more hateful than ever.

There was always something on. She and Charles went with the Alexanders to the bioscope, the races – she looked for Tom, but did not see him. She would walk around the Royal Cape Golf Club course with the men; sometimes she and Freda would swing at a ball and Kate found that they expected her, as a Scot, to be a natural player.

'Not everyone in Edinburgh plays golf,' she told them.

Jerry was a fanatic who often played three or four days a week.

'When does he work?' she said.

'When he's not playing golf,' Charles replied.

Sometimes Jerry and Charles would disappear for an evening 'with the boys', and once or twice Kate found herself alone with Freda at her expensive new home in Newlands. It was then she realised that, although Freda was beautiful, it was only skin deep. She had little knowledge of anything that went on in the outside world. She was obsessed with herself, with her reactions to people and their reactions to her; especially her husband's. After knowing Kate for only a few days, she talked to her with an intimacy in which even friends of long-standing might rarely indulge. She came from a family of wealthy sheep farmers about two hundred miles from Cape Town, but had been to school in the city. At seventeen, she'd had an affair with a married man, at eighteen an abortion performed by a doctor friend of her father's. At nineteen she had met Jerry and soon she was pregnant by him. But she had lost the baby, and most of her womb; now she could not have babies, but she did not mind, because she didn't like children anyway.

'Jerry doesn't want them either,' she said. 'He's going to take me to Ascot next year. We might even buy a flat in London. It's easier without children.'

On another occasion, as they sat in the big club rooms of the Royal Cape waiting for Jerry and Charles to finish eighteen holes, she said, 'He doesn't like me to wear anything under my dress.'

'Jerry?'

The beautiful grey eyes were unfocussed, the short hair curled over her forehead, giving her a *gamine* look. 'He always wants me. He likes to put his hand up when we're in restaurants. Sometimes he wants me in other people's houses.'

Kate realised that she was simply putting each thought into words without any check or filter; a stream of consciousness.

At first she had thought Freda the height of sophistication, but as she came to know her, she realised that she was both selfish and stupid.

And Kate soon learned that Freda wasn't the only one that Jerry wanted. One Saturday night they had been to a dinner-dance at a country club in the suburbs. She had never been to a place like it before. At one time it had been a great house and, with its ornate mahogany staircase and wood-panelled walls, it gave the impression of what she imagined a Scottish hunting lodge must be. Jerry and Freda had had an argument before they arrived and Jerry spent the evening dancing with Kate, or sitting out. It was not a pleasant party. They left about two o'clock to drive down to a roadhouse near the coast for bacon sandwiches and coffee and Jerry threw the keys to Charles. 'You drive,' he said.

Kate found herself in the back with Jerry. It was a cold night and he spread a rug over their knees. Almost immediately she felt his hand between her thighs. She closed her legs and drew away, but his strong fingers held her. She felt the coldness of his hand above her stockings which, in an attempt to be up to date, she wore rolled down just above her knees. She put her own hands down on his wrist and they began a tug-of-war under the rug. Freda, perhaps sensing what might be happening, said from the front seat: 'Do you want to sit next to Charles?'

It was impossible to say yes without insulting Jerry in front of his wife so she said, 'No, this is fine.'

Jerry was smiling at Freda. 'We're keeping each other warm.'

Even as he spoke, he forced his hand up. She dug her nails into his arm, but he twisted his fingers in her hair and pulled. Tears sprang to her eyes.

Abruptly, she said, 'Stop please, Charles. I'm going to be sick.'

He pulled up and she got out and stood by the car. 'I think I drank too much. Cars make me sick.'

'Sit in front then,' Freda said. 'You won't feel sick in front.'

'I'd like to go home.'

The two women changed seats and Charles drove back to Observatory.

'Feeling all right now?' Jerry said as she left the car.

'Yes, thank you.'

He was smiling, but his eyes were hostile and she realised that she was frightened of him.

They did not only go to country clubs and smart parties. Charles and Jerry also knew the seamier side of the city. Once the four of them went to District Six. Jerry was driving and Freda was in front. Kate sat at the back with Charles. 'Don't ever walk up here by yourself,' Charles had said as Jerry turned into Hanover Street, the ghetto's main thoroughfare. 'Not even in daylight, or the *skollys* will get you.'

'*Skollys?*'

Jerry pulled over to the pavement and said, 'Coons. Coloureds. Street gangs.'

'Aren't *you* afraid?' she said, with heavy sarcasm.

He had opened the glove compartment and pulled out a pistol. He held it as though waiting for someone to come up and make trouble.

'See that place over there?' Charles pointed to a large white building with a shop beneath it. 'That's a *shebeen* where you can buy liquor after hours.'

'And that's a brothel over there,' Jerry said. 'Full of coloured girls. The white men come about midnight. And over there is where the *moffies* are.' He laughed. 'Have you ever seen a *moffie* – a man dressed as a woman?'

'No,' Kate said.

'That's one.' He indicated a coloured 'woman' who was leaning against a lamp-post. She was a grotesque figure in a short, tight, pink satin dress which revealed muscular legs and clung over her tiny breasts. On her head was a ginger wig, with kiss-curls plastered on her cheeks.

One evening, when she had gone home for the week-end after some weeks with Mrs. Preller, Charles had taken her to the Crescent Curry House in District Six. Its interior was decorated in the style of an Indian temple and smelled strongly of joss-sticks and cardamom.

'Good evening, Mr. Charles,' the Malay owner said. 'How is Mr. Charles tonight?'

'I'm okay. Have you got my table?'

He had put them in a corner. Charles ordered a curry and rice with roti for them both. After a while Kate had become aware of a good-looking coloured girl, very light-skinned, who was staring at them. Charles turned and the girl smiled and nodded, but he seemed to look through her as though she was not there.

They had been the only two white people in the place. Some of the women, whose mouths were covered by thin veils, looked as though they might be beautiful, with large, liquid brown eyes and oiled hair. Many of those who were unveiled shared a common characteristic she had noticed in some of the women in Helmsdale: the front teeth of their upper jaws were missing.

They had finished eating by eight o'clock.

'You haven't seen my flat,' Charles said. She had made excuses twice before not to go to his flat, now she had none.

It was on the top floor of an old town house overlooking the city and Table Bay. The view of the lights was spectacular. He had taken her through french windows onto a large balcony.

'It's marvellous!' she said.

He was standing a few paces away, looking not at the lights, but at her. She had felt her heartbeat increase. She was on his territory now.

Then the doorbell had rung. He frowned. It rang again, then a knock came.

'I'll get it. You stay here,' he said.

She heard him open the door, then a woman's voice. She could not make out words, but the tone was angry. Charles' voice, answering, was a low rumble at first, growing louder.

'You *have*!' she heard the woman say, then '. . . waiting and waiting . . .' Her voice was heavily accented.

Charles: 'Stop that shouting!'

'. . . car. I *saw* you. You're lying!'

Suddenly, he had appeared in the doorway of the sitting-room, blocking it. Over his shoulder, Kate could see dark hair. She had found herself crouching in the shadows like a criminal.

'Not now, for Christ's sake!' His voice was like a whip.

'You think I don't know why she doesn't want me? You think I don't know why she won't let me come to the house?'

She heard sounds of a scuffle, a piece of furniture was knocked over, then a scream, partly of anger, partly of hurt. And silence. The front door slammed and feet ran down the stairs, and stopped outside.

Kate could see the woman standing in the shadows,

looking up, trying to penetrate the dark verandah, and then she had turned and gone away.

Humiliated and angered, Kate had gone into the sitting-room.

Charles was standing, lighting a cigarette. She took one from his silver case and he lit it for her.

'Sorry about that,' he said. She could feel his rage; his eyes had gone blank.

'Take me home,' she said.

He did not seem to hear her.

She had picked up her bag and gone towards the door. 'If you won't take me, I'll order a taxi.'

'What?' The light came back, life moved into the eyes.

'I said I want you to take me home.'

'Ja. Okay. Fine.'

[7]

'Bloody ostrich feathers,' Smuts said to Kate one morning. 'Who'd have thought that ostrich feathers would make people rich. You women are bloody funny.'

But it wasn't only ostrich feathers that had captured the fashionable imagination. There was a new interest in every kind of decorative feather, from louries and birds of paradise, to exotic pheasant. Ostrich feathers were in such demand that Saxenburg could not produce them quickly enough. Helmsdale was agog with the prospect of real wealth again and Miriam Sachs' death was hardly discussed any longer.

Smuts took on a few extra hands and soon the small dwellings on the far side of the sheds were filled with brown-skinned families. As the price of feathers rose, the pace increased and Kate found herself having to pitch in and help.

The first plucking was something she would never forget. The adult birds were rounded up in their camps and taken to a walled enclosure. Each of the labourers carried a long pole with a shepherd's crook tied on the end with wire. This was used to hook a bird by the neck. The head was bent low, throwing the ostrich off-balance so that it could not attack with its large, clawed feet. Each bird was led to a small, triangular pen into which it fitted closely and to the sides of which it was securely tied. Then a sock was pulled over its head to calm it.

When she heard Smuts talk of plucking, she had envisioned feathers being pulled from the living bird and had felt uneasy about the pain it would cause.

'You bloody townees always get things wrong,' he said. 'Of course we don't hurt the birds. I told you, they're too valuable.' He took a body feather in his fingers and pulled. It came away easily in his hand. 'Body feathers are plucked, but only when they're ripe.' He touched the place from which he had pulled it. 'The nerves have died. The bird would have moulted the feather anyway. Doesn't feel a thing. The wing feathers are different.' He ran his fingers through the long white plumes. 'If we left these to ripen they would grow so long the birds would damage them. But we can't pull them or we *would* hurt the birds. So we cut them.' He cut the feather from the underside of the wing with shears and showed her the two inches or so that remained of the quill. 'In a few months that will ripen and the nerves will die and then we'll take it out. If we didn't a new feather would be damaged trying to push it out.'

Kate's days began to be dominated by the birds as hundreds were rounded up and driven into the plucking 'kraals.' She learned to live in a world of hysterical birds, shouting labourers, snipping shears – and dust. The birds kicked up dust as they were driven from one place to the next; sometimes they would thrash about in the plucking box and for several moments would disappear behind a screen of fine yellow dust; it got into her hair and eyes and up her nose and between her teeth.

Soon her problem was not the ostriches, but the feathers themselves. Smuts left Jonas to deal with the plucking while he organised Kate and Betty and Lena into a team to deal with them. They came first in a trickle of bundles and then in a flood. The dirty white feathers had to be washed, dipped into starch and dried in the hot sun by beating them together in bundles. This made them light and fluffy.

One problem was where to put them while they were waiting to be sorted, and where to store them afterwards. There was so much dirt and dust in the air near the plucking kraal that eventually the clean feathers were taken into the house. For the six or seven days of the plucking, Saxenburg became inundated by them. Whole rooms were given over to their storage: on chairs, the dining-table, the big drawing-room, the hall, the breakfast room. Everywhere there was a flat area out of the wind and dust, Smuts used it for feathers.

But the feathers held dust, too, dust so fine that the interior of the house began to look as though a sea mist had entered it. Dust and fluff penetrated everywhere, including Kate's sinuses, causing her to sneeze most of the day. It was only when she retreated to her room at night and sat by the open window, breathing the ozone-laden air, that she found some relief. It was the same for everyone. Smuts, Betty and Lena went about looking as though they had hay-fever.

Smuts taught Kate how to sort the feathers by length, colour and quality into prime whites, blacks, tails, feminas and chicken feathers.

Other farmers began to restock and refurbish as the new boom held, and Helmsdale shook itself out of a sleep that had lasted for more than ten years. People began to paint their houses; a few shops reopened; two new cars appeared for sale in the show-rooms of Preller Motors; there were more cars in the streets; more diners at the hotel. When she remarked on this, Mrs. Preller said, 'At the moment there is more confidence than new money. But confidence *is* money. You will find that out for yourself one day.' In the months that followed, the trickle of money became a stream that became a river.

Charles came home most week-ends. Kate found it fascinating to see him against his own background, especially his relationship with his mother. Mrs. Preller lived for his visits. On Friday evenings she would become restless as she waited for the sound of his roadster on the gravel drive. He would leave Cape Town after work and be at Saxenburg by eight or nine o'clock, depending on how fast he drove. And he drove fast; he loved speed. The house would revolve around him for the next forty-eight hours. He would spend time with his mother and would often go with her for a drive in the afternoons, usually with Smuts at the wheel.

But Kate was never sure about his reaction to his mother. When they were in company he treated her with deference and respect, but sometimes when he was alone with Kate he would make remarks about her curious, hermit-like existence – 'the spider in her web,' he called her once – that were meant to be funny but left a somewhat sour taste. She began to get the impression that he had an ambivalent attitude to his mother and wondered if it did not spring partly from childhood fears that had never completely gone. She knew that she had similar deep-seated fears of her own mother.

Lena was also pleased to see him and treated him as the young master. She knew his favourite foods and would take his breakfast to him in bed, spoiling him as she must have spoiled him when he was a child. But again Kate realised that what she saw was what she was meant to see. Below the surface there were tensions.

Then one day the relationships had become clearer. Charles had spilt a few drops of gravy on his waistcoat – he was a neat and careful dresser, 'natty', as Smuts called him – and went into the kitchen to have it cleaned. After a moment, Kate followed him to ask Betty to replenish the salt-cellar. The girl was cleaning off the spots with a moist rag. Her sharp breasts were almost touching him and he was looking down at her with a look Kate recognised. After that she noticed for the first time that Lena never left Betty alone with Charles if she could help it.

He would leave again late on Sunday evening, or early on Monday and the house would seem empty. Mondays were always bad days for Mrs. Preller. She would be irritable and jumpy.

One Monday, soon after Kate's arrival, she had called

her up to dictate after lunch. When she had finished, instead of dismissing her, she said abruptly: 'What do you think of Charles?'

'He's very nice.'

'How do you get on with him?'

'We get on well.'

'What do you do when he is here? Where do you go with him?'

'We go swimming.'

'In the pools?'

'Yes.'

'They are dangerous. I hope you will be careful. I have told him many times. So did Boss Charles. We must have the swimming-pool mended here. Then you can use it. And the tennis-court. You can play tennis with Charles. He is not very good. Hugo would have been a champion. He could swim like a fish. What else do you do?'

'He has taken me to dinner at the hotel.'

'And in Cape Town before you came here? I know you saw him there, too.'

'We went to the beach. He took me for drives.'

'In that red car. It is dangerous, I think. He drives too fast. Where else?'

'To restaurants.'

After a moment Mrs. Preller said, 'Long ago this whole area used to be called Prellersdorp. The family owned all the coastline and as far as you could ride a horse inland in a day. It was a huge property. Then a British troopship called the *Helmsdale* was wrecked on the India Reef. Two hundred and thirty-two people died. You have seen the monument down by the harbour?'

'Yes.'

'That is where they were buried. The Preller family went into a decline for many years. They became poor. Almost what we call out here poor whites. But not quite. Things were bad everywhere in those days, especially around here. Then in the 1890s the feather market began to grow. The Prellers became rich again. But Charles's father never completely trusted in feathers. That is why we have survived. That is why I have put Charles into business in

Cape Town. Let him learn how to handle money. One day he will take over all this. The house. The farm. The businesses in Helmsdale . . .' Her voice trailed off. 'One day.' Then she said, 'If Hugo had lived, I would not have been so worried. Even as a child, he could do anything.'

'Worried?' Kate said.

She drew in a breath as though to explain, but changed her mind. 'I'm glad you like Charles. I'm glad you get on with each other.'

Later, Kate tried to analyse the conversation. Why had Mrs. Preller catechised her so carefully? It was almost as though she was questioning a . . . but that was ridiculous.

She wondered what Mrs. Preller would have said if she had known the truth, which was that Kate lived in a constant state of sexual tension when Charles was at home. He was not difficult to manage in the house. She thought he probably feared the all-seeing eyes of the servants and Smuts and what they might say to his mother. But when they were alone, she found herself waiting for his inevitable approach. Not that she always objected. She found him attractive, but the memory of what had already happened to her was too vivid to allow her to relax with him. There was an element of violence in him that excited her, but at the same time frightened her.

He did not always come back alone for the week-end and once brought Jerry and Freda and, to her surprise, Duggie, though she knew they had been seeing each other in Cape Town. He put them up at the hotel.

They had planned to spend the week-end lounging on the beach and eating and drinking, but the weather for once had turned sullen and a black south-easter had blown up.

Helmsdale under these conditions was not an ideal holiday retreat and time hung heavy. On Saturday they had tried to play tennis on the ruined court. Charles had told two of the labourers to sweep it and pull the weeds from the cracks, but the net had long since rotted away and there were no lines. Jerry was determined that they should play and he found a rope to act as a net and tied pieces of rag to it about six inches apart. He then found half a brick and broke it in two, using the red, crumbling baked clay to mark off a singles court according to the dimensions he found in an encyclopaedia. Charles became infected by his enthusiasm. Three racquets were found in an old chest in the house. They were warped, but most of the strings were still intact. They made do with old balls last used about ten years before, but which still bounced on the hard concrete surface.

'Who's going to play?' Freda said. 'There are three racquets.'

'Three can't play,' Jerry said.

'Yes, we can,' she said. 'I'll play with Charles and you hit to us.'

'That's not a game! Charles and I will play.'

But Freda insisted, though she took part only long enough to realise that to be graceful took an experienced player. After missing a couple of balls she dropped the racquet and stood moodily at the side, clutching her white cardigan around her thin, elegant shoulders. Kate and Duggie sat in the shelter of the wall and watched the two men.

Kate had not seen much of her brother and frowned at the sight of his papery skin and the little veins that were spreading like red threads across his cheeks. He kept a flask of brandy in his pocket which he topped up from a bottle in the car. She never saw him drunk and he was always pleasant to her, but he never seemed to be quite *there*. She told herself that the leg was to blame.

In spite of the drink, he was still a good-looking man. Even she, his sister, could see that. He had a thin face that smiled easily. Dressed in plus fours, an old tweed jacket and a tweed cap, he seemed at home with these rich young South Africans, as comfortable with them as he had been on the ship with the gang of hard-drinking miners from Fife.

Bored and impatient, Freda called to Jerry, 'How long are you going to be?'

'As long as we go on playing.'

'You'd think they were playing for a championship,' Duggie said.

Kate knew nothing of the finer points of tennis but was able to see how aggressive the two men were. It was no longer simply a friendly knock-up to pass the time. They argued at least one point in every game, questioning each other's line calls. Freda was appealed to, but she turned away and sat down beside Kate.

'They're always like this,' she said. 'Babies.'

The game came to an end on an acrimonious dispute about a back-line call.

'You've marked the bloody court wrongly,' Charles said angrily. 'It's too short.'

'For Christ's sake, man!' Jerry said. 'You lost!'

But Charles went into the house and brought out the encyclopaedia and this time, instead of measuring the approximate length and breadth with his feet, he fetched a tape measure from Smuts' office and they spent half an hour measuring and arguing. They then piled into the two cars, drove into town and measured the club courts to make sure of the size. Charles remained angry for the rest of the day.

Sunday, too, was cloudy and cool, and they decided to play golf: 'they' being Jerry and Charles. The golf course was only nine holes and built along the cliff tops. The 'greens' were of blue sand and the fairways so poor that players were allowed to tee-up their balls on it. It reminded Kate, in its state of decay, of the tennis-court at Saxenburg.

The club-house was a small wooden building with a corrugated iron roof, and Duggie elected to remain there with his brandy flask.

The primitive conditions made no difference to Jerry and Charles. They played as though they were at St. Andrews, and again there were arguments about lies and strokes and stymies. Towards noon, the black south-easter cleared away and the day turned warm. They decided to have a picnic at the rock pools. Charles found some bottles of cold wine in the paraffin refrigerator at the hotel.

As they were about to drive away, Miriam came along the pavement towards them. She was dressed in a cream-coloured skirt, cream blouse and a black and cream silk scarf worn as a headband, tied so the ends hung down behind her right ear. The creamy colours contrasted with her jet-black hair and olive skin. She looked fleshy and nubile and very different from the two other women. Kate remained half hidden in the car. She told herself there was no need to feel embarrassed, but she knew how Miriam felt about Charles.

They all chatted for a few moments, then Jerry said, 'We're going for a picnic. Why don't you come, too?'

Charles and Kate were in the roadster, Jerry and Freda and Duggie in the big Pierce Arrow.

Miriam seemed to consider the invitation for a moment, then she said, 'Why not?' and got in beside Duggie.

It was lunchtime when they reached the rock pools. Duggie and Charles built a small fire of driftwood and cooked sausages and chops while they all drank the wine.

The day turned hot and the wind dropped. Miriam pulled up her skirt as she had done when she and Kate had been there together, and opened the front of her blouse to expose her skin to the sun.

Kate watched, fascinated, as she flirted with Duggie. She gave him all her attention, used his Christian name caressingly and saw that he had everything he wanted. She sat next to him and asked him to tell her about himself and his life in Edinburgh. He seemed to forget his painful leg. He had always been a man who could charm women and now he turned it on like a tap. From where she sat, Kate could see his fingers touching Miriam's hair. Their voices had dropped and she could no longer hear what they were saying, but occasionally Miriam would laugh huskily.

Charles watched with hooded eyes.

The rock pools were glassy and crystal clear. Kate lay on her stomach and looked down through the water. The pool's sandy bottom seemed close enough to touch. Strands of weed waved in the wake of tiny fish, pink anemones lay like open flowers; here and there in the rock crevices she could see the purple spines of sea-urchins.

'Is anyone going to swim?' Miriam said.

She had rolled up her dress even further and her blouse was open to the fourth button.

'My costume's at the hotel,' Freda said. 'I didn't think it would be swimming weather.' None of the others had brought bathing-costumes, either.

Charles passed the wine. Kate felt the sun and the wine loosen her muscles and undo knots in her brain.

'Why don't we take our clothes off?' Jerry said. 'Come on, Miriam, I will if you will.'

She smiled at him. Her eyes were large and black. 'I've often swum in the nude,' she said.

'Come on, Charles,' Jerry said. 'What have you got to hide?'

Charles was lying on his back, his head on Kate's cardigan. 'I don't feel like it.'

Jerry looked at Kate, who shook her head.

'So it's only Miriam and me?'

Freda watched sullenly as he started to take off his clothes. His powerful, chunky body looked pale in the bright sunshine. He dived into the water.

Miriam pulled off her blouse and head-scarf, and dropped her skirt. She was wearing a white brassiere and a pair of the new, brief knickers, pictures of which Kate had seen in advertisements. Swiftly, she removed them and dived in.

They watched her play with Jerry in the water. They were like two friendly seals, splashing and somersaulting. Duggie watched Miriam, a half smile on his lips, but Charles lay with his eyes closed against the sun.

As Miriam, giggling, climbed onto Jerry's back, Freda stood up abruptly. 'Tell Jerry I'm going back to the hotel.'

'I'll drive you,' Charles said.

'I'm going to take the car.'

Kate watched her walk bare-footed across the beach. Then she put on her sandals, climbed the path up the cliff and vanished.

In the late afternoon, they all piled into the roadster, Miriam laughing as she squeezed between Duggie and Jerry in the dickey. Charles drove into Helmsdale and dropped them outside the hotel.

'Come for a drink,' Miriam said, looking directly at him. 'My father's away. I need company.'

He frowned and shook his head. 'I promised mother I'd be back early. She hasn't been feeling well.' He turned to Duggie. 'I'll pick you up later.' As they pulled away, Kate saw Duggie and Miriam walking up the street together.

Charles drove her back along the cliffs. The wine and sun had produced an effect in which her mind, for once, was not on her constant fear of pregnancy.

He stopped the car outside one of the ostrich houses. 'Have you ever seen over one of these places?' She shook her head.

He drove through the open gates and onto the overgrown drive. The house loomed ahead of them: mock-Tudor, with heavy, fake beams. The garden was overwhelmed by grass grown yellow in the sun. A wind had come up and thorn trees tossed their branches. Some of the windows were broken, but what panes remained shone like copper in the last of the sun.

He had stopped at the back of the house and taken a bottle of wine and two glasses from the picnic-box in the dickey-seat. The back door was locked, but he pulled a key from his pocket and opened it. The lock looked new and Kate saw a dark stain of oil on the wood around it. They entered a back passage. 'Mind where you put your feet,' he had said, pointing to holes in the floor-boards. She followed him through an arched doorway and came into the front of the house. Here the sunlight streamed through the dirty panes. Dust covered everything. To her left, a great marble staircase, many of the treads cracked and broken, rose to the first floor. Some of the window panes were broken and the winds had blown in spray from the sea and the summer sun had bleached and warped the wooden panelling. Originally the place must have been almost as grand as Saxenburg.

'This way.' Charles had taken her hand.

They went onto the first floor and along a gloomy passage. Paper had come away in strips and the walls were stained with water that had soaked in from blocked gutterings.

Once this house would have been filled with members of a family, she thought. The rooms would have echoed with laughter, perhaps with anger, but would have echoed with *something*. Now she heard only the whine of the wind as it found its way through the broken glass and round dark corners.

Charles opened a door.

She had stood on the threshold, transfixed. This room was entirely different from the others. They were bare of furniture, their walls peeling and cracked. But this beamed room, with its bed and chairs, its carpet and its curtains, looked as though whoever lived there had just gone out for a few moments.

'How . . .?' she began.

He had closed the door behind her and put the wine on a table. 'I did this. It's where I used to come to smoke.' He had taken out his case and offered her a cigarette. 'I found the furniture in other rooms and brought it together. The Berrangés used to live here. He shot himself at the end of the last feather boom.'

He opened one of the bottles and spread newspaper on the table-top as a cloth.

She went to the window. The sun was going down in a mass of red and yellow cloud. She said softly, ' "Sister Ann, Sister Ann, do you see anyone coming?" '

He handed her a glass of wine. 'You'd better drink that before you frighten yourself.'

'I've done that already.' She had shivered. 'I think it's knowing that someone killed himself here. Did you know them?'

'The Berrangés? Of course. We knew everybody. This was Louise's room.'

'Who was she?'

'One of the daughters. We used to play tennis and swim together when I came home during the school holidays.'

She had thought of Miriam, who had told her she had not seen Charles once he had gone to boarding-school. Perhaps it had been because he had Louise.

The room was filling with the dusk of evening. Only the area around the windows was still lit by the last of the day. She lay back in the large armchair and stared idly at his silhouette. She felt her muscles slacken. Carrying the bottle, he had crossed the room and sat on the arm of the chair. He poured her half a glass of wine and she swirled it round and round. 'It's beautiful.'

He had bent and kissed her. Her lips were still wet from the wine. She was finding it hard to breathe as though a hand had closed over the upper part of her abdomen.

'I'll take your glass.' He had put it down on the floor and kissed her again. Now he was sitting with her in the chair. She had put her arms around him and returned the kiss. She felt as though she were floating, drugged, yet excited. She felt his hands on her breasts. She was hardly aware that the buttons of her blouse had been undone until she felt his cool touch. His hands were expert and excitement mounted. They stayed as they were for a long time. Darkness had fallen, but the moon was already up and the room was bathed in a cold, silvery light. She had seen a pale reflection in the windows and realised it was her own skin. She had seen her breasts and his hands. She discovered with some surprise that she was naked from the waist up. His hands moved constantly. She felt one on her thigh. She told herself she was still in control. The hand moved. She gasped and caught his wrist.

'Why not?' he whispered.

'I don't want you to.'

The hand had moved again and again. She used all her strength against him.

'Please!'

'What's wrong?'

'I don't want to.'

But the hand was moving all the while. She had felt suddenly stifled; he was smothering her. She had felt the first flutterings of panic. She had twisted and turned. Her wiry body was strong. The arm of the chair gave way and Charles fell to the floor. In a moment, she was on her feet, buttoning her blouse.

He stood up. The blankness that she associated with his anger came into his eyes. He had grabbed her and dragged her towards him. 'Why did you come here? You could have said no!'

She had felt his rage and his strength and been suddenly

afraid. She let her body relax against his. 'It's not that,' she whispered. 'I've got my period.'

There was a pause, then she had felt him begin to slacken.

They drove back to Saxenburg in silence and she went up to her room and locked the door. He remained downstairs and she heard him calling for water, ice and brandy. Much later the roadster's engine revved up and she heard the harsh noise of its tyres speeding off down the gravel drive.

Such outbursts of temper from him were infrequent, but when they came, they were alarming. She recalled one in which he had lost his temper first with Jonas and then with Smuts.

She had been working in her office at the back of the house when she heard his raised voice. It appeared that he had told Jonas to wash his roadster and that Jonas had not done so because he'd had his own work to finish.

'Don't you give me any of that shit!' Charles was shouting. 'When I tell you to do something, you do it!'

'Master told me to fill the heaters with paraffin.'

'I don't give a fuck about that. I told you to clean the car, man, and you haven't done it. You bloody do it now or I'll kick your arse. Verstaan?'

At that moment, Smuts had come into the yard. Jonas immediately appealed to him.

'He's right,' Smuts said. 'I told him to check the incubators.'

'I want my car cleaned. I told him half an hour ago.'

'If he's got time, he can do it later.'

'What!'

'You're not taking one of my boys away from his work just to clean a car. We've got too much to do, Charles.'

'Christ Almighty! First I get a bloody argument from a coloured and now you. I'm telling you, I want that car cleaned and I want it cleaned now.'

Smuts said evenly, 'You're not *Boss* Charles, you're *Master* Charles. You don't give me orders.'

'You! God, my father picked you out of the gutter! That's where you would still be! I'm a Preller. You're bugger all. When I say something, I want it done!'

Again without raising his voice, Smuts said, 'You want me to go and ask your mother? You want me to ask her who gives Jonas orders, you or me?'

For a moment Kate thought Charles was going to attack him, then he turned and walked into the house. Jonas stood firm, a look of satisfaction on his face. Smuts shook his head and said, 'All right, get on with your work.'

These gusts of anger did not seem to bother Smuts or the coloured folk on the farm as much as they did Kate. Perhaps they were used to them, she had thought. She was to get used to them herself.

Under Smuts' tuition, she learned to drive the motor and during the second week of December she was driving Mrs. Preller to Helmsdale when the old lady brought up the subject of Christmas: 'It is a time for family gatherings, no? In Vienna, if the weather was cold, my father would take us skating in the Turkenschantz Park. I remember once I fell and hurt my elbow. Such days! You must go to your mother and father for Christmas.'

Kate thought of the little house in Observatory with the smell of drains and old cooking. She thought of Tom and knew she did not want to be anywhere near him at Christmas.

Mrs. Preller went on, 'You know we have a holiday called Second New Year? That is the day after New Year's Day. You must take that, too. You can leave here on Christmas Eve and you need not be back until the third of January.'

Kate was appalled at the thought of such a long period with her family. 'What about you, ma'am? I think I'd rather stay here with –'

'Do not pity me!' Mrs. Preller's voice cut at her like a whip. 'I have got on well without you for years. I can get on . . .'

'I didn't mean that at all.'

'Do not interrupt. Charles will be here with me. I do

not need anyone. Do you understand me? Not Smuts, not you, not Lena, not anyone!'

'It wasn't meant that way, ma'am. It's just that the Scots don't keep Christmas. There's no holiday in Scotland on Christmas Day, everything is the same as usual. It's New Year that we keep, that's when we have our celebrations.'

'It is a strange custom.'

They had reached Helmsdale and Mrs. Preller was distracted from the conversation when she saw a group of people standing outside the little courthouse. There were two cars and an ambulance with Cape Town plates.

'What is happening?' she demanded. 'Who are those people?'

The group broke up and got into the cars. Kate saw Arnold Leibowitz, the attorney, Mr. Sachs and the local police sergeant. The cars drove up the street, followed by the ambulance. Dr. du Toit, in his own car, was about to follow them when he saw Mrs. Preller and came towards her.

'What's happening, Hennie? Who is sick?'

He was frowning. 'No one is sick.'

'Then why the ambulance?'

'They're digging up Miriam Sachs' body.'

There was a moment of total silence, then she said, 'What?' as though she had misheard.

'Sachs got a special court order.'

'But why?'

'He says she was not buried according to Hebrew rights. He's going to have her re-buried.'

'But that's nonsense!'

'It may be, but it's true.'

'To dig up the poor girl! What next? Has he no respect for the dead?'

'He's her father, Augusta.'

'Ever since it happened he's been . . . peculiar. He's not the same Sachs I knew.'

'He's taken it hard.'

'He collapsed,' she said, with contempt.

'She was his whole life.'

'What if I had collapsed when Hugo died?'

'Ja, that's true.'

'But why the ambulance? Are they going to bury her in Cape Town?'

'Apparently he's asked a pathologist there to examine her.'

'Cut her open? Hennie, what a terrible thing to do!'

'He thinks there may be something wrong.'

'Wrong? How?'

'He doesn't think she drowned.'

'He's mad! Of course she drowned. I told her when she was a little girl not to go near the rock pools. You know she used to go there with Charles. He would not have gone if she had not tempted him.'

'Sachs says she would never have swum that night at high tide.'

'Come, Hennie, you know what she was like. She was a . . .'

Dr. du Toit looked at Kate and said, 'Augusta, she's dead, you know.'

'I mean, she wasn't one of *us*.'

'That's true.'

'What could they find?'

'God knows.'

'I think it is unChristian.'

'I don't think that matters, Augusta. They're Jewish.'

'Ja, but Jews should also be Christian, if you know what I mean. How long will it be before they know?'

'Probably a few weeks.'

The fact that Miriam had been dug up and removed by ambulance to Cape Town was a greater sensation in Helmsdale than her death had been. The town was used to the occasional knifing in the coloured fishing village, the occasional skull split open by a wine bottle, but this was something different. There had been nothing like it since Hugo Preller had died. Mystery still surrounded his death and now mystery surrounded the death of Miriam Sachs. What made it even more fascinating was that her death should have taken place on Saxenburg. When it had happened, the fact that it had occurred there had only added a pinch of spice, for Saxenburg was a source of abiding interest in the town, especially since the Prellers had dominated its history for so long. But now this! To be examined, to be cut open, to be looked at through a microscope! The wildest rumours circulated, none of which lasted for more than a day or two. The most persistent was that Miriam had been pregnant, that the foetus had been found by the pathologist. Therefore, there was only one reason for her death: suicide. She had gone to a place she knew and had drowned herself.

[8]

'She's taken to you,' Smuts said to Kate a few days before Christmas. 'She respects you, and that's bloody rare, my friend. It's because you work like a kaffir. You know, we haven't had a proper Christmas since, oh, before Hugo died. You'll see, when she does something, she does it properly. It's going to be like the old days.'

Kate expanded under his praise. No one had spoken to her in such a way for a long time. She had been praised for her work at school, but once school was over, there had been little enough. She felt the old stirrings, the need for praise and the concomitant drive that followed, the one fuelling the other.

Smuts' prediction was right. For a few days the house was transformed. Lena and Betty opened up the drawing-room and the dining-room, dusted and cleaned, and let in more fresh air and sunlight than Saxenburg had seen in many a year.

Mrs. Preller made lists of food and wine and reminisced about Christmases in the old days, with tennis tournaments and swimming parties, and sometimes her mind would go back to others she had spent in Vienna. Kate had never seen her so animated. There were visits to Helmsdale and telephone calls to shops in Cape Town to order cheeses, tins of foie gras, smoked ham, Bath Oliver biscuits, tinned asparagus and other items which must be put on the train in good time. One day Smuts took Kate into a cellar she had not known existed. Part of it had been shelved and there must have been nearly three hundred bottles of wine lying on beds of straw.

'Rhine wines,' he said, touching a bottle reverently. 'You couldn't buy these today even if you had the money. I had some once. Like bloody nectar, my friend.'

He consulted the piece of paper on which Mrs. Preller had written her choice, and took up half a dozen bottles. 'I told you she would do things properly.'

Kate shopped for presents and delivered an invitation to Dr. du Toit, who looked at her in surprise and said, 'Augusta's going to . . . Good God! Yes, of course I'll be there. I never thought . . . well, well. I was going to have my Christmas dinner in the hotel as usual. This will make a change.'

Charles arrived on Christmas Eve, and set himself out to be charming.

'Smuts tells me this is all your doing,' he said. 'Mother must have taken a shine to you. She doesn't often.'

She was flattered, and when they were alone in the drawing-room, she did not resist his kiss. There was a hunger in it to which she found herself responding, and she realised for the second time that she did not have as much control over her needs as she had thought. After a moment, she broke away and went to the window overlooking the cove.

Charles joined her. 'Have you been swimming?'

'Not in the pools. Not since Miriam drowned.'

'I don't blame you. But you can't let that influence you for ever. She drowned. It's sad, but the world goes on.'

'It's not that easy,' she said shortly. 'I found her, remember.'

'Try and think of her as she was in life.'

'I had just about managed that until . . .'

'Until what?'

'The exhumation. The post mortem. It's macabre.'

'The *what*?'

'They dug her body up. Didn't you know? I thought someone must have told you.'

'Dug her up? What for?'

'Her father said she had not been buried according to Hebrew rites, so he got a court order.'

'I don't understand. What has that got to do with a post mortem?'

'Mr. Sachs doesn't think she drowned.'

'You found her. She was drowned, wasn't she?'

'She looked drowned, but I'm not an expert.'

'I know you're not an expert, but . . .'

'Mr. Sachs has asked a Dr. Fleischman to do the post mortem.'

'I've heard the name.'

'Dr. du Toit doesn't think it's necessary.'

'I don't either!' Charles said vehemently. 'Jesus, I hate the thought of her body being . . . Why couldn't they have left her alone?'

So he did care, she thought. Deep down below the surface, he did care about Miriam. She found herself somewhat relieved.

Christmas Day was hot and windy and they had decided to have their dinner at night. Lena traditionally went into Helmsdale in the afternoon to attend the service at her church, which lasted for most of the evening, so everything was left to Kate and Betty.

Dr. du Toit arrived at seven, dressed in a dinner-jacket, and was followed by Smuts, who wore tails. Both men looked uneasy in their tight-fitting clothes, and Smuts' had the rusty look of old age. 'They used to belong to my father. We had them cut down for him,' Charles told Kate softly, as he poured Smuts a brandy and water. He himself was in a white tuxedo with a claret-coloured bow-tie and a matching handkerchief.

Softly lit, the drawing-room was huge and shadowy. The blues and purples gave it an opulent look, a feeling of luxury which suited Kate's mood, for she had, the day before, bought a new black dress at Paris Modes in Helmsdale's main street. It was the first non-utilitarian dress she had ever bought and she had been wavering about it for days. Finally she had given in to temptation and now she knew she had been right. Charles had told her she looked pretty and she was wearing the dress in the right surroundings: not a small, wretched house in a run-down suburb, but a great mansion which had been briefly brought to life. Why did it have to be brief, she thought? Why did Saxenburg ever have to return to the dim, lifeless place it had been before?

'Well, Charles, it's like the old days,' du Toit said, holding up his glass.

'Just what I was saying,' Smuts said. 'Like the old days.' He had finished his brandy and Charles took his glass.

'You're always talking about the old days, Smutsy,' he said.

'We'll have them again. You'll see.' He took a fresh drink, and turned to du Toit. 'Any news?'

'News?'

'About Miriam Sachs.'

The doctor frowned. 'I don't think –'

'I didn't know,' Charles said. 'It's bloody awful, isn't it?'

'Ja. But these things happen. I don't think we should talk about it, you know. Not at Christmas. I don't want your mother . . . Here she is!' He moved to the door. He bent to kiss her cheek and Kate saw him murmur something in her ear. She shook her head slightly.

Her long, dark blue dress reached the floor and her hair had been brushed so that it covered part of her face. She wore a piece of lace at her throat and matching lace gloves. Very little of her skin was visible, but again Kate was struck by the whiteness and thickness of the powder she had applied, which contrasted so dramatically with the slashes of red on her lips.

'Darling,' she said, coming forward to Charles.

He made to kiss her, but Kate saw him turn away fractionally at the last moment so that his lips did not quite touch her.

'We were saying how long it's been, Augusta,' du Toit

said. 'Man, it must be . . . we haven't fore-gathered here since the accident.'

'I thought it was time, Hennie.'

'What will you drink, mother?' Charles broke in.

Kate noticed that her hands were shaking. 'Have we any vermouth? Yes? Then I will have a dry martini.'

'Augusta, you . . .'

She turned to the doctor. 'It is Christmas and my son is home.'

There was a moment of tension, an uncomfortable little silence. Then, holding up her glass, she said, 'Merry Christmas!' They drank the toast. 'That was delicious, Charles. You make them almost as well as your father did.' She held out the glass. Dr. du Toit pursed his lips.

Kate decided that the sooner she served dinner, the better, and she went into the kitchen, where Betty was dressed in her best. 'You look lovely,' Kate said.

Then she saw a shadowy figure in the half darkness at the far end of the kitchen. 'Good evening, Jonas.'

He came into the light. He was no longer in working clothes, but in a shirt and tie, and looked a different person. The clothes hid his physical power.

The dining-room looked better than she could have hoped. She and Lena and Betty had spent long hours cleaning it. They had polished the refectory table Smuts had told her came out of the *Nicobar*, then they had taken down the drops from the chandeliers – from the *Saxenburg* – and washed them in vinegar water, and used beeswax on the sideboard. Everything glowed, and points of light from the glittering chandeliers were reflected in dark, silky surfaces.

After consultation with Mrs. Preller, Kate and Lena had transported a complete English traditional dinner into the hot African night: soup was followed by goose and plum pudding. The wines were in a beautiful teak cooler which had come from yet another wrecked vessel. There were no elaborate decorations, but a small paper Christmas tree stood in the middle of the table. It was the most festive setting Kate could imagine. She had never known such surroundings.

The talk was general and she sat back, drinking her wine and listening. She was interested in the talk, but more so in her own reactions to the atmosphere. It was as though she fitted in naturally. And again she thought, as she had when she sat by the ruined tennis court and the cracked swimming pool, how much she would like to recreate Saxenburg and bring it back to its original splendour.

'. . . cold enough, my father would take us skating,' Mrs. Preller was saying. 'My father always bought a cake at Demel's . . . a "creation" is more the word. I remember one that was a valley in the Tyrol: the little houses made of chocolate, the meadows of cream, the snow of marzipan.' She had drunk several glasses of wine and her speech was rapid, her manner excited. Kate noticed that Dr. du Toit was frowning. '. . . fried carp. But that was for Christmas Eve dinner. No one knows how to cook carp in this country. And coffee . . . there is no comparison. Mr. Preller found a shop in Cape Town with Viennese coffee. Whenever he came back from Cape Town, he brought me coffee. He was always giving me presents. But he had so little time to be here towards the end. Business, business. That was after Hugo died. Do you know, I still . . .'

'Augusta –'

'All right, Hennie, all right.'

There were undercurrents in the conversation that Kate did not understand.

Mrs Preller staggered as she rose, and du Toit steadied her. 'Miss Buchanan and I will leave you to your cigars. We will have coffee in the drawing-room.' Words and syllables had begun to run into each other.

Dr. du Toit gave Kate a glance that needed no interpretation and she moved forward to let Mrs. Preller take her arm. 'I am not crippled,' she said.

When they were in the hall under the huge *Saxenburg* figurehead, she stopped. 'I will join you in a minute.' Kate watched her go along the passage into the downstairs cloakroom.

She carried coffee through from the kitchen, telling Betty to start clearing the table. Jonas was already at the sink. In the drawing-room, she put the coffee down, emptied ash-trays and removed glasses. When she had finished, she stood in the doorway, frowning, then moved to the cloakroom door. The light was on, but she could hear no sound.

She called: 'Mrs. Preller?' There was no reply. She knocked gently, then louder. She heard the men come from the dining-room and drew the doctor aside.

'Is something wrong?' Charles said.

'We don't know. Your mother may have fainted,' du Toit said. He knocked and called, then twisted the door handle. 'I'll have to break it.'

He put his huge frame against the door and pushed. It was made of heavy teak and the lock was solid, but there was a splintering sound and it burst open.

Mrs. Preller was lying on her side in the middle of the room, her hair covering her face, her long dress caught up under her knees.

Du Toit knelt beside her. 'It's the wine, on top of martinis. I told her she shouldn't drink much. Augusta!' He slapped her wrists. 'We must get her upstairs.'

'My God, what's happened? What has she done?' Smuts said from the doorway.

'It's all right, Smutsy. Too much wine,' Charles said.

Dr. du Toit picked her up easily. 'Charles, you wait down here with Smuts. Miss Buchanan, come with me.' He paused at the bottom of the stairs. 'Tell Lena to come.'

'She went to church. She won't be back until late.'

'Then Augusta may be in trouble,' he said grimly.

Kate had not been in Mrs. Preller's bedroom before. Her impression was of lace everywhere, curtains, hangings above the bed, lace that billowed and moved like the ostrich feathers in other parts of the house. The bed was large and high, with pillows piled up against the headboard. Du Toit placed her against them.

'Help me undress her and get her into bed.'

There was a sound from the sitting-room and Charles called, 'I've told Smuts to go. I'll be downstairs.'

'Send Betty up.'

'She left a few minutes ago.'

Mrs. Preller's dress was fastened at the neck. Kate undid

it and slipped it over her head. She found a night-dress under the pillows and started to remove her undergarments.

'Oh, God!' she whispered, as she saw her body. She wanted to look away, but couldn't. Mrs. Preller was painfully thin and at first Kate thought she was wizened, like someone very, very old. Then, in the shadowy lamplight, she saw the skin of her chest – there were no breasts to speak of – and upper arms and back looked as though candles had been dripped all over her and the wax allowed to harden. It had the same dead-white, ridged and shiny appearance. She saw something else: blotchy bruises on the inner arms, some red, some purple and some a sulphurous yellow.

She hurriedly pulled the night-dress down and Dr. du Toit drew up the sheet.

'Not feeling ill, are you?' he said.

'I'm all right. It was just seeing –'

'Ja. Well. You've seen what third-degree burns can do.'

'Oh, God,' she said again. 'What happened?'

'Has no one told you?'

'People are always talking about an accident, but that's all.'

'You sleep upstairs, don't you, in the old nursery? It happened in the room next door. The two boys had it as their bedroom. I'm not sure of the exact details, but it was winter and a fire was burning. A piece of coal or wood must have fallen from the grate. I was told that there was some washing drying on a clothes-horse in front of the fire. Apparently it caught alight. Man, the next thing, the whole room was in flames. She got those burns trying to save Hugo, but it was no use.'

'What happened to Charles?'

'He was only a child. He says he –'

The telephone rang and they heard Charles answer it downstairs. They listened. Then du Toit said, 'I'm damn sure that's what killed her husband. I don't think he ever recovered. Nor did she. Man, they loved that boy.'

'It's for you, doctor,' Charles called.

'She's all right for the moment,' du Toit said as he picked up the extension in Mrs. Preller's sitting-room.

When he returned, he looked annoyed. 'On Christmas night! Now I've got a confinement. The pains have started. Listen, there is not much to do here. She may vomit. I hope she does. You must lift her head, otherwise the stuff will get into her lungs. The main thing, though, is that you must turn her over every half hour or so. It's important. When they go into this kind of coma, they can't turn themselves. The nerves can be damaged and cause a Bell's palsy. You understand?'

'I think so.'

'Just stay awake. I'll be back as soon as I can.'

He left and she heard him talking to Charles. Suddenly, for no reason she could explain, she did not want Charles there. When he came to the door, she said she would call him if there was anything he could do.

'I'm sorry about this,' he said. 'Not a very nice Christmas for you.'

'Nor for her.'

She sat by the bed. Every half hour, she put her hands under Mrs. Preller's body and heaved her over onto her other side.

By two o'clock the doctor had not returned and she was exhausted. She dozed, then came awake suddenly, flustered and frightened, only to see by the clock that she had slept barely a minute or two. She rose and turned the old lady. Mrs. Preller opened her eyes.

'So,' she said. 'Where is Lena?'

'She went to Church.'

'I fell. I remember falling.'

'That's right. You must have tripped. You fell in the cloakroom.'

'Who found me?'

'I did. Then Dr. du Toit broke the door down.'

'He would have enjoyed that. He was a rugby player. He always talks scrum . . . scrum . . .' She lay back, her white, wasted face matching the colour of the expensive linen pillow-cases. 'Who undressed me?'

'Dr. du Toit and I.'

'Where is he?'

'One of his patients is having a baby.'

'So. On Christmas. It is not possible to conduct these things.' She paused and looked directly at Kate. 'Then you saw?'

'Yes, ma'am.'

'It is not pretty. You know, once I was like you, thin, but with a good figure. Maybe like a boy's, but good. Young. Strong. I used to walk like you. Quickly. As though there was never enough time to get where I wanted to go. Did Hennie tell you about it?'

'He said it happened the night your son died.'

'What did he say exactly?' Her voice was suddenly sharp.

'That there had been an accident in the nursery. A piece of coal or wood had fallen on some drying clothes. You went in to save your son.'

'No more?'

'No, ma'am.' Kate was out of her depth. The room, the scarred and twisted body, the fall, the house, the wind that was howling around the corners; everything was alien. Yet she also felt a bond developing between her and the woman in the bed, feeling a pity for her and an admiration that she had not known before. She realised suddenly that she had been so caught up in her own life that she had felt almost nothing for anyone else since she had broken with Tom.

'Can I get you anything?' she said.

Mrs. Preller ignored her, pursuing her own thoughts. 'Once I loved to run and swim and play tennis.' She yawned and rubbed her arm in a gesture that Kate had already learned to know. 'How old do you think I am?'

It was something she had often wondered about. Given that Charles was twenty-seven or twenty-eight, his mother, judging from her appearance, would have been about forty when she had borne him. And yet, when she spoke of Vienna and her marriage to Boss Charles, Kate had the impression that she had been young then.

'I couldn't say, ma'am.'

'Guess.'

Kate thought she looked between sixty-five and seventy, but she said, 'Fifty-five.'

'Has Hennie been speaking to you?' Mrs. Preller asked harshly.

'No, ma'am.'

She lay back, scratching her arm. 'You have done well here, Kate.' It was the first time she had used her Christian name. 'Sometimes I see myself in you when I was young. You have the same . . . how shall I put it? Hardness? Strength? I do not mean it in a bad way. I needed such hardness. Now you can see why. Maybe you will need it, too, who knows?' She shivered in spite of the warmth of the room. 'Go and see if Lena is back and send her to me.'

Kate went out in the hot, windy darkness to the workers' dwellings. There was no answer either from Lena or Betty.

Mrs. Preller looked agitated when she returned to the room.

'Is Charles still here?'

'Do you want me to call him?'

'No, no.' She looked closely at Kate. 'Now you must do something for me. Look in the cupboard.' She pointed to the bedside cupboard. Kate opened the door and saw a kidney-shaped enamel dish, a syringe, ampules of a colourless liquid and a piece of red rubber tubing. For a second her stomach clenched as she remembered the red rubber tubing in the dirty room at Fat Sarah's.

'It will not bite you,' Mrs. Preller said. 'Have you never seen morphine?'

'Ma'am, I –'

'Come.'

She picked up the syringe and the small bottle and held them out to Mrs. Preller.

'No, no. You must do it.'

'Me?'

'Of course. If Lena was here she would do it. Look, I will draw it in.' She took the syringe and drew the morphine up, then handed it back. 'Now you must find the vein. Take the rubber tube. Put it so.'

The inner side of her arm was, as Kate had already

noticed, covered in blue-black, purple and yellow bruising. Now she could see old puncture marks.

'Tighter. Pull the rubber tighter. Look for the vein.'

She twisted the band and the arm began to swell. Thin, threadlike veins filled with blood and stood out from the skin. 'Come, child, don't be frightened,' Mrs. Preller said.

Kate touched the skin with the needle. It seemed at first that it would not go in, then suddenly it slipped into the vein and blood rose in the syringe. She pressed gently on the plunger and the mixture of blood and morphine slid down the tube and into the arm. She removed the syringe and placed it in the dish. Mrs. Preller was rubbing her arm. 'Have you never done such a thing before?'

'No, ma'am.'

'Where do you think I get the morphine?'

'I don't know.'

'From Dr. du Toit. Did he not tell you where the scars came from? Did he not tell you about the fire? Can you imagine the pain? No, you cannot. They had to give me morphine for weeks. After that, you cannot say no to it. You cannot live without it. You learn to live with it. So. You know my little secret now.'

Her voice had become drowsy and she closed her eyes. 'You can go now.'

But Kate sat on. She did not know whether or not she coud continue to turn the sleeping woman and decided that she should. She sat watching the small figure and gradually she absorbed the terror and horror of that night long ago in the room next to hers. She saw in her mind's eye the flames and heard the screaming. Year after year of needles and bruising, and the fight to keep sane, the fight to bring up her child, to hold onto Saxenburg. Until that moment, Kate had thought she had plumbed the depths in Fat Sarah's house. She began to realise that she had scarcely sunk below the surface.

She was awake, sitting stiffly in the chair, when Lena came in. It was a little after three o'clock.

'What is Miss Kate doing here?'

'Mrs. Preller fell. Dr. du Toit told me to sit with her.'

Lena came towards the bed and saw the syringe on the

bedside cupboard and a look of such fierce anger came into her eyes that for a moment Kate thought she was going to attack her. She bent and gently placed the bruised arm under the covers.

'Miss Kate must go to bed now.' Her anger seemed to have abated.

'Dr. du Toit said I should turn –'

'Does Miss Kate take me for a fool?'

'No, Lena, of course not.'

She went up to her room and lay in bed, but she could not sleep. She could not get out of her mind that night all those years ago. Her imagination was so vivid, her senses so sharp, that she even seemed to smell the fire. Could the smell still be in the room next door, a scent of charred wood, an old smell, a smell that would be there forever?

She spent the New Year holiday with her parents in Cape Town. She arrived there on New Year's Eve, bringing a basket of crystallised fruit as a present. The house was even worse than she recalled. The city was experiencing a heat wave and the tar bubbled in the street outside and heat seemed to collect in the small, dark rooms. But the family seemed genuinely glad to see her and the house had been tidied and swept.

'Come away! Come away!' her father said, putting his arms around her. Mrs. Buchanan kissed her and Duggie gave her a hug. They took her into the front room and she had a glass of sweet wine and her mother brought in some Mowbray haddock cooked in milk. Kate was unused to such attention at home and was touched. But she saw in their eyes something beyond this brief affection and she could not place it. They seemed to wait for her to speak, to hang on her words. They made her tell them about Saxenburg. It was as though she lived in a far-off kingdom and had come to give them news of an enchanted world.

She spent the following day at home and gradually the old values reasserted themselves. She found herself in the kitchen cooking most of the dinner, she discovered that the family stopped talking when she came into a room; she began to feel the claustrophobic quality she had always felt at home. But home, she realised, was no longer here. If it was anywhere, it was at Saxenburg and she saw herself in her new black dress, a glass of Rhine wine in her hand, sitting at the great refectory table in the dining-room. *That* was where she longed to be; *that* was where she ought to be.

Late in the afternoon a Coloured messenger delivered a letter for her. She took it to her room. She knew, before she opened it, that it was from Tom.

'Darling,' she read. 'I telephoned Helmsdale and they told me you were spending the holiday with your parents. What's happened to us is plain ridiculous. We must see each other. I know it and, in your heart, you know it. Come to the office tomorrow morning. I'll take the day off. I love you so much it is like an ache that never goes away. Tom.'

She read and re-read the letter. She smelled it and thought she caught the faintest trace of his skin. She knew that ache. It had never left her either and now, as though in ambush, it struck her forcibly enough to make her catch her breath.

Of course he was right. They *had* to see each other. She did know it in her heart. She thought of tomorrow. She could make some excuse to leave her family. She would go to his office. He would take her in the car. They could spend the whole day together. Hours and hours. She would go early, straight after breakfast. They could go to a hotel. Have food sent to the room . . . a bottle of wine . . .

There was a knock at the door. She hastily hid the letter. Her mother came in and sat at the end of her bed, something she had often done when Kate was a child. For a moment she was a little girl again, young enough not to know how much greater her mother's love was for Duggie than for her.

Mrs. Buchanan began by asking if she was well, if she was happy, and then the real reason for her visit emerged. Her father had not worked for more than two weeks, Duggie not for a month or more. They were living entirely on what Kate had been sending them.

'But it's Duggie I've come to talk about,' she said. 'It's

his leg. It's no' getting better, just the reverse. The pain's terrible. I took him to a specialist. It's called osteo-myelitis. It means the bone has gone rotten. He wants Duggie in hospital and the surgeon will take out some of the bad bits and then they'll treat him in a nursing home. It'll take weeks. Months maybe. It's either that or he'll lose the leg.'

Kate stared at her. She saw, instead of the domineering woman who had caused her so much unhappiness, a pathetic old lady who had lost her way. This was at the root of yesterday's behaviour: they had all lost their way and they looked to her to find it for them. And suddenly she knew it was she who had lost it for them; she who had forced them out of an environment which they had known and with which they might have coped, to this alien terri-tory where everything was unfamiliar and where it was easier to allow themselves to sink than to swim.

'Tell the specialist to make the arrangements,' she said. 'I'll find the money somehow.'

'I knew you would,' Mrs. Buchanan said, touching her knee. 'I said to Duggie, Kate'll no' let us down.'

The following day she took them to the seaside at Muiz-enburg and watched her father paddle and Duggie lie on the sands by the bathing-boxes, his handsome face waxen from drink and trying to cope with pain. Briefly, fleetingly, she thought of Tom waiting in his office and the ache was like a stone at her heart.

She caught the late train back to Helmsdale and Smuts was waiting for her on the station. It was unusually brightly lit. Cars' headlights illuminated the rear of the train and she saw dust rising and moths flying in and out of the beams. A group of people had collected at the guard's van. Something was being unloaded. Kate went closer and saw that it was a coffin.

'They've brought Miriam home,' Smuts said.

He helped her into the motor and started the engine. She sat back in the deep plush seat. There was a wild banging at the window and she saw Mr. Sachs' face. She tried to roll down the window, but it stuck. He banged again. She thought that his face was covered in sweat, but quickly realised that the sweat was tears. He was sobbing and choking and mouthing words at her. She started to open the door but Smuts let out the clutch and the car shot forward.

PART TWO

The Second Inquest

Helmsdale received the news that there was to be a second inquest into the death of Miriam Sachs in an atmosphere brittle with tension. Over the centuries the little town had been host to a dozen wrecks and to their dead and living, but Miriam's murder was in a category by itself – and that is what they were calling it: murder. No one knew how the word had first come to be used, but it was on everyone's lips, though Sachs himself had not used it. After his outburst at the station he had re-buried his daughter next to her mother in the Helmsdale cemetery and had taken himself off to live with his sister in Cape Town. The police were saying nothing, either.

Mrs. Preller was reinforced in her belief that Miriam had brought her fate upon herself. 'How you die depends on how you live,' she said to Kate. 'I knew something would happen to her. Right down here in my heart. I said it to Boss Charles long ago. I said it to Smuts.' Kate felt that she gained some satisfaction from being proved right.

In the Evergreen Cafe and the Helmsdale hotel, in Paris Modes and Preller Motors, the talk was of Miriam.

Then two things happened at Saxenburg within a day of each other. The first was that Betty became ill after eating contaminated shell-fish, and was sent to her aunt in Caledon, about sixty miles away, to recuperate. The second was that Jonas was arrested.

When the police arrived, Kate was helping Smuts in the incubator shed, Jonas was working in the plucking kraal, mending one of the plucking boxes. There were four of them, Sergeant Van Blerk and three constables Kate had not seen before. They came in a dusty truck and stopped in the yard.

Kate followed Smuts as he went to meet them.

Van Blerk stood by the truck, the others made a small group on one side. Each was armed. They were all big men, including Van Blerk. His body was gross and there were dark patches on his khaki shirt where he was sweating.

'I'm looking for one of your boys,' he said.

'Which one?' Smuts said.

'Koopman.'

Kate did not connect the name until Smuts said, 'Jonas? What's he been up to? Drunk again? He's a bugger for the *vaaljapie* and when he's drunk, the women better watch out.'

'Where is he?'

'On the other side of the sheds.'

They walked round in a group. Jonas was working with his back to them.

'Jonas, you got visitors,' Smuts said.

He straightened up. He had a hammer in one hand and a handful of nails in the other. His eyes were hostile.

'Is your name Koopman? Jonas Koopman?' Van Blerk said.

Jonas looked directly at Smuts, ignoring him.

'They want to talk to you,' Smuts said. 'You been drunk again?'

'It's more than that.' Van Blerk stepped towards Jonas. The other three policemen fanned out.

'Jonas Koopman, I'm arresting you for stealing a . . .'

'No, master!'

Jonas was looking directly at Smuts, appealing to him. 'No, master!' he repeated, more loudly.

'Stand still!' Van Blerk said.

Jonas was backing away, the hammer raised. Kate saw one of the policemen unbutton the flap of his holster.

'They lie, master!' he shouted. He flung the hammer at the nearest policeman and the nails at another, leapt the fence surrounding the plucking kraal and raced away through the ostrich camps.

'Don't shoot him!' Smuts shouted. 'For Christ's sake, don't shoot!'

The urgency of his tone reached the police. Instead of firing, they gave chase. Van Blerk stopped after about twenty yards but the other three, young and powerful, spread out and coursed Jonas as though they were dogs coursing a hare. They caught him within half a mile. Kate saw a sudden flurry of dust and, for a few moments, nothing else, then the three policemen emerged from the dust, dragging Jonas by the arms. His face was covered in blood and his clothes were torn.

'He fell,' one of the constables said. 'Hit his head on a rock.'

They threw him into the back of the truck and two of the policemen climbed in with him.

'He's a bugger, that one,' Van Blerk said.

'Your men hit him,' Kate said. 'Three of them against one!'

'He fell,' Van Blerk said. 'Didn't you see? He fell and hit his head.'

Jonas rose on his knees in the back of the truck. 'Master!' he called to Smuts. 'Master must help me!'

'Sit!' One of the policemen pulled him backwards.

'Listen!' Smuts said. 'What's he supposed to have . . .?'

'You'll find out,' Van Blerk said, starting the truck.

The second inquest into the death of Miriam began on a day of gale force winds. Out of the wind, the heat was stifling. In the wind, it was cooler, but dust was everywhere, blowing up the main street of Helmsdale in clouds, lying in a thin veneer on the shiny wood and green leather of the courthouse.

There was a different atmosphere about this investigation, dominated as it was by the prisoner in the small gaol on the outskirts of the town.

Jonas had been in custody for a week and during that time rumours began to circulate that his arrest for theft was no more than a holding charge for something more serious. It was soon being said that the something more serious was Miriam's death. Helmsdale split into two racial camps: the coloured fishing-village and the town itself. A group of white youths burnt an effigy of Jonas on the jetty of the small harbour and carelessly set fire to the rigging of one of the boats. The following day a white farmer was stoned by coloured youths as he was driving out of town. His windscreen was smashed, but he was unhurt.

In the bars, the white farmers drank brandy and told each other what they would do if there was any further trouble. 'They're talking like bloody vigilantes,' Smuts said to Kate. 'I don't hold with coloureds murdering white women, but these chaps would run a bloody mile if there was any real trouble.'

'You sound as though you thought Jonas was guilty.'

He looked at her with surprise. 'Do you think they would have arrested him otherwise? Everyone says he did it.'

Kate was suddenly angry. 'Who is everyone? I never liked Jonas, but do you think he'll get fair hearing here?'

'I wouldn't say that too loudly in town,' Smuts said. 'You don't want people to get the wrong impression, my friend.'

It was in this atmosphere of hostility that the second inquest began. There were several advocates in black gowns in the court. One had come from Cape Town to represent Mrs. Preller's interests. Leibowitz was there with Sachs and a young attorney called Stoltz was representing Jonas. On the exhibits table Kate saw a bundle of what looked like laundry, then she realised that she was looking at the clothes which she and the police sergeant had found on the beach.

The coroner, Dr. Armstrad, entered briskly. He was a man of about forty-five, with short grey hair and a hard, lined face. He gave the impression of someone who would get to the root of any question, or know the reason why.

Miriam's father, frail and ill, was the first to give evidence, referring particularly to Miriam's clothing, which had been found far from the rock pools. 'My daughter would never have swum at high tide,' he said. 'She would never have walked naked along a beach for fifty, a hundred yards. Why? If she was going to swim she would have taken off her clothes by the pool. But not at high tide. Never. Never. It's impossible.'

He was followed by Van Blerk, then the hearing was adjourned for lunch. Dr. du Toit took Mrs. Preller out, and Kate followed. She found herself in a press of people.

She heard a voice say, 'Kate!'

She turned to look into Tom Austen's face. He caught her arm and pulled her towards him in the crush. She felt her breasts press against him and twisted away as Mrs. Preller looked back for her.

'Have lunch with me,' he said.

'I can't.'

They were carried through the doorway on to the pavement. She introduced him to Mrs. Preller and Dr. du Toit, feeling flustered.

He towered over Mrs. Preller. He bent towards her and smiled. She returned the smile and for the first time Kate saw her reacting to a good-looking man as he said, 'Would it inconvenience you if I kidnapped Miss Buchanan and carried her off for lunch?'

They had lunch under the slowly-moving fans in the hot hotel dining-room. The menu made no concessions to the weather: soup, fish, roast, treacle pudding.

'Do you want a drink?'

She shook her head. 'I have to give evidence this afternoon.' She sipped a few spoonfuls of soup and pushed the plate away. 'Why didn't you let me know you were coming?'

'You resent my being here. I sensed it in the courtroom and again on the pavement.'

'I suppose I do.'

'Why?'

'Because I've been learning to do without you. And now you come bursting into my life again.'

'Why didn't you come to me at New Year? I know you got the letter. I checked up with the messenger.'

'Yes, I got it.'

'I waited all day.'

The soup plates were taken away and the fish arrived. She picked at it. 'Aren't you hungry?' he said.

'No. It's too hot. You're not, either.'

'For God's sake, Kate,' he said, lowering his voice. 'Let's stop this. You know why I came. I could have lifted the story of the inquest from the Cape Town papers if I'd wanted it. I came because of you. I came because I love you and this was the only way I could get here, because of . . .'

'Of Joyce.'

'Precisely. It doesn't have to be this way.' He pushed away the half-eaten fish and placed his long, cool fingers over hers.

'Not here.' She slid her hand away. 'Most of these people know me by sight.'

'I don't give a damn about that.'

'I do. I live here.'

'All right.' She saw him control himself. 'But tell me one thing: You accused me of bursting into your life again. Tell me honestly: have I ever been out of it?'

'Don't force me to answer questions like that.' She felt her hands begin to shake.

He looked triumphant. 'There you are. You haven't got over it.'

'I'm trying.'

'But you haven't. That's all I wanted to know.'

'It's not as simple as that. I *want* to get over you. That's the difference between us. You want us to go on and on, and always there's Joyce in the background.'

'Now you know I can't help –'

'Of course you can't. But equally it doesn't help me. There's no future in it. Month after month. Year after year. Hotel rooms. The car. Or are you going to set me up in a flat and visit it on the way home twice a week?'

She knew she had angered him then, for he said quietly, 'Do you want anything more to eat?'

'No.'

'I really do have work to do and the hearing resumes in forty-five minutes.'

She walked slowly back to the court-house. She knew she had sounded hard, but inside she felt mushy and weak. It would have been so easy to have slipped back into her earlier relationship with him, but always now at the back of her mind was the figure of Fat Sarah.

Mrs. Preller's vermilion lips stretched into a smile that split the white face when she saw Tom. 'Finished your work, Mr. Austen?'

'Well, part of it,' he said. Kate watched him. The expression on his face was hard to read, but his eyes were no longer angry. 'I've come not only for the inquest, I want to do an article on the resurgence of the feather business. Perhaps you would let me pick your brains.'

'I have not much to pick, but you are welcome. You should have seen this place in the old days. Talk to Smuts about it. Miss Buchanan has seen the old houses. She can also help.'

'Perhaps she could show them to me,' he said.

Kate suddenly recalled the room in the Berrangés' house: her bare breasts reflected in the windows; Charles.

'Mr. Smuts knows much . . .'

'I only have this evening,' Tom said. 'I'd be very grateful.'

'Come.' Mrs. Preller took Kate's arm. 'We must not be late. It is that old fool, Dr. Richards, who is to give evidence.'

Kate had not seen Richards since the first inquest. He appeared even smaller, more stringy and gnomelike than he had then. He started in the same positive, rather hectoring manner that she remembered, but Dr. Armstrad was having none of it.

'You did not carry out a post mortem?'

'No, I did not.'

'You assumed that Miss Sachs had drowned?'

'I didn't "assume." It was an educated assessment of what had occurred.'

'But you could not be sure.'

Richards threw up his hands and smiled at the spectators. 'Who can be sure of anything in this life?'

'District surgeons,' Dr. Armstrad replied sharply. 'At least they can be certain whether or not someone drowned. Do you recall what time the tide was high on the Sunday night?'

'Some time after midnight. The sea was calm. There was no wind to speak of.'

As she listened to the evidence, Kate realised that she must have been awake that night in Saxenburg House while Miriam was dying. That was the night after the picnic, the night of her scene with Charles in the Berrangés' ruined house. She remembered how hot it had been when the black south-easter had dropped. She even remembered getting up and opening the window because she had been unable to sleep. She had lain in her bed, half expecting Charles to come to her room, but Dr. du Toit had arrived to check on Mrs. Preller, who had summer 'flu. Then she had heard the roadster leave and some time later Dr. du Toit's car, and had been able to relax for the first time that evening. But still she had not been able to sleep. Eventually she had got up and gone to the kitchen to make herself a cup of tea.

She had hardly put the kettle on when there had been a banging at the back door and she had heard Lena's voice. The woman had been upset.

'Has Miss Kate seen Betty?'

'No, Lena. Isn't she at home?'

'I been to church. Betty is not there.'

'What the hell's going on?' Smuts said from the doorway. 'Lena, what's all this?'

'She's looking for Betty,' Kate said.

'Well, for Christ's sake, look for her in the morning. How can I get my sleep?'

Lena turned on him in fury. 'You don't care what happens! Nobody cares! Jonas isn't here, too.'

'What?' Smuts shouted. 'That bugger! He's supposed to watch the temperatures.'

He flung open the door and ran out to the shed. Kate knew that Jonas was supposed to check the ostrich eggs in the incubators each night to see that the temperatures did not vary from 103 degrees Fahrenheit. Hurriedly, she lit a lantern and followed Smuts. He took it from her and held it up. The big wooden incubators reminded her of a mahogany chest-of-drawers her mother had left in Edinburgh.

'Christ, this is a hundred and five,' he said. 'So is this. This one's nearly a hundred and six. We'll lose the whole bloody lot in a minute. I want buckets of water. Tell Lena.'

But Lena was not in the kitchen and Kate filled two big tin buckets and carried them out to the shed. There was an opening at the top of each incubator and Smuts dashed the water into it. Kate ran to get more. They waited, watching the thermometers.

'This one's going down,' she said.

'So is this.'

Slowly, the temperatures began to drop: 104.5 ... 104 ... 103 ... 102 ... 101 ...

Smuts turned up the paraffin heaters slightly. Soon the temperatures stabilised at 103. The two of them sat like mother hens with the eggs for most of the night.

And while they sat, Miriam had been dying, perhaps was already dead. Kate shivered in spite of the heat in the courtroom.

At last Dr. Armstrad was finished with Richards. Kate was called next.

'According to your earlier testimony, you were with Miss Sachs once before when she swam in the nude at the rock pools?' His voice was coldly professional.

'Yes.'

'Did she say anything to you at that time about swimming at high tide?'

'She said ... well, it was a warning, really. She warned me never to swim at high tide because you couldn't see the bottom of the pools.'

'That is what I told you!' Mr. Sachs called out. 'I said she ...'

Leibowitz quietened him. The coroner turned back to Kate. 'What would have been on the bottom?

'Sea-urchins. She said the spines would give me blood-poisoning if I stood on one.'

'And you wouldn't see the bottom at night.'

'No.'

'About the clothes. Sergeant Van Blerk says they were about a hundred yards from the pool.'

'About that.'

'Do you recall seeing a scarf among Miss Sachs' belongings?'

'No.'

'But she had been wearing one the day before?'

'Yes. As a headband.'

'Thank you.'

For the first time, she looked at Tom. He smiled and nodded.

'Professor Fleischman,' a voice called.

There was silence for a moment and then she heard the rear door of the court open. All heads turned, for no one had yet seen the most important figure in the inquest. He came slowly down the aisle towards the box, a tall, stooped figure who walked with his head thrust forward. Kate judged him to be about sixty years old. He was thin and his head was disproportionately large for his narrow shoulders. He had a sharp face, incised with lines, and a prominent nose. His head was bald, except for tufts above his ears, and he wore heavy spectacles. His face was cast in an expression of permanent disdain.

'Can you tell the court how you became involved in this matter?' Dr. Armstrad said after they had established Professor Fleischman's credentials.

'I was approached by the deceased woman's father.'

'On what grounds?'

'He was not satisfied with the results of the first inquest. He had been unable to attend, being in hospital at the time with a cardiac condition.'

'And he asked you to perform a post mortem?'

'That is correct.'

'Are you familiar with the findings of the first inquest?'

'I am.'

'Then you know that a verdict of death by accidental drowning was handed down. Do you agree with that?'

Professor Fleischman's mouth turned down even further. 'No, I do not.' He consulted a small notebook and said, 'The cause of death was a fracture of the hyoid bone in the neck.'

'Could it have been caused by a fall?'

'It can only be caused by pressure. It is commonly

associated with strangling, not with a ligature, but with the hands. The fracture is caused by pressure from the thumbs.'

In the silence, the scratching of Armstrad's fountain pen was uncommonly loud.

'Could it have been caused by a blow, say an accidental blow?'

'No. I found bruising on the tissues of the neck characteristic of finger grips in strangling. A single blow would have produced massive bruising in one area. The bruising I found is of a type commonly associated with manual strangling.'

'So there is nothing, in your opinion, to the theory of drowning?'

Professor Fleischman's cold eyes searched the courtroom, seemingly, Kate thought, to discover where Dr. Richards was sitting, and then said, 'Nothing whatsoever. There was no water in the lungs, which would have been the case if Miss Sachs had drowned.'

'In the first inquest it was stated that the damage to Miss Sachs's face and shoulders was caused by a fall onto rocks. Would you tell us your opinion?'

'No fall would have caused wounds such as those. If Miss Sachs had fallen from a height sufficiently high to cause such massive discoloration and bleeding, I would have expected to find fractures of the cheek and jaw bones. This was not the case.'

'What, in your opinion, caused the wounds?'

'They are cuts and abrasions, not impact wounds. Miss Sachs' face was damaged by scraping over sharp or abrasive objects which removed the top skin layer of her cheek.'

Into Kate's mind flashed the picture she had been so assiduously trying to erase, the raw meat of Miriam's face: red, turning to blue and purple.

'Would you like to suggest how those abrasions occurred?'

'I have examined the pools where the body was found. On the farthest pool the seaward rocks are covered in mussels and limpets. Miss Sachs' wounds could have been caused by being washed over an area of rocks with such sharp protrusions.'

'Is that how you think it happened?'

'Yes. I think her body was washed into the outer pool at high tide and scraped on shell-fish and sharp, rocky protrusions by the surge of the waves.'

'This would mean that her body entered the rock pools from the seaward side?'

'That is correct.'

'It has been stated that she might have gone for a swim, slipped, fallen and hit her head, drowned, and then been washed, first out to sea and then back again. What is your opinion?'

'I have said that she could not have drowned; there was no water in her lungs. And I have stated that the wounds on her face and body were consistent, not with a fall, but with scraping on rocks.'

'What does that add up to, Professor?'

'It seems to me that the body was placed in the water after she had been strangled.'

'In the rock pool?'

'It is my opinion that the body was put into the open sea and that it was brought to the rock pools by tide and current action, and that it scraped over the outer wall as the waves pushed it forward.'

'What other findings were there, Professor –?'

'In cases like this it is usual to examine the sexual organs of the deceased.'

'And did you?'

'Yes, I did.'

At that moment there was a scraping of chairs to Kate's left and she turned to see Sachs and Leibowitz holding each other's arms. At first it looked as though they were performing a grotesque dance, then she realised that Leibowitz was supporting Sachs. Slowly, he led him out of the court.

Armstrad waited until the court had quietened, then said, 'And what did you find?'

Fleischman consulted his notebook. 'I found bruising on

the walls of the uterus, which is usually associated with forcible penetration.'

'Had the deceased been a virgin to that time?'

'No. Examination showed that she had practised regular sexual intercourse. I also found some bruising of the vagina. There was further bruising on one buttock consistent with pressure against some hard object.'

'Such as?'

'Oh, a floor, a flat rock, anything hard.'

'What you are saying is that Miss Sachs had been raped?'

'That is precisely what I am saying.'

'Could you indicate briefly what you think occurred?'

'I think Miss Sachs was raped and that during the rape she struggled. To quieten her, her assailant put his hands up to her throat and, intentionally or unintentionally, fractured the hyoid bone, causing her death. He then took the body to the cove, undressed it and placed it in the sea, hoping that it would be thought that Miss Sachs had drowned.'

It was out at last. Miriam *had* been murdered. Not only murdered, but raped. Professor Fleischman walked back along the aisle, head thrust forward, lips slightly twisted as though the information he'd had to impart had left him with a bitter taste in his mouth.

'It's a terrible thing!' Mrs. Preller said. 'Terrible. I told Miriam many times. I said, you must take care. But this! My God! They will hang Jonas for this. Hanging is too good. If I had my way . . .'

A voice called, 'Lena Lourens.'

Mrs. Preller turned sharply. Smuts, too, swung round. Kate followed their eyes. From the back of the courtroom, where the coloured people were standing, Lena walked to the box.

'Did you know about this?' Mrs. Preller hissed at Smuts. He shook his head.

'Mrs. Lourens, you had been to Church, is that right?' the coroner said.

'Yes, master.'

Lena looked very black in the shadowy court. She was

wearing her best dark blue frock. Kate looked at her in this unusual setting, seeing her with fresh eyes. The two missing teeth gave her a predatory, fish-like appearance, and there was a look in her eyes Kate had not seen before, a hardness, a bleakness; eyes that seemed to be full of hate.

'What did you do after Church?'

'I walked home.'

'What time was this?'

'Maybe ten o'clock.'

The coroner looked surprised. 'Was that not a long service?'

'In my Church, we have very long services, master. Sometimes all day, too.'

'I see. So you walked back along the road. What happened when you reached home?'

'The house was empty.'

'Your house?'

'Yes, master.'

'Who should have been there?'

'My daughter, Betty, master.'

'What did you do then?'

'I went to Jonas's house. But she wasn't there, and neither was he. I know that Jonas must watch the temperatures in the incubators. If they go too high, the ostrich eggs die.'

'What did you do?'

'I told Mr. Smuts.'

'He is the manager of Saxenburg?'

'Yes, master. Mr. Smuts and Miss Kate, they go out to the shed and throw water in the incubators.'

'And while they were doing this, what were you doing?'

'Looking for Betty, master. Down by the beach.'

'Did you find her?'

'No, master.'

'Did you see anyone else?'

There was a heartbeat's pause and then she said harshly, 'I see Jonas.'

Oh, God! Kate thought. This had happened while they were saving the eggs. Miriam was dying or was already dead and her body was floating on the tide.

'That is . . .' Armstrad looked down at his notes. 'That is Jonas Koopman?'

'Yes, master.'

'What was he doing?'

'He was by the rocks.'

'Fishing?'

'No, master. He was coming out from the water.'

'But he was dressed?'

'Yes, but he was wet on his trousers.'

'Did you speak to him?'

'No, master. He did not see me.'

'You didn't ask him where your daughter was?'

'No.'

'Why was that?'

'I am afraid for Jonas.'

'You're afraid of Jonas Koopman? You were afraid he might hurt you?'

'He can cut people with a knife.'

'We won't go into that. You didn't find your daughter on the beach, so where did you find her?'

'In my house.'

'In bed, where you expected to find her the first time, isn't that right?'

'Yes, master.'

'Do you know where she had been?'

Lena looked down as she answered and was inaudible. Sergeant Van Blerk rose from the front row and bent his head to listen to her.

'She says her daughter had been outside relieving herself.'

'I see. Where is your daughter now?'

'She is sick, master. With her auntie in Caledon.'

'I have one more thing to ask you. You went to the police with this information of your own decision?'

'Master?'

'I mean, no one forced you, no one even knew what you had seen. You just decided to go to the police, is that right?'

'Yes, master.'

'Then I must ask you why you didn't go at the time of the first inquest?'

'I was afraid, master.'

'Afraid? Of the police?'

'Of Jonas, master.'

'Thank you, Mrs. Lourens.'

Above the fishing harbour on a low cliff path there was a small, white-washed cairn with a stone cross at the top. On a brass plaque were the words, 'In memory of the men, women and children who perished in the ship *Helmsdale* when she struck the India Reef on the evening of 15 October, 1879. "For those in peril on the sea." '

Tom read the words aloud, then wrote them in his notebook.

'The place was called Prellersdorp before that,' Kate said.

'I prefer Helmsdale.'

He was a different man from the one who had faced her at lunch. He had not referred again to their conversation. Instead, he was coolly professional.

'That's the India Reef.' She pointed to a line of white water. The wind was still blowing hard, as it had been throughout the inquest, and now in late afternoon they could see the waves strike the reef and shoot up into the air.

The inquest had ended just before three-thirty with a verdict of murder, as had been expected. Groups of people had stood in the hot wind under the gum trees, discussing it for a long time, but slowly they had dispersed, most already looking forward to the next instalment in a month or so, when Jonas would be brought before the local magistrate at a preparatory examination of a charge of murder.

Kate had taken Tom and shown him where the body had been found – she had not gone down onto the beach with him – and now they were walking along the cliff path to the ostrich houses. She showed him the derelict exteriors of several and then they stopped at the Berrangés'.

'My God!' he said, turning into the overgrown drive. 'Stock-broker Tudor, all the way from Surrey. You

wouldn't be surprised if you saw this place outside Guild-
ford or Reigate, but here . . .'

She followed him unwillingly. It was late afternoon and
the windows were sheets of red mirror as they reflected the
sinking sun.

'I'd like to get into one of these places, to see what the
innards are like,' he said. 'I read some old newspaper
articles about them before I left the office. The owners
spent money like water: marble stair-cases, oak panelling,
walls of mountain stone.' He tried the front door, then
wandered towards the back.

'They're all locked up,' Kate said.

At the back door, he said, 'This lock looks relatively
new.' He tried the handle. Kate remembered that Charles
had used a key. This time, to her surprise, the door opened.

'Come on,' he said.

'I hate these places.'

'Don't be a baby.' He took her hand and drew her in.

They walked through the ruined rooms downstairs. 'Isn't
it sad?' he said. 'Let's go upstairs.'

'Tom, I've had enough.'

'Just ten more minutes, then I could use a drink, and so
could you, I should think, after the inquest.' He began to
climb the stairs, still holding her hand. 'By the way, I
forgot to congratulate you on the efficient way you gave
your evidence. I'd wager that's the first time a Helmsdale
court has heard an Edinburgh accent.'

They reached the first floor.

'Someone's been here.' He pointed at footmarks in the
dust. She thought she could recognise her own. They led
directly to Charles's special room and Tom opened the
door. 'Good God! Someone's been using this place. Look.'
He indicated the empty wine bottle, which Charles and
Kate had shared. The room still bore the evidence of their
struggle.

She took her hand from his and went back to the door.
'This place gives me the shivers. Berrangé, the man who
owned it, shot himself when the feather business collapsed.'

'Berrangé? That sounds French.'

'It is. They say he shot himself on the tennis-court.

Apparently he was a fastidious man and didn't want to get blood on the carpets.'

Again he was professional, and made notes.

They went down the stairs and out into the garden.

'How are you getting on with Charles?' he said.

'Fine.'

'See a lot of him?'

'He comes back most week-ends.'

They returned along the cliffs into town. 'I must write my piece and telephone it to Cape Town,' he said.

'And I must be getting back.'

'No, no! Mrs. Preller released you from school for the entire evening. Don't worry, I'm not going to molest you.'

'But . . .'

'No buts. I'll book the call and we can have a drink while I'm working. Then dinner.'

He had a large, old-fashioned and rather spartan room overlooking the main street. On a table against one wall was a portable Underwood typewriter. He took a tray from the room-service waiter and closed the door. 'Tom Collinses, to remind you of the ship.' He put the tray on the table and turned to her. Then he bent and kissed her. She could taste the warmth of his mouth. She had longed for such a kiss, but instead of relaxing into his embrace she twisted away and said lightly, 'I thought you weren't going to molest me.'

'I lied!'

As she picked up her drink she noticed that her hand was shaking. 'Keep your mind on your work,' she said.

He looked at her for a moment and then nodded and sat down. 'Cheers. Here's to love.' There was a bitter edge to the toast but she pretended not to hear it and held up her glass.

He turned a piece of paper into the machine and began to type. She watched him from the window. This was what she had always wanted: just to be with him. She had wanted to be with him in his house in Cape Town; had wanted to furnish it for him, create a home for him, have his children. She had wanted to travel with him and sit in hotel rooms like this with him when he worked. And now she *was* with him, and nothing was right. He was huge in the small, hard-backed chair, yet all his actions, typing, changing the paper, were delicate and precise. He was completely absorbed in what he was doing. She leant against the window-sill, feeling the warm wind ruffle her hair, aware of the small town coming to the end of this hot, windy and exceptional day, and thought how she would like to go up to him and put her arms around his neck and make love to him on the narrow bed under the window and let the warm wind cool their sticky bodies when it was over. She had never loved him as much as she did at that moment.

They went down to dinner. The dining-room was filled with farmers who had come into town for the inquest and they were all drinking brandy-and-water with their greasy mutton chops. The air was hot and the fans in the ceiling did nothing but stir it. They were put at a corner table and several of the men looked at Kate with approving eyes. One smiled and nodded.

'Who's your friend?' Tom said as they sat down.

'The bank manager.'

'Those are the friends to have.' He read from the menu: 'Vegetable soup, fried stockfish, beef olives, cold meat. We'll have a bottle of cold white wine as well.'

They talked about the inquest for a few moments and then a waiter arrived to say that Tom's phone call to Cape Town had come through. He took his copy and went into the lobby. He was away for longer than Kate had expected. When he returned he drank a glass of wine in one long pull and motioned the waiter to fill his glass. Then he said, 'I spoke to Joyce.'

The name hung in the air like a shadow between them, 'I wanted you to know why I'd been so long, in case you were wondering.'

'I wasn't.' Then she said sharply, 'That isn't the real reason you told me.'

'No, it isn't. I wanted to mention her name because we don't talk about her and I think that's half our problem. We treat her as though she doesn't exist, yet we know she does. It gives her an importance in our relationship that she shouldn't have. We've made her separate, a kind of brooding presence, a spectre at the feast. And it shouldn't be that way. We should talk about her naturally and then perhaps we could be natural with each other.'

'I don't want to talk about her.'

'There you are. By not talking about her you can't erase her. She's there, all right.'

'Oh, for God's sake, Tom . . .'

'It's true.' He crumbled a piece of bread in his fingers and said: 'Ask me how she is. That's what people do when they meet. They ask about wives and husbands. It's the natural thing to do, so why don't we be natural?'

'All right. How's your wife?'

'Joyce?'

'Yes.'

'Well, say it. That's half the bloody battle, isn't it? She's got a name, you're still treating her like a disembodied spirit.'

Kate gritted her teeth and said, 'How's Joyce?'

'Would you really like to know?'

'Yes, please.'

He opened his mouth to go on with the game and then stopped.

'What's wrong?' she said. 'Do you want to change the subject?'

'Christ, no. I've got to tell someone. Why not tell the one person who really matters to me?'

She felt an ache above her heart. 'Go on, then.'

'Where do I start? The problem with this kind of discussion is that it's difficult to keep a whine out of one's tone, difficult to preclude self-justification and self-pity. If you hear anything like that, kick me under the table.'

As he began to talk, she realised that she had never given his day-to-day life with Joyce much thought. He was right: she *had* avoided thinking about her. He spoke flatly without any sign of self-pity, painting the story in word pictures brilliantly lit and coloured and suggestive of emotions and hatreds and guilts which she had barely guessed at. He spoke as he wrote, sparely, but with a magic that made scenes come alive. She began to see the pictures, began to understand what made up the mosaic of their lives.

Their days and nights were filled with one long, endless argument. It was never loud or angry, sometimes it was not even expressed, but it lay in the house ready to ambush them with its low-keyed nagging. It rose from trivial things. He told her that one thing he looked forward to every morning in the hot weather was a shower out in his garden. There was an arbour formed by hydrangeas and plumbago and he would go down there in the early hours and hose himself. His description was so well-drawn that she could see the big, shadowy garden, smell the rubbery, earthy smell of the water.

But Joyce did not care for it. She had seen him from her bedroom window and had told him she thought it undignified.

'She said, what if one of our maids or those next door saw me naked? And I said they'd probably seen better equipment, anyway. And she told me I was being vulgar and it wasn't fair to her to allow my dignity to be eroded. It's that sort of argument. About damn all.'

She had her own bedroom and would spend large parts of the day in bed, sometimes not getting up at all. 'When I tell her that both her doctors – oh, yes, she has two – feel she should exercise the leg as much as she can, she tells me I'm unfeeling. So we argue about that. And we argue about me playing the gramophone and about how you treat servants and about whether the curtains should be open or not in case the sun fades the carpets. And we argue about going out or not going out.'

He told her about a recent morning when he had gone up to Joyce's room after he'd had his breakfast. It was still in darkness, the shutters closed, the curtains drawn. 'She was beautiful once,' he said. 'So beautiful it hurt almost to look at her. It was a kind of misty, pre-Raphaelite beauty. But now . . .' He paused, and said, 'I suppose it's all the time she spends in bed. She's put on a lot of weight and, of course, that makes the leg weaker.'

Kate began to get a picture of a puffy figure in a dim, hot, stale-smelling room. A kind of younger, fatter Mrs.

Preller, who lived out of the world, but without that lady's toughness.

'The other morning I went up to her after breakfast to say good-bye, and she said, "This is the only time I see you during the day and it's always just to say good-bye. You never sit down. You can't wait to go." And I said something like we wouldn't get the rent paid if I sat down instead of going to work and her eyes filled with tears and I said, don't bother, it might have worked once, but not now. It was a bloody awful thing to say and I felt ghastly about it all day. That's the problem. I often say things that hurt her and then feel dreadful. But the moment I recover, I do it again. Then I apologise. And so on. You see, the danger is, if I go too far she'll try again.'

'Try what?'

'Sleeping pills. Her wrists. She tried once in London, and once about a month ago.'

'You never told me.'

'As far as you were concerned, Joyce was a non-person, remember? They're not serious attempts. By that I mean she knew that I or someone else was going to be around to save her. But all the same, it's pretty bad. That's why I have to have a damn good reason for going on a trip like this. She'd never have believed me if I'd said London was interested. But I went along to George Ascher on the *Cape Times* and told him I'd thought of doing an article on the new feather boom and that I could do the inquest for them at the same time. He jumped at it.'

They had finished dinner and were drinking a bitter mixture of coffee and chicory and she was waiting for the next stage of the evening. She wanted nothing more than to go up to his room with him and yet the thought of what had happened in Fat Sarah's still made her break out in a cold sweat.

And then he said suddenly, 'I'm going to take you home now.'

She remained silent and he smiled and said, 'I hope you won't mind. But talking about Joyce and thinking about her sometimes makes me feel like a eunuch. Perhaps I should never have brought the subject up.'

'I'm glad you did. I'd never realised what it was like for you.'

'There you are, I've made you feel sorry for me.' It was said lightly, but again there was an underlay of bitterness. 'Come on, before I change my mind and take you upstairs and rape you.'

He drove her back to Saxenburg and looked up at the big house standing starkly against the night sky. 'My God, it looks like Bluebeard's Castle. Sister Ann . . . Sister Ann . . .' Then he kissed her once, hard, and drove away.

She lay in bed listening to the wind. Sister Ann . . . it seemed to say . . . do you see anyone coming . . .?

[2]

Charles came back for the week-end. She had not seen him for several weeks and was wary of him, but he put himself out to be charming and seemed to have forgotten the incident in the old house. He was plumper than she remembered. His face was growing heavy and the sensual cast of his lower lip seemed more pronounced.

He wanted to talk about the inquest and asked her to walk down to the beach with him. She had not been close to the rock pools since she had shown Mr. Sachs the spot. Charles said, 'It's sad. Of course it's sad, but these things happen. If one didn't go to places where some tragedy or other had occurred, there'd be no place to go at all.'

'That's where we found her clothes,' she said, pointing midway between the rock pools and the far headland.

'When does that bloody Jonas come up for trial?'

'In the autumn. That's what they're saying.'

'They'll hang him all right. The bastard.'

It was strange walking down by the sea shore without seeing Jonas and the big sea-pole silhouetted against the sky. She wondered where he had strangled Miriam. On the beach? Among the rocks? Perhaps he had not meant to kill her. Perhaps he had been fishing there that night when she had stripped and walked across the beach in the moonlight. The sight of Miriam's nubile body would have been an invitation to many men. She remembered the day she had watched her swim naked. Jonas had been around then. In fact, he may even have seen Miriam. Kate remembered mentioning it to her and the off-hand way she had dismissed his presence, as though he did not count because he was a servant. Or – and the thought came sharply to her – had Miriam been aware of him all the time? Had she undressed slowly, garment by garment, knowing she had a male audience? Kate wondered if she should mention such thoughts to Jonas's lawyer, Mr. Stoltz. Perhaps he would want to cross-examine her about that day when the preparatory examination was held.

'Have you heard from your family?' Charles asked.

'Mother isn't much of a correspondent. I get an occasional letter.'

'Did you know that Duggie went into hospital yesterday?'

'I knew Mother was making the arrangements.'

'I went to see him. He's in a lot of pain.'

'Poor Duggie. He's been in pain ever since he came back from the war. I'll telephone the hospital tonight.'

'I've promised him a good time once he gets out of that place.' He paused and said thoughtfully. 'Although good times are getting scarcer these days.'

There was something in his tone that caught her attenion. 'Why so gloomy?'

'It's a gloomy time. Haven't you heard about Black Friday?'

'Black Friday?'

'The stock market crashed last week and a lot of people got badly burned.'

'You?'

'Including me.'

'I'm sorry, Charles.'

'So am I.'

They walked back to the house in silence. He spent the afternoon with his mother, but later he had a drink with Kate, sitting on one of the window seats of the blue and purple sitting-room. The sea was calm and the India Reef no more than a ripple on its surface. She was very much aware that they were alone together in the high, shadowy room and that all he had to do was shift along the window seat and she would be facing the same problem she had before. But nothing happened, and she told herself he would not try anything in the house itself; there were too many eyes.

Perhaps some similar conjunction of thoughts were going through his mind, for he said, 'I hear Betty's sick.'

'She's staying with an aunt in Caledon.'

'Is she coming back?'

'Lena hasn't mentioned it.'

After a moment he said, 'Mother tells me you know about the morphine.'

'I've known since Christmas night.'

'So you know what happened – before?'

'Only what Dr. du Toit told me, which wasn't much.'

He began to pace up and down the room. His heavy face was flushed and she realised he had been drinking upstairs. 'It's Hugo's birthday today – or it would have been if he was still alive.' He was moving restlessly and seemed almost to be talking to himself. 'My father always sent me a card on Hugo's birthday. He never forgot. Even when I was at boarding-school. Not a birthday card, but a bloody mourning card. Edged with black. And the words were always the same: In Memoriam, Hugo Adolphus Preller, who would have been eleven years old – or twelve or whatever it was – today.'

She thought of the little boy opening his envelope every year until his father died, and felt a surge of pity for him.

'Do you remember anything about that night?'

'I'm not sure now whether I remember or whether it's what Smuts or Lena or my mother has told me.' He lit a cigarette and poured himself another drink and continued his pacing, making the dyed ostrich feathers stir and wave in their vases. 'Have you ever seen a picture of Hugo?'

'No.'

'My mother keeps one. Only one. It was taken just before he died. I remember we went to a photographer's studio in Cape Town and they took one of each of us and the two of us together. She keeps the one of Hugo in her bedside table. Maybe she'll show it to you one day. If she does, you'll see why my father . . .' He broke off and she noticed that sweat had broken out on his forehead. 'My father thought the sun shone out of his . . . well, you know what I mean. Jesus, I hated him!'

She was shocked by the violence in his voice. It came on a gust of passion in a way she had noticed before. One second he was normal, the next in the grip of violent emotion. She remembered him in the Berrangé house and the difficulty she'd had in calming him. And it had happened again in the yard with Jonas and Smuts. There seemed to be no bridge between normality and this sudden flare-up.

'You hated your father?'

'No. That came later, when he started on me. It was Hugo I hated. I'll tell you this: I wasn't sorry when he died. It's a hell of a thing to say, but it's true.'

The violence seemed to be leaving him and he wiped his face with his handkerchief. 'It was always Hugo this and Hugo that. What Hugo was going to do when he grew up. How Hugo was going to increase the fortunes of the family. He was ten years old, and I was eight. Only two years younger and they spoke like that in front of me! They thought I was too young to know what the hell they were talking about.

'My father had always talked to him like that. By the time he was ten you'd have thought he was a prince or something. He ordered Lena about. It made my father smile. Sometimes my mother would get worried about me, I suppose, and give me more attention. Hugo hated that. He was so used to getting it all that he would become angry. He had a bloody awful temper. He got it from my father. Anyway, he made my life a bloody misery whenever that happened.'

Without warning, he ripped off his right shoe and sock and held his foot out to her. 'See that?' He was pointing at two white scars about half an inch apart. 'You know what they are?'

Kate shook her head, slightly bemused at the outburst and the sight of his naked foot in front of her.

'Snake.' He sat down and put his sock on again. 'A bloody night adder in the upstairs bathroom. You tell me how it got into the house and up the stairs and into the bathroom. People *said* it must have come up the waste pipe.'

'You mean you think your brother put it there?'

He poured himself another drink. 'I'm not sure. Of course, I didn't think so at the time. Snakes are common around here. But afterwards I thought, how the hell would a night adder get up the waste pipe? It was under the bath. When I went in, it hit me in the foot.'

She shuddered.

'Even now I can remember the pain. Smuts sucked it and they took me to hospital, but the fangs hadn't gone in properly, so I was all right.'

'Was it in my bathroom? The nursery bathroom?' She felt a prickling sensation on her scalp.

He nodded. 'They've put wire mesh over the opening to the waste pipe. There's no way anything can get up now.'

The telephone rang, three shorts and a long, the party-line signal for Saxenburg. He went into the hall to answer it. 'It's your call to Cape Town.'

After she had spoken to the staff nurse at the Rondebosch Cottage Hospital she told Charles: 'They operated on Duggie's leg this afternoon. They took a piece of bone out. The staff nurse says he's still drowsy from the ether, but otherwise comfortable. Mother and father were there.'

'It's going to take time.'

'I know.' Then she said, 'I asked Lena to make us a plate of sandwiches. Would you like them now?'

'I'm not hungry. You?'

She shook her head. 'I'll have one of your cigarettes, though.' She sat back, smoking. 'Do you mind talking about Hugo?'

'I hardly ever talk about him. Mother does. When I go up to her room, she sometimes wants to remember him. Like today, on his birthday. She has the photograph and his school cap and a flute he made out of a reed. She usually drinks too much.'

'Do you think I should go up?'

'Lena's there. It's dangerous if she drinks with the morphine. It's easy to take an overdose. But Lena knows what to do.'

'Her scars are terrible.'

'That's my fault. According to my father.'

'That's a terrible thing to tell a child.'

'It was the sort of thing he did. He was a very big man. Almost as big as Hennie du Toit. Heavy body and heavy face. At least, that's how I remember him. Most people called him 'Boss,' but some called him 'Bull' Preller. He played rugby when he was young.' He paused, then said, 'It *was* partly my fault. If I'd run straight to my parents . . . hell, there's no point in going over it now. It's too late. They say Hugo's death was what eventually killed my father.'

'Charles, you shouldn't let this thing eat into you. People have told you about it, you've overheard talk. The important thing is what you yourself remember.'

'That's the bloody problem. I don't *know* what I remember. Hugo was sick. I remember that. It was winter and he often had bronchitis in winter. He had a weak chest. He was sleeping in the room next to yours. I was sleeping in your room because he was sick. They had lit a fire in his room and left the door ajar. I remember that because I saw things in the light of the fire.'

'What sort of things?'

'Shadows. I woke up and heard a noise and saw shadows and I was frightened. I put my head under the blankets. I don't know how long. Maybe I even fell asleep. The next thing I knew, I was smelling smoke and there were more shadows. I suppose they must have been made by the flames as they caught the washing hanging in front of the fireplace. Big, jumping shadows. So I ran. I wasn't running away from the smoke, so much as the shadows. I wasn't running *to* anyone, but *away* from things that frightened me. I ran down the stairs looking for Lena. She used to sleep in the house in those days because she was our nanny, but she wasn't in her room. Of course, by that time the fire must have been blazing. My mother ran in and got Hugo out, but he was dead from the smoke and her nightdress had caught alight.'

She had been listening with growing horror. 'But couldn't your father have helped?'

'He was out at the incubator shed.'

'Yet he blamed you?'

'Because I hadn't called for help.'

'You ran for Lena. You did go to get help.'

'Yes. Only she wasn't in either.'

'But you *tried*!'

'Not hard enough.'

He left for Cape Town on Sunday evening and she watched the plume of dust from the red roadster as he speeded along the cliff road. In a way, she was sorry to see him go.

During the week she had a letter from her mother. It was stiff and formal, like the ones she had infrequently received at school:

'Dear Catherine, Your brother had his operation on Friday. Your father and I went to see him when he came out of the ether. He was in pain. I spoke to Mr. Fincham, the surgeon, and to Dr. Milner. They told me that they had removed a piece of bone six inches long. They do not know if the operation has been a success, but are hoping. It will be some weeks before we know. I prayed, and so did your father. I hope you will, too.

'Douglas comes out of hospital in a few days and he will be taken by ambulance to the False Bay Convalescent Home at St. James. We have booked him in for three weeks. It is very expensive. Your father has not worked since before Christmas. Your loving Mother.'

Kate read the letter twice. Now that she was away from her family, she felt a stronger emotional tie than when she had lived with them. She felt great pity for Duggie. The awareness of her own role in the family fortunes, which had come to her so sharply at New Year, had not left her.

She felt increasingly responsible for them. Every penny she could spare was already being sent. She cast her mind over her possessions. She had nothing to sell, but she regretted buying the black dress at Christmas. That had been a terrible extravagance. To help her mother and father, she would have to borrow. She decided that the next time she went into Helmsdale she would approach the bank manager. She wondered how much she would need. Fifty pounds? Would that pay for the surgeon and the specialist and the doctor and the hospital and the convalescent home; would it enable her mother to pay the rent and buy food? She realised she would need closer to a hundred. But how could she pay it back? She felt a kind of dread at the thought of borrowing. In spite of the fact that her father had spent a proportion of his wages on drink in Edinburgh, he had been in work, so that he had not needed to borrow. Debt was a terrible word in the lexicon of her childhood. She could remember other families on the stair on which they lived, who had struggled against debt all their lives. One fifty-year-old woman, the wife of a labourer, who had seven children, had been found at the bottom of the basement area one day. Some people said she had fallen, others said she had thrown herself down. When the bailiffs came, they had taken everything. Nothing belonged to the family. Kate did not know what had happened to them after that, but she had seen the woman's body. Now violent death was associated in her mind with debts. She felt she was moving into a world of which she had no experience and which she feared.

'They say they've had to move that coloured man to a gaol in Cape Town,' the bank manager said, 'They found him trying to rip out the window-bars last night. He must be a powerful chap.'

Kate nodded, remembering the strong body she had seen so often on the beach.

'They say the hearing's to be held in the autumn. Did you hear about the scarf?'

'The scarf?'

'Miss Sachs' scarf. They say it was found in his shack. That's why they arrested him in the first place.'

She recalled vividly the black and white headscarf which Miriam had been wearing at the picnic. She could see in her mind's eye Miriam taking it off and shaking her head to settle her hair before she swam.

'They're all talking about it,' he said.

'Poor Miriam.'

'A terrible tragedy.'

Mr. Hamilton had emigrated to the Cape from England two years before and felt that this gave him something in common with Kate. He was a plump, middle-aged man with a Kitchener moustache and had a habit of smoothing it to the sides of his mouth with his hand. The bank was in his house, or his house was in the bank, whichever way one preferred it. He liked to tell his customers that he 'lived above the shop.' His staff consisted of one teller and one secretary. Now, sitting in his office, Kate could hear someone washing dishes beyond the wall.

He received her story about Duggie sympathetically. 'That *is* bad luck. A war wound, too. I was in the infantry. Well, now, do you have any insurance?'

'No.'

'No policies you could borrow against?'

'No.'

'You say your family has a house in Cape Town; they could borrow against that.'

'It's rented. That's why I've come to you.'

He looked down at her bank statements. 'And this is the money you send your mother every month. It doesn't leave you much, does it?'

'Not much.'

'Do you have any collateral, Miss Buchanan?'

She had never heard the word before.

'When we lend money, we need something to lend it against: a house, jewels, land . . . just in case something goes wrong, you understand. For instance, say I lent money to someone and that someone was knocked down by an omnibus, I would have the house or the jewels or the land to sell in order to recover my loan. You see that, don't you?'

She looked at him, stony-eyed. 'I don't have a house or jewellery or land. If I had any of those things I wouldn't be here now.'

'Banks have certain rules, Miss Buchanan. We do not offer unsecured loans. I'm sure you can appreciate . . .'

'It's only a hundred pounds. I'm not asking for a fortune.'

'If it was my money, I can assure you . . .'

She rose. 'Thank you,' she said.

'Remember me to Mrs. Preller,' he called as she went out.

It had taken her a couple of days to screw up her courage to go to him and now she was angry and humiliated. Later, she would feel the touch of fear again, though this time it was not so much fear of borrowing as fear that no one might lend. She went down the main street, her strides long, her dark hair blowing in the wind. Now there was only one person she could go to: Mrs. Preller. But what if she said no? Would it not make her position in the house awkward? She could not risk creating any such difficulty. She and her family only existed because of Mrs. Preller.

She hated indecision above all things, but she had never faced such a problem as this. When she reached Saxenburg she decided she must sleep on it, perhaps tomorrow she might be able to see a solution.

But the following morning she had other things to think of: Smuts was injured.

One of the labourers had hooked a big male ostrich called Red Wing and was putting it into the plucking box so Smuts could examine a gash on its thigh. The bird was angry and fought every step of the way. Eventually it was forced into the triangular pen and Smuts was about to tie a leather strap around its neck and put a sock over its head to quieten it, when it broke loose. Kate was standing a few yards away and saw it burst from the plucking box and lash out at Smuts.

Its single long claw caught him in the chest and ripped downwards. He was flung back and the bird began stamping on his chest and arms. In a moment, one of the labourers had caught it with his crook and pulled it aside, but the damage was done. Smuts lay in the dust, unconscious. Two of the hands carried him into the house and put him in his bedroom. Kate hurried to Mrs. Preller's apartment.

'How bad is he?' she said. 'Have you telephoned to Dr. du Toit?'

'Lena is doing that.'

Mrs. Preller followed her downstairs. She was not often seen out of her rooms in the mornings, especially in a dressing-gown and with her hair awry. The scarring on her cheeks was very visible. 'Don't touch him,' she said to Lena. 'Wait for the doctor. Bring me water and a rag.' She sat by Smuts' side, gently washing his face with cool water. Twenty minutes later, Dr. du Toit arrived.

'Hennie, do your best for him, then come and tell me,' she said.

She went upstairs as he cut away Smuts' clothing. The single claw had gouged the flesh from the bone in a long rip down the chest. The force of the kick had caused purple bruising that extended on either side of the wound and covered the heart. There were other cuts and bruises where the bird had stamped and kicked when he was on the ground.

'Lucky he's a small chap,' du Toit said, cleaning the wound and beginning to strap up the chest. 'If he'd been much taller the kick would have landed on the abdomen. I doubt that he could have recovered from that. I've seen the results of an ostrich kick before; worse than a horse in some ways.' He worked on. 'He probably has a couple of cracked ribs, but it's the internal damage I'm worried about.'

When he had finished he sat down by the bed and Lena brought coffee.

'I've never seen Mrs. Preller so upset,' Kate said.

'He's been with her a long time. He's special. He worked for Boss Charles. In fact, he worked for the Prellers even before Boss Charles took over. He came from a family of poor whites in the Knysna yellow-wood forests further up the coast. He really lost his heart to Augusta when she arrived from Austria. I mean it. I think he was in love with her. Oh, he didn't do anything about it, couldn't, but I suspect he saved her once or twice from Boss Charles.'

'Saved?'

He seemed to sense that he might have gone too far. 'I don't mean *saved*. But Boss Charles was not an easy man, if you know what I mean. And when he was drinking he sometimes became violent. You know how it is with people like that. And Smuts would try to calm him down or get between him and Augusta. She's never forgotten what he did.'

'You mean her husband would hit her?'

'Listen, I've talked too much. Forget what I said. These things happen. As I say, he wasn't an easy man.'

After he had left and Smuts was resting more easily, Mrs. Preller sent for her, wanting a full description of the accident. Then she said sadly, 'It would never have happened in the old days. He was like a cat then. But it has happened and now there are things I have to do. Hennie tells me that it will be a month, perhaps two months before he can be back at work. Even then he will not be able to take on as much as he does now. No one knows exactly how old he is, not even Smuts himself, but he must be sixty-five. So I will have to find . . .'

'Mrs. Preller, let me try.'

'Take over Smuts' work? A young woman like you?'

'I've been thinking about it. You know I've worked with Mr. Smuts ever since the boom began. I've still got a lot to learn, but at least let me try.'

'You'd be taking on a man's job.'

'Not entirely. The boys know what to do and Mr. Smuts is here to help with advice. After that it's just hard work, and if that's what a man's job is, I'm capable of it, too.'

'And money?'

'That's the other thing. You wouldn't have to pay me as much as you'd pay a man.'

Kate watched her. This was the crux, for Mrs. Preller was sharp about money. A calculating look came into her eyes.

'Give me an idea of what you would want.'

Kate knew what Smuts was paid because she helped Mrs. Preller with her accounts and she knew that any other competent foreman would command the same wage, if one could be found, for now that the boom was under way experienced men were scarce.

'Half what you'd pay a man,' she said – knowing this would be three times what she was presently making – 'and if you're satisfied after two months, we can discuss it again.'

Mrs. Preller smiled. 'All right. You may try.'

It was then that Kate discovered, for the first time in her life, what hard work was. She had known that once the plucking was over and the feathers sorted and cleaned and sent off there would be a nine-month break before it all came round again. What she had not realised was that, like any other organisation, the farm had layers of work of different kinds. She had to keep the books and pay the hands; see that the house had enough food; see that the food supplies were ordered for the hands and their families; if something went wrong with a tap or a fence or a door, one of the servants would come to her and say, 'The tap doesn't work, Miss Kate,' or 'The fence is broken, Miss Kate,' or 'The door is stuck, Miss Kate' and would wait for her to do something about it. Apart from such duties she was expected to drive Mrs. Preller into Helmsdale most days.

Had anyone told her she would enjoy working as hard as this, she would have laughed. But now her slender, long-striding figure was to be seen all over the farm. She hardly ever sat down. She ate like a horse and slept like the dead and had never felt so alive in her life.

Smuts improved, but the periods between her visits to him for advice grew longer as she learned the running of the farm. A fortnight after he had been injured, she drove him around the camps. It was his first expedition outside the house. She showed him the birds, she showed him the lucerne coming up green after rain, she showed him the incubators and the last of the sorted feathers. He was silent for a long time and at last he spoke. 'It's not bad, my friend, not bloody bad at all.' She felt as though she had won a major prize.

The hard work was not without its lighter moments. She would never forget her first incubator hatchings. The eggs were put into a different kind of incubator for the last two weeks, called a 'finisher,' and one morning she heard unfamiliar sounds coming from it: faint tappings, like the point of a pencil being tapped on a table. She leaned down and put her ear to the eggs and heard squeaks and scrapings. Ten days later the eggs were broken and the new chicks pecked their way to freedom. She was as delighted with the small, grey, fluffy bundles as if she had personally created them.

Occasionally when parents abandoned a chick in one of the camps the orphan would be brought to the house and reared by hand. She did this with a chick she christened Jackie. He was a pleasure to have around the place when he was small, but when he began to grow he quickly became a nuisance. He developed a taste for human food and would go into the kitchen and harass Lena while she was preparing a meal, snatching things from the table. In this way, he swallowed a tea-strainer, several coffee spoons and a small salt cellar. He enraged Lena, who would drive him from the kitchen with an iron frying-pan. Finally, she took to closing the kitchen door, but that made the room, with its big black range, so hot in summer that she had to leave the window open. Jackie, with his long neck, found he could often reach through it to loaves of bread and other foodstuffs left on the work tops. Lena fought a war of attrition for many months against his incursions.

When he was not harassing her, he would wander around the sheds, grabbing anything that caught his fancy. He liked to snatch pipes out of the mouths of the coloured labourers and once pulled a scarf from Kate's neck.

Eventually, he came to an unpleasant end. Lena was careless one day and left the kitchen door ajar.

He pushed his way in and found a pot boiling on the stove. It was rice. In an instant he had scooped up a large lump with his beak and swallowed it. He flailed about in agony for a few seconds and then charged from the kitchen, flapping his wings and roaring in pain. He tried to jump a fence, broke his leg and had to be shot.

Kate remembered how she had felt when Smuts had ordered a bird to be shot soon after her arrival. She had fewer qualms now. The life was making her tougher, both physically and mentally.

[3]

Summer drew to its end. The south-east wind dropped away and the days became still. The sea was a translucent green over the slowly shelving sand, but once the water grew deep, around the India Reef, the green gave way to the deepest blue. The air became filled with creamy sea mists, so light that they could only be seen at a distance, but they held the tang of the kelp and brine so that to stand on the verandah of Saxenburg House and breathe in deeply was to taste the distillation of the sea itself.

But Kate had little time to stand on the verandah and indulge such fancies. The work never ceased, for the farm was not only an area of land divided into ostrich camps, but also a complex of buildings of which Saxenburg House was the largest, the fabric of which was Kate's responsibility too. And there were the families who lived and worked on the estate; there were feuds to be settled and sick children to be cared for. There were arguments about food rations and requests for higher wages. One or two of the men tried to test Kate's nerve and found, to their chagrin, that she was as perceptive as Smuts had been and as quick to pounce on any dereliction.

A labourer called Hans was persistently late in the mornings and was often drunk by mid-afternoon. She warned him several times, but he seemed to treat her warnings as a joke. She thought of sacking him, in fact, she discussed it with Smuts, who was in favour of it. However, when Hans worked, he worked well, and she was loath to dismiss him. Instead, she went to Tilly, his wife, who sometimes helped Lena in the house. Betty, according to Lena, had contracted a fever and was still at her aunt's house in Caledon.

Tilly and Lena got on well enough together and, after consulting Lena, Kate offered Tilly a permanent place in the house, but only on condition that she controlled her husband.

'I want him on time, and I want him sober. If you can manage that, then you both work here. If you can't, neither of you does. Do you understand me, Tilly?'

Tilly was almost square, with arms like hams and, again, the curious barracuda-like jaw with the missing front teeth.

'I understand, Miss Kate,' was all she said, but her voice had an ominous ring to it.

From that day, Kate had no more trouble with Hans.

'My God, that's a woman's trick,' Smuts said, laughing. 'I never heard anything like it.'

'It worked though,' Kate said.

One morning in March she was crossing the yard after checking the incubators when she saw a cloud of dust on the cliff top, which signalled the approach of a motor. It was not Friday, so it could not be Charles. For a moment her heart raced at the thought that it might be Tom, but as the car drew nearer she saw that it was a large limousine and was driven by a black chauffeur. The car drew up and the chauffeur opened the back door. A small, birdlike man emerged. He took off a long white dust-coat and gave it to the chauffeur. He was elegantly, almost fastidiously, dressed. He wore a pearl-grey Homburg, a light grey suit with a cream waistcoat, black pointed shoes of Russian leather which twinkled on his tiny feet, and grey spats. In his button-hole was a red rosebud. He carried a pair of yellow chamois gloves and a walking stick with a silver top. When he saw Kate, he bowed and took off his hat. His bald head was nut brown, as was his face, the proportions of which were narrow and pointed. His nose was thin and the bones of his cheeks pronounced.

'Mendel,' he said.

It was so unexpected that for a moment Kate was confused.

'Isidore Mendel.'

'You mean . . . Mr. Mendel? *The* Mr. Mendel? From London?'

'My dear, you flatter me.' He put out a hand and she felt the cool dryness of his skin. He had an attractive, slightly goatish smile and she noticed that his brown eyes were darting and quick and again she was reminded of a bird.

'You have the advantage,' he said.

She introduced herself and took him into the house.

'Mrs. Preller isn't down yet, but I'll tell her you're here,' she said.

She rang for Lena, sent her upstairs and then went to the kitchen to order coffee from Tilly.

She had shown Mendel into the drawing-room, but found him standing in the hall looking up at the sculptured prow of the *Saxenburg*. He seemed tiny under the Amazon-like woman whose white bosom dominated the room.

'Very robust,' he said. 'I remember her. Yes, she is not easily forgotten.'

'This isn't your first visit?'

'I was here about fifteen years ago. In the big boom. Now it is a little boom, but getting better – I hope. So I said to myself, Mendel, it's time to go out.'

They walked back past the stirring ostrich feathers into the drawing-room.

'I tell you, my dear, travel is not my favourite occupation.' He brushed a little invisible dust from his coat sleeve. 'Ships I don't mind, but the hotels . . . Oi!'

'I think you'll find the one here quite good.'

'I hope so. I arrived last night. For dinner, barley soup, stockfish, mutton chops, treacle tart . . .'

Kate smiled. 'I think we can do better than that. You'll stay for lunch. I'm sure Mrs. Preller . . .'

'Of course. We have to talk.'

For only the second time since Kate had been at Saxenburg, Mrs. Preller came downstairs to eat. Smuts was also there and they lunched at the refectory table in the big dining-room. Kate herself had not eaten there since Christmas.

Lena had done well at short notice and the main course was grilled yellow-tail served with parsley butter. Mrs. Preller had told Smuts to bring up two bottles of Spätlese to go with it.

Mendel had courtly manners and was consistently gracious to Mrs. Preller. Kate noticed that while she and Smuts were reserved at first, he soon broke this down. It transpired that he loved gossip, especially about people in high places, and his talk was laced with the indiscretions of the rich and titled. Mrs. Preller's eyes soon shone with amusement and even Smuts laughed and said, 'That's a good one!' at the end of each story.

Kate watched as he took his first sip of wine and was pleased to see a look of reverence come into his eyes.

Over coffee, they began to talk business.

'Is it going to be a real boom, Mr. Mendel?' Smuts said, asking the question that was in all their minds. 'Or is it just a flash in the pan?'

'If I knew, I would tell you. Believe me. I personally, think it is going to last, though not so big as before. There are problems we didn't have last time and we have been greedy. We have wanted more and more feathers, more and more wild-bird feathers. You never saw such feathers: scarlet ibis, parakeet, lyre-bird, bird of paradise, orioles, humming-birds, even larks. Everyone has been shooting and trapping birds. I've seen whole wings, sometimes whole stuffed birds on ladies' hats. Look in Cape Town, you'll see the same. Little yellow finches, the heads of small owls, sea-birds.

'I kept out of that trade as much as I could, but other dealers bought and finally I was forced to buy too. My customers wanted sooty terns and blackbird feathers. If I didn't have them, they would go elsewhere.

'Well, I mean, what can you expect? The outcry began. The Audubon Society and others grew stronger and stronger. So now we have the Anti-Plumage Bill.'

'We've read about it in the papers,' Mrs. Preller said. 'But will it affect ostrich feathers?'

Mendel shook his head. 'Never. At the moment, some people believe you slaughter the ostriches to get the feathers, but the hysteria won't last.'

'Bloody fools,' Smuts broke in angrily. 'Forgive my French.'

'Germany is taking more and more, so are France and New York. Queen Mary has said she will not wear feathers any more, but we'll see. I think the end has come for exotic feathers, but not for ostrich feathers, and that makes it even better for us. Without the wild birds, the ostriches will take the market.'

Kate had hardly spoken and now she said, 'So the Anti-Plumage Bill could really be good for us?'

'In that way, maybe yes. But the real problem is what it has alway been: you ladies. If you want to wear feathers, then everything is all right, but if you don't . . . It's the same with diamonds. I mean, what is a diamond? A piece of coloured crystal. Who needs it? If you ladies said, we don't like diamonds, De Beers would go bust. That's where Rhodes was so clever. He knew that if he could control the amount of diamonds going onto the market he could maintain a scarcity and keep the prices up. Open the floodgates, and down would go the prices. It's the same with feathers. But we have no Rhodes in feathers.'

He accepted more coffee, then said, 'This is good! No chicory.'

'We have it sent from Cape Town,' Mrs. Preller said. 'It is Viennese.'

'Have you been back there?'

She shook her head. 'One day. But in a way I am frightened. We lived in such luxury. What will things look like now? Is there still luxury since the war? Maybe it is better not to go back.'

'Talking of going back,' Mendel said. 'You know that Sachs will no longer be coming back here to buy? Such a tragedy.'

'They say he's in Cape Town with his sister,' Smuts said.

'I saw him three days ago; looks eighty and like a pencil, so thin.'

Kate was fascinated by the fastidious way he picked up his cup, the small, birdlike sips.

'I must appoint a new agent. Do you know Lippman from Oudtshoorn?'

'I've heard of him,' Smuts said. 'I believe he's a good man.'

'For twenty years I've known him. Nothing bad. I'm going to see him in Oudtshoorn tomorrow. We'll talk.'

An idea had been forming in Kate's mind. She had pushed it aside once or twice, but it forced its way back. She found herself breaking into the conversation: 'Mr. Mendel . . .'

'My dear?' He watched her over the coffee cup. She groped for the right words.

'Mr. Mendel, this may sound stupid, but it's something I've just thought of.'

'Please . . .'

She saw Mrs. Preller turn to look at her. Mendel's eyebrows rose as he waited.

'You were talking about the way diamonds are controlled. Well, it just seemed . . . as though we *might* be able to do something similar.'

'How, my dear?'

Again she searched for the words. 'Say you didn't have an agent. Say we worked directly with you in London. Exported directly to you. We could agree a price between us, no need for agents or middlemen of any kind. So we'd save those commissions. But the most important thing would be, we would know how much to produce, because you could tell us.'

There was silence around the table as the three stared at her.

'Go on, my dear.'

'That's all, really. It's just that Mr. Smuts has often told me it's boom or bust, glut or famine in this business. You'd get the pick of our feathers at prices agreed between us. And we'd know how much to produce.'

'But what if we agreed on a price and the market fell?' Mendel said.

'What if it rose?' Kate said.

He smiled. 'What do you think, Mrs. Preller? You've got a real business lady here.'

'The point is, what do *you* think?' Mrs. Preller said. 'You are in the centre of things.'

Mendel turned to Smuts. 'Such a pupil!'

'I better get back to work soon, or she'll have my job for good.' Smuts said it with mock irritation, but Kate could see he was pleased.

Later, as Mendel was pulling on his gloves and donning the white dust coat, he turned aside to Kate and said, 'Let me think about it. Maybe there is a way. Maybe if we formed a company between us, with contracts binding us together . . . maybe it would work. The only problem is, what about the other farmers? Maybe they would try to undersell us. What then?'

'You're the biggest dealer in Europe and we're the biggest farm in the world. We'd break them in the end.'

He looked at her approvingly. 'You're going to do well, my dear. Very well. Even if this comes to nothing, we're going to work together, you and me. We're going to make profits.'

She watched the dust trail along the cliffs as the car sped back to town. She felt a hand on her arm and turned to see Mrs. Preller. She was suddenly embarrassed at what she had done, and began to say so.

But Mrs. Preller held up her hand. 'Boss Charles used to say, "Never apologise, never explain." You had something to say, you said it. He listened. Mendel is no fool. He *listened*.'

They walked through the gate that led into the old garden and she took Kate's arm as they went slowly up the ruined paths. She seemed older and more frail than even a few months before. 'Yes, he listened,' she repeated. 'I liked him.'

'He's the best kind of Jew. Come, take me back to the house now.'

March turned to April and the fine, calm weather held. The interest of Helmsdale was still centred on the forthcoming trial of Jonas, though no one knew when it was to be. It was said that Professor Fleischman had pleurisy and he would have to recover before it could be held. There was another interest: two of the old ostrich houses had been bought by farmers from the interior and one of them was already being refurbished.

'It's not the Berrangé place, is it?' Kate asked Smuts.

'It's the old Williamson house. My God, it'll be good to see those places put right. We've been living with ghosts for too long.'

In April, Charles came back for good. Kate had been in Helmsdale and when she arrived at Saxenburg she saw the red roadster in the yard. It was not a Friday, or a public holiday, for Easter was past, and she wondered why he was there. As she went into the house, she saw Lena.

'Is that Mister Charles back?'

'Yes, Miss Kate.'

'Anything wrong?'

Lena did not reply, but went through the door into the kitchen. Kate started up the stairs to Mrs. Preller's apartments with the overseas mail, and heard raised voices: the deeper voice of Charles and the high tones of his mother. She paused, turned, and went down again. Then she heard a door bang as Charles went into his own room. She let Lena take up the overseas mail and went on with her work. She had no wish to become embroiled in a row between Mrs. Preller and her son.

She was lunching alone in the small dining-room when Charles came in. She greeted him warily. He refused anything to eat, perched on the window-sill and took one of Smuts' cigarettes. He smoked for a while, then said, 'I've come home.'

She waited, but when he offered no further explanation she said, 'You mean, on holiday?'

'No. For good. I resigned. Got fed up. I'm not cut out for office life.'

He stubbed out the cigarette and left the room as abruptly as he had arrived.

Kate had developed the pleasant habit of visiting Smuts after she'd had her bath at about six o'clock. He had a big room on the seaward side of the house, with easy chairs and a low table near the windows. It was the part of her day that she enjoyed most and she had become fond of the little, elderly man who had, in his own curious way, been kind to her from their first meeting. He had quickly corrupted her into having first one brandy and water, then two. 'Spots,' he called them. 'It's time for spots,' was one of his phrases. She would have a drink and talk over the events of the day and pick his brains about problems she knew were looming.

He had not really recovered from his accident and he was beginning to look his age. He walked with a marked stoop, as though by straightening he might stretch and hurt the muscles and tendons which had been injured by the ostrich. Now, as he poured them both their first drink of the evening, he said, 'What do you think about Charles?'

'He told me he'd resigned. He said he'd got tired of the job.'

'If you believe that, my friend, you'll believe anything. Cigarette?'

She took one. 'You lead me astray. First brandy and now cigarettes.'

'If you're thinking of anything else, you'll be disappointed,' he said. 'I'm too old for that sort of game.'

She smiled. 'What happened to Charles?'

'If you ask me, I think he got the push. Times are bad. The market crashed a while back. Anyway, Charles was never the boy for an office.'

'He said as much himself.' She thought of Jerry and Charles and the other young men she had met in Cape Town. Golf and tennis, riding, swimming. All the hard work done by coloured people. It was a strange, anachronistic kind of life. When Mrs. Preller spoke of that kind of existence she was recalling her childhood, long before the war. Here, it still existed.

Her feelings about Charles's permanent return to Saxenburg were ambivalent. On the one hand, it renewed the tensions she felt when he was around, but on the other it helped her to cope with a problem that had begun to loom larger and larger as the brief autumn ended.

Helmsdale lay in the winter rainfall area, and as the golden days petered out, the storms gathered from the north-west and rain lashed down as she had never seen it in Scotland. The squalls followed each other, battering at the windows, flooding areas of the farm and making the ostriches generally unhappy and irritable, especially if they were sittng. Sometimes nests were washed away and, although Kate tried to tempt the birds back, they ignored the eggs and she had to try to hatch them in the incubator.

'In the old days they used to make a coloured woman go to bed for a couple of weeks and hatch them,' Smuts said. 'Don't you believe me? It's gospel.'

Mostly the eggs did not hatch and they also lost a good number of chicks in the cold, damp weather. Sometimes she would look at the bedraggled birds with their wet, drooping feathers and wonder how they would ever return to the magnificent black and white plumes of the summer.

The house had been built to withstand heat and the clammy weather penetrated to the farthest rooms, and Lena and Tilly spent part of each day bringing in coal and wood and seeing to the fires. There were beautiful days when the sun shone and everything had a washed look and the sea was tranquil and light green. On these days, because the work of the farm had slackened considerably, Kate went for long walks along the cliffs or the dunes that lay on the far side of Helmsdale. The walks tired her out and helped her to sleep. Her problem had become loneliness.

She would have her two brandies with Smuts, by which time it would already be dark, and the evening would loom ahead. Smuts, she knew, had one or two more brandies after she left him and would then doze by his fire. Lena would give her a plain supper, often on a tray, then she would lock up. Kate would be left to her own devices.

She did her mending, she did the farm accounts, she read some of the farm journals that arrived in the mail pouch, she wrote her diary and she read book after book. Then she would go to bed. She had never been lonely before. In Edinburgh, living in a teeming warren, she had longed for solitude. And even when she had first come to

Saxenburg there had been the strangeness and interest of this new world to keep her mind occupied. And then there had been visits from Charles and Jerry and Freda and other friends who came from time to time. Now visitors were rare. There was not even Mr. Sachs. Dr. du Toit came regularly, but he was always closeted with Mrs. Preller and Kate was not invited to join them. She would even have been pleased to go up to the old lady's room and read to her in the evenings, but Mrs. Preller had never asked for her.

She had begun to smoke as a regular habit and sometimes she would find herself considering whether or not to have a third brandy as she sat alone in her small office or up in her room. Sometimes she felt a sense of despair. This was the time of her life when she should be marrying and having babies.

These thoughts would, by association, bring Tom very close to her. If he had written then, or even telephoned, she would have gone to him, even though she knew there was no future in their relationship. But he did not, and she found she could not break her silence to make the contact.

She began to feel more and more remote. The outside world seemed unreal. Edinburgh, Prince's Street, even Cape Town might have been on another planet. All she knew was the sea on one side and the great plain with its mountain barrier on the other.

This changed when Charles came back. Instead of three people living in their separate apartments, his presence turned the house back into a home. Whatever initial irritation Mrs. Preller had felt at his 'resignation' soon disappeared and he was once again her little boy and Lena's Master Charles, to be spoilt and cosseted. Sometimes he took his mother for her drive to Helmsdale and freed Kate from what had become something of a chore. In the early evenings he would dig Smuts out of his room and bring him into the drawing-room for a drink, or he might join Kate and the old man in Smuts' room and sit in front of the fire. Later, he and Kate would play two-handed poker or Lexicon or listen to the Victrola.

A day or so after he arrived he trapped her in her small

office and kissed her. She responded for a moment, then pushed him away.

She had known that the situation would arise sooner or later, and had prepared for it. She held him off and said, 'Not here. Not now.'

'When?'

'When I say so.'

She saw the anger mount in his face until the strange and frightening curtain dropped behind his eyes.

But she was prepared for this, too, and squeezed past him. At the door she turned. 'Charles, I like you and it's nice having you here. But I couldn't stand it if you were waiting to pounce around every corner. Life would become unbearable. So let's see what happens in its own time. Don't push things.'

The curtain lifted and he smiled uncertainly. 'You don't make me feel very welcome.'

'I've told you it's nice having you here. That's a welcome, isn't it?'

When she reached her room she found herself stiff with tension, but she had said something which needed saying and she thought she might have got away with it.

The problem with Charles was that he did not have enough to do. He began to talk about taking over the business interests in town and relieving his mother of the responsibility. But nothing seemed to come of that for Mrs. Preller still made the daily journeys, driven either by Kate or Charles or, with increasing frequency as he regained enough strength to handle the motor, by Smuts.

In the mornings, Charles would occupy Kate's office, ringing brokers in Cape Town, but she never knew if he was trying to find another position or whether he was playing the market. Sometimes she would take a break from her work and have coffee and a cigarette with him. They were moments she enjoyed. It was pleasant to have another person in the house and she missed him on his occasional visits to Cape Town. He still retained his apartment there – though, as she found out from Smuts it was not and never had been his own, but belonged to Preller Estates and was the one his father had used.

Jerry and Freda came down one week-end. Freda had had her hair marcelled and had picked up from one of her friends just returned from London the current smart word: amusing. Everything was amusing; Jerry was amusing, the hotel was amusing, the flooded golf course was amusing.

The weather was grey and drizzly and there was not much to do, so Jerry and Charles collected as many golf balls as they could, buying every second-hand ball at the Club and every ball for sale by the little coloured caddies who spent hours beating the tussocks and bush of the rough. They took the balls back to Saxenburg, stood on the verandah and, using wooden clubs, lashed them out to sea.

Kate discovered that they were competing for the longest drive. There was an uncovered rock about two hundred yards out to sea and this was their target. She watched each drive ending in a small splash on the calm water, and usually in an argument about which had been the longest. They drove a bucketful of balls before they grew bored. She thought she had never seen anything so pointless and wasteful in her life. But Freda found it amusing to sit watching the two men.

Later she told Kate that Jerry was having an affair with another woman. 'It's amusing to watch him pretend,' she said. 'He's been much nicer to me.'

But Kate did not think she was amused. When she spoke, it was with bitterness. She was also drinking and smoking more than she had.

On Sunday Kate had to go and see one of the coloured children on the estate, who was ill. When she came back, she found Freda and Jerry preparing to leave.

'Aren't you staying for lunch?' she said.

'We must get back,' Jerry said. 'You know what the roads are like in this weather. It's going to take hours.'

Freda came to kiss Kate and whispered: 'They've had a row. Jerry offered him a job and Charles told him to stuff it up his arse.'

As the days passed, Kate began to feel a sense of unease. Although Charles had never expressed any interest in farming, she could not help feeling that she was usurping his function. He was the son, the farm would eventually be his responsibility. So she tried, as best she could without forfeiting her own position, to discuss the day to day working of Saxenburg with him. But he was not interested. Instead, he would usually shift the conversation to the profits made by the hotel or the garage; to how he planned to enlarge the bar; how he hoped for the Ford franchise; how he would build a canning factory down at the harbour. His plans were big, and she encouraged him to talk.

On one lovely, crisp winter's day they walked down to the cove and along the beach to the rock pool. Now, in winter, there was a different feeling in the air, the colours had changed, the beach itself was partly covered in driftwood. Jonas was no longer standing among the rocks with his big sea-pole, the sun no longer beat down, the south-easter no longer blew the sand in eddies across the beach. She had partially recovered from her horror of the pools, though she knew she would never swim in them again.

The tide was low and Charles said, 'Let's go to the sea cave.'

'I don't like it.'

'Come on, there's nothing else to do.'

He helped her across weed-covered rocks, wet and slippery, and encrusted with limpets, and they crawled through the small tunnel. The sun was westering and the cave was filled with a strange green light. 'You only get this light in winter,' he said. He was standing near the mouth where the wavelets hissed on the shingle.

'It's beautiful.'

'I know people who have seen grottoes in Italy and they say this is more beautiful.'

She turned away. 'It makes me feel claustrophobic.'

'Wait.' He caught her by the shoulder and turned her to face him. 'I want to kiss you. I want to kiss you all the time.'

'Kiss me, then.'

He took her in his arms and her fear of him returned. They kissed, but it was he who broke away. 'Kate, there's something I want to ask you. . .'

She knew what was coming, and held up her hand. He

took it in his. His face looked heavy and satyr-like in the green light.

'I think I know what you're going to say,' she said.

'Well, if you know . . .'

'Please don't. Don't complicate things just at the moment.'

'What things?'

She thought of Tom and her parents and Duggie. How could she explain? 'My life is in a muddle. Please don't make it worse.'

She could see his mouth begin to turn down in anger. Oh, God, she thought, if he takes me here, there's nothing I can do. She put her face up to his and kissed him.

'Soon,' she said. 'I promise you things will change soon.'

As they walked back to the house, which loomed darkly on the cliffs, she felt the need to get away from Saxenburg, from Charles and from Mrs. Preller. She decided to go home the following week-end.

But on the Thursday, Mrs. Preller sent Lena to find her.

[4]

Lena called her before lunch, which was an unusual time. The old lady – Kate still thought of her as that – was in her chair, her face half-hidden by shadow, the lamp glowing on the table beside her, the screen behind her. Another deviation from normal was that a bottle and two glasses stood on the table.

'Come, my dear,' she said. 'Sit here by me.' She indicated a comfortable chair. 'Now pour us each a glass of Madeira.'

Kate poured the drinks. Her mind was racing. She had no idea what the purpose of the meeting might be.

'I first tasted Madeira in my father's house,' Mrs. Preller said. 'He used to take it with a biscuit about eleven o'clock in the morning. Sometimes my mother would join him. Perhaps friends would call in. It was more usual in Vienna in those days to take cofee with cream. Such cream! But my father preferred his Madeira.' She sipped her drink. 'You would have loved that house. It was in an area called the Cottäge, in Gustav Tschermakgasse. Half a city block the garden alone. A lily pond the size of my tennis court. Red squirrels in the trees. Sometimes my father would take his Madeira in the summer house before the day grew too warm. I would sit on the steps and watch him, and he would stroke my hair. "One day, *liebchen*," he would say. "One day you will have this house."

'But it was never to be. One day never came for me, but it came quickly for him. And when he died, my mother found that he was so great in debt that she had to sell the house. All the years we had been living in that big house on borrowed money, and we did not know it. Then, suddenly, it was the end. House sold. My sisters and mother gone. We – my family – had been in that house two hundred years. While Mozart and Beethoven and Schubert and Brahms had lived in Vienna. But no more.'

The thin white face and the vermilion lips were still for a few moments and Kate waited for her to continue. She knew that more was to come, for Mrs. Preller had a habit of circumlocution whenever she wished to discuss something important.

At last she said, 'You have done well, Kate.'

It was one of the few times she had used Kate's Christian name. Was she going to offer a raise in salary? As always, Kate was excited by the praise.

'Much better than I could have thought,' she continued. 'Smuts says you have done wonders. Mr. Mendel was impressed. Truly impressed.'

'Thank you.'

'It is we who must thank you.'

'Mr. Smuts taught me everything.'

'There are many who could not have learned. So . . .'

Now it was coming. Would the raise be substantial?

'Do you ever think of marriage?' Mrs. Preller said.

'You mean, in the abstract or to someone in particular?'

'You have nothing against it?'

'Of course not.'

'You know, my dear, your age is the best time for a woman to marry. Having babies is easier than it would be later. A woman begins to dry up as the years go by. You understand what I mean?'

'I understand.' She had, in fact, expressed Kate's own recent thoughts.

'Tell me, how is your family?'

Kate told her briefly about Duggie's operation and convalescence.

'That is sad. Does your father work?'

'I don't think so, at the moment.'

'Times are hard. They say things will get even worse.'

She paused, as though to make sure she chose the right words.

'Sometimes I think that my situation here is similar in many ways to Vienna. There a family lived in one house for so long, but not in trade, you understand. Here is also one family for a long time. In trade, ja, but not shop-keepers. Two families with position, money, a little bit of power. Comfort. Wealth. Then suddenly, *kaput*. I ask myself sometimes: What if I had stayed in Vienna? But I know that in those days I could have achieved nothing there. Women were flowers or donkeys, no more. Here I *had* to do something, and found I was able to do it.

'Then I say to myself, what would have happened in Vienna if I had been a person like Kate? Could I have done more? You understand me, my dear?'

'I think so.'

'We needed a Kate. Someone like you, ambitious, trust-worthy, clever, hard-working . . . no, no, my dear, I mean it. We had property in the Salzkammergut, we had a small estate in the Waldviertel. Things could have been done to save them. But no one thought. My father died. And the end for my mother and my sisters was a small apartment in Nussdorferstrasse, near a railway bridge. No more cream after that.

'And now here is a situation that reminds me of those days. Except for one thing: I have seen it before, so I recognise it. So what to do? Smuts is an old man, I am an old woman . . .'

'Mrs. Preller, you're —'

'Please . . . morphine makes you old before your time. And so I look around me. Who can save Saxenburg, I ask? Charles? He is my son. I love him, but if I am honest, I must say he is more like my own father than myself. You see, my dear, there is a paradox in life. If you come from the top, you can only sink; from the bottom, your struggle is upwards. That is what this place needs, someone who will struggle. And there is still another problem: a person will seldom struggle hard to make others rich.'

She drained her Madeira. 'So . . . I am sorry to talk for so long. It is tiring. But think about what I have said. It is important for both of us.'

Kate spent the remainder of the day analysing the conversation, trying to probe the meaning behind Mrs. Preller's words, the thoughts in her subtle Viennese mind. She wondered whether Charles had inspired them. Had he dared to go to his mother and say, 'I want Kate. Buy her for me'?

The thought infuriated her, but that evening when she was having her 'spot' with Smuts, he came in and remarked, 'I might have guessed you'd be at the brandy!' It was said so guilelessly and matter-of-factly that she was convinced he'd had nothing to do with the conversation. Charles was less than subtle.

That night, she could not sleep. She believed she understood what Mrs. Preller had offered, and its magnitude, the difference it would make to her own future, was overwhelming. And yet . . . could she be wrong? Had the old woman simply been maundering on, had she only wanted company? But she had specifically asked if Kate understood her. There had been the references to her family and to marriage. The whole structure of the conversation seemed to have been carefully thought out. Again Kate checked herself: Were her ambitions not racing ahead of her, muddling her thoughts? Did Mrs. Preller really intend her to marry Charles? And what if she did? Might she not be worse off than she was now? At least she had her independence, such as it was. What if Charles controlled the purse-strings and she had to go to him for every penny?

The following day, as they were driving into Helmsdale, the old lady said, 'Have you thought about our conversation?'

'Yes.'

'And what did you think?' The voice was chilly, businesslike. Today there were no 'my dears', and no Christian names.

'I think that you're probably right. You do need someone permanent to look after Saxenburg, someone who doesn't simply work for wages.'

'Someone with a personal interest.'

'Yes. But say this person was a woman . . .'

'To have a personal, a genuine personal interest she would have to be married to Charles.'

'Yes, I can see that.'

'Tell me, as a young woman yourself, would that be appealing?'

'It might to the right person. Someone who loved him.'

'All marriages are not based on love, you know. Some of the best had nothing to do with love. Do you think the Hapsburgs married for love?'

'I understand that. But if the person, say the woman, was the kind of person you would want, who would hold the estate and the business interests together, then that woman would not want to have to ask her husband for a pound here and a pound there.'

Mrs. Preller laughed softly. 'The kind of person needed would have to be of independent means, naturally. And the estate would see to that.'

On Friday, Kate went home for the week-end and arranged for Smuts to take her to the station, but when Tilly helped her downstairs with her bag, it was Charles who met her at the door. 'I'll run you into town,' he said. 'I'm going, anyway.'

He was dressed in his long, leather driving-coat and his tweed cap, which suited him well. He took her case and put it in the dickey while she got into the front seat. They drove along the cliffs for a mile, and then swung inland towards the mountains.

'What are you doing?' she said. 'The train leaves in twenty minutes.'

'I'm taking you to town.'

'You know this isn't the way.'

'I said I was going to town. Cape Town. We'll be there long before the train. Relax. You're off duty now.'

He was right. She *was* off duty. A feeling of release and freedom came over her as they headed across the flat sandy plain covered in *fynbos*. Charles reached behind him and gave her a heavy tartan travelling rug. 'You'll need it if it's cold in the mountains.'

She snuggled down under the rug and pulled her heavy coat around her. Her hair was covered by a black beret and she, like Charles, wore leather gloves.

It had rained heavily the day before and the brown dirt road had turned to mud. Charles drove fast, but with care. Again, as she had been in the train, she was struck by the emptiness of the land, but there had been a shift in her emotions. It was no longer an alien landscape. She identified with it and had learned to like its bleak beauty. At first the dun-coloured plain and the brown mountains had seemed to be monochromatic, but she had learned to distinguish the subtleties of a range of colours from cream through fawn and chestnut to mahogany and back again to dusty yellow. Now, as they began to climb away from the coastal plain, the browns and light tans were contrasted by the first of the wheatlands, bright, almost phosphorescent green in the grey afternoon light. The road was lined here and there with gum-trees, all leaning away from the south-east winds.

Charles fumbled in his pocket, pulled out a silver cigarette case and offered it to her. She took two and lit them before passing one to him.

'I'm sorry, I've left some lipstick on it.'

'It won't be the first time.' He put it in his mouth and she felt a sudden moment of intimacy, as though he had touched her. She closed the case and was passing it back to him when she saw engraved on it, '*To C.P. from M.S*'.

Miriam? It had to be. She leaned back and watched him through half-closed eyes. Miriam had wanted him so badly. She thought of the day of the picnic when she had flirted with Duggie and then with Jerry, trying to make Charles jealous. Miriam would have married him like a shot. But Miriam had not been granted the opportunity, and she had. Why not take it? Because, she thought, the shadow of Tom was between her and Charles. Yet . . . she was ready to make someone a good wife, ready to have his babies. She believed, as Mrs. Preller did, that the longer one left it, the more difficult it would become.

After Caledon, they began climbing up towards the Houw Hoek Pass. The muddy road was badly cut about by lorries and Charles sometimes had difficulty keeping the motor out of the ruts.

When he dropped her at her parents' house, he said, 'I'll be at the flat. Why don't we eat and go to a nightclub?'

She was tempted, but reminded herself that it was to have a break from Charles and from Saxenburg that she had come. 'I can't,' she said. 'Not this time.'

It was as though she had never left the cramped little villa; the same smells hung in the passage, the same poor lighting gave the place a cold, depressed look, the same grease seemed to have remained in the kitchen, the same cold, damp atmosphere prevailed, the same small coal fire burnt in the sitting-room grate.

Her mother looked bonier, more gaunt than she remembered. 'Supper's ready,' was her greeting as Kate put down her suitcase.

'Where's Dad?'

'Next door.' It was said with tight lips.

Kate knew that a family named Bremer lived in the neighbouring villa.

Her mother said, 'He goes there a lot. They're coloureds, you know. He owns a removal business. Well, you wouldna call it a proper business. One wee lorry. He gives your father work from time to time.' She picked up a heavy ladle and banged on the wall. 'That'll fetch him out. He sits there aw' the day when he's not working and the two of them drink white port.'

Her father came through the kitchen door from the yard. He was wearing an old grey cardigan and a white striped collarless shirt with a copper stud at the neck. He was thinner and older and more worn than when she had last seen him.

'Ma wee girl!' he said, putting his arms about her. She flinched at the smell of him.

They ate mince in which there were heavy white dumplings, and a dish of cabbage. 'I bet you havena had dumplings for a long time,' Mrs. Buchanan said.

'No, Mother.' They were heavy and sticky in the middle and Kate was barely able to get them down.

After she had done the washing-up, her father borrowed a pound from her and went out.

'He'll be away to the Railway Arms. You shouldna have given him the money,' Mrs. Buchanan said.

They sat in the front room and Kate listened to a catalogue of complaints: the roof leaked, the fire smoked, the rent was going up, her teeth were hurting, Mr. Buchanan was hardly ever in work, her chest was playing up, Duggie was no better, worse if anything. 'We'll go to see him tomorrow,' she said. 'And you can see for yoursel'.'

By nine o'clock, Kate had excused herself and gone to bed. The sheets were cold, the room damp.

The following day, she and her mother caught a train down to the sea. Mrs. Buchanan had asked for a couple of pounds 'to get a wee something to cheer him up'.

They left the train at St. James, which had always reminded Kate of pictures she had seen of Devon and Cornish fishing-villages, and walked up a long flight of steps cut into the side of a hill. Duggie's convalescent home was a double-storeyed house with a verandah that commanded a view over False Bay. He was sitting, wrapped up in a basket chair, taking the winter sun. He was thinner, like his father, and looked wasted. Kate kissed him and asked after his leg.

'Not bad. They say it could be worse. The whole thing could be rotten, you ken, not just the one patch of bone.'

He spoke with painful bitterness and her heart went out to him. This was her big brother, the charmer, who had gone off to the wars like a stainless knight and had come back with a wound that had affected not only his leg. She remembered him in Helmsdale, with Miriam sitting close to him, feeding him tit-bits from the picnic. She remembered his smile, the conspiratorial conversation between the two of them, she remembered him limping off up the street with Miriam when they had been dropped at the hotel. Had he gone home with her? Had she made him happy? She hoped so.

'Have you brought anything for me?' Duggie said to his mother.

'Just a wee something,' Mrs. Buchanan said, and passed him a package wrapped in brown paper. He excused himself and when he returned he seemed calmer, slightly more cheerful. But his limp was worse than Kate had seen it, and there was pain in every movement.

'They want to take it off,' he said. 'Just about there . . .' He put his finger below his knee. 'They say the bone'll go on getting worse and worse. They havena a hope of stopping the infection.'

Twice more he excused himself in the following hour and twice more he limped painfully back. Kate wondered how long it would take him to finish the bottle.

On the train going back her mother said, 'Now you know.'

'Have you spoken to the doctor?'

'Of course I have. It's as Duggie says. If they dinna take it off, he'll die.'

They were silent for a spell and then she said, 'I've not seen him happy since that Jewish girl died.'

'Miriam?'

'If that was her name. Your father and I didna ken any Jews – didna want to, you understand – but she was good to him.'

'In Cape Town? She saw him here?'

'Oh, aye.'

'I didn't know.'

'He was in a terrible state when he heard. I've never seen him like it.'

For a few seconds she seemed to look down the wrong end of a telescope into the future. It was going to be months before Duggie regained his strength. First there would have to be the operation, then the artificial limb-fitting, and convalescence. And once it was all over, who was going to employ him? And then there was her father. He did not seem able to keep a skilled job – according to her mother, coloured people were being employed in preference to whites because their wages were lower. For a moment, she had an urge to leave the train, to change her name and disappear into the vast continent that lay to the north.

The following day, Sunday, she telephoned Tom at his home, something she had never done before. He sounded guarded and surprised, but agreed to meet her in Claremont Gardens during the morning.

It was chilly, with a north-wester building up, and she stood under a palm tree in the light drizzle. She watched him come up the path between the lawns, a tall, broad-shouldered figure with sandy hair, and she felt the old excitement. She managed a shaky, lop-sided smile.

'May I join you under your tree?' he said.

'Hello, Tom.'

He put her hand to his lips.

'I wanted to see you, otherwise I'd never have telephoned your house,' she said.

'Joyce isn't up yet, so it didn't matter. Anyway, I often go for a walk on a Sunday morning. It must be important.'

'Yes.' She wanted to tell him how often she had thought of him, how often she had taken up a pen to write to him, only to put it down again, how often she had heard the telephone ring and hoped against hope it might be him. But she couldn't. If she faltered now, everything would be lost. 'It is important. I'm going to marry Charles.'

She saw him flinch. He stood for some moments, letting the news sink in, and then said, 'Why? You don't love him.'

'Lots of reasons.'

'Give me one.'

184

'Duggie has to have his leg off. He'll never work again.'

'That's hard on him.' Then he said: 'Once before you came back and refused to see me. Your family seem to have a strange effect on you.'

'At least this time I'm seeing you. I don't think you realise how difficult that is.'

'You're right. I don't. Largely because you made your feelings clear enough when I was in Helmsdale. But don't let's fight. I should be wishing you good luck. And I do.'

'There's no other *way*,' she said, fighting back the tears.

'I suppose not.'

The drizzle became heavier and rattled on the palm leaves.

She put out her hand again. He took it and tried to draw her towards him. 'Don't,' she said.

'Kate . . .'

'No! For God's sake, just leave me alone!'

He dropped her hand. 'Will I see you again?'

'I don't know.'

[5]

Kate would remember her wedding-day always, for reasons which had nothing to do with her marriage. The ceremony was on a June day of gales and rain. It was set for eleven o'clock in the registry office at the courthouse. Her mother and father had come to Helmsdale and were staying at the hotel. Apart from Dr. du Toit, Smuts, and Jerry and Freda, there were to be no other guests. A special room in the hotel had been set aside for the wedding luncheon and after that she and Charles were to leave for Cape Town.

It had been at her insistence that it was to be a very private wedding. She had flatly refused Charles's suggestion that the ceremony should be at the Cathedral in Cape Town, and Mrs. Preller had supported her, as Kate had known she would, not wanting to be seen by crowds of people.

On her wedding-morning she was dressing – she had bought a grey silk dress, waistless, with pleats flaring from the hips and a matching cloche hat, and Charles had given her a silver-fox stole – when Lena came in.

'Miss Kate must be very happy.'

'Yes, I am.'

'I just come to wish Miss Kate good luck.'

'Thank you, Lena.'

'Everything going to be all right now. I pray for Miss Kate. God has heard my prayers.'

'You mean you prayed that Mister Charles and I would get married?'

'Right from when Miss Kate first came. Madam don't pray, but Madam also wanted it. Madam is very happy.'

Everyone was happy, Kate thought. Charles, his mother, Lena, even Dr. du Toit. 'It's the best thing that could happen,' he had said kissing her on the lips when the announcement had been made. 'The very best.' Everyone except herself. There had been moments in the past weeks when she had been on the verge of calling it off, when she had looked into the future and seen herself in Mrs. Preller's rooms, alone, fighting as the old woman fought now, to keep the estate together. Is this what she was forging by marrying Charles: iron clasps binding her to the house, to the family, to the tradition, to the name? Would she one day also end up in the mausoleum in the dusty cemetery at the edge of town: CATHERINE PRELLER née BUCHANAN, and then the dates of her birth and death? She put a pin into her hat and arranged a grey veil over her face. This was not what she had planned for herself. Life seemed to have swung off-course and was taking her farther and farther from anything she had imagined.

She watched Lena in the mirror. The woman was looking at her with burning eyes, and Kate felt momentarily uneasy.

'It's a pity Betty isn't here,' she said, to fill the silence.

'A big pity, Miss Kate.'

'How is she?'

'She getting better. She helps her auntie in the house.'

'When will she be coming back?'

'Maybe in the summer.'

The telephone rang and Lena went to answer it. She came back after a few moments.

'It's for Miss Kate. A call from Cape Town.'

It was Duggie, she thought, phoning to wish her well. 'Is it my brother?'

'No, Miss Kate. I didn't catch the name too well, but it sounds like Easton.'

'Could it have been Austen?'

'That's the name.'

Kate turned back to the mirror.

'Miss Kate?'

'Tell him I'm out.'

When Lena returned, she said, 'I told him. He says when Miss Kate comes in, Miss Kate must be sure to telephone him. He says it is very urgent.'

'Thank you, Lena.'

Smuts drove Mrs. Preller and Kate to town. Charles took the roadster, with their luggage.

Dr. du Toit was standing in the shelter of the doorway when they arrived. The north-wester was lashing the gum-trees and squalls of rain battered at the window. They hurried inside, straightening hats and brushing drops of water from their clothing. Her mother and father were in the waiting-room and she saw that Charles was already there with Jerry and Freda. Jerry was his best man.

The ceremony was quickly over and when they emerged into the passage again, Lena was waiting with a brown paper bag in her hand. 'Good luck, Miss Kate. Good luck, Master Charles,' she said, and threw confetti over them. Kate realised that she must have come in Charles's car. It was kind of him to have brought her. For a moment everyone was enveloped in a cloud of multi-coloured confetti, laughing and brushing it out of their hair. Until then the wedding had been something to be endured, now it suddenly took on a festive atmosphere and Kate felt her spirits rise. Charles took her arm and hurried her forward. At that moment, the big exterior doors burst open. Three men stood on the threshold; two were burly policemen and between them, manacled, stood Jonas.

For a second or two, everything was still. Kate found herself staring at Jonas as though he were an animal, and this was the impression she carried with her afterwards, of a wild animal. The rain was dripping down his face and his eyes were red and staring. Lena screamed and ran down the passage away from him, dropping her bag of confetti which burst like a bomb.

The two groups eyed each other, then Jonas slowly sank to his knees. He was looking directly at her. 'Miss Kate,' he said. 'Help me!'

One of the constables jerked him to his feet and pushed him along the passage. The other turned to Mrs. Preller and said, 'Excuse us. We got to take him before the magistrate for remand. Then he goes back to Cape Town until you got a safe cell for him here.' A door closed and they were gone.

The wedding-party trooped out into the street, but no one threw confetti now. The spirit of festivity had gone. Dr. du Toit did his best to make the wedding luncheon cheerful but for Kate, watching her father in his old grey suit and her mother in her black hat, trying to efface themselves, there was little to feel cheerful about. Charles was attentive to her and boisterous with Jerry, and Smuts became animated on two glasses of champagne. But the spectre of Jonas hovered over the table and she was glad when the festivities were over and they were in the roadster heading for Cape Town.

'Why was Jonas at the courthouse?' she said. 'I thought he was being held somewhere else.'

'For remand, the constable said. They're probably fixing a date for the trial. I hear that Fleischman is better.'

'What do you think will happen to him?'

'They'll hang the bastard.'

'Everyone's so sure he did it. What if he simply picked up the scarf on the beach? What if he didn't even see her?'

'That'll be his defence, you can bet on it.'

'Who will defend him?'

'The court appointed Stoltz.'

She sat back, watching the road unwind. People had already made up their minds about Jonas and there had not even been a trial, not so much as a preparatory exam-ination. She could not get out of her mind the red, staring, animal eyes, the cry for help.

'He was one of our people,' she said. 'We should do something.'

'Like what?'

'We could get him a decent lawyer. It's the least we could do.'

'Don't meddle in something you know nothing about,' he said. 'It's got nothing to do with you. Anyway, it would cost money.'

She did not reply. She knew there would come a time when she would not allow such a reprimand to pass unchallenged, but not yet. She had married Charles and she had every intention of making things work. She would not start their life together on a sour note.

'Of course, money doesn't mean much to a rich woman like you,' he added. It was said lightly, but there was an edge to the joke.

She *was* a rich woman. Or by her own standards, anyway. And by the standards of her mother and father, and Duggie and, she supposed, even by Tom's standards. Within reason, she could buy what she wanted. But at this moment, with the wedding only hours old and the spectre of Jonas on her mind, she did not want anything. What she required was to be happy, to enjoy this, her wedding day. And she knew, as she had known when she first arrived at Saxenburg on that strange and upsetting evening, that the future depended on herself.

The curious thing was that Mrs. Preller had said nothing more to her about the conditions of the marriage. It was as though she had dreamed their conversation. But there was nothing dreamlike about the call she had received from Mr. Hamilton, the bank manager in Helmsdale. This time there had been no talk of collateral, of jewellery or houses to back a loan.

'Do you know why I have asked you to see me? No? In that case, I have a pleasant duty.' He had spread his Kitchener moustache with his plump thumb and fore-finger. In the background she had heard a sizzling noise and the office was filled with the smell of frying fish. He had opened a file and read to her a letter from Mrs. Preller's attorney in Cape Town, Mr. Godlonton. It was written in legal phraseology and she had found it difficult to follow. When he had finished he dropped it onto his desk and said, 'Well, there you are. I think you'll agree that this means the start of a new life for you. And, I suppose, your family, too. How is your brother? It was your brother, wasn't it, you spoke of before? A war wound, I think?'

'May I read the letter?'

He had handed it to her, saying: 'By the way, I have not congratulated you. I hope you'll both be very happy.'

She had read it slowly and with concentration. It appeared that as from a date two days previously, Preller Estates (Pty) Ltd., were to pay her an annual salary of six hundred pounds, split into twelve monthly payments. From the day of her wedding a second company, Preller Investments (Pty) Ltd., was to be formed, of which she was to be a director, along with her husband Charles, and Mrs. Preller. At that time she would receive twenty per cent of the equity of the company, the other eighty per cent to be shared between Mrs. Augusta Preller and Mr. Charles Preller on the basis of three to two, which would give Mrs. Preller the controlling share. Kate's allocation, the letter had stated, was to be her wedding present from Mrs. Preller.

'What does equity mean?' she had said.

'The share capital. If the company is in profit, you will receive dividends, the amount of which you and your fellow-directors will decide.'

Equity. Fellow-directors. Share capital. She was moving into a world she knew nothing about.

Mr. Hamilton had held up a cheque. 'As I understand from Mrs. Preller, the six hundred pounds has nothing to do with the other matter. This is your salary. Do you want it paid into your current account or shall we open a deposit account? And then I'm sure you will want to talk about payments to be made . . .'

She had written to her mother later that day telling her

to telephone Saxenburg. Two days later, she had spoken to her.

'Do you know what this is costing?' The voice had come to her faintly, and in her mind's eye she could see her mother standing in the Greek café on the corner of the street.

'Yes, I do, Mother. I'm sending you enough to cover it, and more.' And then she had told her about her engagement.

There was silence for a moment, then her mother said, 'Getting married? Did you say, married?'

'Yes, Mother.'

'Oh, ma wee Catherine! And to Charles! Oh, my dearie, what a thing! Wait till I tell your father and Douglas. They'll be so . . . they'll be jist . . . I canna say what I feel. Are you coming home first?'

'No. I'll write, though, and let you know the date. It'll be here in Helmsdale.'

As Charles drove her over the mountains towards Cape Town, that all seemed a long time ago.

When she thought back on her honeymoon in future years, her memories were coloured by the events that followed, and it was difficult to tease out the reality. But at the time, she enjoyed herself. And if she was clear-sighted enough of the past, she could sometimes remember herself feeling happy. It was never the passionate, overwhelming happiness she had found with Tom, but a happiness made up of things which were important to her then, and reached through her own decision to do her utmost to make her marriage work. She wanted no half measures. She had reservations about Charles, that was true enough, but she felt, as Mrs. Preller did, that marriages were not made in heaven, but that there were practical aspects that could compensate. After all, Mrs. Preller should know, if the stories about Boss Charles were anything to go on.

Her happiness emerged in unexpected ways, from negatives and positives alike. For the first time in her life she felt that she had true security. Even at school at the Academy she had known that the idyll could not last. But now she could look forward to a future of financial stability and, if she worked hard enough and did not demand too much, emotional stability as well.

She had set aside a certain amount of money to be paid each month to her mother. This meant that Duggie could have his operation, that the rent of the house would not fall into arrears and that there would be enough left over to feed them, thus removing the guilt which had hung over her since she had caused the family to be uprooted and brought to the Cape. Later she found that having bought the removal of guilt, she could not face visiting the house in Observatory. She and Charles drove down several times to see Duggie in St James, but she never went to the house, arranging instead to meet her mother in the city.

In her relations with Charles, she found almost immediately that his love-making was pale and anaemic compared with Tom's. But she forced herself to put Tom out of her mind and when she lay with Charles she tried to give him what she thought he expected. If there was pretence, it came from the best of motives. Charles's sensual face belied the reality. He was a lover without much finesse and the acts were quickly over.

But on their honeymoon, he was attentive. He seemed naively pleased to be married, as though he had joined some kind of club. He took her about the city, to parties, to lunches and night-clubs, and showed her off. This flattered her.

He bought her clothes and, with her small breasts, she wore the current, boyish shapes with elegance. She had her hair marcelled and she began to smoke cigarettes in a long, amber holder.

As she came to know her husband better, she found him a curious mixture of naiveté and sophistication. He carried on his endless sporting duel with Jerry to the point of absurdity, like a small boy. But he knew his way around menus and wine lists and had the confidence of a man who had been educated at the best school, been dressed by the best tailor and been used to money all his life. During the two weeks of their honeymoon the violence which she knew lay just below the surface of his psyche did not surface.

She discovered that he was afraid of the dark and liked to sleep with a night-light. She wondered if she could protest about this, but decided not to, remembering how he had told her what had happened the night Hugo died; how he had buried his head under the blankets because he was afraid of the shadows in the adjoining room. Probably his fear sprang from that. However, she was not used to going to sleep with a light on and after a week she asked if they might leave the light on in the hall instead.

'I've always had a night-light since Hugo died,' he said. 'I used to have nightmares. Dr. du Toit would come and sit with me. I remember he used to hold my hand and tell me I must be a little man. He gave me the night-light. Do you think it's silly?'

'Of course not,' she said.

Allied to his fear of the dark was fear of being alone. That, too, happened at night, and she thought it might spring from the same experience. If they were out with Jerry and Freda, he would want to go on and on, first to a night club and, when that closed, to a road house for sandwiches and coffee, or he would insist on bringing them back to the flat and keep them there, talking and drinking unil Kate would excuse herself and go to bed. It was even more of a problem when they were alone. He would talk and talk and she would feel her eyes grow heavy until sometimes she would go to sleep on the sofa while he stood on the verandah with a drink in his hand, willing the city to stay awake with him.

He slept badly. Sometimes she would wake and find him reading a novel or one of the English magazines he bought when the mail-boat came in. The result was that he slept late in the mornings. This was when she would go out and stroll through the early-morning streets, often part of the commuter crowds. She would find herself looking for a tall man with sandy hair, but she never saw him. She liked these morning walks, loved being in a large city and feeling that she was not some amoeba-like creature who could be crushed by it but was, in a small way, dominating it.

The flat was on a hillside above the city and the views, especially at dusk, when the lights came up all the way down to the pier that jutted out into Table Bay, were breathtaking.

Sometimes, when Charles was still asleep, she would take a tram down the hill and window-shop. She did not buy much, but loved the thought that she could have this dress or that hat, that leather handbag, those imported shoes, if she wanted them. Then at mid-morning she would go into one of the big department stores, Stuttaford's or Cleghorn and Harris, and have her coffee overlooking Adderley Street, one of the city's main arteries.

All in all, it was a pleasant time, better than she could have hoped, but she was not sorry when the fortnight came to an end and they put their bags in the dickey-seat, locked up the flat and drove back to Saxenburg.

[6]

It was during the first few weeks after returning to Cape Town that Kate began to see the pattern of her future forming, and she did not like what she saw.

She remembered how Freda had once said to her in Cape Town, when she was depressed and angry with Jerry: 'Once you marry them, it's different.'

Freda was not the most perspicacious person but, in her own way, Kate began to understand what she meant. What she had thought were merely sexual tensions between her and Charles before they were married were revealed as something more complicated. It was as though they lived in two different worlds: the city and the farm. The city had always been Charles's territory; she had met him there, he had taken her about with him, it was where he lived and operated. The farm had become her world. Weeks had passed between visits from Charles, weeks in which she had been alone, or almost alone, and in which she identified – because she could not and would not identify with her parents' little villa – with Saxenburg itself. The house had become her own, Helmsdale her territory.

On top of this was a new layer of tension: she had been running the farm under Smuts' guidance for months before her marriage. She had become used to having things done her way, of making all the decisions, only consulting Smuts on problems she had not encountered before, and Mrs. Preller on matters of finance. But when they returned to Saxenburg together, she felt that a subtle change had taken place: this was more Charles's home than hers, it was eventually his inheritance, and she felt constrained by his constant presence.

For the first few days, however, she was too busy to notice anything much outside the running of the farm itself. Smuts had kept things going, but relinquished the reins to her with obvious relief.

She and Charles had moved into the guest suite, which was in the east wing and consisted of a large bedroom, dressing-room, bathroom and sitting-room. She'd had the suite repapered and repainted in cool greys and pale colours and had had two sets of curtains made, one in green and yellow for summer, the other of heavy red velvet to give warmth in winter. When it was finished Mrs. Preller came in, looked around and finally said, 'It is all right for young people, but personally I like the old styles.'

'Does that mean I can't re-do the drawing-room and the dining-room downstairs?' Kate had said it only half-jokingly. The rooms had oppressed her from the start and she itched to get her hands on the drawing-room, with its magnificent great windows overlooking the cliffs and the sea.

'No one will touch those rooms while I am alive,' Mrs. Preller said.

But Charles liked their suite and said, 'You have a flair for this kind of thing. I'll work on mother about the ground floor. What about the gardens and the pool and the tennis-court? Why can't we do those as well?'

'Money,' Kate said.

'We might be able to put it through the farm account. Everyone says the boom's going to last. Anyway, you're a wealthy woman.' Again there was a cutting edge to the remark.

She was not sure what Charles really thought of the increase in her salary and her twenty per cent holding in the company. In the beginning he had appeared to be pleased. Now perhaps he was jealous that she had received anything at all. Perhaps he felt it gave her too much power, too much independence. She recognised this as a danger area in their relationship in which she would have to tread carefully.

She fitted back quickly into the pattern of life. She rose early, saw to the distribution of the work and dealt with any problems that might have arisen during the night: sick or injured birds, the incubator heaters – they were a continual headache – a leaking roof, wind-damage, a thousand things that needed decisions. Then she would come back to the house for breakfast. At first, Charles had joined her, in his dressing-gown, but this soon stopped and she found herself breakfasting alone while Lena took a tray up to Master Charles. Sometimes he did not get up until ten o'clock. This had the inevitable result of keeping him wide awake as midnight approached, while Kate was limp with exhaustion. Sometimes he would play the Victrola and she would pretend to read, but her eyes would droop. When she wanted to go to bed, he wanted her to stay up, he wanted company, he did not want to be alone.

When he did get up in the mornings, he took over her office. In the time he had spent at Saxenburg before their marriage, he had often worked there, but there had been a clear, though unspoken, understanding that he was borrowing it. Now he installed himself. Often, when she needed to work at papers or accounts, Charles would be at the desk talking on the telephone to friends in Cape Town. He made her feel like an intruder and would sit with his hand cupped over the mouthpiece while she took what she needed and left. She found herself doing her paper-work on the big refectory table in the dining-room, surrounded by the furniture from the wrecks.

She told herself that all marriages began with periods of adjustment and said nothing, but sometimes she remembered the panic that had gripped her before the wedding. Then she had been afraid of the future; now that it had arrived, she no longer felt the panic, but she did often feel worried. She wondered if the fact that she was living in the same house as her mother-in-law contributed to these difficulties. Given the choice, she would have liked to start in a place of her own. But she had not had the choice and there was no point in brooding about it. So she kept her peace while Charles's breakfast trays were taken up to him, while he talked and drank and wanted her to play Lexicon or poker or gin-rummy into the small hours; she smiled when she went to her office and saw him with his feet on the desk and the telephone in his hand.

At dinner one night, he said, 'You know, we could run another two or three hundred birds if we had more water.'

She was delighted to talk to him about the farm. He had often seemed bored by it and she had felt that if she could draw him into a shared interest much of the tension of who ran what would disappear; ideally it would be a joint enterprise. She had once herself mentioned the lack of water to Smuts and he had shrugged and said, 'Talk to the old man up there, my friend,' pointing to the heavens. The problem was that all the rain came in winter, but the ground was sandy and it soon disappeared so that in the hot, windy summer months it was not there when it was needed.

'If we put in a dozen or more bore-holes and windmills we should be able to run birds *and* irrigate more lucerne,' Charles said.

For several days he consulted farming books and magazines and made telephone calls and talked to people in Helmsdale.

Then Smuts got wind of it. 'Do you think we haven't tried to find water?' he said to Kate. 'We've tried all over the place. There's no underground water here.'

When Kate told Charles, he said, 'Smutsy isn't running the place any more. We are.'

A week later a traction-engine trundled onto the farm towing a drilling-rig and set up in the north camp. For a month Kate listened to the thud-thud-thud of the distant engine working all the hours of daylight, except when a bit was lost down the hole. Altogether the rig's owner tried in seven different places, lost two bits and part of his drilling gear, before Charles called it off.

During that month, Kate did not protest, but when the bill came in, it was enormous. Charles had signed a contract at a high rate per foot, whether water was found or not. He had also undertaken to pay for any damage to the machine.

'Bloody fool,' Smuts said. 'Any kid knows how easy it is to lose the bits and how expensive they are. You *never* stand to pay for lost or broken gear. That's the owner's responsibility.'

When Kate spoke to Charles about the cost he said, 'You're putting it through the farm account, aren't you?' as though this was some magical way of conjuring money from the air.

Kate waited for Mrs. Preller to send for her, because she went over the books with a fine comb once a week, but no summons came.

This was only one of several occasions when Charles either tried to make changes in the farm or questioned Kate's decisions, which meant appealing to Smuts, the repository of knowledge. Invariably, she was proved right, and it was in this atmosphere that they had their first major row.

One raw and misty day after a frustrating morning when things had been going wrong, and with the thud of the boring-machine in her ears, she was not in the best of moods when she came in to lunch.

Charles was wearing a new tweed suit he'd had made in Cape Town on their honeymoon and was looking very elegant. Dr. du Toit had dropped in to see Mrs. Preller and the two men were having a sherry in the drawing-room. In her work-clothes, Kate felt dowdy by comparison with them.

'I hope you'll stay for lunch,' she said, accepting a sherry, and really hoping the contrary.

'No, no, thank you,' du Toit said, smiling his dimpled smile. His mane of silver hair shone in the light from the window and he looked huge, dwarfing Charles.

'I only dropped in for this.' He held up his glass. 'I use

Augusta as an excuse. I hear your coloured boy, Jonas, is back.'

'Here? In Helmsdale?' Charles said.

'Ja. He came back last night.'

'That must mean the magistrate's hearing is soon.'

'Next month, they say. They brought him back early because the gaol has been strengthened. They say the cement had rotted round the bars and he could have pulled them out with his bare hands. Now there are new bars.'

She and Charles saw him to his motor.

'What do you think of Jonas's lawyer?' Kate said.

'Stoltz? I wouldn't want him if I was Jonas. But what difference does it make?'

He started the engine and drove off.

'What difference!' she repeated angrily.

'He's right. We don't want one of those attorneys from Cape Town coming out and getting him off.'

Kate clamped her lips together and walked into the house with long, agitated strides.

Smuts had been to town and had brought back the leather post pouch with the day's mail. Charles sorted through it and gave her a pile of circulars. They opened the envelopes as they ate.

'What the hell's all this about?' he said, and tossed a letter across the table to her. She glanced at the letterhead: ISIDORE MENDEL & CO. *Importers of Exotic Feathers.* Then she saw the first line: '*Dear Miss Buchanan,*' and felt a surge of anger.

'This was addressed to me,' she said.

'What does it matter?'

'A great deal.'

'It had Mendel's name on the envelope. I knew it had to be farm business. What the hell's it all about anyway? You never told me anything about this.'

'It was addressed to me. It was my private letter. I will not have you opening my mail.'

'Why? Have you got something to hide?'

'Don't be silly.'

'I can't see what you're getting all lashed up about. There's nothing private in a letter from Mendel. Anyway, it's just as well I did see it. This isn't the way you do business. Gentleman's agreement! What the hell's the use of that? This is farm business and we run the farm.'

There was a heart-beat's pause, and then she plunged. '*We* don't run the farm. *I* run the farm. I've been running it for months, with Mr. Smuts's help. I'm paid to run it.'

'Hang on . . .' A shutter seemed to drop behind his eyes, but it was too late to stop and she was too angry to care.

'No, you hang on. If you want to run the farm, then say so. *You* get up at six in the morning and tell the boys what to do. *You* make all the decisions. And *you* take the responsibility if anything goes wrong.' She had risen and was standing by her chair.

'Who the hell do you think you're talking to?' He rose to face her. 'You do this and you do that. Whose fucking farm do you think it is, anyway? It's not yours just because I gave you my name!'

She refused to be led away from the central issue into areas where they could do permanent harm to each other.

'I want to know what you propose to do.'

'Do? What the hell are you talking about?'

'I want to know if you're going to run the farm. Because if you are, you'd better think about some changes. Like who is going to get you up in the morning. You can't run a property like this and have breakfast in bed.' She shook the letter at him. 'And don't you ever open one of my letters again.'

There was rage and violence in his eyes, but she turned and walked out of the room. She went into the drawing-room and lit a cigarette with shaking hands, expecting him to come bursting in, but instead she heard him go up the stairs. He would be going to his mother for clarification, she thought. Well, that's what they all needed.

She opened the letter again and forced herself to concentrate. Mendel had thought over her idea of forming a direct link between his firm and Saxenburg, but felt he could not commit himself to the formation of a formal and binding contract because of the price fluctuations and uncertainty arising from the Anti-Plumage Bill. Then he went on: 'But having said that, I confess I am attracted to the idea of a link between two of the oldest and, may I say, best of the feather organisations. How would you consider a gentleman's agreement on the lines discussed when I drank such lovely hock at Saxenburg?'

She read the letter twice more. It was long and there were several paragraphs about safeguards on both sides which she would need to think about. But its main thrust was that the idea was feasible in the form Mendel described. She felt a thrill of pleasure in the knowledge that it had been her idea.

Above her, she heard a door slam and Charles's footsteps on the stairs. Now that she'd had her say she suddenly felt ashamed of having lost her temper and went into the hall to apologise. But he was already out of the house and she heard the roadster's engine cough into life.

She sent the letter up to Mrs. Preller and went out into the misty afternoon to inspect one of the gates, which had been hit by a lorry.

Mrs. Preller asked for her in mid-afternoon. As she went up the staircase she felt a fluttering in her stomach. It was caused, not by apprehension, but by anticipation. She had never had a row with Mrs. Preller and did not wish to have one, but if the old woman was sending for her to reprimand her or to take Charles's side, she was ready for a fight. For the first time, she realised how strong her position was now in comparison with when she had first come to Saxenburg.

Mrs. Preller was sitting in the half-darkness of the room, with Smuts beside her. She motioned Kate to another chair.

'This is very interesting,' she said, holding up the letter. 'Mendel seems to have taken a fancy to you.'

'It must have been the wine,' Kate said.

'Well, what do you think? It was your idea.'

Kate relaxed, realising there would be no conflict. 'It sounds exciting. All our feathers taken at a fixed price near the top of the market, not subject to fluctuation except after certain time limits. He knows the price, we know the price. It allows us both to plan for the future.'

'He also talks about the contract with Johnson & Co.,

for feather dusters. That means he'd take all our fine feathers *and* most of the 'chicken' feathers. He also says that with the new dyes even the poorer feathers are finding a market.' She paused, and looked at Smuts. 'What if something goes wrong?'

'You mean this "gentleman's agreement?" No, Miss Augusta, I would trust old Mendel completely.'

'Yes, yes, he's trustworthy enough. I mean, what if something went wrong and he couldn't take the quantity?'

'We could sell on the market again, or let Rothenstein in Paris take the whole lot. He asked us before, you remember.'

'He's harder to please than Mendel and he was always a bad payer. Still, we'd get rid of everything to him.'

They talked for another hour, then Mrs. Preller let Smuts go. When he had closed the door, she said, 'I don't see you as much as I used to now that Charles and Smuts are here to drive me. Are things well?'

'On the farm? I think so. I take Mr. Smuts round once a week.'

'Yes, yes, I know about the farm. Smuts reports to me. You have done well. That I know. That is why you are paid so much. No, not with the farm, with you?'

'I'm just fine.'

'I'm glad. It is nice that things are working as they should.' She stopped, but as Kate stood up to go she said, 'It is difficult for Charles, you know.'

'Yes, I know.'

'He has always had women around who gave in to him.'

'You? That's hard to believe.'

'Sometimes.' The thin vermilion lips twisted into a smile. It was a knowing smile and Kate carried the impression of it in her mind as she closed the door. Later she wondered about it: it was as though they had shared a secret, come to an understanding, forged a bond. But then another thought had come to her: Charles was better at business than farming. Why did Mrs. Preller not let him take over some of the company's business affairs?

She was in bed when he came back. She heard him stumbling about the bedroom, but pretended to be asleep.

When he got in beside her she could smell the brandy on his breath and assumed he had spent the time in the hotel's bar.

She did not see him the following morning, but he sat down to lunch with her. They hardly spoke. Her impulse of the previous day to apologise evaporated under the pressure of his mood, instead she talked as if there had been no row at all. But he asked Lena for the *Cape Times* and sat reading it ostentatiously.

Halfway through lunch he tapped the paper and said, 'There's a paragraph about Jonas. The magistrates' hearing starts on the twelfth. Typical of this bloody place that you have to read about it in a Cape Town newspaper.' She waited for him to continue, but he put the paper down and went out to the office. She picked it up and looked for the paragraph. As her eyes skimmed the columns they were caught by another heading: BRITISH JOURNALIST LEAVES CAPE TOWN.

She read the story:

Mr. Tom Austen, correspondent in Cape Town for the London *Chronicle*, returned to Britain in the *Glendower Castle* yesterday.

He arrived a year ago with his wife, Joyce, and lived at Kenilworth.

It is believed that his return is a result of his wife's death some weeks ago, after a short illness.

Mr. Austen has written several highly-regarded books of travel and politics, notably about the East. He was also a well-known war correspondent.

He was the only newspaper reporter to land with the first wave of troops at Gallipoli.

It is unknown yet who his replacement will be.

She sat, staring numbly at the black print until her eyes filled with tears and the page became grey. Joyce dead. A short illness. Some weeks ago. The phrases went round and round in her head.

She remembered with clarity Lena saying, 'A Mr. Easton.'

She had never returned his call because she could not, at that moment, have borne to hear his voice. But had he been calling to tell her of Joyce's death or to wish her well? No, he had said it was urgent. She was to telephone him urgently. It *had* to be Joyce.

What if she had telephoned? What if he had told her then, an hour before her marriage? Would it have changed anything? Duggie would still have needed the money, so would her father and mother. She didn't know ... she couldn't tell ... And now he was at sea. The ship was sailing slowly up the African coast, each minute taking him farther and farther away. This time the feeling of panic was real. It caught her in the throat. As long as he had been only a few hours away from her, she had felt safe, but now ... She wondered if she would ever see him again and felt she could hardly bear it if the answer was no.

A few days later Smuts came back from town. 'You'd never credit it,' he said to Kate as she took the mail pouch.

'What?'

'Bloody fools.' He was clearly upset.

'Who?'

'Some bloody idiot tried to kill Jonas last night. Poured petrol into his cell and then threw in a match.'

'Petrol!'

'Ja. You know they strengthened the cell window? Well, they still haven't put the glass in, so it was easy.'

'Is he badly hurt?'

'They say not. They say he was sleeping under his blankets, head and all, when it happened. He got burnt on the arms, but not too badly.'

'It's a terrible thing to have done!'

'They never bloody learn, my friend, never. When they had him here before, there was trouble. You remember the bonfire down in the harbour? Now they're at it again. Christ ... I don't know!'

Kate brooded about this all day. There were two pictures of Jonas which haunted her: his arrest, when the police had overpowered him on the farm; and the sight of him on her wedding-day, bursting in from the street, rain on his face, looking more like an animal than a human-being. She could not get it out of her mind that everyone considered him guilty and that the hearing and the trial that would follow at the Supreme Court in Cape Town would be mere formalities. Everyone seemed to have made up their minds that Jonas not only would hang, but deserved to hang. The following day, she decided to try to see him and find out whether he would like a new lawyer. She told no-one.

The little gaol-cum-police station stood on a rocky outcrop on the landward side of the town, with just enough distance between it and the first houses to produce a sense of isolation. It was a single-storey building of brown mountain stone with a red corrugated-iron roof. Half-a-dozen gum trees had been planted to give it shade, but now in winter, against the brown landscape and the grey sky, it was a cheerless place.

Sergeant Van Blerk was working at an old, ink-stained desk when she entered and asked to see Jonas.

'Jonas Koopman?' He rose and came to the counter. His heavy body bulged under the dark blue winter uniform. 'What for, Mrs. Preller?'

Kate was still a new enough bride to find herself surprised when called 'Mrs. Preller', and was only beginning to get used to the fact that people did not mean her mother-in-law.

'I want to see if he needs anything.'

'He's got everything.'

'I want to find out how he is after being burned.'

'He's all right.'

'Sergeant Van Blerk, Jonas is a Saxenburg employee, or was, and I wish to see him.'

He gave in suddenly. 'I'll tell you one thing, he's dangerous. Keep away from the bars.'

The gaol was split into two. In the main house was a single cell reserved for white prisoners, but there had been no white prisoners for the past twelve years and it was used as a store-room. The non-white cells were outside and round the back of the police station. Three of them comprised a small block with a flat roof on which the Sergeant's pumpkins were stored. They reminded Kate of stables. The barred doors opened onto a narrow concrete passageway. Each had a window on the far side. The first two cells were empty, Jonas was in the third. There were black burn marks on the walls near the window. He was lying on his bunk on a mattress which consisted of a single piece of dark blue felt about two inches thick. He had his blanket up to his neck, but his bandaged arms were in full view.

'Jonas,' she said.

He had been looking at the roof of the cell and now his eyes dropped to peer at Kate. His face had become thin and his cheeks sunken. His eyes were red-rimmed and curiously unfocussed.

'Jonas, I've come to see if there's anything we can do for you.'

The eyes shifted away from her, back to the ceiling.

'He hasn't spoken for weeks,' Van Blerk said.

'Perhaps he would if you weren't here.'

Van Blerk shrugged. 'Okay. I'll go to the end of the passage. Don't go near the bars. He's very quick, that one.'

She waited until he had walked away, then she said, 'Jonas, is there anything you need?'

He ignored her.

'Are you satisfied with your lawyer, or would you like me to find you another one?'

Silence.

'Jonas, won't you let me try to help you? Everyone thinks you killed Miss Miriam. I don't know whether you did or not, because they haven't tried you yet.'

Slowly, he turned his back on her.

'Jonas, no one else will help you.'

She stood there in the chilly winter morning for a few minutes longer, but he did not move, and finally she left.

She went to see Arnold Leibowitz, Mr. Sachs' solicitor. She had to wait fifteen minutes while he dealt with another client, then she was shown into his office. Leibowitz uncoiled his long frame and rose from behind his desk.

'I haven't seen you to congratulate you,' he said, taking her hand. 'I hope you'll be very happy.'

'Thank you.' She told him briefly why she had come.

He ran his fingers through his short, wiry black hair and said, 'I'm not sure how I can help you. I mean, you say the boy didn't speak. In other words, he didn't ask for another lawyer. Anyway, you know I couldn't do anything, even if I wanted to, because of Morris Sachs.'

'Of course. I just wondered if you know someone better than this Mr. Stoltz.'

Leibowitz studied his finger-nails and did not answer.

'Isn't there something called a watching brief?' she said. 'Couldn't I hire a lawyer to attend the hearing and advise me, or Mr. Stoltz, or both of us if things were going wrong? It's just that I feel Jonas is ... well, that it's all settled. Helmsdale thinks he did it, and that's that.'

'Helmsdale can think what it likes. It's the Supreme Court in Cape Town that has the say.' He paused. 'But if you really wanted to ...'

'Do you think I'm being stupid?'

'No, not at all. I agree. As far as everyone here is concerned, he's ready for the gallows.'

'It seems so unfair.'

He looked up at her from under his eyebrows. 'It's easy to see you're a new arrival, Mrs. Preller. Fairness? For coloureds? But there is someone, an attorney called Brinkman over at Bredasdorp. He might agree to come. He won't be cheap. But at least if the boy is sent for trial you can then get him for the Supreme Court and he'll brief counsel in Cape Town.'

She left Leibowitz to make the contact and went back to Saxenburg. The cost worried her. Charles's joke about her being a wealthy woman did not bear much examination, not after the money for her family had been taken out. And there would be no dividends until the summer, when the feathers were sold.

She decided to say nothing about her plans either to Mrs. Preller or to Charles, but she needed someone to talk to, so she went to Smuts.

'I wouldn't spread it about if I were you,' he said. He seemed to search for words. 'People talk, you know.'

'Talk?'

'You've been here less than a year. You're running the farm, you've married the heir to the biggest property in the district. They're waiting to see what changes you're going to make. They're interested in you. You can't blame them. You're news, my friend.'

'They can't have much else to talk about.'

'It's a small town. This murder's the biggest thing that's ever happened here.'

'Let them talk, then!' Kate said angrily.

Jerry and Freda came for the week-end. They arrived before lunch on Saturday in driving rain. It was clear that they'd had a row on the way.

Freda told Kate about it when she went upstairs to change. 'He's always like this now,' she said. 'Arguing, shouting.' Kate watched her as she took off her long fur coat and cloche hat and combed her cropped hair. She looked as smart as paint, and with her pale colouring, smoky grey eyes and her thin, elegantly-dressed figure, she was more beautiful than ever.

'The road's cut from the rain. And, all right, I did get stuck in the diversion. It wasn't my fault. The wheels went round and round. Jerry had to push, and you'd think the end of the world had come. Then he wanted *me* to get out and push!'

In the afternoon the two men went out in the rain to play golf. Freda talked endlessly about Jerry. At first Kate was amused, but finally it became boring and she was glad when Jerry and Charles came back, even though they were argumentative and frustrated because the weather had stopped them after a few holes.

The afternoon dragged on, with games of cards and Lexicon, and she was relieved when it was time to bathe and change for dinner. They all drank too much during the meal and after they'd had coffee and Tilly had cleared away, Jerry said, 'What are we going to do now?'

He was like a child, Kate thought, needing constant entertainment.

'What about carpet bowls?' Charles suggested.

The game started slowly, but became increasingly energetic. Woods were rolled under furniture, chairs were shifted, they laughed a great deal, shouted, argued about points.

Suddenly, at the height of the game, there was a loud knocking at the front door.

'I'll go,' Charles said. 'Watch Jerry and don't let him cheat.'

Kate went to the drawing-room door as he opened the big main door. The rain was lashing down. He stepped back and was followed in by a figure in dripping oilskins, holding a rifle.

It was Sergeant Van Blerk. They spoke for a moment, then Charles said, 'Jonas has escaped.'

'You mean that coloured who's up for murder?' Jerry said.

'Ja.' Van Blerk shook water off his hands. 'He got away a couple of hours ago when he was given his food. Usually two constables take it, but it's Saturday and one was off duty. The bugger jumped my man. Gave him a hit here at the back of the neck that's put him into hospital.'

'We haven't seen or heard a thing,' Charles said. 'Is he armed?'

'No, thank God. What about your people?'

'Smuts is asleep and I'm not going to disturb my mother.'

'I'm talking about the servants.'

'I'll get them together in the shed.'

He hurried out, followed by Kate and Jerry, with lanterns. A police vehicle stood in the drive. There were two constables in the front seat, holding carbines. As Kate passed the rear she could see several tracker dogs jumping up at the wire mesh of the sides.

The farm-workers assembled in the incubator shed. In the lantern light, their faces were apprehensive, their eyes wide. There were about thirty of them, including children, some of the tiny ones still wiping the sleep from their eyes.

Van Blerk climbed up on a box, big and menacing in his oilskins. Kate saw that most of the servants were looking apprehensively at the gun.

'Have any of you people seen Jonas Koopman? he said.

No one answered. Lena was standing next to Tilly. Her eyes were frightened and Kate wondered if she feared Jonas's retribution for what she had told the magistrate at the inquest.

'He's got away from the cells. If any of you see him, you tell me. You understand? *Verstaan julle?*'

There were mutterings of 'Ja, master,' and then he stepped down. 'Okay,' he said to Charles. 'You keep them here while we search their houses.'

The search was quickly over, and they were allowed to return to bed. Charles said, 'Where are you off to now?'

'Up the road. He might be making for the mountains.'

'We'll come with you. Jerry, let's get the guns.' Charles's eyes were alight.

In a matter of minutes, they were back, each carrying a gun. Van Blerk looked at Charles's rifle. 'You hit him with that and there'll be nothing left to hang.' Jerry was loading a shot-gun with buckshot.

Kate followed Charles as he went to fetch his heavy coat. 'Why are you taking a gun?' she said.

'Because I'm going to shoot the bugger.'

'Leave that to the police! That's their job.'

'You heard what the sergeant said. Jonas has injured a cop as well.' He pushed past her. 'Hey, Jerry, we'll go in my car. It's faster than yours. Ten quid to whoever sees him first.'

Jerry slapped the butt of his shot-gun and laughed as he climbed into the car. There was a roar as the lorry and the car started together, then they disappeared through the driving rain along the cliff road.

Kate and Freda stood in the doorway and watched the lights flicker in the distance.

'They're like children with a new game,' Kate said.

She and Freda looked at newspapers and magazines as they waited for the men to return.

'Didn't you know Tom Austen?' Freda said idly.

'Yes. Why?'

'He left this week.'

She had tried to put Tom out of her mind and she did not want to talk about him now.

'It was sad about his wife,' Freda went on.

'Yes.'

'Probably for the best, though. We heard about . . .'

Kate stood up abruptly. 'I'm going to bed.'

She was aware of Freda's eyes on her as she left the room, but she did not care.

She was asleep when Charles returned about three, but he switched on the light and woke her. He was wet and muddy.

'Did you catch him?' she said.

'Didn't see a bloody thing. We'll get him tomorrow, though.'

When he climbed into bed beside her she could feel he was tumescent. She had made a pact with herself when she had made up her mind to marry him that her part of the bargain would be never to refuse him if she could help it, never to have a headache, never to be feeling too tired. So now, as he put his arms around her, she lifted her nightdress and slid under him. There was no love in this mating, nor love play; it was, for him, fierce and cathartic and soon over, leaving him lying limply on her. She felt his weight increase and heard the regularity of his breathing and knew he was asleep. After a few minutes she gently turned him on his side and got up.

She stood for some moments by the window. The rain had stopped and the moon had come out from behind a bank of heavy cloud. She wondered where Jonas was. Could he have come back to Saxenburg? Could he be hiding somewhere on the property? After all, he knew it better than almost anyone else. Could he be here in the house? She shivered. In one way, she wanted him caught, but in another, she wanted him to stay free. She would never have been able to explain that to anyone and it was hard to explain it to herself. She had thought of Jonas as a caged animal. But wasn't Saxenburg a cage, too? Hadn't it caged Mrs. Preller? And Smuts? Was it her cage, too?

The following morning after breakfast she went into town with Jerry and Charles. Freda stayed in bed. A knot of whites had collected down at the harbour. Most of them were carrying guns, either rifles or shot-guns. She recognised the manager of the hotel, and Mr. Hamilton from the bank, carrying a walking stick. Dr. du Toit came up to them. He was dressed in a corduroy jacket, gum-boots and a trilby hat. He carried a rifle on his arm.

'They're searching the village,' he said, pointing up to the white-washed houses of the coloured fishing village. A crowd of coloured people stood at one end of the village and watched the police and the dogs go through the houses. 'There's going to be trouble if they don't find him soon.'

A police-car came bouncing down the main street, sending up splashes of muddy water each time it hit a pot-hole. Van Blerk emerged and blew a whistle, summoning the police back from the village.

'What's happening?' du Toit said. 'Are we still going through the old ostrich houses?'

Van Blerk shook his head. 'He's been seen on the Agulhas road. Old Dr. Richards was fishing down there early this morning and saw him near the road.'

The police ran back with their dogs and people started getting into cars and revving up the engines.

Charles said, 'Jerry, you go with Hennie du Toit. I'll follow. There's something I want to do first.' They watched the cars follow each other in a line up the main street and then take the left fork towards Cape Agulhas.

'Why aren't you going with them?' Kate said.

'If they believe old Richards, they'll believe pigs can fly. He can't see across the bloody road, never mind recognise anyone. No, I'll have a look around the ostrich houses. When I woke this morning I was thinking what I'd do if I was Jonas. I wouldn't go too far. He knows this area well. He can get food from the coloureds in the village. It's safer for him here, then when everyone is looking for him somewhere else, he can slip out of the district. Come on, you drive.'

He made her stop at each of the old ostrich houses on the cliff road but, to her relief, told her to stay outside in the road with the engine running. It took him nearly two hours to satisfy himself that there was no one hiding either in the rooms or the ruined gardens.

She drove back slowly along the cliff tops. Charles searched the sea shore through his binoculars. It was about noon when they reached Saxenburg. They were leaving the car when Charles said thoughtfully, 'I wonder if the bugger would try it?' He was staring down at the cove with its jumble of rocks and rock pools. He pulled the gun from the dickey, checked the magazine and went down the cliff path. Kate watched as he crossed the sand and began searching among the rocks. Slowly, she followed.

The storm of the night before had died away, but the waves were still restless and crashed on the India Reef. In a few hours everything would be calm once more. As usual after rain and high tides the beach was clean and white, as though someone had come along, picked up all the flotsam and then smoothed it over. She took off her shoes. The sand was cold underfoot.

Charles was about a hundred yards ahead of her, making for the far point. She had not been down to the cove for weeks. She walked on past the rock pools, remembering that hot summer morning when she had found Miriam, and thinking that nothing ever really ends. Here she was, still part of the chain of circumstances which had begun in these rock pools. Men were driving all over the Cape Agulhas area for the same reason. And somewhere in Cape Town an old Jew was waiting for an Old Testament revenge for his daughter's murder.

She saw Charles suddenly stop and drop down into a crouch. He rose and looked right, then left, and behind him. He ran back towards her.

'What is it?'

'I think he's around somewhere. I've just seen footprints.'

The line of prints came from the broken cliffside behind the beach and went in a straight line towards the far point. They were prints of bare feet. She put her own foot next to one. It was much larger than hers. For the first time she felt afraid.

'Where do you think he is?' She found herself whispering.

'I know damn well where he is. Or where he went, anyway. He made for the sea cave. But that might have been sometime last night or early this morning when the rain stopped. Otherwise we wouldn't see the footprints.'

'Or when the tide went out.'

'What time are the tides today?'

'I don't know, but it looks as if it's already turned.'

'You stay here.'

She watched him walk slowly towards the point where the sea cave was. He did not approach it in a direct line, but started to climb the headland on the landward side. This had collapsed over the millennia due to the battering of the sea and rocks had piled on each other in an unplanned mass.

He moved towards the tunnel entrance to the cave from above. For a moment, she thought he was going to crawl through the narrow opening, but he stopped just above it, put down his gun and began to heave at a small boulder. Although she was fifty yards away she could almost see the strain on his face and hear the breath whistling from his lungs. The stone moved, rolled and stopped, blocking the opening. Now the only way out of the cave was through the mouth which gave onto the sea. He jumped down until he was level with the blocked opening, and shouted. She could not make out the words. Then he climbed one of the rocks from which Jonas used to fish, which gave a partial view of the farthest section of the headland.

She climbed up beside him. He was lying on his stomach, with the rifle at his side. She realised that anyone coming out of the sea cave would be visible.

'What are you going to do?' she said.

'I'm going to wait for the tide to come in.'

'But he'll drown.'

'He doesn't have to drown. He can come out now. I told him so.'

'If he comes out, will you shoot him?'

'He can give himself up.'

'He'll be terrified. He probably thinks you'll kill him anyway.'

'For Christ's sake, I'm not even sure he's in there.'

The sea was still high from the night before, but the waves were coming in evenly, big, silky green swells that gathered as they slid towards the beach, arcing and arching until the leading edge dropped in a welter of foam and turbulence. Each wave crept slightly farther up the beach and, she knew, farther into the sea cave.

They waited in silence for half an hour, then she said, 'You're treating him like an animal! You're making a sport out of it.'

He turned, and there was anger on his face. 'If you don't want to stay, then don't. But for Christ's sake, don't tell me what to do.'

She climbed down the rock. Already the water was lapping around it.

'It's nearly lunch-time.'

'I don't want any lunch.'

She walked back along the beach and climbed the cliff path. At the top, she stopped and looked back. He had not moved.

She went into the house and made herself a sandwich, but could not eat it. Freda was still in bed so she went out onto the big verandah. She was too far away to see Charles. Like a rabbit drawn to a snake, she returned to the top of the cliff path and sat down on the thin turf. She could think of no way of stopping whatever plan he had for capturing Jonas.

One hour passed, then another. The tide rose higher and higher, the foamy water reaching farther up the beach. In the cave, it would already be waist-deep. By mid-afternoon she could stand it no longer and ran down the path and across the beach.

'You've got to stop this!' she called. 'Charles, let him out! If you don't, I'll get the boys from the farm to come and roll the boulder away!'

'Mind your own fucking business! If you bring any of the boys I'll . . .'

She heard a shout and turned to see Jerry and Dr. du Toit coming across the sand.

'Did you find him?' Charles said.

'No. Have you seen him?' du Toit said.

'I saw footprints. I think he's in the sea cave.'

'The water must be up to his neck by . . .'

A cry like a seabird's came over the water to them and suddenly Jonas was visible in the water at the tip of the headland. He was two hundred yards from them. They could see his arms raised above his head. Charles lifted the rifle. Kate grabbed at it. They wrestled for a moment and then she was half deafened by an explosion. She turned and saw that du Toit had already sighted along his rifle barrel as Jerry loaded his shot-gun. Du Toit squeezed off another shot.

'Stop it! Stop it! she cried.

Du Toit slowly lowered the rifle. His face was white and his hands were shaking.

Jonas was struggling in the crashing breakers as the undertow pulled him out to sea.

'The current's taking him to the reef,' Charles said.

'He'll drown before he gets there,' du Toit said. 'The sharks will get him.'

The men all had binoculars and they watched the bobbing head, dark against the white of the foam and the green of the swells.

'He's finished,' Jerry said. 'He's not even trying any more.'

'Ja. He's finished,' du Toit said.

Kate could barely make out the black dot of the head as it receded farther and farther towards the reef where the waves struck and the spume rose in the air.

Then Charles said, 'Are you sure he's finished? He seems to be moving sideways.'

'Hes not swimming,' Jerry said.

'Then a current's caught him.'

The body began to move parallel with the beach. They watched it for more than an hour, until it was in a direct line with their rock.

'Christ, he's coming in!' Charles said.

'He's dead,' Jerry said.

'Then he's being washed in.'

Slowly, inexorably, the body came towards them. They

watched, hypnotised. As it floated closer, Kate could see that no life remained. It was washed one way, then the next at the whim of the sea.

Finally, it reached the outer rock wall of the far pool. A wave lifted it and rolled it, then receded. It lay amid the barnacles and mussels. The next wave broke and pushed it a little farther. The next, farther still. Finally, it slithered into the pool. It moved through the channels until it reached the last pool of all and bumped against the rocks. There was nowhere farther to go.

[7]

The death of Jonas put an end to a chapter in Helmsdale life. The rape and murder of a white woman by a coloured man had never occurred there before and it was devoutly hoped that it never would again. It was considered that the peculiar and grotesque circumstances of the murderer's death were almost as effective a deterrent as if he had been tried and hanged; better in some ways, since the trial and the hanging would have taken place in Cape Town, whereas now people believed that the manner and place of his death indicated that the society in which the crime had occurred, had caused justice to be done.

The town, after discussing the matter for a little over a week, gradually forgot about it and went on with its own business of making money in the feather boom.

But if it was the end of the affair as far as Helmsdale was concerned, it was not so for Kate. What she had seen had disturbed her profoundly. Her own background could hardly have been described as gentle, but what violence she knew had resulted from drink, or poverty, or over-crowding. The manhunt and death of Jonas was something outside her experience. There had been a matter-of-factness about its acceptance that she could hardly credit. Since her arrival from Scotland she had felt, without personal evidence, a latent violence in Africa, a harshness in the light, the landscape, the lives of many of its people. Now she had seen for herself how quickly and extremely violence could break through.

Underlining this feeling, she became aware of stories in the newspapers that she had not seemed to notice before: murders, rapes, assaults, reported almost every morning.

What had shocked her most was Charles's part in the affair. Although he had not fired his rifle – in fact, it was discovered that no bullets had hit Jonas, he had drowned – she held him basically responsible for the death. She fought the feeling, telling herself that Jonas was probably guilty of murder and would have been hanged in any case, that his attack on the policeman indicated how violent he was, that she had seen that same violence in his eyes before, and, finally, that Charles had shouted into the cave, telling him to give himself up. In spite of telling herself all this, she was unable to exonerate her husband.

The reason, she decided finally, was that he had made a kind of contest out of it. He had sent Jerry away with the police while he had stayed behind, his feeling for landscape and the psychology of the hunted telling him that Jonas was somewhere near. Then, when he had him cornered, it was as though he had tried to force him to run, to add to the excitement of the hunt. When Jerry had arrived, she had felt that they were in competition, as they had been when they had hit golf balls out to sea. Who would be the first to wing Jonas?

Not everyone, she was pleased to discover, shared the general triumph and support for the hunters. 'What a bloody example to the rest of us,' Smuts had said contemptuously when he heard what had happened. 'With these young buggers growing up, you wonder what's going to happen to the bloody country.'

For the moment he seemed to have forgotten that she was married to one of these young buggers, but she said nothing, for she agreed with him. However, it occurred to her that the only person who had actually fired a shot was not young and he was a respected member of the community, supposedly dedicated to saving lives.

There were others in town, including Leibowitz, the

hotel-manager, Van Staden and even Mr. Hamilton, the bank-manager, who had gone man-hunting with a walking stick, who disliked the way things had gone. Lena, Tilly and the farm-workers kept their feelings to themselves, and the fishing-village was quieter than usual.

Although Kate managed to recover her equilibrium after a few days, she found that her attitude to Charles had changed. If she had not been in love when she married him, at least she had been fond of him. Now even this had been eroded and replaced by a feeling of coolness. Nevertheless, she kept her side of her own bargain, and when he wanted her in bed, she gave herself to him; she was compliant, but uninvolved. She knew it was not the best recipe for marriage, but told herself that things might have been worse, for he seemed chastened by what had happened and by her reaction to it. He kept out of her way when he could and was more than usually considerate. Jerry and Freda had disappeared back to Cape Town and it was a week or two before she saw Dr. du Toit. He gave no sign that he even recalled his part in the affair, treating her with the same friendliness, the same rather overblown graciousness as he usually did. Eventually, even in her mind the memory of Jonas faded and became, with Miriam's death, part of the past pattern of her life at Saxenburg.

And that life was thrusting on as it always did, carrying her with it. The farm could not stop for deaths or for anything else. The birds needed attention, eggs were laid and incubated, chicks hatched and grew, feathers grew, were plucked, were sorted, were shipped. Winter turned to spring; summer arrived and the whole cycle of farm life began once more.

The demand for feathers showed no signs of slackening. Kate now subscribed to all the major fashion and society magazines and would go through them every time the mail-ship arrived, watching for any sign of change but, if anything, interest seemed to be increasing. Pictures of dinner parties and garden parties given by the Rockefellers and the Vanderbilts in New York and by Lady Cunard and Lady Londonderry in London, showed ostrich feathers worn as stoles, trimming dresses, carried as fans. They were everywhere.

The new arrangement with Mendel worked well and was her personal triumph. She was able to increase profits by nearly twenty per cent so that when the three directors sat down and discussed the affairs of the company, of which the farm formed a part, they were able to vote themselves cash dividends which Kate had never thought to earn in her life. She sent part to her family, put some into gilt-edged stocks on the advice of the bank manager, and still had enough left over to buy herself several new outfits in Cape Town.

One late afternoon when the heat of the day had gone, she and Mrs. Preller were walking in the ruined garden.

'Don't you think it is time to do something about this?' Mrs. Preller said suddenly.

Kate looked at the tennis court and the old swimming-pool with grass and weeds growing from the cracks. It would be nice to have a pool, she thought, for she would never swim in the rock pools again and the open sea was too dangerous. The tennis court had formed the basis of her earlier fantasies, she remembered, of week-end parties with friends from Cape Town, but contact with Jerry and Freda had cured her of those.

'It is a garden for young people,' Mrs. Preller said. 'One day there will be young people here again.' She linked her arm in Kate's and they strolled slowly along the path. 'You've done well, my dear. Very well. Better than I could have hoped. Even Smuts was doubtful, though he likes you very much.'

'I couldn't have done it without him.'

'That is true, but maybe it takes a little of a man's pride to see how well a woman can do his job. With Hennie du Toit, it was different. He said to me that a woman could not do it. He thought I would give it all to Charles. I said, "Hennie, I have run the estate, farm businesses, every-thing, since Boss Charles died, and now you come to me and tell me a woman cannot do it." You should have seen his face.'

They walked on in silence. Over the past six months,

they had grown closer. It was a strange bond, part employer-and-employee, part mother-in-law and daughter-in-law, part age and youth, and part genuine friendship, for Kate found much to admire in Mrs. Preller, not the least her strength and determination to hold onto Saxenburg when all about her the big ostrich estates had crumbled.

There was only one source of disunity and this was mainly on Kate's side. It stemmed from a phrase Mrs. Preller had used only a few moments before, and which was often on her lips: 'young people,' by which she meant her future grandchildren.

Although she never made any direct allusion to them, Kate was aware of the old woman's longings. And who could blame her? She had survived so much, both physically and mentally, that the real reward, that of seeing her grandchildren running about the house, hitting balls on the court, diving into the pool, bringing young life to what had been, when Kate arrived, an old, decaying world, should not be denied her.

Kate longed for a child herself, longed to have someone to love before it was too late and her body 'dried up', in Mrs. Preller's phrase. But all the time, in the back of her mind, was the question: had Fat Sarah damaged her in some way with her probing needles? Could she have a child? The guilt she already felt for abusing her body in the way she had was exacerbated by Mrs. Preller. She began to feel inadequate in this one, all-important area. She felt that all she could do was go on trying to conceive – but Charles was not helping much.

Their marriage jogged along and as the months passed he made fewer sexual demands on her. She wondered whether her own coolness had communicated itself to him. She tried to inject more passion into the sexual act, but it did not seem to have much effect on Charles. Had she not wanted a child so badly, she would have been relieved by his indifference.

Winter arrived again. She saw less and less of him. He had long since given up any interest in the farm and his mother still refused to allow him to deal with the business side. He was now promoting an idea of a fish-canning factory. It was to be on the same lines as Kate's arrangement with Mendel – and directly inspired by it. Fishermen caught as many fish as they could, whenever they could, and this sent prices down. Why not have a contract between them and the canning-factory whereby the factory could agree a general price with the fishermen and control the amount caught. There would be no scarcities and no gluts and the price would not fluctuate wildly.

Mrs. Preller backed him to the extent of telling him that if he could raise the capital for the building of the factory she would make a present of land near the harbour on which to build it. What she would not do was invest her own money or allow him to borrow against the farm; it had to be outside capital.

Charles seemed happy with that, and it was to raise the capital that he now spent more and more time in Cape Town. Often, when he returned, Kate thought he looked worn out and would wonder if he was getting enough to eat, or whether he was drinking too much with his business contacts.

He would stay in the Cape Town flat for four or five days at a stretch, and even then not make love to her when he returned. She would force herself to take the initiative, but often their love-making was still ineffectual, and it was in the sadness of these untender, mechanical moments that she would feel the chill dread of the future and see herself, a childless old woman moving about the dim corridors of Saxenburg without family, without even a friend like Smuts. By comparison, Mrs. Preller's situation looked positively rosy.

Her life slowly reverted to a pattern she had adopted before she was married. Whenever Charles was away she would go to Smuts' room and have her 'spots' with him. He seemed to lay great store by her evening visits and would have the brandy and water ready when she came in. 'Sundowner time!' he would say as he poured her first drink. He still smoked heavily and had a cough that shook his entire frame.

'Don't you think you should stop smoking?' Kate said once.

'Everyone's got to go,' he replied. Dr. du Toit had also advised him to give up smoking and drinking, but he said, 'You might as well take me out and shoot me.'

He loved his brandy and his cigarettes, though he could no longer hold his liquor and four or five drinks would make him almost incoherent. Kate would often leave him dozing in his chair in front of the fire.

He liked to talk about the old days when Mrs. Preller came as a young bride to Saxenburg. 'Now there was a beautiful woman. Fresh. With a white skin and pink cheeks. The sort of complexion we never see here. Everybody loved her, but she looked so sad . . .'

She was probably homesick, Kate suggested, though it was a feeling she had never known herself.

'It was more than that. You felt there was something wrong. I mean, you wondered how someone like her came to a place like this. She never complained. But you could see the sadness in her eyes. Lena knew. She used to worship her, you know. Still does, but she's gone a bit peculiar in her old age. To me, they were like beauty and the beast, I mean Miss Augusta and Boss Charles.' As he gave himself another drink, Kate could hear the slight slurring of the vowels.

'Was he as bad as that?' she said.

'As what?'

'You called him the beast.'

'He was a bastard.'

She waited for him to continue; he had never been so indiscreet before. 'I mean, a real bloody four-square bastard. I always wondered how someone like him got someone like her. The way he treated her – Jesus, you wanted to shrivel up! He spoke to her like a bloody servant. And once or twice he used his hands on her.'

'You tried to stop him, didn't you?'

'Who told you that? Charles? Well, it's true. Sometimes he'd get drunk. Those were the worst times. Once he nearly knocked me through a door; a closed door, my friend.'

'He made Charles's life a misery, too.'

'He made everybody's life a misery. No wonder she looked . . . elsewhere. You could hardly blame her.'

'You mean another man? A lover?'

'That's exactly what I mean, my friend.'

She suddenly recalled something that Dr. du Toit had said about Smuts worshipping Mrs. Preller. Could she have turned to him? Could Smuts have been her lover all those years ago? She waited for him to go on, but he said, 'Ah, what the hell, it's no good looking back. It's just water under the bridge.'

During the winter when there was less to do on the farm, she spent more time in Cape Town. The flat had remained unchanged since Boss Charles's time and was dowdy. She decided that if she could not redecorate the big public rooms at Saxenburg, at least she could brighten the flat. She spent several happy week-ends searching out wall-paper and curtaining and when she finished, it reflected her love of colour: cool yellows and greens for summer, with a change to oranges and reds in winter.

She also saw more of her family. Duggie's leg had been removed just below the knee. He had spent months as both an in- and out-patient of the orthopaedic ward of the Somerset hospital and now he could use his artificial leg with a certain dexterity. He walked with a limp and used a stick, but otherwise he was able to lead a normal life. With the absence of pain his drinking had become less of a problem and through a fellow-patient he had secured a clerking job in a ship's chandlers near the docks.

Her father, too, was in work. His neighbour, the coloured man who had the small removal business, had begun to do well enough to expand. He had bought two old lorry chassis and had hired Buchanan to build the bodies. There was talk of moving to a better house in a less run-down suburb, but nothing came of it.

She enjoyed these breaks from Saxenburg and would have enjoyed them even more had it not been for the fact that she had no real friends of her own. Jerry and Freda were Charles's friends, so were the others she had met. She had only had one friend of her own and he had been more than a friend, and he had gone and she had tried to forget him.

But as the weeks passed she found that when she went away she worried about Mrs. Preller. The bond that had grown between them had weakened the bulwarks which the old woman had built around herself over the years. When Kate had arrived at Saxenburg she had been simply an employee, but now she was a member of the family and Mrs. Preller seemed to depend more and more on her presence. She told herself that she needed the breaks and that Lena and Smuts between them could handle any problem that arose. But she worried nonetheless.

There had been a change in Lena, as Smuts had said. She had always been religious and had never failed to attend the long services at the mission in the coloured village. Recently she had become increasingly devout, until her enthusiasm bordered on fanaticism. Kate would some-times find her on her knees, praying, in the kitchen. On occasions, alone in the drawing-room, she would sense a presence, turn and see Lena in the doorway staring at her, her eyes burning with a strange fire that seemed to put her beyond reach.

On Sundays, dressed in her dark frock and her black straw hat, hymn book and Bible in one hand, shoes in the other, she would hurry bare-footed along the cliff road so as not to be late for the service. Occasionally, Kate drove her. Sometimes she would come back at nine or ten o'clock in the evening, sometimes it would be midnight.

Thinking of her walking through the night, alone, and remembering Miriam, Kate said: 'Aren't you afraid?'

Lena did not answer.

'If you telephoned me, I would come and fetch you.'

'God has spoken to me, Miss Kate.'

Once when Kate was having a drink with Smuts they heard her singing hymns in the kitchen. 'They'll put her in the loony bin one of these days,' he said.

Betty came back towards the end of the winter and Kate hardly recognised her. When she had left to stay with her aunt she had been a pretty adolescent; she came back a woman. At nineteen or twenty, her beauty was startling.

Her pale, café au lait skin was perfect, her cheek-bones were high and her face heart-shaped. In the house she wore a light dress and the shape of her body beneath it was clearly visible. Remembering a moment she had once witnessed in the kitchen, Kate found herself glad that Charles was spending so much time away from home.

Lena's burning, angry eyes followed the girl everywhere and she seemed to double the intensity of her care whenever Charles was home.

If Betty noticed her mother's unease, she did not show it. She ignored Charles as she ignored the rest of them. She lived in her own private world, emerging only to do battle with Lena. Their fighting was worse than ever and the reasons soon emerged.

Betty was causing havoc among the coloured farm-workers. The men flocked around her as though she was a bitch in heat. But that wasn't all. Kate found out that she was stealing liquor from the house both for herself and for any man she was with. Smelling it on her breath, she began checking the levels in the bottles and saw how rapidly they went down.

There was a recklessness about the girl that had not been there before. Kate was sorry she had come back and would have been pleased to see her return to her aunt. But she was loath to say anything in case Lena took it into her head to leave. Kate herself could have managed with Tilly, but Lena was like Mrs. Preller's left hand. So all she could do was try and keep the lid on a situation which would, she knew, either resolve itself or have to be resolved.

[8]

Spring that year was wet and cold. Late snow fell on the mountains to the west and bitter winds blew down on Saxenburg. The birds hated the damp and the cold, and both chicks and young birds began to die. Kate brought them into the big incubator shed, into the garage and even into the house itself, turning the office into a creche where the chicks could dry out and get some warmth.

All this meant a great deal of extra work and worry for her. They had increased the size of their flock, buying in stud birds and putting in two new incubators. They had also built a dam in the northern section of the farm where there was winter run-off from higher ground. This had cost a considerable amount of money, much of it borrowed from the bank.

Mendel was calling for more and more feathers. He had taken on agents in Paris, Berlin and Vienna and was rapidly expanding the ostrich-feather side of his business as the lobby against the use of exotic and wild-bird feathers caused that trade to dry up.

Kate was running an overdraft on the farm account, something that gave her nightmares. She hated the thought of borrowing. To be in debt in her stratum of society in Scotland had been a cause for shame. Now, it seemed, you could be in debt to a bank for thousands of pounds if your name was Preller and be looked upon by Mr. Hamilton with affection and respect. It hardly made sense to her.

It was against this background of physical weariness and worry that she had a major row with Charles, with results that no one, least of all Kate herself, could have foreseen. He was still trying to put together the necessary capital for the canning factory and had decided to take a trip up the West coast of the country, where there were at least three large canning operations which he wanted to study. He came to Kate for money. She was both embarrassed that he should have to do such a thing on what amounted to his own farm, and also irritated, because his income from the joint company was greatly in excess of hers.

'I'm sorry,' she said. 'You know I would if I could, but my mother's feet are needing attention and I have those bills to pay above the other money that goes to them.'

'I don't mean I want your own private money,' he said. 'Christ, don't be silly. It can come from the farm account.'

'But I can't authorize that sort of expenditure. Anyway, even if I could, the overdraft's enormous.'

'Of course you can authorize it. And all farmers run an overdraft.'

'Charles, every penny has to be accounted for.'

'You could put it down to repair for the sheds or something like that.'

'You mean, lie to your mother? You know she goes over the books.'

'Jesus, I'm not asking for charity. I'll repay it once I've got the factory going.'

'I'm sorry.'

'Listen, you talk about doing up the tennis court and the swimming pool. Is that *your* money or the farm's?'

'The farm's, of course.'

'Well, don't you think it's more worthwhile spending it on something like the factory?'

'What I think doesn't matter. Anyway, nothing's been done about the court or the pool, and it wasn't my idea in the first place. Your mother suggested it. If she wants to use the money for that, she's entitled to. She's worked hard all her life keeping this place together.'

'You don't have to tell me. Christ, she's told me often enough herself!' There was anger in his eyes and she found herself matching it.

'If you'd put money aside when you got your dividends you'd not have to ask now. Instead, you run around with your friends in Cape Town, golfing and dining and God knows what.'

'At least I'm welcome there. Living with you is like living with a bloody iceberg. You have no warmth. Even when we're in bed, it's like fucking a . . . I don't know what. Not a woman. Certainly not my wife.'

She had to go to Helmsdale to see Mr. Hamilton about a payment that had come through from London and when she got back, the red roadster had gone. Lena told her that he had left for Cape Town. For once she did not go to Smuts' rooms for a drink that evening and when he came to look for her, told him she had a headache. She went to bed early but in spite of her physical exhaustion, she could not sleep. Her mind fretted at the argument, turning it this way and that, examining its underbelly. She came eventually to the conclusion that Charles was right, she had been cold to him since Jonas's death, and that was not fair. She had married him for her own reasons, the least she could do was continue to try to make a success of it. The following day she caught a train for Cape Town.

The train got in about seven. The rush-hour was over, the station deserted and gloomy. As her taxi ground up the mountainside, she began to wonder if she was doing the right thing. She had no real plan, it was just that their happiest time together had been on honeymoon and she had thought she might be able to recreate some of the atmosphere and kindle some warmth between them.

The flat was in darkness, but that did not surprise her. she had telephoned before she left, but there had been no reply. She let herself in. It was dark and cold and she went round switching on lights and electric fires.

She put down her small case in the bedroom. The bed was unmade and there was a bottle of brandy a third full on one of the bedside tables. With it was a jug of water and a glass. She supposed Charles had drunk himself to sleep the previous night.

She began to tidy up. Some of his underwear was lying on the floor and she scooped it up. There were a couple of towels in the laundry-basket which she could not recall leaving the last time, and a comb with a frizz of hair in it. She picked it up with distaste and threw it into the waste-paper basket. She went back and made the bed. As she did so, she saw a second glass wedged between the top of the bed and the headboard. She stared at it for several seconds, then she picked it up and examined it. There was no trace of lipstick around the rim. Charles might have rested it there, forgotten where it was and fetched another. There could be a dozen explanations.

She returned to the sitting-room, which opened onto the large verandah and the magnificent view of the city lights. The white curtains were drawn back, but the room lacked warmth. She shivered in the chilly air. She did not feel at home in it, even though she had redecorated it. It was Boss Charles Preller's room, and Charles's, not hers, and perhaps it never would be. Her mind reached into the future and she saw herself come into the flat with a small child on each hand, turning it into a home. But the picture lacked credibility. Standing there, she wondered if she had been right to come. But what else could she have done? Surely it would be a signal to Charles that she was prepared to play a secondary role. His position was invidious, she did not want it to become intolerable.

She made herself a pot of coffee and took a cup out onto the verandah. The spring night was breezy, one of the first south-easters of summer. She stood at the rail, sipping her coffee, absorbing the picture of the lights. She was about to turn away when she saw a figure standing in the garden. It looked like a woman. She seemed to be staring up at the house.

Then a gust of wind shook the leaves of the big oak trees and the woman became a pattern of moving shadows, nothing more. But Kate stood, transfixed, remembering the time when a woman *had* stood there and looked up at the house. She remembered crouching on the verandah like a trapped tart when the wife comes home. She remembered the row between the woman and Charles, even some of the phrases they had used. It came back to her. The black hair glimpsed over Charles's shoulder, the thick, screeching voice. Yes, that was it. The voice. Slowly, an image began to form in her mind. Hazy, red, torn and scraped. The ideas were associated. It had been Miriam's voice she had heard; Miriam had been that woman.

She went back into the sitting-room and closed out the night. She concentrated, trying to recall their conversation, but only snatches came to her. There had been something about someone not wanting Miriam to come to the house. Had she meant his mother?

Just then she heard a noise on the stairs and went to open the door, expecting Charles. It was Freda.

'Thank God you're in,' Freda said, pushing past her. 'I telephoned Saxenburg and they told me you'd taken the train. Thank God you're here!'

'Whatever is wrong?'

They went into the sitting-room. Kate noticed that her

hair was blown and she was agitated. Her eyes were puffy and there were red smudges beneath them as though she had been weeping. She flung down a heavy fur coat and said, 'Have you got a drink? I need one.' Kate gave her a brandy.

'I've got no one to talk to. No one.'

'Sit down. Tell me what's wrong.'

'Everything. Me. Jerry. Everything.'

She paced the room. 'Can I use your telephone?'

She spoke for a few moments while Kate poured herself a drink.

She heard Freda say, 'When? Are you sure? Yes. Yes, yes. No, never. All right. Outside.'

She put down the telephone. Her hands were shaking. 'The bastard!' she said. She helped herself to another brandy and drank it neat, then shuddered. 'Come on.'

'Now, wait! I want to know . . .'

'Please don't ask questions. Just come. We're going to see someone. Please . . . please . . .'

Hysteria lurked at the edges of her voice and Kate sensed that if she argued she might become violent.

'All right. Where are we going?'

'To Wynberg. The car's outside. You'll need a coat.'

Kate followed her downstairs and climbed into an open Sunbeam. Freda drove along the Main Road through Cape Town's southern suburbs, then turned off onto dirt roads. The wind was cold and the noise of the engine made speech impossible. Finally they came to a hedge of Australian myrtle. A man was standing by a small Austin Seven at the side of the road. Freda went to him.

When she came back she said, 'This is the place.'

'Who is he?'

'Someone I pay.'

'Listen, Freda, I don't . . .'

'For God's sake, *help* me!' The phrase rang like a bell and Kate saw Jonas's face, the rain pouring down his cheeks, the wild animal eyes. *Help me, Miss Kate!*

Freda took her arm and they went through the big iron gates. There was a short gravelled drive and a turn-around with a lawn in the middle. Several motors were parked along the drive and there were others at the side of the house. It was old Cape Dutch architecture, with colonial gables and a deep verandah of flagstones broken by white supporting pillars. The main doors let off the verandah. As they came onto the flagstones she recognised the strains of 'There's a Small Hotel' coming from behind the curtained windows.

Freda put her hand to the door-knob. 'Don't you think you should knock?' Kate said. But the door swung open and they were inside.

The music, louder now, was coming from a room to the right. Kate followed Freda across the hall. As in a dream, she noticed the expensive teak panelling, the marble tiles, the carved staircase. She was clearly in an important Cape homestead and she felt embarrassed and out of place. Freda had already reached the room. She caught Kate by the sleeve, opened the door and they went in together.

The room was in semi-darkness. At first no one noticed them. Perhaps twenty people were dancing a fox-trot to the Victrola. It was clearly a private party and again Kate was swept by embarrassment. She was about to move back into the hall when she realised there was something strange about the people. The women seemed larger than they should have been, their bare arms muscular. Then she saw that there were no women in the room. All the 'women' were men. At that moment Jerry came dancing by. He was wearing a lounge suit, but his partner was wearing a long dress that reached to the floor, and he was heavily made up. They were dancing very close.

At that moment, Freda gave a shriek of savage anger and disgust. 'Jerry! Jerry, you fucking homo!' She turned to Kate. 'You've seen! You're my witness!' But Kate's attention was elsewhere. As the dancers parted she saw, across the room, sitting in a large chair by the fireplace, her husband. A young man of about eighteen was sharing the chair and they were fondling each other. For a long moment, she and Charles looked at each other, then she felt bile come up into her throat and thought she was going to be sick on the floor.

A voice said, 'Come in, ducky!' But Freda had grasped

her arm and they were running back through the hall and out of the house. Only the sounds of laughter followed them.

'You're my witness,' Freda was saying. 'You'll tell them what you saw. I'll get every penny from him. I'll tell his father. I'll tell it in court. My God, I'll ruin him!'

Kate climbed into the car beside her. The little Austin Seven had vanished. Freda started the Sunbeam, threw it recklessly round in a circle and sped back the way they had come. She drove with abandon. Kate could hear her shrill voice above the engine and wind, but did not know what she was saying. The memory of what she had just seen was crowding every other thought from her mind.

They plunged back into the city. Freda was driving at nearly sixty miles an hour. The traffic was light, but Kate began to feel afraid. They raced towards a cross roads. A car came from the right. Freda saw it in time and tried to swerve, but one of the wheels stuck in the tramlines.

The Sunbeam hit the other car head-on at fifty-eight miles an hour. Kate was airborne. She saw the windscreen coming towards her and heard the crash of glass as she went through it. She felt the wind of her own flight and sensed the ground race up to meet her. She was unconscious for a few seconds. When she came to she felt a weight on her chest and thought that the car was on top of her. She seemed to come in and out of consciousness like a drugged person. She knew she was badly hurt. She couldn't move. She heard voices. And all the time she felt the drip, drip of her blood running down her face and neck. Oh, God, she prayed, let it not be my face.

Then the weight was lifted and she knew it had been Freda lying on her. Her throat was cut from ear to ear and it was her blood that had been dripping.

A voice said, 'Okay, man, I've got her.'

She felt the stretcher under her, felt the swaying of the ambulance, saw the lights of the casualty ward, the white coats of the doctors. And all the time she was saying, over and over, 'Please, God, not my face . . . not my face . . .' Then she smelt ether, and at last the lights went out.

PART THREE

The Trial

London. A morning in early spring. Kate was woken by a discreet knocking. For a moment, in the dim bedroom, she could not think where she was. Then she knew. She was in Isidore Mendel's house in Charles Street.

The door opened and Mrs. McConnell came in with her breakfast tray and the morning paper.

'How are you feeling today, Mrs. Preller?'

'Fine, thank you.' She raised herself on her pillows.

Mrs. McConnell was in her mid-fifties, a Scotswoman from Ullapool who ran Mendel's house with fine precision. Kate had never seen such a clean house. Everything shone, from the brass door knocker on the gleaming, black-painted front door, to the brass fire-irons and the sparkling crystal glasses.

'It's a bonny day.' Mrs. McConnell pulled open the curtains to let in the pale sunshine. 'But best wrap up if you're going out. The wind's in the east.'

There was something, a boniness, a greyness, about her that reminded Kate of her mother. Now she lifted the tray with its drop sides and arranged it over Kate's lap. 'There,' she said. 'I've done you a poached egg and a wee bit bacon. And here's the paper. Mr. Mendel says he'll be up to see you in an hour. That's at half-past nine.'

When she had gone, Kate looked down at the tray. Tea, a mixture of Lapsang Suchong and Darjeeling which Mendel had blended for him at Jackson's, was in a silver pot. There was a silver milk jug and a silver hot water jug. Pale brown toast stood in a silver rack and Mrs. McConnell's own home-made marmalade was in a crystal

237

pot with a silver spoon. The china was Coalport, the snow-white table-napkin linen.

She lifted the lid of the warmer and saw two poached eggs and crisp curls of Wiltshire bacon. She had said that she only wanted toast in the morning, but Mrs. McConnell obviously felt she needed fattening up.

She put the eggs on her plate, cut them so that the yokes ran, then went into her bathroom and flushed them down the lavatory. She returned to bed, buttered a slice of toast, nibbled at the bacon and drank two cups of tea. Then she lay back, smoking a cigarette.

She picked up a hand-mirror from the table and looked at herself. There were no marks, just the thin, familiar cheeks, the eyes that seemed to flash with an inner energy and the short, black hair. She lifted the hair on the left side of her forehead and there it was, the scar, like a pink crescent near the hair line. She touched it. It had almost no feeling.

It was at times like this that the fears and memories that hid among the shadows of her mind threatened to surface. It took only a word or a phrase or a colour to place her back on that pavement in Cape Town with Freda's blood dripping onto her face and neck. There were other colours – white, for instance – and smells – carbolic – that took her instantly back to the small ward where she had lain in the same hospital where Duggie had had his leg taken off.

From her bed she had stared out of the window with its view of Devil's Peak and watched the wisps of cloud play around the summit, hour after hour. Sometimes one of the nurses would come in and chat. Sometimes they brought her books, but she did not want to read.

She was in hospital for nearly three weeks, and it was a week before she was allowed visitors. Charles had been first. He had telephoned twice and three times a day and had sent so many flowers that Kate had told the nurses to take them to the other wards.

The scar was the first thing he had mentioned. Her head had been shaved for the stitches and then painted with a brown disinfectant. She had not been able to bear looking at herself in a mirror. The nurses told her that once it healed and the hair grew back she would hardly notice it. In her depression, she did not believe them. She thought less about her broken collar-bone and fractured ribs than about her disfigurement.

Charles had put on one of her favourite suits, had a bunch of gladioli in one hand and a box of chocolates in the other. He was edgy and looked pale. Encased in bandages and plaster of Paris, she lay on her high pillows and looked at him dispassionately. He was handsome. She gave him that. But his face was without life or character. What she had discovered about him had turned him from a man into a being she did not understand – still good-looking, still her husband, but a stranger.

He kissed her cheek. 'Is it very painful?'

'Not very.'

'You're not to worry about anything, okay? I mean, we're going to get the best. A plastic surgeon. It doesn't matter who it is. We'll get him.'

'There's nothing to do,' she said. 'It'll fade in time.'

But he was not to be deprived. He said again, 'We'll find the best.' He paused, and she could see the struggle within him. 'Listen. About the other thing. You know. We were only fooling around. I mean, we went there for laughs. If Freda had just asked . . . I mean, we could have told you. It was . . . a bit of sport.'

She let him go on, watching him lacing his fingers and tightening them. So this was to be the mood: contrite, but misunderstood. It was less embarrassing to accept it. But sport? Fooling around? She could see him in the chair as plainly as if it had been a minute or two before. She could see the expression on his face, the lips, the hands, the compliant youth.

'I mean, you don't think we do that sort of thing, do you? Jerry heard about the party and we thought, the hell with it, why not let's go and see what the homos and the *moffies* do?'

Once when she was little she had caught Duggie playing with himself and he had spoken and looked much as Charles did now. 'I was itchy,' he had said. And, in the same breath, 'Don't tell mother.'

Here it was again, the small, guilty boy, half-indignant, half-ingratiating.

'You see, there was this chap Jerry had been to school with . . .'

Too much explanation, she thought. What was it Mrs. Preller had said? Never complain, never explain. Or had it been Smuts? She couldn't remember. But she knew that the more you tried to explain the unexplainable, the worse it became. Finally, Charles simply ran down, and stopped. They looked at each other for a moment and then his eyes slid away. It's not his fault, she thought. It's mine. I should never have married him.

He came to see her twice a day after that and never again mentioned the party. It was understood between them that the subject had been disposed of and need not be touched on again. When she was strong enough to travel he had hired an ambulance and they went back to Saxenburg.

It took much of that summer for her to regain her strength, and Dr. du Toit visited her once a day. His bedside manner was bluff and jovial, but she did not look forward to his visits. She worried about the farm, but he would not let her take up her duties again. 'Charles is doing all right,' he said. 'Don't worry.'

Smuts became Charles's tutor, as he had been hers. They had also hired a coloured foreman from one of the big ostrich farms near Oudtshoorn, who moved into Jonas's old house.

'You just worry about yourself,' du Toit said. 'No, on second thoughts, let me worry about you. Don't you worry about anything.'

At first she had been confined to bed, but as her strength came back she spent hours sitting by the great windows looking at the sea, watching the colours change from light green to metallic blue and dirty grey as the south-easters roared in.

Her mother and father came to see her, so did Leibowitz and, once, even Jerry. He talked about Freda as though she had just gone down the road to post a letter. It unnerved Kate and she was glad when he and Charles went off to play golf.

Her most frequent visitor, and the one she most looked forward to seeing, was Mrs. Preller. The bond between them now became much stronger. Mrs. Preller visited her at least once a day and they would sit talking – Kate mainly listening – for an hour or more at a time. As far as the accident was concerned, she and Charles had agreed on a story which they had told both to the police and to Mrs. Preller: the four of them had gone to the party in Upper Wynberg. Kate and Freda had decided to leave early, taking Freda's car. The rest was as it had happened. Only those present at the party knew exactly what had happened and, in their own interests, were keeping silent.

Mrs. Preller's conversation was either of the past or the future. Kate liked it when it was about the past, for the future now was a blank sheet, but to the old woman it was peopled with grandchildren – 'once we get you better.'

She did get better, at least physically. The collar-bone mended, the ribs knitted, the cuts healed, the abrasions disappeared, and even the scar faded under the new growth of hair. Her body slowly regained its former strength and energy, but her mind did not recover so easily, largely because she was riven by doubts and uncertainties, and she was not used to that. She knew that the future, not only of herself, but of the Saxenburg estate, rested on her. Mrs. Preller depended on her more and more, not as an employee, but as a daughter; it was an emotional bond. And in a way, Smuts depended on her. So, too, did Charles. And Duggie. And her mother and father. She felt trapped, stifled and panicky about what was to come. She longed to get away, she needed time and space to think.

It was then she had a letter from Mendel. It was an ordinary business letter which ended with a friendly injunction that she should think of visiting London one day to see the other end of the feather business. It was like a life-belt. She had written immediately that she was coming.

'You can't go alone,' Charles had said.

'Why not?'

'You're not strong enough yet. Why don't I come with you?' His eyes had lit up.

'I'm perfectly strong now. Mendel has offered me a roof in London so I'll be well looked after. In any case, you're needed here.'

She was right about that. As the weeks had passed, she hardly recognised him as the former well-dressed young man about town. He lost weight and wore dusty farm clothes. He never stayed up late and his temper was shorter than ever; for the first time, he was learning what real work was like.

She had kept to her stateroom for most of the voyage. Memories of Tom were all around her, especially when she went on deck and watched the passengers playing quoits. Mendel and his chauffeur met her at Southampton and she was driven to London in his new Minerva. That had been ten days ago.

She bathed and dressed and was sitting by the window, looking down at the traffic as it moved towards Berkeley Square when, at half-past nine, there was a knock on her door and Mendel came in. As always, she was reminded of a small, neat bird. He was dressed in his usual dove grey suit, white shirt, dark blue silk tie and dark blue handkerchief in his jacket pocket. He wore spats over his shining black shoes.

'Good morning, my dear.' He took her hand and bowed over it. There was something Continental about his manner, though she knew he had grown up in London's East End. During the past ten days she had become very fond of him. 'Had your breakfast? Good, good. Mrs. McConnell says you need meat on your bones.'

He picked up *The Times* from her bed and glanced at the main news pages. As he folded it again he said, 'What would you like to do today?'

'Anything you say.'

Mendel helped to revive her spirits. He was a man of catholic taste and, being a bachelor, liked to fill his evenings with theatre or ballet. He took her to see Diaghilev's Russian Ballet in *La Boutique Fantasque* and to hear Chaliapin as Boris in *Boris Godounov* at Covent Garden. Paul Robeson was in *Show Boat* at Drury Lane and Evelyn Laye in Jerome Kern's *Blue Eyes* at the Piccadilly.

It was a luxurious life. They travelled to and from the theatre in the Minerva and dined at Prunier's or Rule's. Sometimes he would take her to Rumpelmeyer's for coffee and cakes, or to the Ritz for tea. He liked to walk into such places with her on his arm and watch the heads turn. 'They'll say to each other that I must be your uncle, but they'll think differently. They'll think, look at that little Jew with the beautiful young woman. They'll envy me.'

Kate *was* beautiful that summer. The weeks of enforced idleness had filled out her body. She was still thin, but her breasts and thighs were fuller and her cheeks less sunken. Sometimes, for fun, she would play up to Mendel and take his hand in full view of other diners, and he would flush with pleasure. 'Maybe they think I keep you in a love-nest in Maida Vale,' he said.

She had never lived a life of total luxury before and, knowing it could not last, decided to enjoy it. That summer England seemed to match her mood. It was a place of peace, or so it seemed to her. She occasionally read *The Times* and knew that other places were less peaceful. A bomb attack was made on King Victor Emmanuel of Italy, killing seventeen people, but not the target; the leader of the Croatian Peasant Party was shot and wounded in the Yugoslav parliament; in Berlin there was hysteria at the success of a Junkers monoplane crossing the Atlantic; in France Communists were said to have derailed a train outside the Gare du Nord, which injured thirty-three people. Peace, in Europe at any rate, was being promoted in theory by the American Peace Pact, but did not seem to be fulfilled in practice. Kate, however, was unaware of any tensions.

During this time, she also learned a great deal about the European end of the ostrich feather industry. Almost the first thing she saw when she arrived in London was a large hoarding advertising Mistinguett in a Parisian revue. The bill-board showed the famous French artiste almost entirely covered by a great, coral-dyed ostrich feather fan. Feathers were everywhere. The Ritz was full of them, so was Rumpelmeyer's. Mendel took her to the Derby and wherever she looked, she saw feathers. She smiled to herself as she thought of the plucking boxes and the dust and the sweating coloured labourers on the Saxenburg Estate, and wondered what these women would think if they knew where their expensive feathers came from.

One morning, Mendel took her to the heart of the London feather industry at Cutler's Wharf in the Pool of London. There, in a great warehouse amid hundreds of buyers and sorters, she smelled the familiar smells and saw the familiar dust. She had never seen so many feathers. Hundreds of thousands of plumes, black, white and grey, were sorted into row upon row of divided tables. Buyers walked up and down, looking and touching. Some wanted feathers for dusters, some for mattresses, some for fashion houses. Some were buyers from New York and Paris and Berlin. At one end of the warehouse were great bundles of feathers still to be unpacked. Their labels were all South African: Oudtshoorn, Helmsdale, the Sundays River Valley, Beaufort West . . . suddenly the bleak, windswept plains were brought very close.

In fact, although she had buried herself in London, she was never far away from Saxenburg in her imagination, for all her memories were being constantly stimulated by a steady flow of letters. Smuts wrote to her, and so did Mrs. Preller and Charles, when he had the time. Smuts wrote of practical things: the winter rains, the number of eggs, the health of the chicks, the increasing 'strangeness' of Lena, the problems caused by Betty. Mrs. Preller wrote mostly of money and plans for the future and in one letter, told Kate that two thousand pounds had been placed to her name in Barclay's Bank in Cockspur Street. Charles's letters were short, as though he was squeezing them in between work, and were tinged by a note of self-pity. She pictured the winter gales and the loneliness he must be experiencing. She saw in her mind's eye the great house with the two old people and Charles, and at such times depression gathered on her like dust.

There were also stiff, rather formal notes about the

family from her mother. Duggie had lost his job because of retrenchment and had begun to drink again, but her father was in full employment in the removal firm and there was talk of him becoming a partner. Mrs. Buchanan's feet were no better and she was suffering from the damp; otherwise things seemed normal. These letters, too, with their conjured images and smells of the small villa in Observatory, produced in Kate a feeling of unhappiness.

Every letter she received, either from Saxenburg or from her mother, asked after her health and wondered when she was coming back: 'home' as Smuts and Charles and Mrs. Preller described it. She could not answer their questions, either in her own mind or in the letters she wrote in reply. She seemed to be in a kind of limbo. She was enjoying herself with Mendel but even that, as the weeks went by, became less stimulating than it had been. She told herself that after her accident it was only natural that she should be depressed from time to time. Who wouldn't be? But she knew deep down that it was not the only reason. She knew that the accident and what she had learned of Charles had formed a kind of watershed in her life. From the small house in Cape Town where she had existed with her family, Saxenburg had seemed first like a haven and then like a palace waiting for its princess. But from London, both places seemed remote, the palace a forbidding castle. Once she was back, the draw-bridge would be raised and she would be trapped. And what of the future? How would she conduct her life with Charles? How would she continue to sustain a charade in which Mrs. Preller's grandchildren would only be figments of the old lady's mind; for Kate knew she would never sleep with Charles again.

The days slipped away and became weeks. She felt inert, unable to make up her mind, unable to think about her future.

Then two things happened which were to bring her out of this mood. The first occurred casually when Mrs. McConnell brought up her breakfast one morning and said, 'The boy made a mistake and delivered the *Chronicle* instead of *The Times*.' A hand seemed to grip her stomach. She could not even eat a slice of toast. She drank coffee and smoked cigarettes and stared at the paper as though it were a bomb waiting to go off, and in a sense, it was.

She had struggled to keep Tom out of her thoughts and had succeeded, up to a point. During the early months of her marriage, this had seemed important. Later, when things had started to go wrong, she had told herself she must not use Tom as an excuse to escape. But on the ship and now in London he had seemed much closer to her. The ship contained its memories of the passage out; in London she had the feeling that this was his territory, that his tall, rangy figure was walking its streets, driving in its cabs, waiting on its station platforms, eating in its restaurants. Wherever she had gone with Mendel she was conscious that she might see him. It had been part of her bargain with herself that she would do nothing to harm her marriage by seeing, or trying to get in touch with him. She had not sought him. She had not even bought a copy of the *Chronicle*. The fact that Mrs. McConnell had dropped a copy on her bed was not her fault. It was fate. She picked it up and leafed quickly through it, but did not see his name. She went back to page one and this time studied each column, taking her time. Nothing. She felt a sense almost of grievance. She had fought her own desires successfully for so long that now there should at least have been the reward of his name. That was all she wanted, just his name. A few days later, she told Mrs. McConnell that she would prefer to have the *Chronicle* rather than *The Times*. After that, she scanned it from front to back, but each day she was disappointed. She could have telephoned his office, but that would be breaking the rules of her particular game. The newspaper had come to her unexpectedly and not by any overt move on her part.

Then, ten days later, she saw his name on the leader page, under the heading, WHAT NOW FOR YUGOSLAVIA ? THE BULLET OR THE BALLOT ? under it was the sentence, *From Tom Austen, our Middle European Correspondent*, and under that was the dateline, *Vienna*.

She knew where Vienna was on a map: hundreds of miles away. He was as lost to her as he had ever been. All that day she kept to her room, until Mendel felt worried enough to ask if she needed a doctor.

The other occurrence which was to affect her was a week-end she spent at a country house in Hampshire, belonging to Lady Vyvyan Bixby. Mendel had taken her to 'Vyvyan's' a shop just off Hanover Square, to let her see the end product of many of the best of Saxenburg's feathers, for Vyvyan was London's most fashionable milliner.

'An aristocrat,' Mendel told Kate as they were driven through Berkeley Square. 'Mind you, I'm not saying she cannot design hats. No, no. But being a lady helps.'

'Vyvyan's', with its striped awnings in brown and gold, and its gold window lettering, reminded Kate of an expensive box of chocolates. Instead of a window crammed with merchandise, there were only three hats on display, two of which were trimmed with ostrich feathers. The shop's interior was even more elegant than its outside had promised: gold-painted Louis Quinze chairs, occasional tables inlaid in ivory, one or two hats on stands and, in one corner, a Chinese vase holding long ostrich feathers in the Saxenburg manner, except that these were dyed in shades of magenta and aquamarine, cerise and coral and apple-green.

Lady Bixby was almost as elegant as her shop, but in a different way. She was about forty, tall and broad-shouldered, and wore peach-coloured Oxford bags, a cream shirt and a large foulard tie. Her face was square and her hair was cut short. She greeted Kate with a firm and friendly handshake.

'So you're from Saxenburg,' she said. 'Mr. Mendel has told me a great deal about Saxenburg; a great deal about you, too. Come along and I'll show you what we do with your feathers.'

She led the way upstairs to her work-rooms. Twenty or thirty women were working at long tables. One wall was lined with shelves holding boxes of dyed feathers and other trimmings. Lady Bixby pulled out pieces of fur. 'Coney,' she said. 'Nutria. Muskrat. Beaver.' She moved on and lifted a pile of black and white feathers. 'These might even

247

be yours.' There were boxes of cream straw from Tuscany and plaited straws from Java and Manila.

Kate watched the milliners blocking straws and felts, hand-sewing ribbons and delicate silk flowers, trimming and curling the ostrich feathers.

After twenty minutes or so they returned to the ground floor and had coffee. When they were leaving Lady Bixby said to Kate, 'You must come down to my place in Hampshire one day and see the English countryside in summer.'

Three days later an invitation arrived for a week-end in late June.

In her present frame of mind, Kate did not feel like making the effort to go, but Mendel said, 'I've heard of her house-parties. Amusing people. Good food. And good for business, too. Most of her friends are in the hat business or women's garments. Contacts, you know. You can never have too many.'

So she had accepted the invitation. The house was in Alresford and she arrived by train on Saturday afternoon. It was beautiful, an old converted mill set in beds of water-cress so that the garden was, in fact, the shallow and slow-moving river. From the windows she could see large trout finning in the current.

Lady Bixby met her and showed her to her room. When Kate came downstairs after freshening herself up she found that, apart from her hostess, the house was deserted. 'I thought it would be nicer to have the place to ourselves,' Lady Bixby said.

They walked up Broad Street to see the village and buy lobsters at the fish-monger's.

It was then that Kate realised that her hostess had meant it literally when she said they had the place to themselves. There were not even any servants.

Telling Kate to call her Vyvyan, she mixed dry martinis in a silver shaker before dinner. She was wearing white flannels and a blazer with red and gold stripes in the Edwardian manner. Round her throat was a red bandana knotted in the way Kate had seen road-menders tie their handkerchiefs in Scotland. She smoked oval Turkish cigarettes. Her hands were square, the finger-nails bitten back to the quicks.

Kate had never seen a room like her drawing-room. It was large, with great glass windows looking out over the cress beds. The furniture was of tubular steel and black leather, but its most astonishing feature was the floor, which was made of glass bricks under which the river flowed, with its trout and waving weed.

'It makes a talking point,' Vyvyan said. 'Let's take our drinks outside.'

On the side of the house that faced away from the town, a wooden walkway, a kind of verandah without a roof, had been built out over the water. She took Kate's arm and they walked slowly up and down. Kate had the sensation of being part of the river itself.

After dinner they had coffee in the glass-floored room. The curtains had been drawn and the only light was under the water. The room was transformed into an aquarium. Trout swam towards the light and lay in a circle around it, their mouths opening and closing. Kate could even see water snails and larvae.

'It's beautiful!' she said.

She felt Vyvyan's hand on her arm. 'So are you.' Kate turned and Vyvyan kissed her on the mouth. She felt the wetness of her lips and tasted the brandy she was drinking. Her stomach clenched with revulsion but she managed to control her anger and gently removed the other woman's hand. She crossed the room to stand by the curtained window.

'Did you like that?' Vyvyan said, moving towards her.

'My taste is for men.'

'My dear, the two are not mutually exclusive.'

'That's what my husband feels.'

'Ah. And you don't.'

'No, I don't.'

Vyvyan shrugged, then smiled and lit a cigarette. 'Well . . . put it down to experience. Have another drink?'

'No, thanks. I think I'll go to bed.'

'Quite sure I can't join you?'

'Quite sure.'

She locked her door and put a heavy chair in front of it.

The following morning she woke and packed and went downstairs. Vyvyan was up, but in a dressing-gown. She was older than Kate had first thought.

'Do you like a cooked breakfast?'

'Just toast and tea or coffee.'

They ate out on the wooden balcony in the sun. Kate was more relaxed now, for Vyvyan looked, in the hard morning light, less threatening than she had in her exotic drawing-room. She made no reference to their conversation the previous night. She also looked as if she had a hangover, and Kate assumed she had gone on drinking alone.

When they had finished their coffee and Kate was wondering what time the first train left for London, Vyvyan suddenly said, 'Have you heard of Brown Brothers?'

'No. Should I?'

'I suppose not. They're not in London yet, but they will be. They're what's called a chain-store. Horrible American word. It means there are lots of them. Brothers called Frederick and Lester Brown started with a single drapery shop in Manchester in 1903 and at the last count I think there were two hundred Brown Brothers all over Britain, and others opening by the hour, or so it seems.'

'What do they sell?' Kate said politely.

'Everything. They're called multiples. Another American word. Big women's departments, catering for the less expensive end of the market. Massive turn-over. Huge profits in the last five years. Are you wondering what on earth this has to do with you? I'll tell you. A month or so ago I was aproached by Frederick Brown. They want to buy my label, "Vyvyan", and they want me to design and manufacture a range of hats for their stores.'

She broke a piece of toast and threw crumbs into the water. Trout threshed in excitement.

'I've been working towards something like this for years. But first one had to make a name; Brown Brothers are fussy. Well, I've made my name catering for the idle bloody rich, now I'm going to cash in. But there's a problem. The margins are small. The profit comes with high turnover.

So everything has to be cut to the bone. And that's where you come in.'

'Me?' Kate was genuinely surprised.

'At least half of the hats I make will be trimmed with feathers. If I had my choice I'd trim with a whole range from bird of paradise to silver pheasant and jungle cock to ostrich, but I don't have the choice. The Anti-Plumage lobby has seen to that, God rot them. So I'm left with ostrich feathers. And it doesn't take a genius to work out that if I can cut the price of the feathers, my profits will improve. Now do you see?'

Kate said, 'The feather market regulates its own prices. Supply and demand. I don't see how you can get them cheaper.'

'What about if I found a primary supplier at the Cape?'

'You mean a farmer?'

'Exactly.'

'You mean, you want me to supply feathers direct to you, the manufacturer?'

'Why not? I'd cut you in on a percentage of the profits and pay you a slightly higher margin, anyway. No middlemen. Direct from you to me. Benefit us both.'

'But I – or we, I should say – supply direct to Mr. Mendel.'

'Yes, I know. That's what I'm saying. Instead of supplying to him, you supply to me.'

'But we have a contract with him.'

'In writing?'

'No, not in writing.'

'Well, then.'

'But don't you buy from Mendel?'

'You haven't understood,' she said impatiently. 'I want to cut him out.' Kate looked at her blankly. 'It's business. Mendel would do it to me if it was the other way around.'

Kate shaded her eyes from the glare on the water. 'It's very bright out here,' she said. 'I think I'll fetch my hat.'

She went into the house, picked up her suitcase and left by the side door. At this hour of the morning, the village was quiet. She walked quickly to the station. The London train came steaming in seven minutes later.

All the way back to town she thought of Vyvyan and the house built over the river. Last night she believed she had been invited down for a sexual romp. This morning she realised that there had also been a matter of business. It seemed that Vyvyan liked to combine the two.

Mendel arrived back from his cottage in the late afternoon and they were having a glass of sherry before dinner when he asked about her visit. She told him the whole story. When she described Vyvyan's proposition about the direct sale of ostrich fathers, she thought he looked shocked, and told him that had been her own reaction.

'Oh, that,' he said. 'No, not that, that's business. She's right, I would have done it to her. But the other thing. That wasn't nice.'

The experience left her in an even worse state of indecision. That week there were more letters from the Cape. The pressure to return to Saxenburg was increasing, and her resistance to that, combined with a sudden disgust for 'business', caused her to do the one thing she had said to herself she would never do. She went to the offices of the *Chronicle* in Fleet Street.

'The Editor?' said the commissionaire. 'You got an appointment, Miss?'

'No.'

'Oh, dear, you got to 'ave an appointment to see the Editor.' He pointed to a man sitting behind a counter. 'You go and speak to that gentleman. Tell 'im your business and he'll advise you.'

Kate had thought that it would be a simple matter to see the editor, tell him that she wished to contact Tom and be given his address. In fact, the process took much longer than she had expected.

'You tell me what you're wanting, Miss,' said the man behind the counter. 'I'll see what can be done.'

She kicked her heels for fifteen minutes before a middle-aged man, holding galleys in one hand and a heavy lead pencil in the other, appeared and said impatiently, 'You're asking for Tom Austen?'

'Yes. I'm going to Vienna. He's an old friend from South Africa.'

'Well, he's not there. Had a cable this morning. He's gone to Zagreb.'

'Where's that?'

'Yugoslavia.'

'Oh.'

She looked so crest-fallen that his manner changed. 'He'll probably be back in Vienna next week. When were you thinking of going?'

She paused. 'Next week.'

He smiled. 'You'll find the address of our office in the telephone book under *Chronicle*. Have a good journey.'

[2]

'Innsbruck . . . Innsbruck . . .' The voice echoed through the dining-car. 'Innsbruck Hauptbahnhof!'

It was a brilliant July day and Kate was sitting at lunch in the Arlberg-Orient Express. She looked out of the window as the train began to slow down. In the crystal air, the Solstein, which rose sharply beyond the city, seemed close enough to touch.

'Has Madame finished?' The waiter looked inquiringly at her half-eaten plate of Veal Marengo.

'Yes. Some coffee, please. How many more stops before Vienna?'

He counted on his fingers. 'Kitzbuhel . . . Schwarzach . . . Salzburg . . . Linz. Four, madame.'

The lump in her stomach tightened. It had lain there since she had left Victoria Station the previous day. She had been unable to eat at all on the first leg of her journey. In Paris, where she'd had a few hours to kill, she had forced down an omelette in a small café near the Gare de l'Est. Since then, she had only been able to drink a cup of coffee for breakfast just after Zurich.

Now, as she returned to her wagon-lit to sit out the

afternoon, she thought about Tom. Would he want to see her? Would he have someone else? There must be many women among the English colony in Vienna, or even among the Viennese, who would consider themselves lucky to catch him. But the most important question was, had he married again? It was something she had not dared ask her informant in the newspaper office. She could have written to him. She could have cabled. But what if he had said, don't come? When she left the train in Vienna, she would be physically *there*. If she had to contend with a girlfriend, then contend she would. But a wife would be a different matter.

She lit a cigarette, one of the many she had smoked since boarding the train, and stared out at the rich green pastureland and the high, jagged peaks of the Tyrol. She had expected to endure moments of regret and confusion for the decision she had made to travel to Vienna, but there had been none. There was apprehension, certainly, but it was mixed with excitement. She was aware of a ruthlessness in herself she had not experienced before. She wanted to see Tom, she was going to see Tom, and nothing short of a derailment would stop her. The only twinge of conscience she'd had was when she had gone to her bank in Cockspur Street and arranged a letter of credit. The money had come from Saxenburg, but she told herself that it was hers, she had earned it in more ways than one.

Then she had told Mendel her plans.

'Vienna?' he had said, startled. 'By yourself?'

'Mrs. Preller has spoken so much about it. I want to see it for myself.'

'If I'd only known, I would have come with you.'

'I'm a big girl now,' she had said, smiling. 'I've already travelled a long way by myself, and I'm sure the Viennese are no different from other people.' She had put an arm around his shoulders. 'Now don't be so solemn!'

He had taken her other hand and brought it to his lips. 'Thirty years ago, I would not have let you get off so lightly. Never mind thirty, even twenty!'

Now, as she sat in the train, London and Mendel seemed to be disappearing down the wrong end of a telescope. Her every thought was on the immediate future. Would Tom have changed? She tried to visualize him, and found that she was able to create his body in her mind, but not his face. That was ironic, for he had never been out of her thoughts, not for one single day. There had always been part of her that was shut off and enclosed, and his alone.

She closed her eyes and dozed, rocking gently with the swaying of the train. Her dreams were of Saxenburg, of the spume rising from the reef, of a woman walking along the winter beach with blood seeping from a wound in her neck . . .

The train stopped at Linz. She woke with a start, and saw Jonas. He was standing on the platform, his arm upraised, his mouth open. For a moment he was quite still, and then he moved and it was not Jonas, but an Austrian with a long feather in his Tyrolean hat. His face had been in shadow and had looked dark. She shivered in spite of the summer heat.

Vienna was scorching in the late afternoon. The city had an exhausted feeling about it and the air lying over the Danube valley was stale. There was a hot, gritty feel about everything and the smell of steam and engine oil and coal hung over the Westbahnhof.

She had already decided that she would book into a hotel in the centre of the city for the night. At the barrier there were uniformed hotel servants from Sacher's and the Bristol and the Grand meeting passengers from the train. She quickly learned that without a reservation she would have difficulty finding a room. One of the servants suggested she try just outside the centre and gave her the name of a small hotel in Döblingerhauptstrasse.

Within half an hour she was unpacking. Her room looked out over the suburban main street. Clanking trams moved along it constantly. Opposite was a sign saying, Cafe Filz, Gösserbierkeller. Backhändelstation. To her left was a small square with a few plane trees. Their leaves were dusty and drooped in the heat.

Her plan had been to have an early night so she would look her best in the morning, but now she felt she could not wait.

She looked up the *Chronicle*'s address and the hotel porter called her a taxi.

The office was in the First District, in a building near the Dorotheum auction house. When she arrived, the heat had gone out of the day and in the early dusk the air was soft and warm. The building was old, with a large, dark foyer weakly lit by three gas jets. She found a tenants' list, picked out in gilt on a blackboard. The *New York Herald*, the *Allgemeine Zeitung* and *De Telegraf* also had suites in the building. She had barely started to read the list when she heard the gates of a lift open behind her and a group of people emerged. She was half conscious of them, hearing their footsteps cracking crisply on the marble floor. Then she heard a laugh. It was so familiar and unmistakable it wrenched her heart. She would have known it anywhere in the world. She turned to greet Tom. Three men and a woman had emerged from the lift. Two of the men were already on the pavement. Tom and the woman followed. They paused at the door and he took her arm with casual familiarity and led her out.

Moving automatically, Kate went to the entrance. She saw them walk along the pavement, Tom still with his hand under the woman's elbow, talking. Although she could no longer hear it, in her mind there was still the echo of their laughter.

They crossed the road and entered a coffee-house. She followed. Gathered curtains covered only the lower half of the windows and she could see into the interior. It was not large. Men were reading newspapers they had taken from a roll-rack near the door.

Tom was at a table, leaning forward, talking animatedly. Her eyes touched his face. The briefest glance was enough to bring back every line. Then she looked at the woman. She was young, with a youthful plumpness and dark hair caught back in a bun. She was very pretty. Kate stared with such intensity that the woman seemed to sense it and glanced about her uneasily. It was not possible to see whether she was wearing a wedding-ring.

After a few minutes, Kate turned away and walked

slowly along the street. She did not know how long she walked, nor where.

In the train she had asked herself what she would do if Tom had another woman, but had not come to any conclusion. Now it had happened and she still did not know what to do. She walked for nearly an hour, criss-crossing the inner city until it was almost dark, then she returned to her hotel.

She had brought with her a flask of cognac. Mendel had given it to her for 'medicinal reasons,' and now she sat by the window and drank half a tumblerful, knowing it was the one sure way to sleep. As she sipped it and looked out into the evening, she remembered another hotel, another window, another feeling of desolation.

The brandy did the trick. She slept for nearly nine hours. In the morning a kind of nervous energy seemed to pour through her body. Why shouldn't she look up Tom? She was in Vienna and would simply say she had seen his name in the *Chronicle*. It was a natural thing to do.

She breakfasted on coffee and a roll, then set off once more for his office.

The foyer was not much brighter in full daylight, but she was able to read that the *Chronicle* was on the second floor. She took the lift and stepped from it into a long corridor. She could hear the noise of typewriters. As she walked along the passage the noise grew in volume until it seemed there were typewriters all around her. She passed several glass doors on which were the names of newspapers of which she had never heard.

Then she reached one which was labelled, *Chronicle, London*. She knocked and a woman's voice told her to enter.

She went in. The office was divided into two by a partition. On one side was a desk, unoccupied, with a typewriter in the corner; on the other side, a woman was seated at another desk. It was the woman she had seen the previous evening. Close up, she was even prettier than she had appeared in the café. Her skin was perfect, her eyes large, with long lashes and under her summer dress, her breasts were full. For a second, Kate was reminded of Miriam. Her eyes flicked to the woman's hands. There was no ring on the left, but several on the right. She knew that Continentals wore their rings in a different way from the British, but could not remember how.

The young woman had been watching her, and waiting. Finally she said, 'Bitte?'

'Do you speak English?'

'Of course.'

'I was looking for Mr. Austen.'

'He is not in.'

'When do you expect him?'

'I do not expect him. He does not come in today. It is Saturday.'

Kate realised she had lost all sense of time.

'Not at all?'

'Not at all.' There was an arrogant quality in her tone.

'Is he at home?'

'I do not know where he is. It is not my business to know.'

'Could you give me his home address?'

'I am sorry. We do not give away such information.'

'I'm an old friend of Mr. Austen's from Cape Town.'

'Where is that?'

'In Africa. I knew him when he worked there.'

'I'm sorry. I cannot help.'

'When will he be in again?'

'Not for two weeks. He takes his vacation. We close this office today. The work will be done by an associate on *Die Welt*.'

She seemed to decide that she had wasted enough time on Kate, and turned back to her typewriter.

'I can't wait for two weeks!' Kate said. 'I must see him now, today!'

The woman glanced up again. 'I told you I cannot help.'

Recognising triumph in her eyes, Kate turned and left the office, shaking with anger and frustration. Tom was somewhere in this city, but she was not going to be allowed to see him.

The door opposite opened and a man stepped out into the corridor. He was tall and thin and elegant, with a monocle hanging on a black ribbon. As he closed the door she saw the words *Daily Mail, London*, stencilled on the glass.

'Excuse me,' she said. 'Do you speak English?'

He raised the monocle and looked at her, then smiled. 'I believe so.'

'I'm looking for Mr. Austen of the *Chronicle*.' She explained briefly who she was and what had happened.

'Ah, you have seen the beauteous Fräulein Necker. Naturally she would not give his address to another beautiful woman. Fräulein Necker has a *schwarm* for Tom Austen.'

Kate was not sure what *schwarm* meant, though she could guess. The most important word he had uttered was *fräulein*.

'I wish I could help you,' he said. 'He moved recently. I had his old address, which was somewhere in the Genzgasse. Would you like me to find it?'

She followed him into a room similar to the one she had just left, except that this was ankle deep in copy paper and old newspapers which had been read and dropped on the floor. It was in marked contrast to the elegance of its occupier.

'My name's Fellowes, by the way.' He offered her a hand, then went to his desk. The top was covered by a typewriter and pieces of paper. He searched through several drawers, churning up the contents.

'I could do with Fräulein Necker to look after me,' he said. 'We all make advances, but she has her eye on Austen. Never could understand it. Ah, here we are.' He pulled out an address book, wrote Tom's former address on a piece of paper and gave it to her. 'That's the best I can do. Hope it helps.'

The Genzgasse was in the north-west of the city, a street of shops and apartment houses. She was hot and sticky by the time she reached the block of mansion flats where Tom had lived. Again she found herself in a dismal foyer where there was an elderly lift with a slot in it. A notice in German and English stated that it cost one Austrian schilling to use the lift.

She wandered through the foyer and down some steps into a deserted basement. There was no sign of a caretaker. Back on the ground floor, she knocked on one of the apartment doors. It was opened by an old woman dressed in lace and amber beads, who shook her head angrily when Kate asked her if she spoke English, and closed the door.

She went out into the street. Next to the block of flats was a *gasthaus*. In its window a notice said, 'Ici on parle Francais. English spoken.' She went in. A woman was sitting behind a cash register.

'Ach, Herr Osten!' she said. 'Ja, I know him. Every morning he takes coffee.'

'But he has left now,' Kate said.

'That is true. So sad.'

'I'm his sister, and I haven't got his new address. Do you know anyone who has it? Perhaps someone who sends on his mail?'

'But of course! Here is Herr Vogel.' She indicated a man who was sitting at a corner table eating a pastry. 'He is, what do you say? manager of the apartments.'

Kate followed her across to the man and stood silently as she spoke to him in German. He was small and bald and wore heavy spectacles. At first he shrugged and shook his head, looking suspiciously at Kate. The woman's voice grew louder and suddenly he gave in, took a small notebook from his pocket, paged through it, then wrote an address on a white paper napkin and handed it to Kate.

Potzleinsdorf lay in the hills to the north of Vienna. As the taxi drove towards it, she realised she was leaving behind the city's built-up area. The gardens in which the houses stood became bigger, there were trees overhanging the road, vineyards, orchards. By the time her taxi stopped at the end of a grassy lane, she might have been in deep countryside. Behind her lay the smoky haze of the city, ahead the gently rising hills covered in hardwoods. She walked along the lane. The day was warm. Apple and pear branches, heavy with fruit, gave dappled shade.

She reached a gate, and paused. The house stood in a large garden. It was single-storeyed, with a classical pediment, and painted dark yellow. All the windows were open and wooden shutters were pinned back. The garden was an old orchard of gnarled apple trees, tall grass and Flanders poppies. Over everything was the dreamy summer sound of bees and birds.

Her heart was racing as she opened the gate and approached the house. Then, above the summer sounds, she heard the tack-tack-tack of a typewriter coming from somewhere to the rear.

She walked through the long grass and stopped at the corner of the house. She found herself looking at a small back garden. The lawn had been mown and there was a lily pond in the middle. To one side stood a wooden summer house shaded by a horse-chestnut tree.

Inside the summer house, Tom sat, typing. He was wearing only a pair of baggy old shorts. She stood watching him for some minutes, remembering how she had watched him type in the hotel bedroom in Helmsdale. As far as she could see, the typewriter was the same machine he had used there, and she found herself envious of it: wherever he had gone since leaving the Cape, it had been with him.

The fixity of her gaze penetrated his concentration and he turned and saw her. They looked at each other over a distance of about twenty yards. There was an expression of total disbelief on his face.

Slowly, he rose to his feet. To anyone else, he might have appeared ludicrous dressed as he was, but not to her.

'Kate?' he said. 'Is it you?'

'I'm not a ghost.'

He moved tentatively towards her. 'Is your husband with you?'

There was a heartbeat's pause and then she said, putting into words, acknowledging for the first time, something she subconsciously knew had already happened, 'No, I think I may have left him.'

'I don't know what to say . . .' he said. 'I don't know where to start . . . I mean . . .'

She laughed and a blackbird flew scoldingly away. 'That's not like you.'

'You might have dropped from Mars.'

'I have come a long way. You could start by kissing me.'

He kissed her and at the same time lifted her completely off the ground. When she caught her breath she said, 'You'd better put me down.'

'I can do a damn sight better than kisses.'

They laughed together. They stood by the lily pond, laughing, and a red squirrel poked its head out from the branches of a beech tree to see what was happening.

Now began a period that Kate was always to look back on as a time of magic. One brilliant, hot summer day followed another, and they lived a kind of life she had never even known existed.

They turned time inside out. The nights were for talking and making love, and they slept in the heat of the day.

Tom showed her the house that first day with the pride of new ownership. 'I've bought it,' he said. 'There'll be times when I'll have to go away, either for the *Chronicle* or gathering material, but it'll always be here to come back to.'

It was smaller than she had thought, and older. He told her it had once been a hunting lodge. 'They say it dates back to the mid-eighteenth century. They called this colour *kaisergelb*. And look at those floors.'

He saw the house in male terms, she thought: the solidity of the structure, the thickness of the walls, the soundness of the timbers. She saw a rather spartan house, that needed warmth and lightness. She helped him to choose curtains, paint and wall-paper, and did all the things she had longed to do for him when he had moved into the house in Cape Town.

They cleaned out the big lily pond and filled it with fresh water and used it as a bathing pool, floating naked in the shallow water.

They did a lot of their cooking outside, for Tom had

taken to the South African way, and they grilled spicy *debrecina* sausages and frankfurters and drank the good, cheap Austrian white wine.

There were moments when she knew she had never been so happy. And then, sometimes, a shadow seemed to fall as she remembered Saxenburg.

Sometimes Tom would question her about what she was planning for herself. The word 'I' became 'we'. But she did not respond. 'I'm not thinking beyond this moment,' she said.

In those first days, they did nothing but get to know each other, both physically and mentally – and Kate established that there was no other woman in his life.

'Fräulein Necker?' he said, smiling. 'Well, I won't deny I've tried. Every member of the foreign press corps has tried, but she's looking for a *baron*. She knows exactly what she wants. She wants an apartment in Vienna, a mansion in the country, servants, a title, a Rolls Royce and a chauffeur. In the meantime, she's a wonderfully loyal and efficient secretary.'

'And there's no one else?'

'I'd be lying to you if I said there hadn't been. But no one important. There never has been. There never will be.'

He was writing a book about a journey he had made the year before through the Caucasus and he returned to it after a few days. He liked to get up early and work in the cool of the morning. Kate did not mind, in fact, she loved it; it gave her a sense of being part of his real life. She would go off in the mornings to the small group of village shops and bring back hot rolls and give him his breakfast in the summer house. About noon he would stop for the day and they would immerse themselves in the lily pond, have lunch and sleep away the heat of the afternoon. Then he would take her for drives up into the hills to Weidling and Klosterneuburg, Sievering and Grinzing. As the sun dipped, glowing yellow on the gold onion domes of the little churches, they would come back into the foot-hills closer to the city and sit in the *heurigers* under the vines and drink the new white wine.

263

'There's no other city like it,' Tom said. 'Imagine London with small vineyards all over St. John's Wood.'

But the past could not be excluded; the idyll could not be total, the isolation could not be complete.

Kate wrote to her bank in London, giving Tom's address for forwarding mail. She had enjoyed the feeling of having dropped out of the world, but knew it was self-indulgent.

Late one afternoon, as they sat in a *heuriger* overlooking a church in Neustift am Walde, she said, 'Tell me about Joyce.'

He told her, and it was not as she had feared. Joyce had not killed herself, but died of pneumonia.

'When?' she said, feeling that at last she could exist with the knowledge.

'Three days before I telephoned you. Why didn't you call me back?'

'It was my wedding day. Why didn't you telephone again?'

'Who answered my call?'

'Lena, the maid.'

'The first thing I asked was if you were in. She said yes, that she'd call you. Then she came back and said you weren't in and was there a message. Well, that was plain enough.' He refilled his glass from the flask on the table. 'I've often wondered what would have happend if I'd spoken to you that day.'

'I have, too. I'm glad I didn't.' She told him about her family. 'Duggie would have died without the operation. The infection was creeping up his leg. I had to marry Charles.'

The past, having re-asserted itself, would not let them alone. That night, as they lay in the big, wooden bed, he said, 'Are you serious about leaving Charles?'

'Yes.'

'Does he know that?'

'Not yet.'

'You never really loved him, did you?'

'No. But I think we could have lived together. What Smuts would have called "making a go of things." But . . .'

'But?'

She told him about the manhunt, about the three men on the rock who wanted to use the drowning body for target practice.

She lay amid the hot, rumpled sheets, remembering her horror, remembering, too, the feeling that what had happened was somehow her fault, that if she had helped Jonas when he asked her to, he might still be alive. On the other hand, they might have hanged him; perhaps she had done him a favour.

'I suppose he did it?' Tom said, echoing her own thoughts.

'I suppose so. He always denied it. I'd never liked him, you know. He'd always made me feel undressed, somehow. But there were moments when I believed him.'

'If not Jonas, then who?'

'It had to be him,' she said. 'There was no one else.'

'Do you mean no other person, or no white person?'

'Why would anyone want to kill Miriam?'

'Why do men rape women?'

Sometimes in the late afternoons they walked among the beech trees on the hills and would lie down in the warm, scented grass and look out over the city. Once he took her to Tulln, on the Danube, and they had lunch on a terrace overlooking the great, grey-green river and watched the barges come down from Basle on their way to Budapest and Bucharest and the Black Sea.

'When I see them, I always want to move on. Just keep going,' he said. 'What made you leave Saxenburg? What broke the umbilical cord? Or is it broken?'

It was something she had asked herself many times since she had arrived in Vienna. It was one thing to say she wanted to leave Charles, another that she had broken all her ties with Saxenburg – and was the one thing possible without the other? And if she acknowledged the break, was she not already replacing it with a future? If so, what was the future? She did not know.

Leaving Charles could be construed in many ways. She could leave his bed, leave him emotionally, but still live on at Saxenburg. What she could not do was simply walk away from her responsibilities and her guilt.

'The trouble is, it's not Charles's fault, it's mine,' she said.

'You didn't make him what he is.'

'Someone did.'

She told him about the party and Freda's death and her own broken bones.

'My God, I turn my back on you and everything goes to pieces,' he said, trying to inject lightness into what he was beginning to recognise as a nightmare.

She smiled. 'I'm sorry, but you asked about Charles.' After a pause, she said, 'Have you ever had an affair with a man?'

He shook his head. 'Cross my heart and hope to die. At school there were the usual liaisons, but nothing after that. I've known bisexuals, of course.'

'I should have guessed. He was always going to District Six, or talking about it. He and Jerry. Freda thought Jerry was having an affair with a woman.'

They ordered coffee and drank the last of the Kremser and she said, 'I can't help feeling sorry for him. I can't help feeling it all stems from the past, from things that happened to him long ago.'

'Such as?'

'His father seemed to hate him after what happened to his brother Hugo.'

'What happened?'

'I thought you'd know.'

'Drag out your skeletons and let's have a look at them.'

She told him about the fire and how Charles had been blamed for not fetching his mother sooner. The change in his father. The black-edged cards on his birthdays that were not to wish him happy returns, but in memoriam for Hugo.

'I can see what you mean,' Tom said. 'But you can't live with someone out of pity.' He took her hand across the table. 'Look, you've seen the sort of life we could have. You know I want you to marry me. You say you love me; you say you're going to, or have already, left your husband. Yet you won't commit yourself.'

'Give me time to get used to the idea,' she said.

One day they had been shopping in Kärntnerstrasse for linen and Tom had decided to drive home a different way from the one he normally took.

Suddenly, she said, 'Stop!'

Looking anxious, he pulled up. She was pointing to a sign on a tree-lined street to their left. 'Look! Gustav Tchermakgasse!'

'What about it?'

'It's the street where Mrs. Preller lived. Tom, let's go and look at her house.'

'Do you know which one it is?'

'She talked about it over and over. I'll probably recognise it.'

They drove slowly along the short street. There were not more than a dozen houses. They were all substantial, giving an air of wealth and opulence to the quiet neighbourhood.

'This area is called the Cottäge,' Tom said. 'New and old money all mixed up.'

'That must be it.' She pointed to a house behind tall iron gates. An iron fence edged the large garden and she remembered Mrs. Preller telling her it was half the size of a city block.

He stopped the car. She got out and went to the railings. The house, at the top of wide steps, was beautiful, with simple, classical lines, rather like Tom's cottage, but on a grander scale.

He pointed at a notice hanging on the railings. 'It's for sale.'

'Let's go in and look at it.'

The gate was unlocked. A gravel path led to the back of the house, into a formal garden with cypress hedges and lime and horse-chestnut trees. In a shaded corner was the rotunda where, Kate remembered, the family had played cards. It was overlooked by the windows from which the young Augusta had observed them as she practised the piano.

Suddenly, they heard a voice. They turned and saw an old man in a black suit. He was clearly upset and waved his arms angrily at them.

'He's telling us to clear off,' Tom said. 'He's the caretaker.'

'Tell him we know someone who once lived here.'

'What was her name?'

'Her first name is Augusta.'

As Tom spoke, the old man stopped muttering and gesticulating. 'Fräulein Augusta?' he said. 'Fräulein Augusta von Berendorf?'

'Tell him I'm her daughter-in-law,' Kate said.

He listened, unbelievingly, then took her hand and bowed as he talked to Tom.

'He used to be the gardener here. He worked for her family. His name is Vedder.'

Tom's German was fluent, if sometimes erratic, and he was able to piece together what the old man said. 'He worked for them for years. Apparently he came from the family's estate.'

'Ask him if any of them are still alive. Mrs. Preller had two older sisters.'

'He says he doesn't know. He stayed on when they left. A Jewish factory owner bought the house. He died six months ago and the house has been on the market ever since.'

As they said good-bye, the man spoke again.

'He says their old governess is still alive,' Tom said. 'She's English, and she still lives in Vienna.'

'Does he know her address?'

The old man disappeared into the house. When he returned, he handed Kate a slip of paper.

The next morning, as Tom was working at his typewriter, she went shopping. When she had finished, she looked at the name, Fräulein Binns, and the address, in a part of Vienna she did not know. On impulse, she found a taxi and handed the driver the paper.

Miss Binns lived in the bottom half of an old house built above a railway-line. As Kate knocked at the door she heard a roar and a long-drawn wail, then steam rose above the roof of the house as a train went by.

Before the echoes had died away, the door was opened and she found herself looking down at the diminutive figure of a very old woman wearing a dark dress and a lace cap. She was no more than four foot ten inches tall.

'Bitte?' she said.

'I'm looking for Fräulein Binns,' Kate said.

'I am Miss Binns.' She might have been very old, but her voice was crisp and her eyes were bright. She reminded Kate of a bird, in much the same way that Mendel did. 'I do not give English lessons any longer.'

'No, no! I don't want lessons,' Kate said, and explained who she was.

'You know Augusta von Berendorf?' The old eyes shone, the wrinkled skin of her face rearranged itself into a smile of welcome. 'Come in, my dear!'

She led the way along a dark passage into a room which was furnished in the style of fifty years earlier, with lace anti-macassars and aspidistras and oversized pieces of mahogany furniture. A large window overlooked a narrow garden that ran down to the railway tracks. There was a chair facing the window and next to it was a low table on which was an open book containing what appeared to be rows of figures, and a small carriage clock.

There was another roar and a locomotive passed along the end of the garden. Steam rose. The whistle sounded. When the noise faded and the coaches were rattling past, shaking the house, Miss Binns peered at the book through a magnifying glass, and Kate realised it was a railway time-table.

'Number 191,' she said. 'St. Polten . . . Melk . . . Pochlarn . . . Austetten . . . St. Valentin . . . Linz. Three minutes late.'

She settled herself by the window and waved Kate to another chair. 'Do you like trains?' she said.

'I've never thought much about them.'

'I didn't when I came here. But the house was cheap because of the noise. There's a whistle sign just below the garden. I didn't sleep for a week, then I dreamed the trains were in bed with me. But I realised that if I let them worry me, I would go off my head. I said to myself, "Take an interest. Learn about them." Now I know them all. Sometimes when I lie in bed at night I say to myself, that's the Number 2020 or Number 1073. Or that's the Simplon-Orient going down to Constantinople. Or the Arlberg-Orient starting off for Paris. They're friendly things.'

Kate spent nearly two hours with her. They drank coffee and talked of trains, and of the von Berendorf family, of which Miss Binns had been part.

'Of course, none of them suspected that the money was running out,' she said. 'The girls lived the kind of life they had been brought up to accept. There was the estate in the Waldviertel which they hardly ever visited, the holiday house in the Salzkammergut, the big house in the Cottage. Herr von Berendorf had a box at the Staatsoper and another at the Volksoper. They always took season tickets for the Musikverein. They kept their own carriages and would go to Baden for the waters whenever they chose.'

'And no one knew about the debts?' Kate said.

'Augusta's father never discussed his financial affairs, not even with his wife. It was the way the von Berendorfs had always lived. Men never talked business with their wives. Women were not supposed to have the brains to understand.'

Their talk was punctuated by periods of silence as trains passed. On each occasion, she checked the time. Some were up to five minutes late and she made a disapproving click with her tongue before resuming the conversation.

'Well, it all came to an end. All came crashing down. People talked about it as though it were a tragedy, and I suppose it was, for the family, but then came the war and it seemed rather insignificant compared with other tragedies.'

'Mrs . . . Miss Augusta, that is, told me that they lost almost everything when her father died.'

'Everything. That's why they made the bargain.'

'The bargain?'

'For her to go out to Africa with that man – what was his name?'

'Preller.'

'I always forget it. A dreadful man. Uncouth. Like a bull. He fell in love with Augusta, but she did not care for him at all. And so . . . you could say he bought her.'

'Bought her!'

'Not literally, I suppose. But he came to an agreement with Frau von Berendorf. So much money for her and the two other girls if Augusta married him. I remember Bella – that was one of her sisters, the other was Anna – coming to me in tears. "What can we do, Binnsie?" she said. "You can go out to work like me," I said. "Work?" she said. It was like suggesting she might fly.'

'So Mr. Preller supported the family?'

'At the beginning. That was the bargain. There would be enough for Frau von Berendorf and the two girls to buy a small apartment and an amount invested for them to live on.'

'Did the other girls ever marry?'

'Never. They had no dowries. I saw them from time to time, and I wrote to Augusta when each of them passed away.'

Kate had a vivid picture of Mrs. Preller in her isolation at Saxenburg reading of her sisters' deaths and being forced to remember the truth of her past rather than the pretence she maintained.

'She sent money for the funerals. She loved her family.'

'Even though they sacrificed her?'

'Sacrifice is a big word . . .' The Zurich Express crashed along the tracks and she checked the clock, then nodded. 'On time. Girls did that sort of thing in those days. Half the marriages in Vienna were financial arrangements. Some still are. What else could she have done? I suppose there were compensations. He was very rich. And she took a lover.'

'A lover?'

'Of course. That is the natural consequence of such marriages. Everyone does it. As long as the affairs are discreet, no one minds. Society does not – or at least, when there *was* a society it did not expect a fiscal contract to end in love. Oh no, my dear, that is how the middle classes live. To aristocrats, marriage and love were totally separate. She did what anyone of her class would have done. She used to write to me regularly in the early days, then the letters stopped. Yes, she had a lover. Perhaps more than one. I can't remember now. I think she really was very fond of him. She used to tell me how handsome he was. I think she wrote because she needed to tell someone.'

'Did she mention a name? Was he in Cape Town or in Helmsdale?'

'My dear, it's so long ago! My memory is not what it used to be. Once I could tell you where all the trains stopped, now I have to look in the time-table. No, I can't remember a name, and I destroyed the letter.'

In her mind Kate was rapidly rearranging the pieces of information. Mrs. Preller had once had a lover. It did not altogether surprise her. But who? It might have been someone in Cape Town. Then she recalled Dr. du Toit once saying that Smuts had loved her, and it was plain that he still did. Could it have been him? Could the brawls between him and Boss Preller have been over Augusta? She tried to visualise Smuts as a young man. She doubted if he had ever been handsome, but perhaps Mrs. Preller had been looking for something else. If Boss Preller had been uncouth and violent, would Smuts not have been acceptable by comparison? He was a rough diamond, but there was a streak of goodness in him. Or was the whole story simply a fabrication produced by unhappiness and loneliness? Had she not built a world in Saxenburg for Miss Binns as she had built for Saxenburg her story of the rich and handsome young man who had swept her off her feet in Vienna, with no mention of the family tragedy? Could the lover she described have been only a product of dreams?

'After a while, she stopped writing,' Miss Binns went on. 'Bella died when she was quite young. Then Anna went. I wrote each time. She sent money, but no reply. Then, out of the blue, years later, she wrote, thanking me for all I had done. It was a surprise, because I had done nothing. I remember that letter better than the others because it was muddled and unlike Augusta. She said she'd had an accident a year or so before.' That would have been the fire, Kate thought. 'She talked about coming back to Vienna. She wanted to come, because of the scandal.'

'What scandal?'

'I don't know, my dear. It had something to do with another child, or so I thought. You say there were only two boys, but I had the impression that there had been three children: two boys and a girl. I remember something about a sister.'

'I'm sure there were only two children.'

'I told you it was a muddled letter. I had the feeling she might have been drinking when she wrote it. And I've said my memory isn't what it was. But I do remember it as being very bitter.'

Suddenly, Saxenburg was very close. Sitting in the over-furnished room in Vienna with the trains thundering past the window, Kate felt again the dark melancholy of the big house, the secrecy, the mystery, and a mood of bleakness came over her.

It was nearly lunchtime when she got back to Potzleinsdorf. Tom was still typing under the canopy of shade in the summer house. She found a bottle of cold Gumpoldskirchen in the ice-chest and took it out. 'Time to stop,' she said.

'I've missed you. Where have you been?'

She told him. Then she brought out a rug and some wurst and black bread and they lay in the shade and had their lunch. It was a beautiful day, warm, sunny and drowsy with heat. When they had finished eating she lay beside him and put her head on his outstretched arm.

'My holiday is nearly over,' he said.

'I know.'

'What are you going to do?'

'I don't know. May I stay for a while?'

'Of course! You realise I might have to go away?'

'Where?'

'Could be anywhere: Yugoslavia, Hungary. You'd be alone. Would you mind?'

'Not if I knew you were coming back. But we have two more days. Let's not talk about it until then.'

She was suddenly afraid of losing him, and there was an echo in her mind of the day she had left him in Cape Town to go to Saxenburg. 'Hold me,' she said, and he put his other arm around her and held her tightly.

As the afternoon began to cool, he said, 'Let's go to that *heuriger* at the top of Krottenbachstrasse. Then we can go to Anton's in Sievering and eat roast duck. We'll make an evening of it.'

They were getting into his car when a post office messenger arrived with a cable.

'Blast it! They can't even let me finish my vacation,' he said. Then he saw the address, and frowned. 'It's for you.'

She slit open the envelope and pulled out the cable. It was short and had been re-routed by her bank in London. It read: *Charles arrested for murder. Mrs. Preller dangerously ill. Smuts.*

[3]

Another train, another country. Kate sat in her green leather compartment in the brown, dusty coach as it rattled across the bleak windswept plains of gnarled trees and *fynbos* that would end in Helmsdale and Saxenburg and the sea.

A bare two months before she had watched the Austrian mountains slip by as the Arlberg-Orient Express had rushed down the deep valleys. Then she had felt a tight excitement at what was to come; now she was hollow with apprehension.

Unlike the soft evening heat of Vienna, this late afternoon in spring was dry and baking. If she closed the windows she burst out in beads of perspiration; if she opened them, the south-easter blew the engine smoke into the compartment. Her head rolled from side to side to the movement of the train. She seemed to have been travelling for ever. It was nearly six weeks since the cable had reached her in Vienna. She had returned to London, but there was not a berth to South Africa to be had, for the English autumn was starting and the ships were full of migratory rich going out to winter at the Cape. Finally, she found accommodation in a Holland-Afrika liner sailing from Rotterdam, but it had taken the long, slow way via Suez and through the Red Sea, stopping at port after port.

She visualized her journey as a line on a map, starting in middle Europe and going west, then eastward through the Mediterranean, then south and now, finally, southeast. She was tired. More than tired: she was weary to her very core, mentally exhausted by the problems she was trying to face. The ship had berthed that morning, but she had been too tired even to go and see her parents, although she'd had several hours to kill before the train left.

The train slowed. She saw the familiar red and green and black corrugated-iron roofs of Helmsdale, and then they were coming to a halt in the station. She saw Smuts' bantam-like figure on the platform, and waved. He came to the window. 'Thank God you're back,' he said.

He helped her down and they walked to the car. 'I'll send the lorry for the luggage,' he said.

'How is she?'

'Better than she was, my friend, I can tell you that.'

'And Charles?'

'Not so bloody good.'

People in the small car-park were staring at her. She would have to put up with that now: the wife of a man who had been arrested for murder.

'Let's go . . .' She was about to form the word 'home,' but it stuck in her throat. 'Let's go back to Saxenburg and talk there.'

They drove along the cliff road, past the ruined houses, and she saw that another one was being renovated. But the Berrangé place still stood in its desolation. When they reached Saxenburg she said, 'Before I go up, I want to hear everything.'

'Well, it's sundowner time.' She realised that he was making an effort to be his old self.

They had a drink in his room. She told him briefly about her journey, then said, 'If you or Mrs. Preller have written recently, I won't have seen the letters. I haven't heard from Charles. I've no idea what's been happening.'

'I saw Charles three days ago. He asked if we had heard from you. He said he couldn't bring himself to write.'

'So tell me about it, from the beginning.'

'You know that Betty died?'

'Yes. I had your letter about that just before I left. You didn't say how.'

'She had taken up with one of the fishermen in the village. She was drinking a lot. We had some cold weather and one night, when he was at sea, she lit an old paraffin heater. She must have been drunk, because she did not leave a window open. Maybe she went to sleep. The fumes killed her.' He sighed. 'That was the start of everything. Until then, things had been going along not too badly. Charles was doing his best. The season was looking good. Then Betty died. Lena was still here then. She's gone now. You remember she was peculiar even before you left?'

Kate recalled Lena's growing religious mania, and nodded.

'After Betty died, she started hearing voices.'

'In the house?'

'They started at Betty's funeral. Then I found her praying to that damn ship's figurehead in the hall. She said it spoke to her. I used to find her there at odd times of the day and night. She told me God was speaking to her through the figurehead and that she must do God's will. I said *my* will was more important and she must stop bloody praying and get the lunch.'

In her mind, Kate saw Lena huddled in the hall under the great bare-bosomed woman who had once been the prow of the wrecked ship *Saxenburg*.

'Did Mrs. Preller know?'

'Lena didn't spend so much time with her after you left. When Betty died, she went up even less. Only to give Miss Augusta her shots. Then, one day, she put on her hat and said she had to go out. She went to the police. You remember Sergeant van Blerk? He told me later she had come to him and said that she'd been praying for guidance and God had told her to stop lying.'

'Lying?'

'She claimed she'd lied at the second inquest on Miriam. She told Van Blerk that it had not been Jonas she'd seen, but Charles.'

'And he believed her?'

'Not at first, but when she'd told her story, he did.'

'What *is* her story?'

'At the magistrates' hearing she said she'd seen Charles with Miriam.

'That could have been a lie, too.'

'No-one cross-examined her. Charles pleaded not guilty and reserved his defence. There wasn't anything the magistrate could do but send him for trial.'

'Do you think he's guilty?'

'Of course not. Christ, who'd take the word of a bloody mad coloured woman? I reckon Charles's lawyers will get doctors to show how mad she is.'

'How has Mrs. Preller taken it?'

'How do you think?'

'Badly?'

'Ja. Badly.'

'What caused her illness?'

'After Lena went to the police I kicked her arse off the estate. That was a mistake, I suppose, though we could never have let her stay. But she knew about Miss Augusta's shots, how much and how often, you know. After she'd gone, I had to do it. Miss Augusta wouldn't have Tilly near her.'

Kate thought of him moving about the darkened room, filling the syringe, looking for the veins in the thin, wasted arms, the same arms that had, she believed, held him as a lover so many years before. In Vienna, the thought of them as lovers had been strange; here nothing was strange, everything possible.

'I was late one day and when I got to her room she had given herself her dose. It was something Hennie du Toit had told me to watch, because she sometimes gave herself an overdose. She seemed all right at first, but it turned out that there was already some paralysis in her muscles, from lying in the same position too long. You have to move people like her regularly.'

'I know.' Kate remembered that Christmas night when she had sat by Mrs. Preller's bedside, turning her over every half hour.

'Luckily, Hennie dropped in to see her. He's been here a lot in the past weeks. I think he comes because he's lonely. He saved her. She still has a little paralysis, and at first we thought she was getting pneumonia. Anyway, things will be better for her now.'

'Why?'

'Because you're back, my friend.'

Suddenly, she saw her future clearly: Whatever happened to Charles, she was going to be tied to Saxenburg, tied to a sick woman whom she thought of as old, but who might last twenty years, perhaps even longer with loving care; *her* loving care.

It was dusk when she went upstairs. Mrs. Preller was sitting in her usual chair, but the lamp was turned low. Kate leant forward to kiss the dry, scarred cheek.

'I thought I heard the car half an hour ago,' she said.

'The train was late.'

'Has Smuts told you everything?'

'Yes.'

As she looked closely, Kate could see the extent of the paralysis. One side of Mrs. Preller's face was affected by a palsy. The lower jaw was twisted slightly out of alignment, and she had to hold it in place with her hand, otherwise she could not form words. When she spoke, it sounded as though she had water in her mouth.

'Someone put Lena up to it,' she said. 'She would never have done it by herself. Never. Not after all I did for her. They hate us, you know. They have always hated the Prellers. It's because, without us, there would be nothing. We *made* the town. Now they're laughing at us.'

From anyone else the phrases, coming as they did from a semi-paralysed face which was pulled out of shape each time it uttered a word, would have been ludicrous, but not now. Again Kate thought that in Saxenburg almost anything made sense, from a talking figurehead to the acid words of an embittered old woman.

'They'll pay,' she was saying. 'I'll close the hotel. I'll close the garage and the fertilizer factory. See how people will like being out of work and with no petrol for their cars and not able to prop up the bar. See how they'll like that!'

'Have you seen Charles?'

'Of course not. I cannot travel and he is locked up.'

'Has he written?'

'For strangers to paw over before they post the letters? No! Smuts has seen him. The lawyers see him. But he'll soon be home, then we can forget all this. When my grandchildren are here, then we can laugh at it. It's nonsense! Charles could never have killed Miriam. They grew up together. They were friends. Boss Charles and I never liked the friendship – my father never let a Jew into his house in Vienna – but they *were* friends. It could not have happened as they say.'

Kate saw that she was becoming agitated and, to divert her, said, 'I was in Vienna when the cable reached me.'

Mrs. Preller's mind focussed slowly on the words.

'You? In Vienna?'

'I saw your house. It's lovely. I went into the garden and talked to your old gardener, Herr Vedder. He's the caretaker now.'

There was a silence, then suddenly she said shrilly, 'I do not wish to talk about Vienna? Do you understand me? Not now . . .'

'Well, well! So you're back!' With relief, Kate turned and saw Dr. du Toit in the doorway. He came forward and shook her hand. 'Thank goodness you've arrived. We've missed her, haven't we, Augusta?'

'What are they saying, Hennie?'

'They?'

'You know what I mean. I want to go into town. I want them to see me. I don't want them to think I'm hiding here.'

'No one thinks that. And you're not well enough to go out.'

He stood on the far side of the chair and Kate looked at

him in the lamplight. His face was thinner, his hair lank and greasy.

'When can I?'

'Don't rush things, Augusta. You need rest and peace.'

'Peace! Good God, Hennie, do you think because I sit here day after day away from the world I find peace? They have my son. Don't you understand that?'

'Augusta, it makes things worse if you get excited. Only time will get those muscles to function again. But not if you're full of tension.' He turned to Kate. 'You've heard the details?'

'Mr. Smuts told me.'

'Lena's mad, of course. Hearing voices. They'll tear her to pieces at the trial. She's all the prosecution's got.'

'Smuts said they didn't cross-examine her at the magistrates' hearing.'

'Didn't want to tip their hands. And you know what they say about a preparatory examination: even if the magistrate finds there is no case to answer, people still say there's no smoke without fire. But at the trial everything will come out and Charles will be vindicated.'

'He must sue them,' Mrs. Preller said.

'Augusta, we've been through this. Who can he sue? Not the police, they have their duty to do. He can't sue the judge. He can't even sue Lena.'

'Hennie, once he's found not guilty, I want you to have her arrested.'

'That's not possible.'

'Then have her committed to an asylum!'

He glanced at Kate and raised his eyebrows. She rose and excused herself, saying, 'I must go and change.' As she closed the door behind her she heard Mrs. Preller saying, 'You're a doctor. You can do things like that.'

She went downstairs and found Smuts. 'How long has she been like this?' she said.

'I told you . . .'

'I don't mean the paralysis.'

She saw glints of anger in his eyes. 'It wasn't *your* son they took.'

As she went up to her room, she thought about Smuts.

He was no longer the old man she had left. He seemed to have renewed his energy. Perhaps it was taking over the responsibility of the farm again. Or perhaps it was only because she knew that there was a whole relationship between him and Mrs. Preller that was closed to her; a whole life lived out of sight of the world. He was no longer merely a servant. She was glad to see his return to vigour, but did it really help her? He might collapse again any day. In any case, his role was to run the estate. With Lena gone, it was clearly her role to look after Mrs. Preller; a very different Mrs. Preller from the one she had known before.

When she reached her room, the first thing she saw was a pile of letters on her table. They were all from Tom and she knew they must have arrived on the fast mail ship from Southampton even while she was wallowing through the Red Sea. She locked her door and sorted them by their stamps.

They were the first love letters she had ever received and she savoured each word. They were filled with passion and longing. As she read, she could hear his voice, see his face. She smelled the paper and thought she could smell his skin. The phrases brought back the days she had spent with him, the cool water in the lily pond, the soft warmth of the night, the new wine. She remembered the walks on the hills, lunch by the Danube, she remembered everything. They were the only memories she had ever really wanted to keep.

She remembered the day they had parted. He had shown no anger when she had told him she must return to the Cape. He seemed almost to have expected it. He had sat on their big, wooden bed – she thought of it still as theirs – and watched her pack.

'Life has a way of demanding its pound of flesh,' he had said. 'I have a Jewish friend who says, "There's no such thing as a free lunch." It's true.'

'I'll come back,' she said.

He had nodded as though this was part of the formal game of departure; a phrase to be used to soften it, but not to be taken literally.

She finished reading the letters and put them away to be read again.

The following day, she made arrangements to visit Charles in prison.

[4]

Roeland Street Gaol was a bleak, fortress-like building made of mountain stone, with towers and turrets and a heavy steel portcullis that gave it the look of a medieval fortress. It stood above the city on the rising slope of Table Mountain, not far from the Prellers' apartment. Because Charles was a remand prisoner, Kate was allowed to see him alone in a small room that overlooked the exercise yard. It was sparsely furnished with wooden furniture, each piece stamped with a Government mark. It had absorbed the general prison smell of Jeyes Fluid and brown beans. She had been taken there by Mr. Godlonton, Charles's attorney, but she had asked to speak to him alone.

He was dressed neatly in grey flannel trousers and a white shirt, but his face was pallid and there were dark circles under his eyes. She kissed him and he held her for a moment, then she broke away and sat in a straight-backed chair.

'You're looking fine,' she said.

He went to the window and stared at the mountain which reared up behind the prison. A layer of south-easter cloud formed a table-cloth over it.

'You look good, too,' he said.

'The trip was what I needed.'

'Ja. I wish I could have come with you, but I had to look after the farm.' His eyes strayed constantly to the window, only half his attention seemed to be on her.

'Smuts said you're going to have a good season.'

'Maybe.' Then he said, savagely, 'What the hell does it mean to me!'

'You'll be home as soon as the trial's over. You know that.'

'That's what they said before.'

After a moment's silence she said, 'Is there anything you need? Books, magazines?'

'Food. The food's terrible. Stew with beans all the time.'

'I'll ask Mr. Godlonton if he can arrange something. He brought me here.'

'Where is he?'

'Outside in the car.'

'Why didn't he come in?'

'I told him I wanted to see you alone.'

'I haven't seen him for two days.'

'I'm sure he's doing everything he can.'

He was nervous. His fingers fretted constantly at a piece of loose cotton on his shirt. He paced up and down the room, never settling in the chair for more than a few moments, restless, preoccupied. Behind his nervousness, she sensed terror.

'I can't sleep,' he said. 'There's always some bloody noise, always someone talking or snoring or crying. Christ, what a place!' He went to the window again. 'I can't see anything from my window except a brick wall. Did he say he was coming in?'

'Mr. Godlonton? No.'

'Christ! How does he think I feel, left here!'

'I'm sure he knows, Charles. He's done his best for your mother for years.'

'For my mother, maybe, but not for me. I mean, before the preparatory examination he said they'd never believe Lena. Jesus, what a farce! We sat there on our arses waiting for the magistrate to say there was no case to answer, and the bugger sent me for trial! Godlonton could be wrong again.'

'Do you want me to try and find someone else?'

'It's too late now.'

'They say that the barrister is a very good man.'

He nodded. There was an uneasy silence and she was reminded of the visits he had made to her in the hospital. They had never had enough to say to one another and

283

had made each other uneasy and tense. The same was happening now. She longed to leave, but could not. She must relax and try to make him feel better, not worse.

'No one believes me,' he said.

'Of course they do.'

'No, they don't. I've told them over and over what happened that night and they look at me and take notes, but you can see they don't believe me.'

'What did happen, Charles?'

For a moment, she thought he was not going to speak, and then it came out in jerky, almost uncontrolled sentences, and she was taken back to the day of the picnic on which Miriam had tried so hard to make him jealous. She recalled it vividly, especially later, when she had gone into the ruined Berrangé house with him and had had to fight him off.

According to his story now, he had left Saxenburg later that evening, gone to Miriam's house and asked her to come for a drive. They had taken some brandy and he had driven back to the Berrangé house.

'That was where you always took her, wasn't it?' Kate said. 'It was really yours and Miriam's.'

'It had been since we were kids. My mother didn't want Miriam at our place because she was Jewish, and she didn't like me having Miriam as a girlfriend. After I went to boarding-school, I hardly saw her. But then after the Berrangés left and the house fell into decay, we made a room there where we could meet.'

'And you made love there?'

'Ja.'

'That night?'

'No. She came with me, all right, and I thought everything was going to be the same, but she wouldn't. She only came to tease me. She said she'd been with Duggie earlier and they had made love at her house. She said he was a much better lover than me.'

He paused, and she said, 'What did you do then?'

'I really wanted her, you know. So I said I didn't believe her and caught her by the arm, and we wrestled a bit. I thought she just wanted a bit of fun. But she was serious and fought me off and ran out of the house. I caught her by the gate and tried to make her get back into the car, but she wouldn't. She was shouting and swearing at me and saying Duggie was a better lover and that she was going to sleep with him in Cape Town, and Jerry, too. So finally I said, the hell with it and got into the car and drove back into town. Freda had gone to bed, but Duggie and Jerry were still drinking in Duggie's room. I told Duggie to get ready and we drove back to Cape Town.'

'You left Miriam outside the Berrangés'?'

'She wouldn't get into the car.'

'So that's when Lena must have seen you. Either then or when you were going into the house. She was coming back from Church.'

'I suppose so.' Again he paused. 'Kate, I know what you think of me, after what happened in Cape Town, but I swear to you I didn't kill Miriam. I always sort of loved her. I would never, never do that to her. And that's the truth.'

She remembered Mrs. Preller's words: 'Charles could never have killed Miriam.'

She knew he was waiting for her to agree with him, to believe him, but he had lied so easily before. Instead, she said, 'And Jerry and Duggie gave evidence at the preparatory examination, of course.'

'They all did. Everyone from the second inquest. Look, I don't blame Jerry. He had to tell what he knew, but he hasn't been to see me.'

'Maybe he's away.'

'No, he's here. His father died recently and he's taken over the business. I wrote to him. He never replied.'

'Perhaps he isn't allowed to if he's a witness.'

'Maybe.' But he sounded as though this was the final disloyalty.

When they came for him she recognised the look in his eyes as the same one she had seen in Jonas's; a plea for help.

Later that day, she went to see her parents. She had written to them several times from Europe, letters about what she was doing and who she was seeing, and she'd had one formal note from her mother. Mrs. Buchanan's style was unique. If Kate said she had been to the opera, the reply would be: 'You went to the opera with Mr. Mendel, and you enjoyed it. And then you went to the ballet. I'm sorry to hear how hot it was, but you found it was raining when you came out, and that cooled you down.' The result was that her letters contained very little news. It was only when she wanted something that she was specific.

Not knowing what to expect, Kate found that her parents' circumstances had changed for the better. Her father and the man next door were working partners and he was bringing in good money for the first time in many years. They got on so well that the neighbour had helped Mr. Buchanan to redecorate the small villa, and it was no longer the dark hovel it had been.

The two men had formed a friendship beyond their business relationship. It was the first time Kate had ever seen her father with a real friend. True, they both liked a drink, but now it was not the hectic drinking of Edinburgh or the early days in Cape Town. They would sit on the *stoep* in the hot evenings and drink a couple of bottles of cheap white wine, but the tempo had changed. Her father's drinking was slower, more measured, as though he realised that since the money was coming in regularly, he could afford to have a drink at any time, and did not have to fill himself fast when the opportunity arose.

Duggie, too, was in work again. Through a war veterans' association, he had been taken onto the temporary staff of the City Council, adding up rate demands, folding them and placing them in brown window envelopes for posting. There was a chance that he might move on to other, similar jobs and eventually get onto the 'permanent' temporary staff, as Mrs. Buchanan described it.

She was the one in whom the greatest change had occurred. She had never been a neighbourly woman, and even in Edinburgh had not been friendly with other families on the same stair, but Kate had not been in the house for long before there was a knock at the door and a fat white woman in a tight dress and carpet slippers, shouted from the door, 'Can I use the phone, Mrs. B.?'

'The phone?' Kate said.

'We had one put in a month ago because of the removal business. It's in the passage.'

It was the phone that had made the difference, Kate realised. Few families in the street had telephones and they used the Buchanans' as they might a public call-box. There was a box for money and they came and went. They gave the Buchanans' number as their own, and during that afternoon Mrs. Buchanan twice answered it for neighbours and stood at the door, calling their names.

The result was that there was a flow of people in and out. 'Sometimes I canna get my work done for a' the telephoning,' she said. 'Then they'll want a cup of tea and a bit of a crack. It's as much as I can do to get rid of them.'

But Kate could see that secretly her mother was delighted. A whole new world had opened to her.

The irony, she thought, was that it had been in her mind to offer to pay their fares back to Edinburgh. She had felt increasingly guilty about forcing them to come out, especially since Duggie's leg operation. But now she had to face the fact that they had finally settled down better than she had. That it was she, not they, who wanted to break away and leave the country.

Duggie came back about five and after supper she took him to the lounge of the Railway Arms and bought him a whisky. It was a dreary place, filled with cheap furniture; all the tables had cigarette burns.

Duggie had used part of the first month's wages to buy a suit and when he was sitting down he looked neat, handsome, full of the old Edinburgh charm. The last time she had seen him like this was the day of the picnic.

She told him how Charles had described his movements that night, and he could find nothing with which to disagree.

They went over the day and the evening as they each remembered it, searching for some pointer to what had happened later. Finally, she put the question point blank: 'Do you think he did it, Duggie?'

'God knows. It's something I've asked myself over and over. Everyone thought yon maid from Saxenburg . . .'

'Lena?'

'Aye, Lena. Everyone said she was just a mad old woman. But you should have seen her in the box. She didn't look mad to me. A wee bit simple, perhaps. But there was nothing mad about her.'

'People said she had gone peculiar after her daughter died.'

'But she'd seen Charles. There's no disputing it. She placed him with Miriam. And he'd never come forward before. He'd let yon fellow Jonas be arrested and I don't think he'd have come forward even if that lad had been tried.'

'You don't know that.' Again, Kate thought of Charles waiting on the rocks with his rifle for Jonas to emerge from the cave. Even though she had been there with him, even though she had told herself that he could never have known that Jonas really was hiding there, there was something uncanny and inhuman about the way he had worked it out and waited for the hunted man to be forced into the open.

'Will you be giving evidence?' Duggie said. 'They went ahead with the preparatory examination without you.'

'Mine was only the finding of the body. Mr. Godlonton says that if I wasn't at the magistrate's hearing, I won't be called at the Supreme Court. Duggie, there's something I think you should know. Charles says that when he took Miriam out that night, she told him she'd been with you.'

'Aye. I saw her home.'

She remembered the two of them walking up Helmsdale's main street after they had come back from the picnic.

'He says she told him that you'd . . . that . . . that you'd made love.'

Duggie glanced at her, then looked away. He seemed suddenly withdrawn. He toyed with his whisky, swilling it round and round in his glass, then said, 'I don't want to talk about it. Or Miriam, for that matter.'

'But, Duggie, they're going to ask you about it in court.'

He looked suddenly afraid. 'Why? What's that got to do with anyone?'

She spent the night at the apartment. It was hot and stuffy from being closed up for so long and she flung open the windows, letting in the cooler evening air and driving out the musty smell. She sat on the verandah and wrote to Tom, and later when it grew dark, she went to unpack her suitcase.

She was hanging up a frock in the big wardrobe that she and Charles had shared when she came across a garment she had never seen before. It was a kimono in cheap silk. She took it out and looked at it in the light. It was badly creased and stained. She could not remember Charles ever wearing such a garment. Then she remembered the last time she had spent a night in the flat, the night she and Freda had gone to the party. That night she had found empty glasses and a comb filled with hair. She sniffed the garment and caught a whiff of cheap scent, then took it to the kitchen, dropped it into the rubbish bin and washed her hands. The scent did not indicate whether it had belonged to a man or a woman. Either could have used it.

Her distaste grew. She thought of him here with his boys or his girls and suddenly the place seemed more squalid than ever. There was no jealousy in her reaction, just disgust.

She ripped the sheets from the bed and changed the pillow-cases and the towels and then she filled a basin with soapy water and washed down all the surfaces she was likely to touch. She cleaned the telephone and the doornobs and just when she thought she had finished, she would find something else. She became obsessive about it, trying to wipe out all traces of Charles and his friends. Finally, she fell into bed around midnight, exhausted.

She could not sleep. The night was hot, there were mosquitoes and her mind was unreeling the day like a jerky bioscope. She kept seeing Charles in the bleak prison room, saw again the mute appeal in his eyes, the need to be believed. She tried to think logically. If he had not killed Miriam, and if Jonas hadn't, then who *had* killed her?

It had to be someone who had been at the picnic. Yet all the hours during the day and evening were accounted for, except for the time after Charles said he had left her. Had she gone home, and had someone paid her another visit? Duggie, perhaps. She thought of the picnic when Miriam had been so attentive to him, feeding him titbits, whispering to him, apparently attracted to him. Kate had assumed this to be her way of making Charles jealous, but it might have been more complex than that, for she remembered Miriam cavorting with Jerry in the water. Had that scene been directed at Charles or, for some reason she did not understand, at Duggie, whose physical disability precluded such games? Why had Duggie suddenly become afraid when she had mentioned the possibility of being questioned about Miriam? Her mother had once referred to Duggie and Miriam. They could have been closer than she had realised.

Or Jerry?

Had he gone to Miriam's house when Freda was asleep? She recalled his determination in the back seat of the car in Cape Town, forcing his hand between her legs while his wife sat in the front seat. Had he been sufficiently aroused by those games in the water to go to Miriam later? Had something gone wrong there? Had those powerful hands been just too powerful?

Someone had forcibly penetrated Miriam's vagina, damaging the tissues, and then that someone had strangled her. The police said it was Jonas, and that had been wrong. Now they said it was Charles. That could be equally wrong.

Whoever it was, had taken her dead body down to the sea and thrown it – no! It did not have to be that way. Surely whoever it was would have tried to get rid of it, to have it carried out to sea, not brought back. Jonas's body had been brought by the currents to the precise spot where Miriam had been found. Yet everyone said that if you were sucked out of the sea-cave, you would end up out at the India Reef to be eaten by barracuda and sharks. *Everyone* said that, but they were wrong.

The following day she went to see Jerry. The contracting firm he had inherited occupied a series of sheds near the docks. It was burning hot and the fishermen on the pier were casting their lines into a flat and oily sea. He kept her waiting nearly fifteen minutes before his secretary sent her in.

He was sitting behind a large desk covered in papers. He was wearing a collar and tie and there were sweat marks under his arms. He looked the image of a prosperous business man. He greeted her warily, asking about her trip, then she said, 'I saw Charles yesterday.'

'Oh, yes?'

'He says he wrote to you.'

'Ja, I think he did.'

'He's not blaming you. He says he realises you had to tell exactly what you saw.'

'Are you hot? I'll switch on the fan.'

'He misses you, Jerry. He says you've never visited him.'

'It's difficult.'

He played with the papers on his desk. She watched the square hands that were so much like the rest of him: squat, chunky, powerful. He was one of the most sexually aggressive men she had met.

Now he was unable to meet her eyes.

'He would like to see you,' she said.

He glanced at his watch. 'We're pretty pushed now.'

'Jerry, he's your friend.'

'Look, in this business you've got to keep your nose clean. I'm not the only one looking for work.'

'But he hasn't been found guilty. You don't believe he did it, do you?'

'I can't talk about the case.'

'What?'

'It's sub judice.'

'For God's sake, is there anything I don't know that might give me a hint whether Charles did or did not do it? Don't you see, I've *got* to know.'

His mouth turned into a hard, straight line. 'I've just told you, I can't discuss it.'

In the weeks before the trial, she seemed to become several different people. She found herself physically split between Saxenburg and Cape Town. At Saxenburg she had to concentrate on the new plucking season and, with Smuts, see to the washing and starching of the feathers; she had to oversee the house; she had to attend to Mrs. Preller and give her the shots she needed three times a day. Smuts took over when she went into Cape Town to see Charles.

She seemed never to be able to settle. She used the train journeys to catch up on her sleep and to write to Tom. Sometimes, when she returned to Saxenburg, she would find a letter from him.

Emotionally, too, she was split. To Mrs. Preller, she was a daughter-in-law; to Charles, a wife; to Tom, in her mind, a lover.

Her letters to him were, she knew, unsatisfactory, for she could foresee no clear future. If Charles was found guilty and hanged, could she simply leave Saxenburg and return to Vienna? The answer had to be no. What if he was imprisoned for life? Could she ask for a divorce and leave him to rot? Or if he was found not guilty and released? Would she not feel obliged to help him rebuild his life, a life for which she had become responsible when she had married him? And always in the background was her obligation to the old woman in the dim room upstairs, who depended so much on her now: could she simply walk away from that? She felt that circumstances were closing around her, trapping her, cutting off the one escape route to her personal happiness: the route to Vienna and Tom.

On one of her visits to Cape Town she met Charles's counsel, Joshua Prescott, K.C. He was a gross man, a great, rotund figure overflowing the chair in which he sat in his chambers. He wore a black and white bow-tie and a light grey alpaca office jacket, the elbows of which were in tatters. His face was large and moon-like and a toupée was perched above it. The hair at his temples was grey, the toupée dark brown with a parting in the middle. His office was a shambles: books stood in piles around the walls, briefs lay in an untidy mass on his desk. He sweated a great deal and the smell in the room was ripe: a mixture of his body and the Sen-Sen he sucked constantly.

He appeared at first meeting to resemble a large, simple-minded and rather sleepy bear, but Kate had not been with him for more than a few minutes when she felt herself in contact with a muscular brain.

He began slowly. 'Charles tells me you've been in Vienna. I was there some years ago. You know Demel's of course?'

'I never went there.'

'The finest cakes and pastries in the world. Coffee so thick with cream you could stand the spoon up.' His eyes were half-closed as he remembered. Then they opened and he said, 'Did he do it?'

Caught off-guard, she was about to reply when he cut across her. 'No, he did not. That is your answer, Mrs. Preller, to me, or anyone else who might ask you. That is my answer to you and to them as well. He did not.'

'That's what I say to myself,' she said. 'But if he didn't, then who did?'

'Discovering that is not the function of this trial, that is the function of the police. Our – I should say, my – duty, my *function* in this matter is proving the innocence of Charles Preller to the satisfaction of the court. We do not even have to search for the truth, except insofar as it affects Charles. Do you understand me, my dear?'

'Yes.'

'Good.' He began to swivel from side to side then read some notes on the pages of a yellow legal pad.

'You were at both inquests, so we need not worry about them now,' he said. 'None of that evidence implicates Charles. No, our problem is this coloured woman, Lena Lourens. She's the nigger in the woodpile, if I might use the phrase. She lied before, she could be lying again, though Godlonton said she made a fierce impression at the preparatory. Fierce.'

'Charles says his case was badly handled there. So do other people.'

'Mrs. Preller, you would not expect me to criticise a legal brother, would you?'

'I suppose not. But . . .'

'Let there be no buts. Dismiss it from your mind. What is past, is past.' He made a gesture and wiped out the preparatory examination. 'There are two ways, two paths, one follows in a case like this. The first is the better, the easier. We show positively that your husband could not have committed the crime with which he has been charged: alibis, witnesses, hard circumstantial evidence. Impossibility. Irrefutable. Accused could not have done it because he was in Timbuctoo at the time. Here are witnesses who saw him there. Next case, please. But this isn't our path. Our path must be more circuitous, the low road, the negative one, i.e. to attack the credibility of the witness who says he did it, or that he was there at the time, therefore he *could* have done it. Do you see?'

'Attack Lena?'

'Precisely. I want to know everything about her. Every tiny thing, even though you might not feel it to be important. Let me be the judge.'

She told him everything she knew about Lena, and everything she had heard. While she spoke, he made notes. Then he said, 'Tell me about Betty. And again everything, please: looks, age, way of speaking, every little detail.'

Kate felt drained when she had finished for she had been talking for nearly an hour. It was not possible to talk about Lena without discussing the entire Preller family and its recent history. Some of this Prescott seemed to know, but there was much that caused him to raise his eyebrows.

He sat in silence for some minutes, paging back through his notes, underlining phrases, dotting i's and crossing t's.

'You say on the night of the fire when Hugo died and Mrs. Preller senior was so badly burnt, that Charles ran for Lena rather than his mother. Do you not consider this to be odd behaviour? I mean, why would he run for the cook and not his own mother, especially if the cook was living in a shanty some distance from the house?'

'Lena wasn't the cook then, she was the children's nanny. She slept in the house.'

'I see. But she wasn't in the house that night. Where was she, at church?'

'I don't know.'

'That's one thing we must look into.' He paged on, then stopped again. 'These voices that told her to tell the truth. When did they start?'

'Mr. Smuts says it was after Betty died. I never heard her talk about them before I went abroad, though she was always very religious. She used to pray a lot, and sometimes she would sing hymns.'

He offered her the Sen-Sens, but she refused. He popped two into his mouth. 'Unfortunately religious fervour doesn't prove mendacity. On the contrary. And there are one or two judges – great hymn singers themselves – who might see it as a positive virtue.' He smiled, and she was reminded of the smile of a baby in an advertisement for infants' milk.

'Tell me, Mrs. Preller, were you surprised to hear that the turncoat, if one might use the word, was Lena Lourens? From everything you've told me and everything I've heard from Charles, this would seem to be the last thing she would have done, even if she *had* seen him where she says she saw him.'

'Yes, it was. She worshipped him.'

'And Mrs. Preller, too, as I understand it. That's odd. And anything that's odd must be turned over like a stone. Then we can see the worms.'

'Everyone says she's a bit soft in the head.'

'Everyone? I don't. Nor does Godlonton. We have had her examined. So has the Crown. She's perfectly sane. Telling the truth, in spite of the fact that one may have lied before, does not constitute insanity. If this case was being heard by a jury, then of course we might get up to a few tricks, but to make a fool of a middle-aged coloured woman, who has decided to tell the truth about something that she knows will hurt people she loves, before a judge and two assessors would, in my opinion, be suicidal. No, we must get behind the wainscot of her mind, Mrs. Preller, and see what's there: not fantasies, but facts.'

When Kate returned to Saxenburg, she found Dr. du Toit there. Mrs. Preller had had a fall earlier in the day and

Smuts had called him. They talked in the drawing-room. The late afternoon was calm and the sea was deep navy-blue, the India Reef a thin white line.

'How is Charles?' he said.

'Depressed.'

'Naturally. But how is he physically?'

'He's thinner. He doesn't like the food, but we've made arrangements to have some sent in.'

'I've been meaning to go and see him, but how can I leave my patients?' It was said with a note of querulous irritation and she wondered if Mrs. Preller had accused him of neglecting Charles.

'It will be good to have him home again,' he said.

'You seem very sure he will be.'

'Yes, I am. I've known him all his life. He couldn't have done it. To think anything else is disloyal.' She heard a note of reproof in his tone.

'But if he didn't do it, who did?'

'Jonas, of course. Lena's lying. These people always stick together against the whites. You'll see, he'll be found not guilty.'

'But why would Lena lie? She loved him and she loved Mrs. Preller.'

'Coloureds don't know what love is.'

She felt her anger rise, but stifled it and asked after Mrs. Preller.

'She's only shaken up a bit. I'd like to get her into a nursing home for a month or two to keep her under supervision, but she'd never agree. You're going to have to watch her. She might overdose again.'

She had given him a glass of sherry and she noticed a tremor in his hand as he raised it to his lips. Again she was struck by how he had aged. The silver mane of hair, of which he had been so proud, was rank and uncared for.

He was an old man. Smuts was an old man. Mrs. Preller was an old woman. Kate suddenly saw herself caught in this web of old age and old people, unable to break out of it; marooned in this place, caring for them and for the farm, and for a husband she did not love, until she grew old herself.

A little later, she went up to give Mrs. Preller the news about Charles. She was in bed and the paralysis on the one side of her face seemed more pronounced. She was drowsy and her speech was difficult to follow. Kate told her about her interview with Joshua Prescott. When she had finished, Mrs. Preller held her jaw with one hand and said laboriously, 'If he is not careful, Lena will destroy us all.'

In her room later that evening, Kate wrote to Tom. *My darling*, she began. *What am I to do?* She read the sentence twice, then burnt the paper and crumbled the ash.

[5]

Kate was having her breakfast of coffee and a roll on the verandah of the Cape Town flat. An early morning mist covered the city below her, with only the tops of the highest buildings showing. In half an hour it would be gone and the late summer sun would begin to roast the pavements.

She lit a cigarette and picked up the *Cape Times* and looked for the story she had so far tried to avoid. She found it leading an inside page, with a picture of Charles.

'BODY ON BEACH' TRIAL OPENS AT SUPREME COURT

WEALTHY CAPE FARMER ACCUSED OF KILLING CHILDHOOD FRIEND

The trial opens today in the Supreme Court of Charles Augustus Preller, of Helmsdale, Cape Province, accused of murdering his childhood friend, Miriam Rose Sachs. Miss Sachs' body was found on a lonely stretch of beach
. . .

Kate's eyes flicked swiftly over the formal details, which she knew so well. The story recalled the earlier inquests and the preparatory examination, and went on:

This is the most important murder case to be heard in the city for many years and is expected to last for at least a week.

The central figure, Charles Preller, is the son of a well-known family of ostrich farmers who own the Saxenburg Estate, said to be one of the largest feather farms in the world.

His father, 'Boss' Charles Preller, who was known at one time in rugby circles for his robust forward play, was said to be one of the richest men in the district when the feather boom was at its height before the war.

Since then the industry has been hard hit, but is picking up again.

Mr. Preller will be represented by Mr. Joshua Prescott, K.C., and Mr. Robert Smith, the Crown by Mr. C. J. Nel and Mr. T. de Beer. The case will be heard by Mr. Justice De Wet Fourie.

She read it again. It seemed remote in print, as though it was a story about a stranger. She had the impression of 'the central figure' as a different person from the depressed man she had seen in Roeland Street Gaol the day before.

She remembered him saying over and over, 'They're going to crucify me.'

'They won't. They can't. Just tell them the truth, that's what they're trying to find out.'

'You really believe that?' The fleshy face was thinner, the cheeks slightly hollow, the smudges under the eyes were darker, and the eyes themselves seemed set farther back in his skull.

'The truth! You really think that's all they care about. Listen, the police were made to look like fools the first time, they're not going to let it happen again.'

'What the police think doesn't matter. It's what the judge and the assessors think that counts.'

'Anyway, I don't know if I'll go into the box.'

'Charles, there's no one else who can testify for you! No one was with you – except Miriam, of course – and there'll be no one to tell your side.'

He paced up and down the small room. 'Jesus Christ,

no one knows what it's like!' Then he began to cry. It was a soft, helpless sobbing.

She went towards him, to comfort him, but he turned away. She watched him, wondering. Was he putting on an act, or was it self-pity, or frustration at injustice? For the hundredth time, she wondered whether he had killed Miriam.

When she saw that he had stopped crying, she said, 'What are you going to wear?'

'Wear?'

'In court tomorrow.'

'I don't know. I've got my dark suit.'

'Wear that. I'll buy you a new white shirt.'

He shrugged. 'If you like.'

She bought him a shirt and a new tie, new underwear and socks, even a new white silk handkerchief for his jacket pocket. She was pleased to be doing something for him.

She finished her coffee and put on her coat and hat and walked down to Prescott's office, through the public gardens. The mist had lifted, the sun was hot and the sprinklers were on. There was a smell of water on warm grass. Everything was hushed. People walked slowly. Everyone looked so normal, yet she knew there was no such thing as a normal life.

Prescott was wearing his black silk gown and looked a magisterial figure. There was something formidable about his size. She was glad he was on their side.

'You've seen this, I suppose,' he said, flicking a copy of the *Cape Times*. 'A fair summary, I'd say.'

'I thought it made Charles sound like a wealthy socialite.'

He raised his eyebrows. 'Isn't that precisely what he is?' He offered her a Sen-Sen, but she shook her head. 'That's why there's going to be a crush. Nothing the public likes more than to see wealth and privilege brought low.' He paused, then went on, 'We've had a bit of bad luck with the judge. De Wet Fourie is a staunch Calvinist. Still, he's pretty fair, I'll say that.'

'What about the prosecutor?'

'Nel's a sound man. Not a flyer, but pretty sound. It's

going to be a good fight.' He looked at his watch. 'I think we'd better go.'

There was a crowd on the steps of the Supreme Court building, spilling out into the street and holding up traffic. Prescott took Kate's arm. 'If they see us, we'll never get through.' He led her through a side door and into a small, flagged courtyard, then by another door into No. 1 court.

It was smaller than she had imagined from the size of the building, not much bigger than the one in Helmsdale, but the ceilings were high and the wood panelling was light instead of dark. It gave an airy impression. But that was only an impression, for already it was packed, and the heat was solid. Everywhere, people were fanning themselves. Heads turned in her direction. There had been no picture of her in the newspapers, but her presence with Prescott was enough: there was a stirring as people whispered to each other. She was glad she was wearing a hat with a veil.

Prescott showed her to a seat on a bench behind him and he and his junior began untying ribbons and releasing papers and talking in low voices. At the other end of the bench she saw the team for the Crown. Nel was middle-aged, with a small Van Dyck beard shot with grey, and wore rimless spectacles. She saw Prescott walk over and put his hand on the prosecutor's shoulder. He said something and they both chuckled.

She felt outraged that he should have such contact with someone she considered their enemy. But more than outrage, she felt isolated and vulnerable. She looked around the court-room, but saw no familiar faces. This was an audience of strangers come for entertainment. Smuts had stayed at Saxenburg to keep the farm going, and he and Dr. du Toit were looking after Mrs. Preller. Duggie and Lena and Jerry – even Jerry's face would have been welcome – were witnesses and were waiting outside the court-room.

She became aware that someone was talking to her. She turned and saw, sitting next to her, a man in his forties, untidily dressed in a white drill suit. His hair was curly and stood out from his head in a shaggy mass.

'I'm sorry, I didn't hear what you said,' she said.

'You're Mrs. Preller, aren't you?' His accent was English and when she did not reply he added, 'My name's Guy Bedford. I'm the correspondent of the London *Chronicle*.'

'I don't give interviews.'

His round face broke into an infectious smile. 'I haven't come to interview you. I've been told to come – *ordered* to come, by a friend of mine, and of yours.'

'Tom!'

'Yes. He wrote and said he thought you might need moral support. I'm not very good at supporting things and my morals have sometimes been called into question, but I'll do the best I can. He said I was to give you . . .' He smiled again, '. . . his best regards.'

At that moment, they brought her husband up from the cells below the court-room. She thought he looked well in his dark suit, new shirt and tie. But his face was dead white and, as he turned to where she sat, she could see the dark hollows of his eyes. She smiled, but he did not seem to notice her. He was searching for Prescott, who had returned to his seat.

'All rise in court!' an usher called, and Mr. Justice De Wet Fourie entered with his two assessors.

Until that moment, Charles had been the focus of attention. Now all eyes turned to the judge in his black gown. He was a small man, below medium height, with a lined face which gave the impression of being dry and dusty. But his eyes were a piercing light blue. His face was set in what appeared to be an expression of permanent irritation. The court settled, but he took a few minutes longer. He shuffled his papers until he was satisfied with their arrangement, then placed his pad precisely where he wanted it; took out a large fountain-pen and placed it next to the pad. The two assessors, seemed in awe of him and quickly settled down, their faces turned expectantly towards him. At last he was ready. He unscrewed the top of the fountain-pen and nodded at the Clerk of the Court. The case of the Crown v. Charles Augustus Preller had begun.

Like most cases of its kind, it began slowly. In a sense, it was like some behemoth that had to be started into movement, which could only be achieved with much careful, slow effort. Kate had only ever been to one court case, the one in which Duggie had been involved, and that had been a rough-and-tumble sort of affair, with drunks and petty thieves and prostitutes queueing to get into the dock; a kind of justice factory. This was the other extreme. Details which Kate thought were self-evident were picked over again and again. They were looked at and opened up and examined until, in the heat, her concentration began to waver, and even boredom set in. The most dramatic event of the morning was when one of the ushers brought a small chair for Charles.

But there was a strange fascination in what was taking place. The same people were assembling as had assembled for the first and second inquests. Some were a little fatter, some a little thinner, some a little greyer.

Sergeant Van Blerk went on the stand to describe what had occurred after the body had been found. This was where Kate would have given her evidence had she been in the country when the preparatory examination had taken place. She realised now how little of importance she would have had to tell.

The morning was taken up with such details and with an expert from the Cape Agulhas lighthouse, who had studied the tides and the currents in the Helmsdale area for the past twenty years as part of his passion for the exact placing of the wrecks. Both Nel and Prescott examined him exhaustively, quibbling over this and that, until Kate saw signs of impatience on the Bench. The Judge began to rearrange his papers with little, jerky movements. Finally, he burst out: 'Really, Mr. Prescott, we must get on!'

'I shall not detain the witness much longer, m'lord,' Prescott said imperturbably, and went on with his questioning in the same laborious and measured manner. Kate had the impression that he was trying to show that the body might have been placed in the water some distance away from Saxenburg, perhaps in another direction completely, perhaps from the beach at Helmsdale, and had floated from there to the pool.

She sat through that long, hot day, as the story began to reveal itself. Sometimes she had to convince herself that they were actually talking about a part of her own life, about Miriam, about Saxenburg Cove, about Helmsdale. Everything sounded one remove from reality. When the hearing was adjourned, she was as exhausted as if she had been in the box all day herself.

Prescott, Smith and Godlonton were deep in conversation as the courtroom cleared. She had almost forgotten the man beside her, but when he said, 'May I run you home?' she was grateful.

When they reached the flat, he accepted her invitation to come in, and they had tea on the verandah. He was engaging company, and she questioned him eagerly about Tom. He had been on the *Morning Post* before joining the *Chronicle* and the two men had several times been on assignments together, including trips to Singapore and Tokyo. She wanted to know all the details. She wanted to know everything he knew about Tom.

Finally he said, 'Tom would never forgive me if I left you to your own devices tonight. Have supper with us. I'll phone my wife. She's half expecting you anyway.'

She wavered for only a moment. She had been dreading the lonely evening.

The Bedfords lived in a rambling old villa with what seemed like dozens of untidy rooms and small passageways. Jenny Bedford was large and friendly, the mother of three small children. It was bedtime when Kate arrived and she was simply absorbed by the children and their mother as a familiar part of the ritual. She helped in the bathing and the putting to bed, and while Jenny went off to see about supper, she read the children a story. They were entranced by her Edinburgh accent. When she had finished, they wanted another, and another. 'They'd never let you go,' Guy said, coming to remove her. The three adults sat on the flagged verandah that faced the mountain, and ate off their laps.

'Sorry to inflict the kids on you,' Guy said, as he was taking her home.

'I loved it.'

And she had. As she lay in bed that night she thought: this is how Tom and I could live.

The second and third days of the trial were taken up by the medical evidence of old Dr. Richards and Professor Fleischman. It became apparent how Richards had bungled his job, and Prescott struck. Until then he had seemed almost too benign in his cross-examination. Now he was brutal, and Dr. Richards left the stand looking humiliated and angry.

Fleischman was altogether different. Kate remembered him immediately, the stooping figure, head thrust forward, the huge bald head, the thin, lined face, the tufts of hair above the ears, and the disdain that played around the thin lips.

He spoke quietly as Nel took him through the evidence. Every detail was carefully explored in greater detail than by the coroner at the second inquest. It seemed to Kate that the prosecutor was determined to leave no line of questioning open to Prescott.

But when Prescott did haul his huge body to its feet he seemed to ignore the fact that Nel had been examining the witness at all. He went over much of the same ground, and Kate saw the judge begin to rearrange his papers. And then, in the afternoon, as the court was in a state of hot somnolence, the line of Prescott's inquiry became clear.

'Now we come to the sexual aspects of the case.'

There was a stir as the spectators refocussed their attention. This was the part they had come to hear.

'You say that it is usual in cases like this to examine the sexual organs. What do you mean by "Cases like this"?'

'I mean a case in which a young woman is molested and dies from the molestation.'

'So you have examined a number of unfortunate women?'

'I have.'

'Can you give a figure?'

'Not without my records.'

'An estimate. A hundred? Less than a hundred? More?'

'I don't guess at figures.'

'All right, but quite a few?'

'Quite a few.'

'And you've given evidence in quite a few cases of this kind?'

'Quite a few.'

'And rape cases? I mean, where the girl hasn't died, but says she was raped.'

'Yes.'

'Quite a few?'

'Yes.'

'And in some of the cases, did the court find that the girls were, how shall I put it, stretching credibility? In other words, that they had acquiesced in the act, and later, for whatever reason, had been afraid of the consequences and cried rape.'

'Yes.'

'It is a fact, is it not, doctor, that rape is a difficult charge to make stick?'

'That is not my province.'

'But you have just said that some cases, cases in which you were involved, were thrown out of court. That's what you meant, isn't it?'

'I would not use the phrase "thrown out",' Fleischman said, his thin lips pressed together.

'What I mean is, the men were acquitted. Will you have it that way?'

'Yes, that is so.'

'Now you say that you – and I quote – "found bruising on the walls of the uterus and also on the tissues of the vagina, bruising which is usually associated with forcible penetration".'

'That is correct.'

'What do you mean precisely by forcible penetration, doctor?'

'I mean the forcing of the male organ into the vagina against the wishes of the woman.'

'I see. In this instance, was the bruising very extensive?'

'Not very. I have seen worse.'

'Were there lacerations?'

'No.'

'Doctor, would you accept the fact that there are degrees of sexual intercourse?'

'That sounds like "a little bit pregnant" to me.'

There was a gust of laughter, but Fleischman did not seem to think he had made a joke. 'Sexual intercourse is sexual intercourse.'

'Bear with me, doctor, if we go into this matter . . .'

Mr. Justice De Wet Fourie had been shuffling his papers for some moments, and now he said, 'Mr. Prescott, do we have to listen to all this?'

'M'lord, I am trying to show . . .'

'I am perfectly aware of what you are trying to show. What I wish to know is whether or not it is relevant.'

'If your lordship will grant me a moment or two longer, I think I can make this clear.'

Grudgingly, the judge nodded, and Prescott turned back to Fleischman.

'Let me put it another way, doctor, would you agree that there are gentle forms of sexual intercourse, but that there are also rougher forms? In other words, there is a spectrum of activity from gentle to rough. That some men are rougher than others.'

'I suppose so.'

'Do you think that the bruising of which you spoke could have been caused, not by rape, but by rough intercourse?'

Fleischman hesitated. 'It is possible.'

Prescott consulted his papers. 'Can you say with any certainty when this bruising took place: five hours before death? Ten? Fifteen?'

'Not with any certainty.'

'So that the two acts might not have coincided.'

The judge broke in. 'I don't follow you.'

'I mean the rape and the murder, m'lord.'

'Are you trying to separate them?'

'M'lord, I'm trying to show that one is not necessarily the corollary of the other. Dr. Fleischman stated in his evidence-in-chief that Miss Sachs was not a virgin, but, on the contrary, gave the impression of an active sexual life. I am trying to show, m'lord, that she might have indulged in boisterous sexual activity at some time before her death and that the murder itself may have occurred for reasons unassociated with rape.'

'Could that be so, doctor?' the judge asked.

'I suppose so, m'lord.'

'Thank you, doctor,' Joshua Prescott said, and sat down.

Guy Bedford, who had once again joined Kate, leant towards her and said, 'He's trying to throw suspicion on someone else.'

'Who?'

'God knows. Anyone, as long as it's not your husband. It's a well-known trick.'

The prosecutor had risen to his feet. He was a precise, pedantic man, who liked to grip his pointed beard and pull on it gently as he spoke.

'Just one question, doctor. You say you have been involved in "quite a few" such cases. Can you recall any one in which sexual intercourse was carried out by one person and the killing soon after by someone else entirely?'

'No.'

'The rapist was always the killer?'

'Yes.'

'Thank you.'

Bedford drove her home again after she had seen Charles, and she had barely closed the door when the telephone rang. It was Dr. du Toit, from Helmsdale. He sounded angry, and she realised that she had forgotten to telephone Saxenburg the previous night; she had been too caught up with the Bedfords and the chance of contact, however distant, with Tom.

'I've just seen Charles,' she said. 'He wanted something to read . . . Yes, the food is being sent in. They take him back to Roeland Street every night . . . No one seems to know exactly how it's going. It's mostly been the same as the second inquest so far . . . No, Mr. Prescott has said nothing to me. I asked him yesterday what he thought and he said it was too early to tell.'

'What about Charles?' du Toit repeated.

She thought of the pale, nervous man she had seen in the room below the court. Prescott had been there, with Smith, Godlonton and a policeman. She had been a supernumary.

'He's all right,' she said.

'Give him my best. Don't forget.'

'I won't.'

'And love from his mother.'

'Of course. How is she?'

'It's taking its toll of her. The worry. The tension. Listen, don't forget to telephone me tomorrow.'

'I won't forget.'

She stood holding the telephone after he had rung off, her mind on the old woman in the upstairs room and the man in the cell.

'You're coming back with me again,' Guy said.

'I couldn't.'

'Jenny insists, so do the children.'

She was welcomed like a favourite aunt. She read stories again and was part of their rough-and-tumble bedtime games. But some of the joy had gone out of it for her and she asked to be taken home early. She decided not to go to the Bedfords' house again. In some ways, it only made matters worse.

[6]

Douglas Buchanan was making a poor impression in the witness box. He had been given a chair, and initially Kate had felt the sympathy of the court was with the crippled man, but he was so ill at ease and unwilling to meet the eye of the prosecuting counsel that he gave the impression of being shifty and unreliable.

'So what happened when you came back to Helmsdale after the picnic?' Nel asked.

'The others went off. Mr. Preller and my sister were in

his motor, Mr. and Mrs. Alexander went to the hotel. I took Miss Sachs home.'

'How long were you at the house with Miss Sachs?'

'An hour, mebbe.'

'Could the witness please speak up,' Mr. Justice De Wet Fourie broke in. 'I'm getting earache trying to hear him.' There was a ripple of laughter, but the judge turned his angry, bright eyes on the spectators and they quickly lapsed into silence.

'An hour,' Duggie repeated, more loudly.

'And then?'

'I came back to the hotel.'

'Did you see the accused again?'

'Aye, he came back to the hotel about eleven. I was having a dram wi' Mr. Alexander. We all had a dram and Mr. Alexander went up to see if Mrs. Alexander was all right. They'd had a row that day, y'see. He didna return. So we went back to Cape Town.'

'Was there anything odd about Mr. Preller? I mean, in his manner or his dress?'

'He seemed agitated. His shirt had a wee tear near the collar and his hair was ruffled.'

'Anything else?'

'Aye. He had a scratch on his right cheek.'

'Had you ever seen him like that before?'

'Never. He was always very neat.'

'Thank you, Mr. Buchanan.'

Joshua Prescott rose like a walrus. He went back over the picnic. 'Is it true that you and Miss Sachs were making – how can I put it? – a kind of twosome, that day?'

'You could put it that way.'

'But then she went swimming with Mr. Alexander, did she not?'

'Aye.'

'And they played games and teased each other?'

'Aye.'

'How did you feel about that?'

'It was all in fun.'

'You were not jealous, it was just a bit of fun?'

'That's all.'

'And afterwards you went home with her. Was there anyone else in the house?'

'No.'

'And she gave you a drink?'

'Yes.'

'But you had been drinking quite a bit that day, all of you?'

'Well, I canna say that.'

'Come, Mr. Buchanan, you are quite a heavy drinker, are you not?'

'I . . .'

'What was that? Can you speak up? We cannot hear you, Mr. Buchanan. Yes or no?'

'I had a sair leg. It helped.'

'You had a bad leg? Is that it? And alcohol helped?'

'Aye.'

'And the others?'

'They drank a fair bit.'

'Did you have sexual intercourse with Miss Sachs when you took her home?'

'No.'

'Did you try?'

'No.'

Kate remembered what Charles had told her: how Miriam had taunted him about Duggie being a better lover than he, and she knew Duggie was lying. Everyone is the same, she thought, they're only concerned with saving themselves.

'Had you ever had sexual intercourse with Miss Sachs before?' Prescott said.

Duggie looked around the court. Mr. Nel was on his feet, objecting.

The judge said, 'Mr. Prescott, I hope this is relevant.'

'It is, m'lord. If Mr. Buchanan had sexual intercourse with Miss Sachs while he was with her in the house, that would possibly explain the bruising.' He turned back to Duggie. 'I repeat, had you ever been intimate with Miss Sachs?'

'Aye.'

'I put it to you that you took Miss Sachs home that

evening, and that you indulged in rough sexual intercourse.'

'That's no' the truth of it!'

Kate watched him limp away from the witness box. He was sweating, and he kept his eyes away from Charles. As he passed her, he looked up and gave a sickly smile.

Guy Bedford whispered to her, 'Prescott's trying to muddy the water.'

'How?'

'As far as I can see, he has no witnesses of his own, so the only thing he can do is try to confuse the issue, cast doubts, suspicions. It's a better gambit with a jury, but you can never tell even with a judge and assessors. They're only human.'

Jerry was next. Nel took him through the picnic and what had happened later. Then it was Prescott's turn again.

'Now let me see, you're a friend of Mr. Preller's, are you not? An old friend?'

'We were at school together.'

'And you've been close ever since?'

'Yes.'

'But you were tremendous rivals too, weren't you? I mean, in sport, things like that?'

'I suppose so.'

'You suppose so? I put it to you that you spent much of your time playing golf and tennis and competing with each other.'

'Yes.'

'Did you compete in other ways?'

'How do you mean?'

'I mean, with girls? Were they not fair game between you?'

'I don't know what you mean.'

'I'll try to explain. Is it not true that at one time Miss Sachs had been close to Mr. Preller?'

'They grew up together.'

'That is not answering the question. Were they, or were they not, close?'

'Yes.'

'Now at the picnic, Miss Sachs swam in the rock pools, and you swam with her.'

'Yes.'

'Did you wear bathing-costumes?'

'We hadn't brought any.'

'What did you swim in, then?'

'Nothing.'

'I see. The court has heard that you and Miss Sachs played games in the water, enjoyed yourselves.'

'Yes.'

'Did you not find this provocative?'

'It was only . . .'

'A bit of fun?'

'That's right.'

Guy Bedford turned to Kate again. 'He's got us focussed on Alexander now. Anyone, so long as we don't focus on your husband. He's clever, I'll give him that.'

Prescott looked at his notes. 'Let's move on. You and Mr. Buchanan were drinking at the hotel when Mr. Preller returned, is that right?'

'Yes.'

'And he sat down and had a drink with you. He was looking ruffled. Did he offer any explanation?'

'He said he'd taken Miss Sachs down to one of the old houses, a place where they had often been before. He said they'd had a . . . well, a fight.'

'Did he say why?'

'No.'

'But you guessed?'

'Well, I thought he would have tried, you know, to, uh . . . to make love to her.'

'And he told you and Mr. Buchanan he had left her down on the coast road?'

'He said she wouldn't get into the car.'

'I see. Then what did you do?'

'I left them a few minutes later to see how my wife was.'

'Was she ill?'

'She'd had a headache.'

'You and she had had a row, hadn't you?'

'Yes.'

312

'Why was that?'

'Because I had swum in the nude with Miss Sachs.'

'So you went to see if she was all right. And was she?'

'She was asleep.'

'And?'

'I was tired too, so I went to bed.'

Prescott fanned himself for a moment, then said, 'And that's where you stayed? In bed?'

'Yes.'

'So if I were to bring a witness who says he saw you getting into your motor-car about that time, he would be mistaken?'

'I ... uh ...' Jerry looked around uncertainly. Kate could see his big, square hands gripping the sides of the box.

'Mr. Alexander, may I remind you that you are under oath.'

'I ... you see, I couldn't sleep. So I went for a drive.'

The court stirred. Prescott paused, and with an actor's sense of timing, said, 'A drive. I see. Where did you go for your drive?'

'Just along the road.'

'Which road. The coast road?'

'No ...'

'The road that runs past Miss Sachs' house?'

'No.'

'Come, Mr. Alexander, which road?'

'The Agulhas Road.'

'You went out onto the Agulhas Road. What then?'

'I stopped and had a cigarette.'

'In the middle of the night you got up, got into your car, drove out onto the Agulhas Road and had a cigarette?' Prescott's voice was filled with contempt and disbelief.

'Yes.'

'What did you do then?'

'I went back to the hotel. I thought I'd have a last nightcap with Mr. Preller and Mr. Buchanan, but they had left for Cape Town. So I went back to bed.'

'Did your wife wake up?'

'Yes. She spoke to me, asked if anything was wrong.'

'But she is tragically not with us now?'

'She died in a car accident.'

'So we have only your word for all this?'

'I suppose so.'

'Yes, I suppose so, too. Mr. Alexander, I put it to you that you heard what Mr. Preller said about his experience with Miss Sachs, that you got out your car and went down to the coast road and found her walking back to town. You offered her a lift and tried to make love to her. When she fought you off, you strangled her, perhaps accidentally, but she died nevertheless. You then took the body to the cove, undressed it and put it into the water, hoping it would be sucked out to the reef and that she would have been thought to have drowned.'

'That's a lie!'

'Thank you, Mr. Alexander.'

Nel rose to his feet. 'Just two questions, Mr. Alexander. Did you go near the coast road?'

'No, sir.'

'Were you ever intimate with Miss Sachs, that night or any other?'

'No, sir.'

At the lunch adjournment Nel came across to Prescott and said, 'That's the first I've heard of this witness of yours.'

'What witness?'

'The one who's going to say that Alexander went driving.'

'I didn't say I had a witness. I said *if* I were to bring a witness.'

Nel smiled. 'Do you think I don't know your tricks, Josh?'

'Stands to reason that's what he'd be likely to do after what had been happening all day. And that naked swimming. Christ, she was like a bitch on heat.'

They went out of the court together. Kate stood watching them, thankful that Mr. Sachs was not in court to hear them.

'They seem so friendly,' she said to Bedford. 'You wonder they can be on different sides.'

'Don't forget they do it for money,' he said.

In the afternoon there was a witness who was new to her: Constable Le Grange. She supposed she must have seen him in Helmsdale, since he was apparently attached to the police there, though she did not recognise him. He might even have been one of the officers who had come to arrest Jonas, a large young man, darkly sunburnt, with close-cropped curly hair, brown eyes and forearms the size of thighs.

Nel established him quickly, then said, 'After the accused was arrested, you were instructed to do what?'

'I was instructed to make a search of the house.'

'The Berrangé house.'

'Ja . . . I mean, yes, sir.'

'What did you find?'

The constable took out a note-book and read from it in a mumbling voice, which seemed to irritate the judge. 'I and two other constables searched the premises. First we searched the downstairs rooms, then the rooms upstairs, then we went out into the garden and we searched the garden . . .'

'May I stop you there. I don't think the court is interested in the garden.'

The judge leant forward. 'If there is nothing new about the garden, let us forget the garden!'

Nel said, 'Constable, the court would like to hear what you found in one of the upstairs rooms of the Berrangé house.'

'Oh, ja. Well, the upstairs was in ruins, just like the downstairs, except for one room.'

'Go on.'

'In this room there was a bed, two chairs, a table, a carpet on the floor . . .'

'Yes, but what struck you first about this room?'

'It looked as though there had been a fight there, sir.'

'A struggle?'

'Yes, sir. I found an empty bottle of wine and an empty bottle of brandy on the floor. The table was knocked down and the side of an armchair was broken out like someone had been fighting . . . I mean, struggling.'

'Otherwise the room looked as though it had been used?'

'Yes, sir. There were cigarette butts in the ashtray, and glasses. The bed had been lain on.'

'Thank you, constable.'

He turned to look at Prescott, who slowly shook his head.

Kate had listened with mounting apprehension, and when the hearing was adjourned for the day she said to Prescott, 'I must talk to you.'

He looked at her as though he hardly knew her, and she realised that his concentration was almost obsessive. 'Is it important?'

'Very.'

He took her out into a courtyard where there was space to be private. 'What is it?'

'It's about the constable's evidence.'

'Yes, that wasn't very helpful, was it? What about it?'

'Someone did struggle with Charles in that room, but it wasn't Miriam, it was me.'

His shirt was wet with sweat. He put two Sen-Sen tablets in his mouth. 'Go on.'

She told him what had happened after the picnic, how she had gone to the Berrangés' house with Charles, how she'd had to fight him off.

'Good God!' he said.

'So you see, they mustn't be allowed to think it was Charles and Miriam.'

'Mrs. Preller, if I put you into the witness box and you told the court that Charles Preller had tried to rape you in that room, that you had to fight him off with such ferocity that you broke an armchair, do you think they would believe for one moment that he did not try precisely the same thing with Miriam Sachs later on the same evening, with fatal results?'

'Well, I . . .'

'We'd convey the impression that he's a sexual maniac. Doesn't it sound like that to you? First of all he tries one woman, fails, then, mad with lust and frustration, attacks another. If I put you in the box we could give up the case. I think you would be far better advised to prevail upon

316

your husband to go into the witness box himself. Things aren't going too well. All I can do is stir the pot, but that's not enough. We need his side. We've got no witnesses of our own, no one to support him.'

That night, after reporting to Saxenburg, she went to see her parents. She was glad Duggie was out. She told them as much of the case as she could remember.

'Yon telephone's no' stopped ringing since it began,' her mother said. 'Half the time it's the newspapers, asking questions.'

'That's why I told you not to come to the court.'

'Aye, well, I'm no' sorry to miss that. I've no wish to get mixed up wi' it.'

The following morning, Lena took the oath.

Kate had not seen Lena since before she had left for England. She was thinner, and the hair which peeped out from under her black straw hat showed more grey than Kate remembered. She wore wire spectacles and the light in court flashed from the lenses each time she moved. Her skin was very dark and her mouth, with the missing teeth, reminded Kate of a fish. Her expression was severe, and after she had taken the oath, her lips moved in a swift, silent prayer.

C. J. Nel established her background, length of service with Mrs. Preller, the fact that she'd had one daughter, Betty, the work she did. Then he said, 'I want you to tell us about the night on which Miss Sachs was murdered. It was a Sunday, wasn't·it? Where had you been that day?'

Lena's reply was almost inaudible. Mr. Justice De Wet Fourie shifted his papers impatiently. 'Would you please ask the witness to speak up?'

Nel encouraged her, and repeated his question.

'Church,' she said.

'You had gone there in the afternoon?'

'Yes.'

'I think the service is a long one in your church, Mrs. Lourens.'

'A very long one, master.'

'When did you come home?'

'After the service.'

'Yes, but what time?'

'Maybe ten o'clock, master.'

'Was that usual?'

'Sometimes it was later.'

'Which way did you come?'

'Along the cliffs.'

'Along what they call the coast road? The one that passes the old ostrich houses?'

'Yes, master.'

'When you reached the Berrangés' house, what did you see?'

'I heard a noise, master, like feet running. I stopped and hid behind a tree.'

'Why?'

'I was frightened, master.'

'Why were you frightened?'

'A person can get hurt in the night.'

'I see. So you hid and watched. What did you see?'

'I saw Miss Miriam and Mr. Charles. Miss Miriam was running to get out the gate and Mr. Charles caught her and pulled her back.'

'Back where?'

'To the house.'

'Were they saying anything?'

'Miss Miriam was shouting.'

'What was she shouting.'

Lena hesitated.

Nel pulled at his pointed beard. 'What did she say, Mrs. Lourens?'

Lena whispered softly to the Clerk of the Court, who came across to Nel. Nel turned to the judge. 'She says she doesn't like to say it in open court, m'lord.'

The judge smiled at Lena. 'I respect your feelings, Mrs. Lourens, but sometimes we have to do things we don't like to do. Would you prefer to write it down?'

'I can't write, master.'

'All right, you tell the Clerk of the Court and he will say it.'

The Clerk listened for a moment, then said gravely, 'The

witness says that Miss Sachs said, "You're not going to have sexual intercourse with me any more".'

Mr. Justice De Wet Fourie looked down at him and shook his head. 'Mr. Terblanche, are you asking the court to believe that this woman came running out of the house, pursued by someone, and used a phrase like "sexual intercourse"? Come, be a man, we're all adults here.'

The Clerk swallowed. 'Fuck, m'lord. The word was fuck. You're not going to fuck me any more.'

There were a few titters, but one contemptuous look from the judge brought instant silence.

'Thank you, Mrs. Lourens,' he said. 'I can quite see why you did not wish to use the word. Let's get on, then.'

Nel said, 'What happened then, Mrs. Lourens?'

'I went home to Saxenburg, to my house. Betty wasn't there. I looked in Jonas's house.'

'Was she often in Jonas Koopman's house?'

'Sometimes.'

'They were lovers?'

Lena paused, and finally muttered, 'Yes, master.'

'So you went to look for her?'

'On the beach. Jonas was there, alone.'

'Did you ask him where Betty was, or speak to him?'

'No, master, I was afraid for Jonas.'

'So you went home?'

'Betty was there. In bed. She pretended she was asleep, but I shook her and said, where have you been?'

'And where had she been?'

'She said she had been outside making water, but she lied, master. I know where . . .'

'Objection!' Prescott said.

'Don't tell us what you don't know for sure, Mrs. Lourens,' said the judge. 'Just the facts.'

'So you decided to say nothing to the police, because of your loyalty to the Preller family. Why did you change your mind?' Nel said.

'God tell me to tell what I know.'

'You're a very religious person, aren't you?'

'Yes, master.'

'All right, thank you, Mrs. Lourens.'

After the luncheon adjournment Prescott rose to his feet. 'Mrs. Lourens, my learned friend asked you if you were a religious person. A *very* religious person, I think he said, and you said you were. Is that right?'

'Yes, master.'

'Have you always been religious?'

'Always, master.'

'*Very* religious?'

'*Very* religious, master.'

'You see, I ask you that because when God told you to tell the truth, you should have done that already. I mean, it says in the Bible that we must tell the truth, doesn't it?'

'Yes, master.

'So you already knew about being honest before Miss Sachs was killed; you knew it years and years ago?'

'Yes, master.'

'It seems to me that you had a very sudden change of heart and . . .'

'M'lord, I object.' Nel was on his feet. 'This line of questioning doesn't seem to be leading us anywhere.'

The judge peered over his spectacles at Prescott. 'Mr. Prescott?'

'M'lord, the witness has said she has been a religious woman for a long time, a woman who knows right from wrong in the Christian ethos. She knew she was lying earlier. I want to find out if there were other causes – I mean, other than God telling her – for her sudden change. That means going back in time, m'lord, but I submit that we cannot ignore this line of questioning. I am certain there are things buried here, m'lord, which would be much better out in the open.'

'Very well, Mr. Prescott, continue for the moment.'

Prescott returned to the attack. 'Mrs. Lourens, tell me about your daughter's illness.'

'She ate fish, master.'

'And was sick?'

'Yes.'

'And you sent her away –' He glanced at his notes, '– to her aunt in Caledon?'

'Yes, master.'

'That's a . . . a Mrs. Moolman?'

The light flashed on her glasses as Lena moved her head. 'Yes, master.'

'It's a curious thing, but try as we might, we could not find a Mrs. Moolman in Caledon. The police didn't know of her. The post office didn't know of her. We asked lots of questions, but no one knew of her.'

Again, Lena's head swung from side to side.

'We wondered if we might have got the town wrong. It was Caledon, wasn't it?'

She cleared her throat, but did not answer.

'I'm sorry, I didn't hear.'

She remained silent.

'I don't want to distress you, Mrs. Lourens, but the whole thing sounds so coincidental to me. I mean, you send your daughter away, and then almost immediately go to the police with your story about Jonas Koopman. Then we don't see Betty again, because this time she has a, what was it? Oh yes, a fever. I put it to you, that this was simply a tissue of lies, a story to cover up something that really did happen.' He paused. 'Remember, God has told you to tell the truth and you have sworn on the Bible. Now what *did* happen?'

'You must answer, Mrs. Lourens,' the judge said.

Lena turned to him and said, 'She was having a baby, master.'

'You mean she was pregnant?' Prescott fastened onto the fact like a lamprey. 'By Jonas?'

'She said by Jonas, master.'

'And did she have the baby?'

'She had it taken away.'

'An abortion?'

'Yes, master.'

'Why didn't you let her have the baby? Why didn't you let her live with Koopman if that's what she wanted?'

The spectacles flashed.

'I must keep her away from him. She must not live with a black man!'

'How do you mean?'

'He was black, black!' Her voice had risen and was thick

321

with anger. 'Blacker than me. You want me to let my child live with a *black* man? All her life, evens when she is a little girl, I tell her she must never go with a very black person.'

Kate could scarcely believe what she had heard. There was a picture in her mind of Betty lying on the same bed as she had in Fat Sarah's rooms, having her child removed.

Prescott obviously thought he had stumbled at last onto a vein of gold. 'Bear with me, Mrs. Lourens, if I don't seem fully to comprehend this.' The voice was bland, almost unctuous. 'What you're saying is that Jonas was too black for you, is that it? Was Betty pale-skinned?'

'Very pale, master. She could pass for white.'

'And you wanted her to marry someone equally light-skinned, is that it?'

'Yes, master.'

'Was your husband very light-skinned?'

Lena looked away and again light flashed on her glasses.

'I'll repeat the question,' Prescott said. 'Was your husband light-skinned?'

'I never had no husband,' Lena said reluctantly.

'You just decided to call yourself *Mrs.* Lourens. Is that right?'

'Only a married person must have a child.'

'I see. When Betty was born you decided to say you were a married woman.'

'Yes.'

'Can you tell us who the father was?'

C. J. Nel had risen to his feet, but before he could protest, Lena said, 'Boss Charles Preller.' Nel resumed his seat.

'Boss Charles being the father of the accused?'

'Yes.'

With everyone else in the court-room, Kate turned to look at Charles. The shock had drained his face of any remaining colour. His waxen skin reminded her of Mrs. Preller's candle-like flesh.

'So you and Boss Charles Preller were lovers?'

Lena laughed harshly and the spectacles flashed light angrily back at Prescott. 'He force me. He throw me down and put his knee between my legs. Then he force me.'

'You are saying he raped you? When was this, Mrs. Lourens?'

'The night Master Hugo died in the fire. The night . . .'

Nel had risen again. 'M'lord, I must object. What has this got to do with the case on trial? This is old history.'

Prescott said, 'I'm sure my learned friend is familiar with Polybius's pragmatic view of history.'

'I'm sure he is,' said Mr. Justice De Wet Fourie dryly.

'This seems a good example, m'lord, for there appear to be two nights in question that need investigation here. The night Miss Sachs was murdered and that night more than twenty years ago when Mrs. Lourens says she was raped by her employer. It is a case of the past forming the present, with a vengeance.'

'Very well, Mr. Prescott,' the judge said, his light blue eyes fixed on the huge advocate. 'But *you* will doubtless remember the cyclic theory of Thucydides. The court would not wish to be led in cycles or in circles.'

Prescott smiled. 'As your lordship pleases.' He turned again to Lena. 'Did Mrs. Preller know about this?'

'Only later, when Betty was born.'

'How did she know?'

'She guess.'

'Because of the light colouring?'

'Yes.'

'Did you tell her what had happened?'

'Yes.'

'And?'

'She said I must never tell to anyone. She gave me money. She let me stay and look after Betty.'

Kate realised then what the reference to a girl had meant in Augusta's letter to Miss Binns in Vienna. She also saw clearly that Lena had become a kind of prisoner in Saxenburg, held there by a shared secret and by an occasional gift of money. Was she taking her revenge now?

'Would you tell us about the night of the fire please, Mrs. Lourens?' Prescott said.

As the woman began to speak, Kate had the curious feeling of becoming two people, her body remaining in the hot courtroom, listening to Lena with a mounting sense of horror, but in her imagination, being back in Saxenburg, witnessing the events. She remembered what Charles had told her about that night, and now the gaps were being filled.

According to Lena, Hugo had had a bad cough. She was the children's nanny and, on Mrs. Preller's orders, she had moved Charles into the playroom, leaving Hugo on his own in the bedroom. It was a night of high winds and rain, and a fire had been lit to warm Hugo's room. Normally, wood was used in the big dog-grate, but in high winds the flue drew too fiercely, so on this night coal only was used. At about nine o'clock, Lena had gone in to see how the children were.

Earlier she had placed a wooden clothes horse in front of the fire to dry some of the boys' underclothing and shirts.

The fire was burning brightly and much of the coal had been consumed, so she had decided to fetch more from the bunker in the incubator shed. She was turning away from the fireplace when she became aware that someone else was in the room. She had not turned up the lamp and the only light was the flickering of the flames in the grate. The figure had come towards her and she had seen that it was Boss Charles.

He had been drinking. He came forward and put his hands on her breasts. She struggled, making as little noise as possible, but it was only when Hugo had begun to cough that Boss Charles let her go, fearing the boy was waking.

Kate recalled that Charles had told her how, from the other room, he had seen the shadows on the walls, had not known what they were and, frightened, had buried his head under the blankets.

Thinking she would have no more trouble, Lena had gone down to the incubator shed, but Boss Charles had followed her and had raped her on the dirt floor.

She paused in her evidence. No one moved in the court-room.

'And while this was happening to you, the fire had started in the house?' Prescott said.

'Yes, master.'

'What do you think caused it?'

324

'Maybe we had knocked the clothes nearer the fire. Maybe a piece of coal fell. No one knew.'

'When you got back to the house . . .?'

'Madam was burned and Master Hugo was dead.'

Prescott tapped his teeth with a pencil and stared at her for a long moment. 'Then, about nine months later, Betty was born, is that right?'

'Yes.'

'And you gave yourself a married name?'

'Madam said it is better that way.'

'And you agreed?'

'Yes.'

'She paid you money and told you not to say anything?'

'Yes.'

'In other words, she was bribing you to keep your mouth shut.'

Lena looked at him angrily. 'Madam is not like that.'

'A great deal has been made of your devotion to her. I put it to you that you were *not* devoted, that you were kept in that house like a prisoner . . .'

'No!'

'. . . sharing a secret with your employer. I put it to you that you were paid to keep silent.'

'No!'

'. . . that far from being devoted, you hated your employer and that . . .'

'No, no! I love Madam. I look after Madam. I gave her the medicine three times a day. What you say are lies!'

Prescott's face was red and sweat was running down his neck. 'Then why did you suddenly turn on Mr. Charles? Or are you telling lies again? Isn't your whole testimony simply one lie after another?'

Lena gripped the sides of the witness stand. She was trembling.

'I put it to you, that you have lied from the moment you stepped into that box . . .'

'God told me I must!'

'God told you to lie?'

Several things happened simultaneously: Nel leapt to his feet; the judge began to reprimand Prescott; and Lena's voice lashed across the courtroom. For the first time, she looked directly at Charles. 'God told me to tell, because of the bad thing Mr. Charles did to Betty.'

There was immediate uproar. Prescott, realising he had gone too far, tried to shout her down. The judge was banging his gavel. There was a chatter of voices on the Press bench.

But Lena was unstoppable.

'God told me, because the child was his!'

'M'lord, I ask that to be removed from the record.' Prescott had to shout to make himself heard over the din.

But Nel was still on his feet. 'M'lord, my learned friend was quick with his classical allusions a moment or two ago. May I also use one: As ye sow, so shall ye reap. I think the court must hear what Mrs. Lourens has to say.'

The judge looked around angrily. 'If I have any more of this, I shall clear the court. I hope that is understood. Mrs. Lourens, you say the baby your daughter had removed was that of the accused?'

'Yes, master.'

'How do you know?'

'Betty told me the day she died. She was drunk, and she laugh at me. She laugh because I thought it was Jonas's baby. She said she had never been with Jonas because he was too black.'

'M'lord, this is pure hearsay,' Prescott said. 'I request that it be stricken from the . . .'

'It is true!' Lena shouted. 'Fat Sarah saw the baby!'

But Mr. Justice De Wet Fourie would tolerate no more. He rose, and the court adjourned for the day.

The room below the Supreme Court was stifling in the afternoon heat, with only one small window opening at street level. Charles, Prescott and Kate sat around a plain deal table. The lighting was poor and Charles's skin appeared light yellow, as though he had jaundice. Prescott fanned himself with a sheaf of papers and sucked at his Sen-Sens. Kate listened to the two men and a feeling of claustrophobia swept over her.

'This is what advocates fear most,' he said. 'Traps,

snares, quicksands. If we know they're there, we can usually do something to avoid them. But when we don't . . . I asked you more than once, Mr. Preller, if you had told me everything.'

Charles nodded. He appeared to be in a state of semi-shock.

'Everything. And you said you had. Well, it wasn't, was it? You've damaged yourself badly and, for what it's worth, made me look a fool.' Kate saw he was trying to control his anger. 'I'd like to know what you suggest now, Mr. Preller. But first of all, I want to know if there is anything further you have kept from me. Have you fathered any other children among the workers on your estate?'

'No.'

'Is there any circumstance either in Helmsdale or Cape Town, past or present, that I don't know about, that might affect this case?'

Charles glanced up at Kate, and then looked away. 'No,' he said.

'Are you quite sure?'

'Yes. This was what I was worried about. Of course I didn't know she was my . . . my sister –'

'Half-sister.'

'I mean, I swear to God I wouldn't have touched her.'

'I think we've had enough of God in this case, Mr. Preller.'

'We're talking about bloody . . .' He couldn't bring himself to say the word.

'I know precisely what we're talking about. You're not accused of incest. You're accused of murder.'

'Yes, but it looks so bad! I mean, my father and Lena, and now . . .'

'Mr. Preller, we're not talking about social mores, we're talking about the killing of a woman, and possibly a hanging. Can't you get that into your head!'

Charles looked down at his hands, then said, 'What do you want me to do? I'll go on the stand now. I mean, everything's out. I don't mind now.' He swallowed. 'I didn't want anyone to know . . .'

'That you had been sleeping with a coloured girl?'

Prescott raised his hands in a gesture of despair. 'Don't you realise that it's too *late*? At the moment, all we have is hearsay evidence from Lena. It won't go into the record. But if you go on the stand Nel will cross-examine you and he'll drag every sordid detail out into open court. He'll show you to be both a liar and a man of violence like your father; he'll show you up as someone who not only had the opportunity to kill Miss Sachs, but who, in all likelihood, did so. Now, since we keep on invoking the deity, for God's sake, give me something to work on!'

As he stopped speaking, there was a knock on the door and Godlonton came in. 'Mrs. Preller, there's an urgent call for you from Saxenburg,' he said. 'You can take it in the Clerk of the Court's office.'

She hurried after him and, when she picked up the telephone, heard Smuts' voice: 'We need you here! When can you come?'

'I can't leave Charles.'

'If you don't, we can't carry on.'

'But . . .'

'There are other people helping Charles. Miss Augusta is getting worse and Hennie . . . there's something wrong with him. I think he's sick, too. He won't go near his other patients and now he won't see Miss Augusta. She won't have Tilly near her. There's only me. I've got to do everything and I can't run the bloody farm as well, my friend.'

Recognising desperation in his voice, she said, 'There's a train about six. I'll be on it.'

The train was late getting into Helmsdale. She looked up and down the station, but could not see Smuts. The wind was blowing dust along the platform and she was reminded of the night when she had arrived on the same train as Miriam's coffin, and Sachs had shouted at her through the car's closed window. It seemed long ago, and yet the ghosts of the past were everywhere about her.

She found that one of the farm-hands had come to meet her. 'Where's Mr. Smuts?' she said.

'At the house. The old missus is sick.'

They drove through the battering wind along the cliff road then, on the undulating stretch approaching Saxenburg she saw, through the dark gaps in the folding ground, tantalising glimpses of the house. It stood on the end of its headland, ablaze with lights, like some great liner setting out to sea. It seemed that every light in the place was on. And because she had never seen it like that, she realised that something must be very wrong.

An ambulance was parked outside the front door. She ran inside. There was a group of people on the staircase: two men in white coats, a stranger in a dark suit. And Smuts. 'Be careful now! Be careful! Don't you bloody hurt her!' he was saying angrily.

Then she saw the stretcher.

The man in the suit said, 'Shouting doesn't help. She's all right. She's in good hands.'

Smuts' face was drawn and there were tears in his eyes.

'What is it?' Kate said.

He pointed towards the man who had just spoken. 'He says it's pneumonia.'

'I'm Dr. Bekker, from the hospital.' He was short and square and something about him reminded her of Jerry. He was very young and was covering his nervousness with a kind of arrogance.

'Where's Dr. du Toit?' she said.

'I couldn't find him,' Smuts said. 'Miss Augusta was getting worse. So I called the hospital.'

'I wouldn't have come otherwise,' Bekker said. 'She's somebody else's patient. But he said it was an emergency.'

'And is it?' Kate said.

'I'm afraid it is. One lung is badly affected.'

She looked down at the unconscious form of Mrs. Preller. She was small and shrivelled; her breathing was ragged.

'The sooner we get her into hospital, the better,' Bekker said.

Kate took Smuts aside. 'Does he know about the morphine?'

He shook his head. 'I couldn't tell him. You know how she felt.'

'He has to know. It may affect the treatment.'

She caught up with the doctor as he was going out of the door. 'There's one thing you should know. She's a morphine addict. She has been for years.'

'Oh, hell!' The mask of arrogance dropped away. 'Why didn't someone tell me? We must hurry.'

'Should we come?'

'No! Call me tomorrow morning. If Dr. du Toit returns, for God's sake tell him to get up to the hospital as soon as he can.'

She stood in the doorway wth Smuts, watching the ambulance pull out, followed by the doctor in his car.

'When did it happen?' she said. 'You said she was worse, but I thought you meant the paralysis.'

'She started coughing the day before yesterday. It was this bloody trial. She made me get the papers every day. She forced Hennie du Toit to read her every word. Columns of the stuff. That's what made her ill.'

'And you don't know where he is now?'

'I haven't seen him all day.'

'So all we can do is wait.'

'Have you had something to eat?'

'I don't want anything. But I need a drink.'

'So do I.'

They went into the drawing-room and he poured them each a brandy.

'At least no one will be reading her the papers tomorrow,' Kate said.

'Bad?'

She told him what had happened in court, then added, frowning: 'She said a strange thing to me before the trial. She said, "Lena will destroy us all".'

He shook his head. 'It's not Lena. It's more complicated than that. It all started with her husband. Christ, what a pig he was. Charles . . . he's no bloody good. I know I shouldn't be saying that to you, but you must have seen what he's like by now, and in a way it's not his fault. He really loved his father, you know, and his father loved Hugo. Charles couldn't understand it. He would put himself out to please Boss Charles. I remember when he was a little boy he used to pick up shells on the beach and bring them back as presents. His father never looked at them. And when he went to boarding-school he made a chair in his wood-work classes. A nice chair. I saw it once. He worked damn hard. It was going to be a present for his father. But Boss Charles said, "What the hell do I want with another chair?" So it was left at the school. Ja, it all went wrong for Charles.'

She wanted to tell him what had happened on the night Freda had died, but even now she could not bear to talk about it. Instead she said, 'He told me about the cards his father sent him after Hugo died. Black edged. Every year on Hugo's birthday.'

'That was typical. At one time he said he wasn't going to have Charles back in the house. That was after . . .' He stopped.

'After what?'

'I shouldn't be talking like this, not to his wife.'

'Do you think you can say anything now that would make a difference?'

'It wasn't much. These things happen at a boy's boarding-school.'

She remembered Tom's phrase, 'liaisons with other boys', and used it.

'That's right. They were caught. There was talk about making an example of them, but nothing ever happened.'

'Who was the other boy?'

He glanced at her and, even before he opened his mouth, she said, 'It was Jerry, wasn't it?' He nodded.

They were silent for a while. She knew they had to discuss the future and her role at Saxenburg but felt she could not bear it at the moment. She looked at her watch and saw it was a little past one o'clock. 'I'm going to bed,' she said. 'There's nothing more we can do now.'

He nodded. 'There are a couple of letters for you. I told Tilly to put them in your room.'

Fighting a desire to run, she went upstairs to her suite. There was a small pile of letters on the table in her sitting-room. The top two carried foreign stamps. She opened them and read them according to date.

Again she had the sensation of being with him, of hearing his voice and smelling his skin. Since he last wrote he had been to Budapest but was now back in his house. The first letter briefly described his trip along the Danube, and she longed to have been with him. The second was dated a few days later and said that he was going to be on leave in England for a couple of months towards the end of the year. Could she come?

She remembered the sounds of London's streets, the smell of coal fires on cold afternoons, the sparkle of shop windows as the lights came on, so different from her present surroundings, and imagined herself there.

The rest of her post consisted of a couple of bills and a letter without a stamp. It had only her name on the envelope and she did not recognise the hand-writing. There were five or six closely written pages in the envelope. As she started to read, she felt her throat close with shock.

My dear Kate, it began. *I hope by the time you read these few lines, I shall be dead.*

I write to you, and no one else, for several reasons, which will become clearer. Apart from my sons, you are my one living relative, if only by marriage. I always wanted a daughter.

This letter is to tell you two things. The first is the most important, and it is my confession that I caused the death of Miriam Sachs. I will not say murdered or killed, because I did not mean to do either. But the fact is that she died because of me, and you must go to the police with this as soon as possible. To ensure that they will believe you, and so that the case against Charles will be withdrawn, I will give you the details.

She read on, and his words painted with vivid strokes a picture of what had really happened that night so many months ago.

I am sure you recall that day as well as I do. Your friends had

332

come from Cape Town, with your brother. You had a picnic down at the rock pools. It was this, I think, that caused the tragedy.

I was coming to bathe myself that afternoon because it had turned hot. You were all at the pools when I reached the cove. I was about to join you when Miriam and your friend Jerry prepared to bathe.

I have told you that when Miriam was a little girl, I taught her to swim down in those same pools. We used to bathe naked ourselves, until there came a day when she was twelve or thirteen when we could no longer do so, when innocence vanished.

On the day of your picnic, when I saw her naked, I realised how beautiful she was, how desirable.

This feeling in me was not isolated. It was something I have often felt since my wife's death, when I saw Betty and other women around the town. People think you are finished at fifty-three, which is far from the truth.

I stood at the rocks near the pools and watched Miriam. You all took it so casually. Not one of you can imagine how I felt.

I went home, but I could not settle. In the evening I remembered that Augusta had a touch of influenza. I went out to see her, for something to do, something to fill my mind with other thoughts. We spent part of the evening talking about the future. She has such great hopes for you.

About ten o'clock I left to drive home. When I reached the old ostrich houses, I saw Miriam walking towards town. I stopped to give her a lift. I asked her what she was doing in such a place at such a time. She said she had been going to swim at the cove, but she had decided that it was too far. I was not surprised. Miriam did such things. I now know, of course, that it was not the real reason she was there.

I said, before I could stop myself, that I would like to swim, too. I said, why did we not go together?

She pointed out that I had always told her not to swim at night, but I said it was all right if you knew the pools as well as we did. I drove her to the beach in spite of her objections.

When we got out of the car she said she did not have a bathing costume. I said we should swim as we used to swim when she was a little girl. She said, "I don't think so, Hennie," so I told her that I had seen her doing so that afternoon.

She laughed at me and said, did I know what they called old men like me?

333

I did not wish to hear her talk like that. I reached out for her. I think I meant to cover her mouth, but the moment I touched her it turned into something else. I must have killed her when she started to scream. All I meant to do was silence her.

Perhaps you will not believe me when I tell you that it took me some time to realise what I had done. The mind is a curious thing. Not even doctors know much about it.

When it was over, and my head was clear, Miriam was dead. I undressed her completely and put her clothes in a pile. The scarf that Jonas found must have fallen when I was carrying her body to the sea cave. I believed that the tide would carry her out beyond the India Reef.

I have written to you in such detail, and at this time, because I have already caused my son, Charles, enough suffering. Yes, he is my son. Augusta would never acknowledge it publicly because of her feelings for family continuity. Her own family in Vienna had meant a great deal to her and she had transferred her feelings to the Prellers. Charles was all she had if the name was to continue.

I kept the secret for the sake of my own family and because I knew it would ruin my career.

Kate's mind went back to her meeting with Miss Binns in Vienna and her talk of Augusta's lover. Kate had believed that it had been Smuts. Now she saw how wrong she had been. It was easy to visualize the young Viennese woman in this strange and sometimes brutal place, forming a passionate attachment for a good-looking doctor, fresh from London, who at least had a veneer of sophistication and knowledge of Europe.

I like to think that I would have come forward even if he had not been my son. I felt guilty about what happened to Jonas, but when your own life is at stake you do abnormal things.

But everything has come to an end for me. I have looked after Augusta as well as I could all these years. Now her end has come, too. She cannot recover and I think it is best, after what has come out in the trial, that she does not. She is too proud a woman to be brought low through scandal. It is time for both of us to disappear.

I wish that we could have seen a grandchild. I would never have made my relationship public, but I would have known.

The future now is in your hands – yours and my son's.
'Good-bye, Kate. God bless you. Hennie du Toit.

She read the letter again, then sat with it on her lap. How long she sat there she did not know. She was trying to remember him as she first knew him, not as the seedy man racked by guilt and fear that he had become. She recalled her visit to his house, the dismal and unloved room, the rugby photographs, the tasselled caps. She remembered the magazines on the table, the way he had looked at her when she had realised what the pictures were. She remembered the big, strong frame smashing in the cloak-room door on Christmas night; the smooth, young-looking face with the dimpled smile, the silver-grey mane of hair which was combed in so dandified a way. Everything about him had spoken of the male ethos, of virility. He had expressed all his bitterness in the sentence: *People think you are finished at fifty-three* . . .

Remembering him, she felt pity, mixed with revulsion. Again in her mind's eye she saw the scene on the beach: middle age in pursuit of youth. Miriam's stinging laughter as he had tried, and failed, to turn the clock back. She understood, but she could not forgive him for what he had done to Charles. And to Jonas. She remembered him on the rock, firing at the drowning body; the white hands shaking, sweat on his face.

Then she thought of Charles and Jerry at school, the scandal, the threat of expulsion, the counter-threat by Boss Charles not to have the boy back in the house. No wonder Charles had needed a night-light even as an adult. But if Dr. du Toit was right, then Betty was not Charles's half sister. That was something, at least.

She was chilly when at last she rose and went downstairs. She found Smuts asleep in the drawing-room where she had left him. She woke him and handed him Dr. du Toit's letter. He read it carefully once, then went back to the beginning and read it again. He ran his hand over the stubble on his face and his eyes were old and tired.

'Did you know?' Kate said.

'About Hennie and Miss Augusta, or about Charles, or about Hennie killing Miriam?'

'Anything.'

'I knew they'd been lovers. Or I guessed. I think that if it hadn't been for him she would have gone mad in those first years. I think they were lovers right up to the time Hugo died. Even after that he looked after her as though she was still dearer to him than anyone.'

'What about his wife?'

'She was a farm girl. Hefty. Good stock, but not the brains to run the social side of the practice. But I never guessed about Charles. I just thought Hennie was fond of him like an uncle. As for the killing: not in a million years. I really did think it was Charles, you know. Christ, what a bloody mess!'

'I'd better take this to the police.' Kate picked up the letter. 'The sooner they know . . .'

'Hang on. I want to find Hennie.' He tapped the letter. 'We must be bloody sure this is the real thing.'

'Where will you look?'

'At his home.'

'I'll drive you.'

The first faint streaks of grey were showing on the horizon as she drove into Helmsdale. She parked outside du Toit's house, and waited. The wind was dying and the early morning was cool. The street lights were on, but slowly the dark town became grey and the buildings lightened.

After five minutes, Smuts came out. 'He's not there. His car's not in the garage, either, and his shotgun isn't on the rack.'

'What do we do next?'

'We look for his car.'

They drove out on the Cape road and then the Agulhas road, and then along the cliff road, looking in all the little turn-offs. The sun rose, a great red ball coming up over the dunes. They drove past Saxenburg, past the beach, and suddenly Smuts said, 'There it is.'

Kate stopped. She followed his pointing finger and saw a car parked on the opposite headland. She drove along the bumpy dirt road until she drew up alongside it. There was no one in it.

'I think I know where he is,' Smuts said.

She followed him slowly as he climbed down the headland and walked across the beach. She knew where he was going. The tide was low and the sea was flattening out. She took her shoes off and walked to the water's edge. Smuts had reached the tunnel entrance to the cave. He wriggled through and vanished. She stared up at the great house on the other headland. The sun was striking the windows, turning them the colour of blood.

Smuts emerged from the cave and walked towards her. 'He's in there. I'm glad you didn't come. He must have shot himself last night or this morning. There hasn't been a big enough tide to take him out, but the crabs have got to him, poor bugger.'

[8]

In the weeks following the death of Dr. du Toit, Saxenburg was caught up in its own mortality. Eight days after entering hospital, in the early hours of the morning, Mrs. Preller died, quite alone. Kate had spent hours by her bedside, listening to the breath whistle in and out of the infected lungs, sometimes seeing in her eyes the effort she was making to talk. But the palsied jaw had hung slackly. She had never spoken again.

During that time, too, an inquest was held on the death of Dr. du Toit, and Charles was released from custody after the charge against him was withdrawn. Kate went to Cape Town in his red roadster to bring him back to Saxenburg. It was then that she registered that he had changed. The first hint was when he got into the passenger's seat and let her drive. He had loved the roadster with passion, now he seemed indifferent to it. He hardly spoke all the way to Helmsdale. Once at Saxenburg he remained silent and withdrawn.

She had thought he might be euphoric after his release, now she told herself that he was depressed because of his mother's death and the revelations of the trial.

But the depression lingered and had side effects. Instead of taking up his role as manager – the role that had been forced on him by Kate's accident and her trip to Europe – he took no interest in the farm. He would lie in bed until ten and eleven in the morning, content to let the day drift past.

She had not bargained for this. Her own watershed had been the death of Mrs. Preller, which, she believed, had released her from the future she had dreaded. She had decided she would leave Charles and Saxenburg after finishing the plucking season. Now another incubus stood in her path. How could she desert him in his present state? Her feeling of frustration, almost of panic, was exacerbated by letters from Tom. In one he told her he had been offered the post of the *Chronicle*'s Paris correspondent, with a large apartment near the Bois. *It would mean a new beginning for us both and I think we need that*, he wrote. *No memories, no old tracks in the snow. New home, new furniture, new food, new streets, new air, new everything. My French is not too bad, but rusty, so I'm starting at Berlitz here on an intensive course. How's yours? My darling, it's the best thing I can offer you, the best thing I can imagine for both of us. I must know what you think within a couple of months. They won't hold it open for ever. If you say yes, we'll go, but I don't think it'll be much fun by myself.*

Paris! The very thought of being in Paris with Tom made her ache. She knew the city only slightly, but had been caught by its beauty. And he was right, it would be starting anew. *No old tracks in the snow*, he had said. The image was so vivid. For one of the very few times in her life she felt tears start at the back of her eyes; tears of frustration.

That evening while Charles was having his bath, she sought out Smuts.

'Ready for a spot?' he said, indicating the brandy.

They chatted for some minutes about the quality of the birds and the prices being offered by Mendel for the new

338

season and then, after a moment's silence, Kate said: 'I was wondering if it wasn't time to look for a manager.'

His head jerked up. 'What sort of manager?'

'For the farm.'

'I don't understand, my friend. What the hell do we need a manager for?'

'Well, I . . .'

'You're not thinking of leaving us, are you?'

'What if I started a family?'

He looked at her obliquely. 'Am I to congratulate you?'

'No. I'm saying if.'

'We'll cope. We always have. Anyway, the boom seems to be levelling out.' He paused, then said, 'And there's always Charles. He'll have to pull his weight.'

'I'm worried about him. He doesn't seem to understand what's happening at Saxenburg. He's still so depressed, though I've tried to do everything I can to help him get over the death of his mother.' Even as she said it she knew it was a lie. She had felt his need, but she had been unable to fulfil it. There was only an emptiness in her where Charles was concerned.

'I shouldn't say this to you, but I've known him a lot longer than you,' Smuts said. 'He'll always take the line of least resistance. His mother ran the place for him, then you came along to run it. Sometimes I think it might have been better for him if he'd had to find his own bloody way. It could have been the making of him.'

That evening she went upstairs early. She had wanted to write to Tom, but what was she to say? Instead, she got into bed and thought about Smuts' words. If she were to leave, would it be the making of Charles? She remembered how he had coped when she'd had her accident. He had been a different person. But wasn't that the point? If she remained, would he ever pull himself together? Would she not, in effect, be doing him a favour by leaving him? She knew this was rationalisation, yet Smuts, not she, had originated it.

Charles came to bed around midnight. She was still awake, but pretended to be asleep. Then, for the first time

339

in weeks, she felt his hands lifting her night-dress. He had tried to make love to her a few days after returning from gaol and she had refused him. Now, as she felt his searching fingers, any sympathy she might once have harboured vanished, overlaid by disgust at his touch. Images of Charles and Betty, Charles and his young man, Charles and Jerry, flashed through her mind and she moved away, swinging her legs onto the floor.

'Please . . .' he said.

She did not answer. Instead she went downstairs to her office, where there was a small sofa, and locked herself in. The time, she knew, had come to tell him she was going.

But when she told him the following day, he chose not to understand her.

'Going where?' he said.

'Away.'

'You mean to the flat?'

'At first.'

'For how long?'

'As long as it takes to get onto a ship.'

'What do you want a ship for?'

'Charles, I'm going. Leaving the country. Don't you understand? I'm not coming back.'

'I don't believe you.'

In a way, his reaction helped her. Had he broken down, she would have found it more difficult. As it was, his obtuseness, or pretended obtuseness, gave her just the iron she needed. She decided that she would write to Tom that evening telling him she was coming, then she would talk to Smuts and begin to make the complicated arrangements which would finally give her freedom.

She was in the incubator shed late the next morning when she heard the commotion: first shouts, then running feet. 'Miss Kate! Miss Kate!' It was Tilly's voice and she ran to the door as the coloured house-keeper came charging across the gravel yard. 'Miss Kate must come quick!'

'What is it?'

'It's Mister Charles! Miss Kate must hurry!'

'Where?'

'In the nursery bathroom.'

She ran into the house and took the stairs two at a time. She burst into the bathroom. Smuts was already there.

'Don't come in!' he shouted.

But she had seen the blood. The bath was smeared, so was the wall. Gouts of it had dripped onto the floor, the water was the colour of rosé. In the bath lay Charles. He was naked and his flesh was the dirty white of a plant without chlorophyll.

'Call for an . . .' Smuts began. Then he said, 'No, there's no bloody time. Help me! Get something for his wrists. Something we can use as tourniquets.'

There was a small towel under the bath and she grabbed it. Her hands were immediately red with blood.

'Give it to me,' Smuts said. 'You get the motor out. Send a couple of the boys to me.'

She ran out, shouting for Tilly.

They got Charles into the car. His limbs were slack, as though he were a doll. His eyelids were flickering and his breathing was faint. Smuts supported him.

'For Christ's sake, hurry,' he said. She let out the clutch and the car jerked forward. It took less than ten minutes to reach the hospital. She walked by the side of the stretcher until the doors of the casualty ward closed on him. For some seconds she stood, staring at the brown paint, seeing her future.

[9]

On a warm Sunday afternoon about six weeks later, she was in her sitting room at Saxenburg. For the first time in a long while, she had little to do. The season was over and the feathers despatched. She had been reading a novel, but leisure was so foreign to her that she felt guilty doing nothing. Yet she was exhausted and she told herself that doing nothing was exactly what she needed. Her days, as the season grew to its climax, had been filled with work and worry, but above all, with despair.

She put down the book and sat back, listening to the sounds of boisterous laughter coming from the garden. Who would have thought when they had carried Charles into the hospital that in so short a time this would be happening? Who would have thought after seeing the blood-drenched bathroom that he would have been home a few days later, little the worse? They had celebrated his return, of course, making a fuss of him. Tilly had prepared a special meal and Smuts had brought up a couple of bottles of Rhine wine. Kate had forced herself to assume the burden of welcome.

Looking back now at the six weeks that had gone by, she realised that in a sense Charles had controlled their reactions. Neither he nor anyone else had mentioned the act which had nearly caused his death. It was as though it had never happened.

But it *had* happened, and it had changed more than her own future. It seemed to have had a cathartic effect on Charles, as though he knew that now she would never leave him. Within a few weeks, secure at the heart of Saxenburg, he had taken up his life again. This time it was an extension of the life he had been leading before his marriage.

One day he had gone into Cape Town, 'to see that everything was all right at the flat', and returned for the week-end, bringing a car-load of friends, most of them already half drunk. Jerry was among them, with a girl named Valerie, who seemed to be a new edition of Freda.

This had become the pattern of his week-ends.

Kate rose and went to the window. There had been other significant changes. He had pressed the entire farm labour force into service in the garden. The weeds had gone, the flower-beds been reclaimed, the tennis-court had been patched and new stop-netting erected. But the greatest work had been done on the swimming-pool. Now, watching Charles's friends jumping in and swimming, splashing, shouting, laughing, she saw what life at Saxenburg must have been like in the old days.

She had mentioned this to Smuts the previous Sunday. He had come up to her room and found her writing to

Tom. 'I thought you'd be here,' he had said. 'Always inside.'

'You sound like my mother. She kept wanting me to go out and play on fine days.'

They had stood at the window and looked down at the swimmers and the tennis-players, as she was looking now, and she had said, 'You and Mrs. Preller were always talking about the old days. I suppose this is what they were like.'

'I used to make-believe for her. We all did. But the old days weren't so bloody good.'

She remembered the conversation as she watched Charles and Jerry on the court. She could clearly hear their arguments about line decisions. They kept referring close calls to a fair-haired young man standing at one of the net posts. He was wearing a white shirt, white flannels and two-toned shoes. Kate suspected that he was Charles's lover. After his first visit she had said to Charles, 'I don't mind who else you invite, but I don't want Jeremy here.'

'You invite your friends, I'll invite mine, okay?'

Her only defence was to stay out of their way. Last night they had played the Victrola and danced. She had feigned a headache and gone up to her room. It was almost dawn when Charles came to bed.

At that moment, Charles looked up from the tennis-court and she caught his glance. He had been talking to Jeremy, now his face went blank and a stillness held him for a moment. Then Jerry called and the game went on.

She wandered back to her chair, reached into a drawer and took out Tom's most recent letter. She read it through again. It was full of his love for her, but there was no more talk about Paris. Instead he wrote of the first snow bringing silence to the city. She could hardly bear to read it.

She folded it away and took out her pad. She wondered what to write about, and thought of the letters Mrs. Preller had written to Miss Binns. How could you relate the day-to-day activities of Saxenburg to someone caught up in the life of Vienna? She told him about the house, how it had changed, how Charles had turned the old nurseries into guest-rooms, how the ostrich feathers had gone from the drawing-room and the heavy antiques had been carried out into the incubator shed and covered with tarpaulins. *It seems a pity to alter the character of the house in this way*, she ended.

She knew she should be answering the questions which came in each letter: When was she coming to Vienna? Why would she not leave Saxenburg? She did not answer them because she could not.

The laughter from the swimming-pool began to irritate her and she went along the passage, as she often did these days, to Mrs. Preller's rooms. They were kept locked and she had the key.

She wandered from room to room, touching the fabric of the bedspread, running her fingers along the book-shelves. One of the ornaments on the mantelpiece had been moved. There was a small circle of dust on the dark teak. She must mention that to Tilly. She did not like things being moved from their places.

Then the thought came to her that the suite was going to waste. One day the fabrics would rot and the rooms begin to decay. Why should she not move into them? Then she and Charles would no longer have to share any part of their lives. Nor would she have to listen to the shouting and the laughter from the garden.

She pulled Mrs. Preller's chair to the window and sat down. The view was tremendous. The aquamarine sea stretched away to the curve of the horizon. To her right was Saxenburg Cove and the headland containing the sea cave; directly out to sea from it was the India Reef. She sat there for a long time, looking at the swells coming in over the rock pools, remembering Miriam.

She heard the door open, and turned. Charles came in and closed it behind him.

'What are you doing in here?' he said.

'Sitting.'

'I don't like you being in here.'

She rose as he came forward. She could see sweat on his face. His eyes were angry. She recognised the old Charles.

'You're bloody rude,' he said. 'You haven't been down all day. These are our friends and . . .'

344

'Our friends?'

'All right, my friends. And you're my wife. I expect you to treat them with respect and good manners.'

'Respect? Good manners? You must tell me about them one day, Charles.'

'Ever since . . . well, for a long time you've treated me as though I wasn't really here. This is my house now. My estate. You're my wife. You do what I say. I'll never say please again! Never!'

'I'm one of your possessions?'

'If you like.'

'Why, Charles?'

'Why what?'

'Why do you want a wife at all? You don't need one. You've got Jeremy.'

He flinched and she saw again the curious deadness at the back of his eyes. 'What do you mean?'

'You know exactly what I mean. You want me only to give you the respectability you feel you don't have. Are you so ashamed, Charles?'

'Of what?'

'Your nature.'

It was cruelly said, and he reacted. He hit her in the face with the back of his hand. 'If you ever say anything like that again, I'll really damage you,' he said.

She pressed her lips together, tasting blood.

'I want you downstairs for supper. Do you understand?'

'I understand.'

He left the room. She stood at the window, staring out, but seeing nothing.

The cut in her lip was slight and she cleaned it up. Then she went to look for Smuts. He was in his room.

'I want you to take me out in the motor,' she said.

He looked at her strangely. 'The shops are closed.'

'I just want to go for a drive.'

They drove along the cliff road past the old ostrich houses. After a while she said, 'Take me to the graveyard.' They went through the deserted afternoon streets of Helmsdale and came to the little sandy cemetery. Smuts parked under a gum tree and she got out. It was the first

345

time she had been to the cemetery since Mrs. Preller's funeral. She walked along the dusty paths between granite headstones until she came to the Preller vault.

The name was there now, freshly chiselled: AUGUSTA PRELLER (née VON BERENDORF), then the dates of her birth and death. There was plenty of space below it for those to come. Would her own be on it?

She heard the crunch of feet on gravel as Smuts joined her. They stood in silence for some moments and then he said, 'Families go up and families go down. My own family were pioneers. They came here nearly two hundred and fifty years ago. They were educated land-owners when the Prellers were running about in bare feet. You didn't know that my family once owned Saxenburg, did you?'

'No.'

'The Prellers bought it a long time ago but I've always felt I belonged here.'

She touched the newly-chiselled letters. 'I feel she's still here, somehow.'

'Balls!' Smuts said. 'If you'll forgive my French. She's gone. Dead. Buried. Unless . . .'

'Unless what?'

'Unless you force her to come back.'

'What's that supposed to mean?'

'Listen,' he said urgently. 'Don't you understand what's happening to you? Can't you see yourself? *You're* turning into her.' She stared at him, feeling an ice-cold hand close on her heart. 'Every day I drive you to Helmsdale. You sit up in those rooms of hers. Soon you won't come down at all. Don't you understand that this is what she did when she was young? Christ, she talked about the old days as though they were something great. That was her defence. They were bloody awful for her. Boss Charles used to bring his rugby friends to Saxenburg just as Charles is bringing his peculiar friends. She used to sit up in her room, listening to the shouting and the horse-play, and make excuses about not joining them. One day he lost his temper and hit her.'

Smuts came closer and his fingers closed on her arm. She was aware of the piercing noise of the Christmas beetles and of the heat reflected from the gravel at her feet. He had never touched her before, but there was an urgency about him that stopped her drawing away. 'Tell me to shut up,' he said. 'Tell me it's no bloody business of mine, but I can't stand by and let you destroy yourself. You don't love Charles, do you?'

'I hate him,' she said, and it was the first time she had acknowledged it publicly.

'Get out, then! Oh, I know what you're going to say: What about you? What about Saxenburg? Well, we coped before we ever heard of you. You can't shape everyone's life, my friend. Your parents are all right. We'll be all right. Get going as fast as you bloody can.'

'Aren't you forgetting something?'

'What's that?'

'Charles. What if he – tries again? What if he succeeds? I'd never forgive myself.'

Smuts dropped his hand and walked to the corner of the tomb. He stopped, and turned. 'I hoped I wouldn't have to tell you this, but it's better now that I do. That wasn't a real attempt at suicide. Nothing like it.'

'But I saw the blood. I saw Charles.'

'Haven't you ever seen a nose-bleed? My God, you think you've never seen so much blood in the world. But all it is is a nose-bleed. Blood always makes things look worse than they are. Listen, I spoke to Dr. Bekker. Charles had cut downwards.'

'I don't understand.'

'Show me how you'd do it?'

She drew her finger across her wrist.

'Ja. So would most people if they were serious. That way you cut the veins completely. But if you do it this way . . .' He drew his finger down the inside of her arm parallel to the bone. '. . . you don't. Okay, you cut the veins, but you don't sever them. And remember when I asked for something for a tourniquet and you found a small towel under the bath?'

She recalled picking it up and how her hands had become red with blood. 'He'd been using it to smear the blood,' she whispered.

'Ja. That's what I think, too. But there's one thing more.

347

He'd told Tilly to bring him clean underwear. He wanted to be found quickly.'

'So it was only . . .'

'Of course it was. To stop you leaving. Look at him now.'

'Are you sure? Because if you're mistaken . . .'

'Kate,' he said, 'you're not God.'

[10]

The *Conway Castle* came slowly up Southampton Water in the fog, her horn booming mournfully in counterpoint to the shrill whistles of the tugs as they came to mother her.

Kate was on deck with the Reverend Purchase and his wife, whose table she had shared throughout the voyage.

'That's the Isle of Wight,' he said, pointing to flashes of brown and green seen through the shifting mist.

'Is someone meeting you, my dear?' Mrs. Purchase asked.

'I don't . . .' Then she shook her head. 'No. There's no one.'

'We have a compartment booked on the boat train. Mrs. Preller can come with us, can't she, Matthew?'

'Of course. Delighted.'

Kate smiled, but said nothing. They had been kind to her, but she did not want their kindness now. She wanted to be alone, to make decisions, book seats, take trains. She did not want to rest or sleep or even eat. She was in movement like some projectile and had been ever since leaving Saxenburg. There had been a brief pause to say farewell to her parents and then she had started again on this huge journey that would take her the length of Africa and half the breadth of Europe. And all the time she had been frightened: frightened while she was in Cape Town that Charles might find some way of stopping her, frightened that she might be run down and injured, frightened that her parents or Duggie might fall dangerously ill and need her, frightened that the ship might sink, frightened that something, anything, might happen to check her movement.

Everything had been done so fast. From the moment she had made her decision in the grave-yard, standing next to Mrs. Preller's newly-cut name, she had craved speed. A call to the shipping company had resulted in a berth on the *Conway Castle*, leaving on Thursday, just four days away. She had left Saxenburg on the Wednesday, late in the afternoon.

She had left the way she had come, sitting in the back seat of the motor. The same purple everlastings were in the same silver vase, the same lined and sunburnt neck was in fromt of her, the same white dust blew along the road and, for all she knew, the same ostriches stared at her in wonderment. She had turned only once and looked back at the house. It stood massively on its headland, dark and brooding in the evening light, and beyond it she could see the white line of the India Reef. But there was another form in the landscape: the white figure of Charles standing outside the front door.

'No one leaves Saxenburg,' he had said, disbelieving her to the bitter end. 'Not unless they're carried out feet first.'

He had followed her to the door.

'Good-bye, Charles,' she had said.

'You'll feel better after a few days. The break'll do you good.'

She had shrugged. There was no way, it seemed, that he would understand. 'You're right,' she said finally, 'the break will do me good.'

But as the motor had turned out of the drive she had seen his face. For the first time, he seemed to register what was happening, that this time he was on his own.

The moment she reached Cape Town, she had telephoned Guy Bedford and asked him if he could get a message through to Tom.

'Of course,' he said.

'Tell him I'm sailing tomorrow. I'll cable him from London.'

And now she was nearly in London. She knew exactly

what she had to do. First there were the customs formalities, then the boat-train to Waterloo, a taxi across London to Victoria and the Night Ferry to Paris. From Paris, she would take the first train. It didn't matter where it was going, as long as it was in the direction of Austria. She did not mind how many times she changed, how little sleep she would have. There was all her life to sleep. She had to keep going, keep the projectile in motion.

Through the mists she saw the tops of the cranes along the wharf. Half an hour later they had tied up and the gangplanks were down. She stood in the cold morning, looking through the swirling mist at the cloth-capped stevedores, searching for a big man with sandy hair and a loping walk. She told herself not to be disappointed that he was not there. Vienna was now only a matter of days away.

She found a porter in the customs' shed and told him to put all her luggage under the huge letter P. She fretted as an official opened her suitcases and ran his hands along the bottoms, but a few moments later he was making small yellow crosses on them with his chalk.

'Boat train, miss?' the porter said as they left the shed.

The Rev. and Mrs. Purchase were a few paces ahead of her. She supposed she would have to join them.

She opened her mouth to say, 'Yes,' but a voice at her elbow said, 'No. Just take them to the car over there.'

The porter looked at Tom with suspicion. 'Do you know this gentleman?' he asked Kate protectively.

'Yes,' she said. 'He's an old friend.'

'Oh, well, in that case . . . only I wasn't sure, see?'

They followed the barrow. 'Hello, old friend,' he said, taking her arm.

She dug her nails into his flesh. 'Hello, yourself,' she said.

No one went to the sea cave for many months, nor swam in the rock pools. But gradually memories faded. Tides came in and went out. Storms did their scouring and cleaning. Eventually the cove returned to its natural place in the life of the community. People swim in the rock pools today, and there is a sign saying, *To the Grotto*. It is still an unspoiled place, and there are few holiday homes in the vicinity. The wind is what keeps it clean; people don't like the wind. But on a calm day in summer it is as beautiful as can be imagined.